The Best American
SCIENCE FICTION
and FANTASY
2018

The Best American
SCIENCE FICTION
and FANTASY™
2018

Edited and with an Introduction
by **N. K. Jemisin**

John Joseph Adams, *Series Editor*

A Mariner Original

HOUGHTON MIFFLIN HARCOURT

BOSTON • NEW YORK

hmhco.com

ISSN 2573-0797 (print)   ISSN 2573-0800 (ebook)
ISBN 978-1-328-83456-0 (print)   ISBN 978-1-328-83453-9 (ebook)

Printed in the United States of America
DOC 10 9 8 7 6 5 4 3 2
4500746235

"Don't Press Charges and I Won't Sue" by Charlie Jane Anders. First published in *Boston Review: Global Dystopias*. Copyright © 2017 by Charlie Jane Anders. Reprinted by permission of Charlie Jane Anders.

"Zen and the Art of Starship Maintenance" by Tobias S. Buckell. First published in *Cosmic Powers* by Saga Press, April 2017. Copyright © 2017 by Tobias S. Buckell. Reprinted by permission of Tobias S. Buckell.

"Tasting Notes on the Varietals of the Southern Coast" by Gwendolyn Clare. First published in *The Magazine of Fantasy & Science Fiction*, September/October 2017. Copyright © 2017 by Gwendolyn Clare Williams. Reprinted by permission of Gwendolyn Clare Williams.

"The Hermit of Houston" by Samuel R. Delany. First published in *The Magazine of Fantasy & Science Fiction*, September/October 2017. Copyright © 2017 by Samuel R. Delany. Reprinted by permission of Samuel R. Delany and his agents Henry Morrison, Inc.

"The Last Cheng Beng Gift" by Jaymee Goh. First published in *Lightspeed Magazine*, September 2017, Issue 88. Copyright © 2017 by Jaymee Goh. Reprinted by permission of Jaymee Goh.

"Black Powder" by Maria Dahvana Headley. First published in *The Djinn Falls in Love*, March 2017. Copyright © 2017 by Maria Dahvana Headley. Reprinted by permission of Maria Dahvana Headley.

"The Orange Tree" by Maria Dahvana Headley. First published in *The Weight of*

Contents

Foreword

Welcome to year four of *The Best American Science Fiction and Fantasy!* This volume presents the best science fiction and fantasy (SF/F) short stories published during the 2017 calendar year as selected by myself and guest editor N. K. Jemisin.

In recent years, Nora has basically set the genre on fire.

In 2016 and 2017, her novel *The Fifth Season* and its sequel *The Obelisk Gate* both won the Hugo Award for best novel, making her one of only three writers who have ever won the best novel Hugo two years in a row (joining Orson Scott Card and Lois McMaster Bujold). Both of those books were also finalists for the Nebula and World Fantasy Awards, and as I write this, in May, the final installment in that trilogy, *The Stone Sky,* just won the Nebula Award and was named a finalist for the Hugo Award. (World Fantasy finalists have not been announced yet.) If *The Stone Sky* wins the Hugo this year, Nora will be the only person ever to win in the best novel category three years in a row. (The result will be known by the time this book is published, but not before we lock the text for publication.)

Nora first achieved the trifecta of having a book nominated for all three of the abovementioned awards in 2011 with her debut novel, *The Hundred Thousand Kingdoms* (which won the Locus Award). *The Killing Moon* in 2013 was nominated for both the Nebula and World Fantasy Awards, and her story "Non-Zero Probabilities" was nominated for both the Hugo and the Nebula in 2010. So she's had a real knack not only for writing award-worthy stuff but for generating a genuine consensus among the different award bodies that her work is truly among the best of the year.

And so after writing a significant portion of what many readers and critics have considered the best works of the year on an annual basis, it seems pretty fitting that she now gets to weigh in *editorially* as well. But this is not her first go at showcasing the finest works of the genre; indeed, until just recently she was the science fiction/fantasy book reviewer for a little newspaper you might have heard of called the *New York Times.*

In addition to all of the above accolades, which mostly focus on her novel-length work, she is an accomplished short fiction writer as well, with short stories published in a wide variety of publications, such as *Strange Horizons, Lightspeed Magazine, Uncanny Magazine, Wired, Fantasy Magazine, Tor.com, Clarkesworld Magazine, Popular Science, Escape Pod,* and *Weird Tales,* as well as in anthologies such as *Epic: Legends of Fantasy; After: Nineteen Stories of Apocalypse and Dystopia; Steam-Powered: Lesbian Steampunk Stories; The Best Science Fiction and Fantasy of the Year* (Strahan, ed.); and *The Year's Best Dark Fantasy and Horror* (Guran, ed.); not to mention last year's edition of *The Best American Science Fiction and Fantasy.* If you *haven't* read a lot of her short fiction, now's your chance: Orbit is publishing her first collection of short stories in November.

You can learn more about her and her work at nkjemisin.com, and/or you can support her via Patreon (patreon.com/nkjemisin) to get an advance look at forthcoming book chapters and the occasional short story.

The stories chosen for this anthology were originally published between January 1, 2017, and December 31, 2017. The technical criteria for consideration are (1) original publication in a nationally distributed American or Canadian publication (i.e., periodicals, collections, or anthologies, in print, online, or ebook); (2) publication in English by writers who are American or Canadian, or who have made the United States their home; (3) publication as text (audiobook, podcast, dramatized, interactive, and other forms of fiction are not considered); (4) original publication as short fiction (excerpts of novels are not knowingly considered); (5) story length of 17,499 words or less; (6) at least loosely categorized as science fiction or fantasy; (7) publication by someone other than the author (i.e., self-published works are not eligible); and (8) publication as an original work of the author (i.e., not part of a media tie-in/licensed fiction program).

As series editor, I attempted to read everything I could find that met these criteria. After doing all my reading, I created a list of what I felt were the top eighty stories published in the genre (forty science fiction and forty fantasy). Those eighty stories were sent to the guest editor, who read them and then chose the best twenty (ten science fiction, ten fantasy) for inclusion in the anthology. The guest editor read all the stories anonymously—with no by-lines attached to them, nor any information about where the story originally appeared.

The guest editor's top twenty selections are included in this volume; the remaining sixty stories that did not make it into the anthology are listed in the back of this book as "Notable Science Fiction and Fantasy Stories of 2017."

As usual, in my effort to find the top stories of the year, I scoured the field to try to read and consider everything that was published. Though the bulk of my reading typically comes from periodicals, I always also read dozens of anthologies and single-author collections (this year, sixty-plus and thirty-plus, respectively).

Here's a sampling of the anthologies that published fine work that didn't quite manage to make it into the table of contents or Notable Stories list but are worthwhile just the same: *Adam's Ladder*, edited by Michael Bailey and Darren Speegle; *All Hail Our Robot Conquerors*, edited by Patricia Bray and Joshua Palmatier; *Behold!: Oddities, Curiosities and Undefinable Wonders*, edited by Doug Murano; *Black Feathers*, edited by Ellen Datlow; *Catalysts, Explorers & Secret Keepers*, edited by Monica Louzon, Jake Weisfeld, Heather McHale, Barbara Jasny, and Rachel Frederick; *Dark Cities*, edited by Christopher Golden; *Dark Screams*, volumes six and seven, edited by Brian James Freeman and Richard Chizmar; *The Death of All Things*, edited by Laura Anne Gilman and Kat Richardson; *The Demons of King Solomon*, edited by Aaron J. French; *Infinite Stars*, edited by Bryan Thomas Schmidt; *The Jurassic Chronicles*, edited by Crystal Watanabe; *Latin@ Rising*, edited by Matthew David Goodwin; *Mad Hatters and March Hares*, edited by Ellen Datlow; *Matchup*, edited by Lee Child; *Meanwhile, Elsewhere*, edited by Cat Fitzpatrick and Casey Plett; *Nevertheless, She Persisted*, edited by Mindy Klasky; *New Fears*, edited by Mark Morris; *Nights of the Living Dead*, edited by George A. Romero and Jonathan Maberry; *Oceans*, edited by Jessica West; *Ride the Star Wind*, edited by Scott Gable and C. Dombrowski; *Submerged,* edited by S. C. Butler and Joshua Palmatier; *Sycorax's Daughters,* edited by Kinitra Brooks; *Tales from a Talking Board,* edited by Ross E. Lockhart; and *Where the Stars Rise,* edited by Lucas K. Law and Derwin Mak.

In addition to this, the anthologies *Behind the Mask,* edited by Tricia Reeks and Kyle Richardson; *Cosmic Powers,* edited by me; *The Djinn Falls in Love,* edited by Mahvesh Murad and Jared Shurin; *Global Dystopias,* edited by Junot Díaz (published as a special issue of *Boston Review,* so it's debatable whether or not this counts as an anthology); *Humans Wanted,* edited by Vivian Caethe; and *Infinity Wars,* edited by Jonathan Strahan, all contain stories represented in the table of contents in this volume, and several other anthologies have stories on the Notable Stories list, such as *Chasing Shadows,* edited by David Brin and Stephen W. Potts; *Haunted Nights,* edited by Ellen Datlow and Lisa Morton; *Looming Low,* edited by Justin Steele and Sam Cowan; *Mech: Age of Steel,* edited by Tim Marquitz and Melanie R. Meadors; *Overview: Stories in the Stratosphere,* edited by Michael G. Bennett, Joey Eschrich, and Ed Finn; *Straight Outta Tombstone,* edited by David Boop; *The Sum of Us,* edited by Susan Forest and Lucas K. Law; *Visions, Ventures, Escape Velocities,* edited by Ed Finn and Joey Eschrich; *The Book of Swords,* edited by Gardner Dozois; and the XPRIZE Foundation's *Seat 14C,* edited by Kathryn Cramer.

I reviewed somewhere in the vicinity of thirty collections, about half of which contained no eligible material (either because they were all reprints or because the books or authors themselves were not eligible for consideration). The collection that set everyone's mind ablaze in 2017 was clearly—and with good reason—*Her Body and Other Parties,* by Carmen Maria Machado, being nominated for pretty much every major literary award one could think of, including the National Book Award; on top of that, it was the sole collection to provide one of the stories selected for this volume. Other collections that had stories on the Notable Stories list were *The Language of Thorns,* by Leigh Bardugo; *Machine Learning,* by Hugh Howey; *Norse Mythology,* by Neil Gaiman; *Tender: Stories,* by Sofia Samatar; *The Voices of Martyrs,* by Maurice Broaddus; and *What It Means When a Man Falls From the Sky,* by Lesley Nneka Arimah. There was fine work to be found in several other collections, including *Tales of Falling and Flying* by Ben Loory; *And Her Smile Will Untether the Universe,* by Gwendolyn Kiste; *Speaking to Skull Kings and*

Other Stories, by Emily B. Cataneo; *Fire,* by Elizabeth Hand; *So You Want to Be a Robot,* by A. Merc Rustad; *She Said Destroy,* by Nadia Bulkin; *The Overneath,* by Peter S. Beagle; and *Cat Pictures Please,* by Naomi Kritzer.

As always, I surveyed more than a hundred different periodicals over the course of the year, and paid as much attention to major genre publications like *Clarkesworld* and *Beneath Ceaseless Skies* as I did to more recently founded markets like *FIYAH* and *Diabolical Plots.* Likewise I do my best to find any genre fiction lurking in the pages of mainstream/literary publications, which this year yielded notable stories from *Kenyon Review* (and a selection), *Tin House, McSweeney's,* and *Slate.*

The stories presented to the guest editor for consideration were drawn from forty-five different publications — twenty-two periodicals, sixteen anthologies, and seven single-author collections — from thirty-nine different editors (counting editorial teams as a singular unit). The final table of contents draws from fifteen different sources: eight periodicals, six anthologies, and one collection (from twelve different editors/editorial teams).

This year marks the first appearance of two periodicals in our table of contents: *Beneath Ceaseless Skies* and *Kenyon Review.* Periodicals appearing on the Notable Stories list for the first time this year include *Kenyon Review, Diabolical Plots, FIYAH, Omni,* and *Slate.* (Note: I didn't count *Boston Review* in the preceding list because *Global Dystopias* felt more like a separate anthology than an issue of the magazine, but feel free to count it if you disagree!)

Six of the authors included in this volume (A. Merc Rustad, Carmen Maria Machado, Caroline M. Yoachim, Charlie Jane Anders, E. Lily Yu, and Maria Dahvana Headley) have previously appeared in *BASFF;* thus the remaining thirteen authors (thirteen rather than fourteen because Headley appears twice) are appearing for the first time.

Maria Dahvana Headley had the most stories in my top eighty this year, with four (and of course had two stories selected for inclusion); Maurice Broaddus had three, and then several authors had two each: A. Merc Rustad, Cadwell Turnbull, Carmen Maria Machado, Charlie Jane Anders, Hugh Howey, Kathleen Kayembe, Maureen McHugh, and Rich Larson. Overall, sixty-six authors (counting collaborations as a single author) are represented in the top eighty.

Caroline M. Yoachim's story selected for inclusion, "Carnival Nine," was also named a finalist for both the Hugo and Nebula Awards. On the Notable list, Linda Nagata's "The Martian Obelisk" was named as a Hugo Award finalist.

As I've noted in past forewords, I don't log every single story I read throughout the year—I only dutifully log stories that I feel are in the running—so I don't have an exact count of how many stories I reviewed or considered. But as in past years, I estimate that it was several thousand stories altogether, perhaps as many as five thousand.

Aside from the top stories I passed along to the guest editor, naturally many of the other stories I read were perfectly good and enjoyable stories but didn't quite stand out enough for me to consider them among the best of the year. I did, however, end up with about thirty additional stories that were at one point or another under serious consideration, including stories from publications not otherwise represented in this anthology (either in the table of contents or on the Notable Stories list), such as *Hobart, The Dark, American Short Fiction, Nature,* and *A Public Space,* as well as the anthologies and collections named above.

This foreword mentions many but not all of the great publications considered for this anthology; be sure to see the table of contents and the Notable Stories list to get a more complete overview of the top publications currently available in the field.

Given all the stories I have to consider every year, it's probably obvious that I can do this only with a considerable amount of help. So I'd just like to take a moment to thank and acknowledge my team of first readers, who helped me evaluate various publications that I might not have had time to consider otherwise, including Alex Puncekar, Becky Sasala, Sandra Odell, Robyn Lupo, Karen Bovenmyer, and Christie Yant. Thanks also to Tim Mudie at Mariner Books, who all along has kept things running smoothly behind the scenes at Best American HQ but who has now, sadly, moved on to other adventures—*ad astra,* Tim! Thanks accordingly, too, to our temporary behind-the-scenes maven, Melissa Fisch—who came in right at the end of the *BASFF* cycle for this volume but ably managed to put out some fires at the last minute—and to our new maven, Jenny Xu.

*

I thought I'd reiterate here something I said in this space in the previous volume, because it's an important thing to remember as fans: Support the Things You Love. This is especially true of anything to do with short fiction, whether it comes to you in the form of magazines or anthologies. Many endeavors that produce some of our finest short fiction exist mainly because the people publishing them are motivated by love for thc form and the genre. Sometimes they're able to make a little money doing it, sometimes not. But no one's getting rich off publishing short fiction, and any venue you can think of needs—and I can't stress the *needs* part enough—your support.

Support need not always come in the form of spending money on the thing (though naturally it often does); there's also word of mouth (both on social media and among your peer group) and writing customer reviews on sites like Amazon (where reviews seem to have the most impact) or Goodreads.

One easy thing to do to support a magazine is to post a reader review for the magazine as a whole on its subscription page (on Amazon or the like). No individual issue of a periodical is ever going to amass a high number of reviews, but the subscription page *might* . . . and having a good star rating should help new readers decide whether or not to give it a shot. And if you enjoy a particular magazine, encourage your friends to check it out as well; many publications have some way to sign up for a trial subscription where readers get at least one issue for free, and of course many magazines, like *Beneath Ceaseless Skies* and *Clarkesworld*, have extensive archives of fiction available online that new readers can sample as well.

All that said, here are a few of the fallen—publications that gave it a go but have now given up the ghost (or at least gone on an extended hiatus) since we launched *BASFF* in 2015: *Bastion, Crossed Genres, Fantastic Stories, Fantasy Scroll, Farrago's Wainscot, Fictionvale, Flurb, Gamut, Goldfish Grimm, Ideomancer, Inhuman, Jamais Vu, Nameless Magazine, Penumbra, Persistent Visions* (rebranded as *PerVisions*), *Scigentasy, Shattered Prism* (no activity in 2017, presumed dead), *Subterranean Magazine, Three-Lobed Burning Eye, Unstuck, Urban Fantasy Magazine, Waylines* . . . and, well, you get the picture. The graveyard of short fiction publications is many rows deep.

In more nebulous territory are magazines such as *Omni*, a legendary magazine in the annals of science fiction that had been defunct for many years and had just recently been attempting a comeback. Alas, *Omni* put out only one issue before its parent company (Penthouse Global Media) filed for bankruptcy, thus leaving *Omni*'s fate in limbo. (It was around long enough to contribute one story to our Notable list this year, though!)

Still, that's one more magazine on a long list of publications that are on the bubble or already dead. And in the spirit of optimistically hoping that some other newer publications can avoid such a fate, I encourage you to check out some of these newer venues that have been publishing consistently interesting material since launching: *Book Smugglers, Diabolical Plots, FIYAH, Lackington's,* and *Liminal Stories.* Those are just a few of the publications I've been reading regularly that seem to be flying under the radar to some degree, so here's hoping that this little signal boost helps ensure they'll live to fight another day.

Editors, writers, and publishers who would like their work considered for next year's edition, please visit johnjosephadams.com/best-american for instructions on how to submit material for consideration.

—JOHN JOSEPH ADAMS

Introduction

SCHRÖDINGER'S CAT INVOLVES a hypothetical sealed box, a flask of poison, and a thought experiment that was never really meant to be applied anywhere but at the quantum level. That's the problem with good thought experiments, though—the cat doesn't stay in the box. The purpose of science fiction, as Ursula K. Le Guin intimated in her introduction to *The Left Hand of Darkness*, is not to predict the future but to describe the world as it presently is. Or does it do both at once? Can science fiction and fantasy, by helping us examine the present, in turn shape the future—and in particular shape it away from its current destructive path? Right now a shadowy cabal seeking to bring about a fascist new world order has become more than a thought exercise. *They* seem to think science fiction and fantasy are pretty important, to the degree that they've been standing in the schoolhouse door whenever possible; that call has been coming from inside the house for a while. How, then, have science fiction and fantasy answered, in 2017?

With a whole lot of goddamn revolution.

Not that this is anything new. Despite the cabal (or maybe because of it), fantasy and science fiction have long been literatures of revolution—most effectively because casual or unanalytical readers fail to recognize them as such. And as Le Guin noted, most readers presume that one of these genres (and only one) is future-oriented. They aggrandize the predictive nature of science fiction while dismissing fantasy as regressive, when in fact both genres are actually about the present: science fiction through allegory, and fantasy by concatenation (e.g., "War of the Roses" + "dragons" + modern moral relativism; "boarding school" + "magic"

+ the creeping cryptofascism of 1990s Britain). These genres' power to reimagine the present is of course a double-edged thing, because those same unanalytical readers tend to become unanalytical writers who thoughtlessly replicate the worst of the status quo. I am obviously being generous here, however, because the genres also include bad actors who intentionally use the power of science fiction and fantasy to entrench notions like "only white people will ever matter" and "men will always rape" and "disabled people should yearn for death" and "fat people can only be miserable and gluttonous." Fortunately, the powers that be—the fans who record the podcasts and organize the awards ceremonies and buy the books and review the movies—are getting better at acknowledging such readers as uncritical and such writers as harmful. That's good, because revolutionary art forms should be bigger than their hype men.

And what can be more revolutionary than "what if," when that speculation speaks truth to power?

So: herein are contained the twenty most revolutionary short stories from the year 2017. It might be helpful if you knew what I meant by *revolutionary,* though!

As I read through the full set of eighty stories, there seemed to be a number of stories that tackled the theme of revolution in well-trodden or overt ways, like AI turning against their creators, cryptocurrencies disrupting economies, and time travelers going back to kill [insert problematic political figure of choice]. Nothing wrong with familiar explorations; we all need to be thinking about what war will look like in the future. But while these kinds of stories are both enjoyable and necessary, I found myself particularly drawn to those that revolted against tradition, revolted against reader expectation, or revolted against the world entirely.

As an example of a revolt against tradition, Maria Dahvana Headley's "Black Powder" fractures the Scheherazade fairy-tale structure, then kintsugis the cracks with school shooting imagery and rage against toxic masculinity. Kate Alice Marshall's "Destroy the City with Me Tonight" wrings from superhero clichés an excoriation of the demands society puts on its youth.

But then Samuel Delany's return to science fiction sees a revolt against form itself—and propriety, and identity—in "The Hermit of Houston." Other stories are similarly explicit in their rejection of the expected. Kathleen Kayembe layers Congolese folklore about twins onto a revenge tale, with surprising results, in "You Will Always Have Family: A Triptych." In Micah Dean Hicks's "Church of Birds," the one-winged swan prince pleads to be set free from the agonizing expectations of a society that will not accommodate his difference. Carmen Maria Machado's "The Resident" disrupts with more subtle, creeping dread as the protagonist performs that most clichéd of writerly rites of passage: heading off to a writing residency. But by the end of the story (no spoilers), her world has been turned inside out.

Most fascinating to me were those stories that revolted against reality itself by scrapping it and starting over entirely. This is because worldbuilding, as the lone skill set unique to science fiction and fantasy writing, is the core of these genres' revolutionary power.

In a two-hour workshop on worldbuilding that I offer to beginning writers, I start by laying out the basic structure of a world. We talk about the macro scale of worldbuilding—what the physical structure of a planet is like, and how this affects climate—and its micro scale, where we delve into social structures and how these might affect an individual character. Microworldbuilding is usually where we discuss the artificially constructed nature of our own reality. We start by discussing speciation, then significant morphological differences within a species, then raciation (and other insignificant morphological differences), then acculturation, and finally power dynamics. For example, I often point out that, morphologically speaking, there's nothing that makes women inherently incapable of combat. We live in a world that frequently employs child soldiers, after all, who tend to be physically weaker than women yet are brutally effective. Only cultural habits make us reluctant to accept that people other than adult cishet men can be capable soldiers—some of us to the point of conjuring up pseudoscientific hogwash to justify our habits (e.g., women are nurturers and therefore wouldn't shoot back). As another example, I talk about the performativity of social status. In our world—the world that readers know best—people of higher social status literally take up more space than everyone else. Correspondingly, people of lower status are expected to compress themselves, and they often do. But what's one of the easiest ways for a defiant person of lower social status to get on a higher-status person's nerves? Take up just as much space. Stand taller, don't hunch up, actually use that elbow

rest between the airplane seats. Demonstrating a thorough understanding of how social structures like these are constructed—and
how they can be challenged—is key if a writer means to establish
trust with savvy readers.

And here I found even more profoundly revolutionary stories. Like Charles Payseur's "Rivers Run Free," which replaces
oppressed people with dammed/diverted/drained rivers who are
anthropomorphically embodied—and piiiiiiissed about what humans have done to them. Here was Caroline M. Yoachim's "Carnival Nine," set in a clockpunk world whose people are born with
windable springs; like Christine Miserandino's spoon theory, it is
a powerful, haunting parable of disability. "Brightened Star, Ascending Dawn," by A. Merc Rustad, posits a world in which people
can be transformed into obedient starships—and a woman thus
enslaved nevertheless defies her masters for the sake of a stowaway
child. I think my favorite of these were the absurdist worlds—like
the one in which a posthuman CEO and bigot gets his comeup-
pance at the hands of a lowly maintenance robot ("Zen and the
Art of Starship Maintenance," by Tobias S. Buckell). Or Rachael
K. Jones's brilliantly bat-shit "The Greatest One-Star Restaurant in
the Whole Quadrant," in which a cyborg chef tries to manipulate
humans through their stomachs . . . well, just read it. It's too good,
and too gonzo, to spoil.

But these are just stories, some of you will say. Just good clean
robotic/sentient spaceship/clockwork fun. Is it not a stretch to la-
bel this *revolution*, when only a few of these stories feature people
getting shot up against a wall?

To which I reply by pointing at human history. The most revolutionary changes in our world have rarely been imposed quickly
or violently, after all, and the gun has not been the primary instrument of lasting change. *Ideas* are far more dangerous to the status
quo, over the long term. Consider gender as a binary, pseudobi-
ological concept. Why did we ever fixate on the idea of just two?
Well, not all cultures have; seems like they've had the right idea all
along. Consider how it became easier for us to imagine an African
American president in 2008, after multiple popular TV shows and
movies featured one in the 1980s and 1990s. Philip K. Dick's *The
Crack in Space* introduced the idea to the zeitgeist in 1966.

So the shadowy cabal is completely right: fantasy and science
fiction are the means through which we ponder the slow ongoing

revolutions of the present and foreshadow—or incite—the next revolutions to come. Maybe if writers sell enough readers on the idea, we'll soon be able to imagine a woman president. Or a society without gun violence . . . or one in which every human life actually does matter . . . or one in which we prioritize education and health over corporate profits. Maybe as stories and novels plausibly depict decolonized or precolonial societies, we might more easily shed the legacy of four hundred years of colonialism.

And at the bare minimum, maybe we can get rid of the damned shadowy cabal.

Readers and writers who lived through 2017 get what's at stake. Readers in 2018 and beyond get it too—and so they will find much to support them (now) and inspire them (later) in this collection. It's about the present *and* the future. Schrödinger's cat is dead in the box, alive in the box, out of the box, and partying on a beach in Goa.

Meet y'all there when the revolution's done.

— N. K. JEMISIN

The Best American
SCIENCE FICTION
and **FANTASY**
2018

CHARLES PAYSEUR

Rivers Run Free

FROM *Beneath Ceaseless Skies*

WHERE VIORA FALLS used to leap four thousand feet into Lake Aerik, her every pounding breath a climax, a triumph, there is now a citadel. It is the great accomplishment of the Lutean Empire—Viora dammed, chained, all her rage and love harnessed now to power their wheels, their cogs and dials and machines.

"They know we're here," Sainet says, voice soft as if unused to speaking. I'm not sure he had ever taken solid form before I found him in a cave system and brought him out into the light. Some say his past makes him cold, but that's not the sense I get from him.

"We have time," I say, more hope than fact. The Dowsers are doubtless on their way, but they haven't learned to fly. And we need to see this. Or I want to see this. To remember this. Whatever happens next.

"Is it true what they say?" Verdan asks. She's the youngest, used to be a branch of the Burgora before the Dowsers diverted the river, cut daughter from mother. "Can they really kill us?"

"As much as they can stop the rain," Mor says, eir voice like iron. Mor, the most faithful to the old songs. The cycles. Change without death, waters without end.

"They can do bad enough," I say, looking down at Aerik, who is nearly dry, alive only by the gentle touch of Viora's waters, not strong enough even to take solid form. He's just a trickle, our reminder and our warning—see what happens when you go against the Luteans. See what happens when river pits itself against human. Everywhere east, where Aerik used to birth a dozen strong rivers that radiated out, bringing life to the valley, there is only the Dust now. See what happens when you resist, when you defy.

We've seen what we needed to see. We all turn toward that bleak
horizon across the Dust, where far beyond the sea might reside,
must reside. We move.

*A truth about rivers: we have always been able to draw our water together
into solid bodies, to walk on two legs. But it is not without risk, and not
without cost. We lose much of ourselves in the transformation, and if there's
not enough of us to start with, well . . .*

We ride stolen horses over the choked earth.

"It's not working," Sainet says.

They've had our trail since the citadel, and there's been nothing since to help us lose them. Sometimes the Dowsers get confused when waters cross, and using the dry riverbed as a road had
seemed nearly safe. But nothing is—safe, that is. Not since the
Luteans discovered what a resource we are.

"We have to turn and face them," Mor says.

I'm tired of fighting. Tired of losing battle after battle. Friend
after friend. I'm tired of running because if I don't a Dowser will
track me down, put me in irons, force me to push a wheel that will
only make them stronger and me weaker, weaker, gone. I want to
win for once.

I close my eyes. The Dust is full of ghosts these days, and some of
them speak. The riverbed we urge our horses faster over was once
the Malbrush. I can feel his confusion when the waters stopped
flowing. When the sun slowly ate him away, drew him into the sky
until nothing remained. Except his memory. I ask to see through
his eyes, and his ghost grants me, reveals the miles he used to run.
And I see a way.

"We keep going," I shout over the sound of the horses' hooves
pounding the dry earth.

"We have to—" Mor starts to say, but I cut em off.

"We'll make our stand up ahead. There's an old waterfall."

Mor smiles as if reading my mind. If there is a hell like the
humans claim, then we're all going to it anyway. But they have to
kill us first.

*A truth about rivers: there used to be laws that kept the peace between
human and river. Or if not laws, an understanding. We liked company,*

*and they liked the food and relief we offered. It worked for everyone until it
didn't, until it only worked for them, and they never looked back.*

I stand with the horses by the edge of the dry waterfall. Not as tall
as Viora, but tall enough for what I intend. I face away from the
dead drop just feet behind me. A cliff, I guess people call it now.
Like this was all natural. I stand with the horses because the Dowsers will know something's wrong if they don't see them. They're
merciless bastards but they know how to track, so it's me and four
horses all standing there, waiting, when they arrive.

"What took you so long?" I ask as two of the four dismount.
They all draw weapons, but shooting from the back of a horse is
bad business, all noise and smoke and panic. So two remain seated,
probably in case I decide to run for it, and two walk slowly forward,
silent. Why are they always silent? Why does that make it worse?

I tried to convince Mor to take the others and run, just run regardless of how this goes. Chances are that I can handle myself—I
have before. I could catch up. But ey just looked at me and I could
feel the hollowness of my words. Of course they can't run. Isn't
this entire trip, our whole mission, about not having to fight alone
anymore? About being stronger together. We're done leaving people behind. So I stand there smiling like an idiot, and the Dowsers
draw forward while Mor feels their footsteps through the sand.

They keep their weapons trained on me, all iron and salt and
fire, the tools they use to bind us, to track us. That and some in-
nate talent that Dowsers have for finding water. Sometimes I wonder that if we had a way to find them as easily as they can find us,
how we'd use the knowledge. If we'd find them as they slept secure
in their beds, if people would find them dead the next morning,
drowned without an inch of standing water to be found. I don't
think it would be more than they deserve.

One of the two approaching me pulls out a pair of iron man-
acles. I smile. Mor acts. Ey rises. From behind their horses a wall
of water jumps to life, splashing from the sands, a sudden torrent
that rolls like an avalanche. The riders have no time at all to react.
In a second they are swept by the wave, pushed forward. I stand
still, which is what dooms the other two, who if they reacted immediately could have run to the side, escaped the wave. But they
pivot, eyes on the wave and then on me, and it's as if they can smell

there's some trick to this, that if they watch me I'll give away how I plan to survive and they can do likewise.

I sink into the sand. Do they think to try that before the wave catches them as well? If they do, it doesn't work. They are swept along. As are our horses. And they all go over the cliff. I don't watch, don't want to see the terror in the horses' eyes, don't want to face that we're all merciless bastards.

I rise, see Mor kneeling in the sand right at the edge watching them fall, eir body heaving from the effort that must have taken, from the water ey has lost. But it worked. And from the falls we can look out at the Dust and see it spread to the horizon like a gray blanket. Huge. Desolate. Nearly featureless except, far in the distance, a collection of buildings betrays what must have been a town once. What it is now, we'll just have to see.

A truth about rivers: all waters are alive to some degree, though not all can stand and talk. It takes volume and movement and force to birth a river, to bring water to full awareness, but the potential is always there. In our oldest stories, it was water that gave soul to humans, falling on their clay bodies and infusing them with some touch of the divine. In our new stories, that was a mistake.

The town is like most things in the Dust—a ghost of what it used to be. Malbrush used to flow down through two dozen farms and near the thriving town center, but now only a handful of the buildings remain, the rest claimed by what looks like fire. A common occurrence where wood used to be the primary building material.

"This is—" Mor's words are eaten by a fit of coughing that wracks eir body, but I know what ey means.

"A mistake," I finish for em. Perhaps it is. But losing our horses means we'll be easier to Dowse, and most places in the Dust hate the Luteans as much as we do. It wasn't just the rivers to have suffered when the citadel was erected. Viora wasn't the only one damned by that treachery.

"I just need—" ey starts to say but can't finish. Time? Rest? Rain? All rather impossible at the moment. But the town is here and might have rain stores they'd be willing to share. So we limp into town and aren't surprised to find a woman wearing a star on her chest and resting a Lutean rifle against her shoulder.

"We're not looking for trouble," she says, which is its own sort of hello out here.

I nod. "We're not bringing it," I lie.

Her eyes narrow as she studies us. Like most people in the Dust, her skin is a pale tan, not the slightly blue tinge of our own. She knows what we are, and must know that the rifle she carries offers her some protection. And she's careful. I can feel at least five other people hidden in the mostly deserted town.

"Traveling on foot?" she asks. I have questions of my own, like where she got the rifle. The Luteans don't just hand those out, so it means she's either working for them or took it off the dead. I'm betting it's the second of those, but can't be sure.

"We lost our horses at the falls," I say.

"That's a shame," she says.

"Well, we lost a team of Dowsers too, so it sort of evened out," I say.

She nods, then lowers the rifle so it's pointing at the ground and walks forward.

"Then you have my thanks." She extends her hand and I take it, feel her firm grip. Her eyes don't leave mine and I can tell she's weighing me. Testing me. I hold her gaze until she smiles and gives a sharp whistle. The five people hiding all step into the street, weapons lowered. We pass the test, I guess.

"I'm Sheriff Arleth Yates," she says. "Welcome to Abbotsville."

A truth about rivers: I do not know the first river the Luteans managed to chain. The notion was so foreign a concept we didn't even know to fear it. Like an infant whose first experience with water is to be completely submerged, it took us too long to realize the rules of our world had changed, and that we were in great danger.

I sit at the table the sheriff has set for us. The food is more than I would have expected from a place like this.

"Where are you headed?" Deputy Owens asks. He's a large man with light eyes that seem always squinting. I catch the sheriff shooting him a warning look, but I shrug. There's no real harm in telling them. After the falls, after everything, maybe it will help them all to hear it out loud.

"To the sea," I say. The word is like a cold draft through the room, and all of us straighten in our seats.

"Sounds like a long way to go," the sheriff says, studying my face like she's reading a map. "I've only heard stories, and none that I could really credit. Doesn't hardly seem possible, all that water in one place."

"It's real," I say. I can feel Sainet's eyes on me. Verdan's. Mor's.

"I suppose it makes sense, looking to run away," the sheriff says. "What with those Lutean bastards. Some things, there's no real fighting."

"We're not running away," I say. We're not. What would that do? The Luteans won't be content with just the rivers in what's now the Dust. Their citadel will grow taller, their wheels larger, until the whole world is empty of free waters.

"Didn't mean anything by it," Sheriff Yates says, raising her hands.

"We're going to bring it back," I say.

The sheriff's eyes widen. Sainet sucks in a ragged breath.

"Beyond the Dust," I say, "and beyond the mountains and beyond the forests and farther still, there's the sea. So vast and so powerful that the waters of it know no fear. And we'll tell the sea of what's happening here, and it will feel the pain of its children and it will rise and flow across the land. Over the forests and the mountains and the Dust and it will tear down the dams and the dikes and the locks and the citadel. And the Dust will be green again, and the Luteans will drown and . . ."

I realize that I'm breathing heavily, that I'm leaning over the table toward the sheriff, that there's a storm inside me. It's my prayer, my hope. I look up, see Sainet staring at me. He's breathing hard too, pupils large.

"Excuse me, I think I need to lie down," I say. I stand, flee the table and the pounding in my veins and the ghosts of the dead and the hope of the sea. I find the room the sheriff has left us and fall inside, everything in me shaking. I sink to my knees, feel part of myself leaking away. I'm crying.

I feel a presence behind me, turn to see Sainet standing there, his face a mask of hunger and despair. He closes the door. I rise to meet him.

What ever made me think I could forget this? Sainet's mouth on mine, his hands tearing at clothing. What made me think this was something I had forgotten how to do? Was it the running? The death? Was all I needed this short respite without Dowsers on our heels to remember? This refuge in Abbotsville?

I react, curving myself against his body, fitting myself to him. Mouth, neck, chest, stomach, hips—we're touching at every point, our bodies liquid and solid and pulling. Somewhere else Mor is sitting with Sheriff Yates and Deputy Owens, and ey has to know what is happening. We aren't human, can't ignore the signs, the way the earth seems to hold its breath, the way the dry night air is suddenly humid, hot.

There is a creak of the door opening, and I know it's Verdan without having to look to see. Peeking at the doorway. I don't stop. She's old enough to know, and I'm not sure I could stop now anyway. Not with the way Sainet's hands are sliding over my ass, working at the pull of my belt.

I think of our last time. How long ago now? I remember darkness, meeting in a rush. Like this. Always like this, hidden from the sun and the Dowsers and any chance of discovery. How long since I have met with another without fear? But they are all unfair questions with Sainet tugging down my pants, pushing me to the bed, onto my back.

I don't cry out as he enters me. I don't whimper or moan. What releases from my lips is a sigh, short and soft, and then I'm pulling him down to kiss me again. It makes the movements awkward, inelegant, but at this moment I need the taste of him, crisp and cool and clear. He is stone and mineral and a hint of salt and perfect, like how the sea must taste. I let him go and we find our rhythm, our flow, his hand around me and him inside me, and my mind is finally free of questions.

And then I feel the rising deep within me, a well that is suddenly overflowing, moving up and up and we do cry out then, voices twined and reaching. Toward each other and toward something else, somewhere else that we're not even sure of except in the hope that lives and dies in the pleasure spreading through us, our skins disappearing and reappearing in a thunderclap of climax. And slowly we come back to each other. To the bed, the room. To Verdan breathing heavily at the door and Mor sitting flushed, talking to the sheriff and deputy.

And somewhere beyond that, another presence as well, an echo of someone we hadn't noticed before. And they're crying for our help.

*

A truth about rivers: There's water nearly everywhere. In the air and in the ground and in the morning songs of the birds who no longer fly here. Too small, too diffused to speak on its own, we can still use it to speak to each other, and to see what humans hope is concealed.

It's early when we slide from the old inn and make our way across town. The sheriff is hopefully still sleeping, but even if she's not, we can't put this off. The call is clearer now, and only we can hear it. The town is silent as we follow the voice to its source. Of course it's the well. Was there any doubt it would be? I look at Sainet, but he won't meet my gaze, keeps his head on a pivot, watching for signs the town knows what we're up to.

"What is it?" Verdan asks, but even she knows the answer. None of us speak, and she doesn't ask again as we examine the well, a shaft of stone piercing the earth. Ever since the Dust has been the Dust, the wells have been dry, but we can all feel the water below.

"Look around for some gearbox," I say. The well has been modified since its original construction, augmented with gears and piping, a faint clicking that belies Lutean technology. It feels like there's a storm inside me, a tempest. I clench my jaw and Mor grunts as ey pulls up a wooden board covered by the sand. Underneath, the clicking intensifies.

"So they're working for the Empire, then?" Sainet asks.

I shake my head, examining the materials used. It's Lutean made, definitely, but it's cobbled together from bits and pieces. Probably the town had managed to ambush a patrol or a caravan. Or maybe raid one of the small Lutean outposts that separate the Dust from the Empire. Probably the sheriff had been telling the truth about just how much they hated the Luteans. This was . . .

"We need to break it," I say. There's a wrench left next to the gearbox, no doubt in case they need to make repairs. I pick it up and bring it down as hard as I can against the metal case. Once, twice, each strike a bell letting the town know what we're doing. But it needs to be done. After three strikes something clangs inside, and the clicking stops.

"Get them up," I say, and instantly Sainet and Mor are sliding down the well, bodies liquefying. I'm almost afraid to see who they bring up.

"Why did they do it?" Verdan asks from beside me. The wrench feels hot in my hand. I can't answer. Only the sheriff will be able to answer for this.

When Mor and Sainet return they're pulling another with them. Verdan and I step forward, place our hands upon them, and share what water we can spare. The moment our waters mingle we know them. Druun. From the borders of the Dust. I see their journey, their flight from the Dowsers. I see them walk into Abbotsville and see Sheriff Yates welcome them with open arms.

A bell begins to ring. A warning. A promise.

"We're getting out of here," I say.

Sheriff Yates is waiting for us in the street.

"You should of just left well enough alone," she shouts as we keep to the shadows. I can feel more people around us. More than the five from before. Did she call them as soon as she knew what we were? Had she been hoping to profit from our visit in more ways than just sending riders out to loot the Dowsers' bodies? Druun doesn't look so good, though they seem much better now that they're out under the open sky. What they've been through —I shudder. It's no worse than the Luteans and so much worse.

"We're not looking for trouble," I shout back, knowing that it's too late for that. Too late for so much. I adjust my grip on the wrench in my hand.

I motion to Sainet to separate, enter the dilapidated buildings. The dark is his home, and I know no one is a match for him there. What to do about the sheriff is another matter entirely. I look at Mor, who is helping Druun but is hardly recovered emself. Which leaves me and Verdan.

"Well, I'm bringing it," Sheriff Yates says, taking aim at us with her rifle. "You put them back in the well or this is going to end in blood."

"I thought you were better than this," I say. "Better than the Luteans."

"I am better than the Luteans!" she nearly screams at me, the barrel of her rifle wavering. "You think we want it this way? We're just making the best of a bad situation, and not one that we caused. What were we supposed to do? Die? Wait for you to show up with your magic sea and save us? What good would that have done any- one? With the power that river gives us, at least we can fight. We can fight to keep the Lutean bastards from taking anything more."

"The citadel's a long way from here," I say. "And it's not a Lutean you've been torturing." My fingernails dig into my palms from where my fists are clenching. I look at Verdan. Her face is set, her body rigid. I can hear something in her, the rage of rapids pounding over rock. She's old enough for this too.

"What do you expect?" Yates calls. "Their power, their weapons . . . how are we supposed to fight them without using what they use? It's not like you lot were out here volunteering to help."

"So this is our fault?" I ask. I nod to Verdan, who starts inching forward along the side of the building. We need to separate, to give the sheriff multiple targets, to draw her attention away from Mor and Druun.

"I don't care whose fault it is," the sheriff says, "as long as me and mine survive it."

"Then you're no better than the Luteans," I say. "Only different."

And then I charge her.

I feel the shot but it doesn't stop me. In the shadows Sainet is killing and in the light I am swinging the wrench in my hand. It's fitting, the sharp shock of impact, the wet thud. The wrench isn't mine and it's not theirs, but it has doomed us both. I keep hitting until my arm is numb and the wrench slips free into the sand. I'm on my knees again, leaking.

No. No, this is not how it ends. I push myself to my feet. This is not the end. Around me there is a new chaos, and I can smell something burning. Abbotsville. The town is burning. Good. I put one foot in front of the other, and then Sainet is there, face spotted with ash.

"We have to go," he says, and there's something in his voice, a ragged hurt and desperation. Not cold at all.

Pain causes me to groan, nearly collapse, but I manage a nod. We'll run, run until we are free.

A truth about rivers: There's so much gone now. Not just our dead but all that we held. The fish and the plants—the life. What remains is only dry earth and memories, and maybe there will come a day when not even those are left.

I keep my mind on Sainet's voice and the feeling of putting one foot in front of the other. I'm leaking. Fucking sea I'm leaking, ripe wet droplets of me sinking into the sand. Gut shot. That's what I am. That's what— I stumble and cry out and Sainet's arms catch me, keep me from falling.

Everything's jumbled. I can't keep it straight.

"Wasn't supposed to be like this," I say. It was supposed to be . . .

"It's nothing," Sainet says. "You're going to be fine." He calls for Mor and Verdan, but they have their hands full with Druun.

A merry bunch we all make. Each step I take wets the sands, causes my feet to stick in earth that's ravenous for moisture. I would kill for a horse, but I'm afraid I've killed for far less, far more, far far away where rivers run free. There is blood on my hands and mingled with the water spilling from me with each step. Whatever the bullet is, inside me, I can feel it doing its work.

"Have you ever been to the sea?" I ask. To Sainet, or maybe to Druun. To anyone. What does it matter anyway?

"The sea is a myth," Sainet says. Of course he doesn't believe. I want to ask him why he came then, but I'm afraid of the answer. Even now.

I take another step, another. I will not die here. I will not die here. Behind me I feel the heat of the flames. It's almost inviting. I don't look back.

"One day the sky will take us up one final time." It's Mor. Ey is suddenly standing there, one of Druun's arms draped over eir shoulder. Ey seems mostly recovered now, but there's a slight quaver in eir voice. "And the wind will take us out to sea, and we will fall as rain into the endless waters."

"I'd like to see it," I say. I falter again. More hands steady me. There's Verdan, eyes still wide. Why is it they have to learn so young to be hated?

"I'm sure you will," she says. "Just like you said. We'll find the sea and we'll bring it back with us, to tear down the dams and the dikes and the locks. Just like you said."

I smile. Just like I said.

A truth about rivers: Sometimes we lie. And sometimes we tell the truth. And sometimes we hope so hard we can't tell where one ends and the other begins.

I'm on the beach, reclined, my head in Sainet's lap, my eyes closed. He runs a hand through my hair. If I open my eyes I will see it, the endless expanse of the sea. I will hear the countless voices speaking as one and they will tell me it will be all right.

"I'm tired," I say, and realize just how true it is. How did I ever get this tired?

"Don't quit on me now," Sainet says.

I smile. *I'm not quitting,* I want to say. *Just taking a rest. A little rest. Haven't I earned that?* But words won't rise in my throat.

"Open your eyes," Sainet says. I hear other voices too. Of course. Mor is here, and Verdan, and Druun too. All here. "Open your eyes."

There's an edge to Sainet's voice. I want to tell him to relax. We've come so far. We've come so far. But Sainet's right. We're not done yet. I move my hand over the fine sand of the beach. It almost feels like dust.

I open my eyes. The sea is so very far away.

"Take me there," I say, though it hurts to say anything. Soon I'll be gone into the Dust, but right now I can hold together long enough to . . . "Take me to the sea."

They crowd around me. Mor and Verdan each take one of my hands in theirs and Druun touches my shoulder. I will make it to the sea, even if I never see it.

"Thank you," I say, and close my eyes. I let go. I let it all go, and I think of Viora and freedom. I am a waterfall bound for the thirsty sand, nearly gone, nearly gone.

Until they catch me.

Through them all, I am. I give, like we gave to Druun after we pulled them from the well, and all that I am they catch, my hopes and my dreams—my waters, until I am just a wave passing through them, soon to crash and fade but for this moment alive in them all, connecting them.

They—now we—all look down at the dry earth, vacant now but for my empty clothes. We stretch, bodies suddenly refreshed, wounds gone as if washed clean. We stand and look back at Abbotsville burning.

"Let's go," Mor says, and we turn toward the horizon, and the mountains beyond that, and the forest beyond that, and the sea beyond that, and start walking.

KATE ALICE MARSHALL

Destroy the City with Me Tonight

FROM *Behind the Mask*

CASS GETS THE diagnosis in high school, three weeks shy of eighteen, full of dreams about Paris and London and New York. She's always had the aches. Growing pains, her mother tells her— normal. She repeats it to herself as they wait for the X-rays— *normal*—in a waiting room with a broken air conditioner— *normal*— and an antiseptic smell. She repeats it when the nurse calls them back— *normal*—while the doctor looks down at his notes— *normal* —all the way until he says the words.

Caspar-Williams Syndrome.

The city is mapped on her bones, to lines that wrap ribs, tibia, mandible. A dense knot of streets engraves her sternum; a lonely road carves a notch in her clavicle. An intersection splays like a starfish below her left eye, and she stares at the shadow of it on the X-ray as the doctor explains. Rare condition. Few known cases. Well, we've all seen the news.

Her mother gives a strangled laugh, covers her mouth. "It's only," she says. "It's only, I thought I was going loopy in my middle age, but I guess . . ."

Cass thinks of the times her mother has forgotten to pick her up. Has seemed startled that she's in the room. Has stuttered over her name or only stared a moment, bewildered, as if she does not know who this stranger is.

Normal.

"The pain will get worse if she doesn't leave. She might have weeks or months or years before it's unbearable," the doctor says, but Cass doesn't wait around. She's never liked long goodbyes.

It takes her a week to find the right city, searching maps for familiar streets, matching them to the osseous grooves beneath her skin. It's not London or Paris or New York; it's nowhere she'd choose to go, but she buys a one-way ticket. Her doctor gives her the name of a local specialist, but she never calls the number. There's no cure, after all, and she's had enough of tests.

She gets a job at a diner and an apartment barely big enough for a bed. The street she lives on sits snug in the crook of her left elbow. For the first time in years, her bones don't ache.

She waits.

It's six months before the visions start. The city starts her out easy: a little girl lost ten blocks from home. Cass walks her back and leaves her at the doorstep. It's stolen suitcases next, dumped in the bushes, money scraped out but otherwise intact. A few weeks after that, it's a mugging. She takes a fist to the stomach, punches back, feels the man's bones break. She doesn't even bruise.

Her boss forgets to give her shifts. Then he forgets she works there at all. But that's all right; her landlord's forgotten she's there too and stops collecting rent. Cass spends her nights riding buses, always tucked in the rearmost seat, waiting to be where the city wants her. She never once fights it.

Two years in, the symptoms are getting worse. Her fingerprints have smoothed out, vanished. Her features blur in photographs. She can stand in a room for an hour before people notice her.

She's always wondered why you'd bother with a mask; now she gets it. It's not to be concealed, it's to be seen, to be remembered. Her mask is pale blue, the hint of feathers at the edges; she gets wings tattooed across her shoulders. When the name arrives, it's Seraph. She takes to it, ditches Cass entirely. No one's called her by name in over a year anyway.

The city offers up a better apartment, right on Main Street. The former tenant is dead, a tunnel taking the place of his right eye, the killing too quick for the city to catch on. She drops the killer off at the police station and cleans up the blood. The walls are decorated with black-and-white photos: New York, Paris, London. She frames her X-rays and hangs them next to Big Ben.

The next day she gets shot. It's the fifth time, but it still stings.

*

The apartment on Main has been "vacant" for six years now. At some point the former tenant's family showed up for his things, but they somehow forgot to take the bed, the couch, the TV, the photos. They looked uneasy when they left, and they lingered, engine idling, for nearly an hour. She almost wished they'd come back and demand she get out, but like everyone else, they shook it off and left.

Seraph's skin is a map of its own now—scars too deep to heal clean. Bullets, knives. Rebar that punched through just under her ribs. Not enough to kill her, though she knows that they can die. She watched it happen once, on the news, the one called Glaive, body slicing downward through the air for a few graceful seconds before gravity and asphalt put an end to her momentary flight. Death breaks the amnesiac contagion; in death, she is remembered, known. Her name was Danielle and no one pushed her.

Seraph gets a recording. Watches it on repeat and wonders when she'll get too weary of being forgotten. When she goes, she decides, she doesn't want to be witnessed.

Another winter passes.

He shows up in April, when the streets are wet and cool. Another Caspar-Williams. The Rothschild variant, though it hasn't been proven that the variation is one of pathology rather than psychology. Every city produces a Rothschild eventually. An echo, a reflection, the destruction to her protection. Whether it's a matter of balance or just a fluke mutation of the virus, no one knows.

Shadows seethe around him when he moves. He's faster than her, hard to keep a fix on; his symptoms are advanced. That worries her, as she steps over the bodies he's left for her; she should have known about him before now if he's been infected this long. He kills bad men, but not exclusively. He doesn't seem to have any point or purpose but destruction.

Their first real fight is at the arboretum. She gets dirt in her hair and a broken arm and doesn't land a blow. Then the Main Street Bank, then the subway, then the football stadium, and by then she can't taste anything but her own blood, and her ears won't stop ringing.

"Why bother?" he asks her, before dislocating her shoulder with a twist. She doesn't have an answer.

She sits in the diner where she used to work, arm in a sling. No one comes to serve her; they never do. Symptom of the disease. She's not wearing her mask. She's no one. So it takes her a while to hear the voice calling her.

"Cass." The woman's said it three times before Seraph looks up. The woman is middle-aged, tired. She's clutching a page ripped out of a school yearbook. Distantly, Seraph remembers the faces on the rear side. Recognizes a few names too.

"Mom," Seraph says. Not sure if she's surprised or glad or anything at all. She's spent years trying to forget her family, her friends, as thoroughly as they've forgotten her. No use clinging to what she can't have. Now the memories hurt like a half-healed wound wrenched open again.

The woman sits down across from her, smooths the page out on the table between them. One picture is circled. The girl looks vaguely familiar. *Cass,* the woman has written, letters traced and re-traced until they're thick and manic. Arrows point to the picture, more words. *Cass your daughter cass CASS casS don't forget CASS.*

"I don't know if I'll remember long enough," the woman says. "So I wrote it all down, everything I wanted to say." She slides an envelope across the table, stuffed thick with folded paper. Her eyes are already getting distant. "There's treatment now. Maybe a cure. That's what they're saying."

Seraph allows herself a moment of fantasy. In her mind, they talk for a while. Catch up. The woman, her mother, says that she's proud of what Seraph's done. That she misses her.

In reality, she only gets those few sentences. Then the woman gets a puzzled expression, stands. She shakes her head a little, like she's forgotten something, and picks up the envelope before wandering away. She leaves the page from the yearbook.

Seraph folds it neatly into eighths and tucks it in her pocket. She doesn't cry; even she has trouble remembering Cass these days.

She goes to the cathedral and sits at the peak of the roof, the wind tugging at her hair. There's nowhere in the city she can't get. It's in her bones, after all. She's not surprised when he shows up, but she is surprised when he sits down next to her.

"My mother came to see me today," she says.

"That's a head trip," he says, and she nods. He offers her a cigarette; she declines.

"She says there's a cure."

"You going to take it?"

It's already the longest conversation she's had in years. "Would you?"

He shrugs. "I'm faster and stronger than anyone alive. I can heal a bullet wound with a nap."

"And you just use it to cause mayhem."

"And I'm supposed to what, save kittens from trees?"

"If you don't get the cure, I can't," Seraph says. "I can't let you run amok."

"Amok?" he laughs. "Okay. I'm your fault, you know."

"How are you my fault?"

"You infected me," he reminds her, and for a moment, it works. For a moment, she remembers.

Three weeks shy of eighteen, dreams of London and Paris and New York. He wants to see the Great Wall; she wants to see the Grand Canyon. He draws a map across her skin with one finger.

He sits in the waiting room with her. He holds her hand. Normal, *she whispers; he squeezes her fingers tight.*

The doctor tells them sexual transmission is unusual but not unheard of. Her mother turns scarlet; Cass looks away. He just nods. At least they'll get to take one trip together. A pair of one-way tickets, but they don't talk. When they get to the city, they rent an apartment barely big enough for a bed. She waits tables; he washes dishes.

When the visions start, she goes out to meet them. He stays home, digging the heels of his palms into his eyes, trying to blot them out. She tries to convince him not to fight them: it's easier if you give in.

The city finds her a new place. She looks at photos of London and Paris and New York and wonders if she should get anything from the old apartment. But she can't think of anything she cares about enough to bring.

She blinks. The memory is gone. He's still there, but not for long. He's standing, stubbing out his cigarette.

"I'm your fault," he says. "I've done everything I can to remember you, but you never even tried to hold on to me. You left me behind."

She can't remember whether that's true, but she doesn't argue. She goes home instead. Smooths out the yearbook page. She finds his photo. The name beneath it isn't familiar, but he's signed next to the picture. *Can't wait for the summer.* A sloppy heart.

The morning paper arrives. They've given him a name: *Night-*

blade. Dramatic. She thinks he'd like it, though she can't say why. She frames his picture, puts it up on her wall next to Paris and an X-ray of the bones of her right hand.

The nights they're too weary to fight, they meet at the church. Half the time she can't remember why she's there until he shows. They don't talk much. Shared silence is revelation enough.

She watches a special on Caspar-Williams. It's still misunderstood, the mechanism of transmission imprecisely imagined. They're the only two in their city, but elsewhere there are more. Dozens. New York, London, Paris. Men and women with maps on their bones, cities that own them. Most are like the two of them, strong and fast and quick to heal. But she sees a woman sheathed in flame, a man whose skin sprouts plates of armor like a beetle's carapace.

She pauses on a blurred image of herself in mid-leap, shadows streaming behind her like wings. She can't even see herself clearly in mirrors anymore.

"I have an idea," he says that night. "We can keep our powers and escape the city. See the world together, like we planned."

She pretends to know what he's talking about. Some nights she remembers. Tonight isn't one of them. "How?" she asks.

"You'll see."

She doesn't see him for weeks. She keeps hearing about the cure. Watches an interview with a former Caspar-Williams sufferer. His cheeks are hollow, eyes sunken, but he smiles, arm around a wife who thought she was single the last three years. She doesn't seem to know what to do with herself.

"What has your life been like, the last three years?" the reporter asks her. She hesitates a long time. "It was good," she says at last, not looking at him, not looking anywhere in particular. "I didn't know I missed him."

Seraph crouches on the cathedral steeple, waits for him to show. The city calls to her; for just one night, she doesn't answer. Winter passes.

It's spring when he finds her again. Things have been quiet without him; she's lost the habits necessary to survive such utter isolation. When he tells her to follow him, she doesn't hesitate.

The machine is a nest of wires and clear tubing. Phosphorescent liquid churns at its core; it clings to the wall like a starfish, like a tumor. It pulses with the heartbeat of a dying titan. Seraph runs her hands over the cold metal; the city's fear is electric in her blood.

"Destroy the city with me," he says. "Destroy the city, and we'll be free. We'll still be strong. But we can go wherever we want."

She presses her body to the machine, fitting her limbs among its protuberances, laying her cheek against its thrumming heart.

"I can never remember your name," she confesses. "I put your picture on the wall, and I still can't remember."

"We loved each other," he says.

"I can't remember that either." She steps away. "I have to stop you."

"You don't have to do it for me," he says. "Do it for yourself. See London and New York. Just think about it."

She tells him she won't, but she does. The notion itches, scratches, burrows.

Haven't I done enough for you? she asks the city. Its fear grows more urgent with every hour; her dreams are filled with glowing liquid and a heartbeat that shudders with promise.

She gets the number of the man she saw interviewed. He agrees to meet. By the time he gets there, he's forgotten why he's come, but he answers her questions. He doesn't regret it. She asks him what made him do it.

"I was lonely," he says. Then he shakes his head. "That's not it. Honestly, I couldn't stand seeing that everyone I loved got along fine without me."

She tells him about the machine. He asks what she's going to do.

"I could give him the cure," she suggests, but he shakes his head again. It's not a syringe of blue liquid you can jam in his thigh; it's months of drugs and radiation. She looks at his skin, paper-thin, his color like a day-old bruise. She wonders how much life he's traded to have any life at all.

"The thing is," she tells him, though he's lost track of her now, doesn't register her voice, "the thing is, if I stop him, I've got to kill him. Or else I've got to stay here forever. Because he won't go for the cure, and he won't stop trying."

She stares at her hands, her fingers gnarled from fractures that have healed over wrong.

"I've never killed anyone before."

He laughs at something on his phone. She leaves him with the bill and walks down a street that stretches from the nape of her neck to the base of her spine.

It is not, in the end, a beautiful city. It has no real soul to it; it is forgettable, indistinct. It clings to her, infests her, gives little in return. No one on this street knows her name.

He joins her. They walk the city, stand at the edge, where the pain sets its teeth gently against their throats.

"It's ready," he tells her. He takes her hand. "Cass. Destroy the city with me tonight. Destroy the city, and be free."

She almost remembers him. In a way, it makes it easier, or else nearly impossible, when she turns to him, kisses him, hands on either side of his face. When she wrenches her hands to the side. When she feels his neck break.

It's not enough to kill him. There is no magical serum to make him weak, no stone from the orbit of a distant sun, no incantation. There's only brute strength and the crack of bones. Too much damage to heal.

When it's done, she goes to the church steeple. The city thanks her with a sunrise more brilliant and more beautiful than any she's ever seen, flooding light over men and women who are alive because of what she's done. Because of the blood drying to grime in the creases of her hands.

Not one of them knows her name. Not one of them knows about the machine still under their feet, waiting for a switch to be flipped.

The city shows her something new. Six hundred miles away, someone's matching her streets to the map on their bones, praying for an end to the ache. It's a promise, a gift. The city's consolation prize. *You won't be alone.*

She leans back. Wonders what part she'll play when they get here. Maybe they'll work together. She'll get a sidekick, and they'll get a mentor who knows every brick and shadow. They'll get each other. They won't have to be alone.

Except she was never alone, and she was. He was always here, and it wasn't enough.

Except that she hasn't taken apart the machine. She should have headed straight there. Scattered its pieces, destroyed its blueprints. She hasn't. She's finding that she likes the option. The switch she could flip and opt out of this whole dance.

Except that she knows, if she's willing to admit it, that someday —not soon, but someday—she'd smile. She'd hold out her hand. And she'd say, *Destroy the city with me tonight.*

She could fight it—for a while. But she's got one death to her name now. Another would be easy. Another hundred wouldn't be hard. Her disease is advanced; she has trouble remembering herself these days, but she remembers enough to know that isn't the way she wants to be.

She smokes his cigarettes until the sun comes up. The city calls to her to reconsider, but she's made her choice. She walks to the clinic, blood still caked beneath her nails.

There's no paperwork to fill out; they move too quickly, the only way to ensure the treatment actually gets started before the disease wins out.

The needle slides into her arm. No blue liquid; it's clear, and it slithers into her blood like poison, hot and acidic. Her bones begin to ache, and the city grieves.

In another city, far away, a woman runs her fingers over the letters carved in her kitchen table. CASS, they say, and she begins to remember.

Further still, six hundred miles and more, someone buys a bus ticket. They step on board, searching for the streets etched on their bones.

KATHLEEN KAYEMBE

You Will Always Have Family: A Triptych

FROM *Nightmare Magazine*

Isobelle: The Whispers of Dogs

UNCLE SAYS THERE'S a pit bull in Mbuyi's old room, but he's lying, and his eyes are scared. Dogs aren't pets in Congo, they're for guarding — it's why Dad never got us one, and how I first knew Uncle had no pet dog. I tried to learn what he was hiding, but the more I asked questions, the worse his lies got, until I finally asked if I could just *see* the dog, and Uncle snapped. His fear and frustration exploded into an angry lecture about respecting my elders; and how I'm too much like spoiled American kids; and that I'd better be careful — no self-respecting man wants a woman who badgers him with questions, and that's true no matter what country you're from.

I bore the tirade in silence, which my American friends didn't understand. Dad and Uncle were close friends in Kinshasa; although he's not blood, he's *family,* and his lectures carry near-parental weight. His French and sociology lectures at UMass are far more pleasing, of course, but to hear Uncle at his best, watch him gather folklore. Once he's turned in spring grades, he travels the country collecting stories of other people from Congo, living off of grants for the eventual book these stories will become, and on the hospitality of those he interviews. Uncle records oral histories, conducting interview after interview and transcribing them.

Uncle loves stories about The Way Things Were — my favorites — but he loves stories of the old religions and witchcraft more. Those are the stories my grandparents never told their children except through actions and naming, and superstitious talk in outdoor markets with other adults about rain and harvest and what evil magic can be done to you if you don't properly dispose of your hair when it is cut and a witch gets hold of it.

Those are the stories Uncle is really seeking. They're what made him lean forward in his seat, dark eyes narrowing and hands stilling over the scuffed cherry wood of our kitchen table. He didn't look down at his list of questions the entire time Dad and Aunt Ntshila talked about their strange dreams the week before my grandmother died. He listened—really listened—when they told him their mother had asked them to gather all of her children and bring them back home. When Dad said sometimes he feels her spirit with him, Uncle even seemed to understand.

I watched Uncle as avidly as he watched them.

And then I watched him lie about the dog shut in the upstairs bedroom. I watched his fear when I stood on the stairwell to move my suitcase from his path. I watched his panicked insistence that I stay closed in the office bedroom from midnight until dawn whenever I slept over.

Something makes noise in Mbuyi's old bedroom, but I know it is not a dog.

I climbed the stairs once, to the second floor of Uncle's apartment, when he left to buy goat meat to teach me to cook. I wanted to see what was up there, but in case he asked, the downstairs bathroom—mine for the summer—was out of clean towels, and they are stored in the upstairs hall closet. I climbed the wood stairs, black twisted railing under my hand wobbling the whole way up, and stairs creaking under my feet. I stood at the closet door with closed bedroom doors on either side of me. On the right was Uncle's bedroom. On the left was his son Mbuyi's room, before Mbuyi disappeared.

Now it is the dog's room, Uncle says.

But dogs don't bang on doors with the sound of a shoulder or a fist. Dogs don't rasp obscenities in jagged French with a voice as sweet as sugarcane. Dogs don't make fear rise up in your bones from somewhere so deep you didn't know it was there. They don't make you afraid to turn away from whatever space they could inhabit, or to sit with your back to the door they are behind, or to close your eyes—even to blink—for fear they will be in front of you when your eyes open again. They don't fill your chest to bursting with a haze of adrenaline and sluggishness. The whispers of dogs are not meant to haunt our dreams.

I never did open that door.

That night, like every night, Uncle said, "This is an old superstition," and he blessed me with wrinkled fingers pressed to my forehead, hung a necklace of beads on the lintel, said goodnight, and gently closed the door. That night, the summer of my freshman year at UMass, Uncle's odd superstition suddenly held new meaning—and wasn't enough. I locked my door. I spent that night huddled on the futon in the downstairs office, for once all too happy not to open my door until dawn, even if I had to go to the bathroom. I wait to lock it now until I hear him moving upstairs; I don't want to seem rude. I also don't want to sleep with the door unlocked while something lives up in Mbuyi's old bedroom.

I often played in Mbuyi's room when I was little. While Uncle sat with my parents downstairs, he let Mbuyi and me play mancala with his nice board, the one of polished wood with hand-carved faces of men and of women with cornrowed hair, their nimble fingers wrapped around flowering vines. Mbuyi's scarred right hand could always hold all the beads, and he chose which hollow to scoop from faster than I did. Still, though I was younger, we were almost evenly matched. I took a long time to move each turn, but strategizing for the game came naturally to me. He was more reckless, but didn't mind losing to a girl who was younger as long as we both had fun.

Mbuyi was my favorite cousin, and although given the name for an older twin, he remained Uncle's only child. When I asked Mbuyi —once—why he had no younger twin, no Kanku, he rubbed his long scar. Then he left and stayed gone long past dark. When he returned and Uncle yelled at him, Mbuyi asked something in Tshiluba. Uncle immediately shut himself inside his room. No one spoke of it again. Mbuyi never explained his obsession with returning to Congo, but at twenty-three he finally did. He stayed in Kinshasa with my grandfather and boarded the plane to return to the States after seven weeks meeting family I have yet to meet, eating food I'm still not skilled enough to cook, and being exposed to a way of life my father says will "show you how some people live." That is to say, one cannot go to Congo and return as spoiled as one left.

Only Uncle knows if Mbuyi came back less spoiled; the day after his return, Mbuyi was declared missing. None of us have heard from him since. He had no car to find by the side of the road or in a ditch or the Connecticut River. His friends knew nothing about where he'd been. Uncle was distraught and cut himself off from my family almost entirely. Not until I came out to school here, where I could take a bus down from UMass to his apartment and Uncle had to let me in because I am family, did he begin to repair the rift he had created. He welcomed me with open arms and haunted eyes when I knocked on his door, and when the banging started from Mbuyi's old bedroom, Uncle told me he'd adopted a dog.

After the first afternoon I spent in Uncle's house, poring over the books in his office and avoiding the handwritten journals and the room with the dog, I visited his apartment often. Determined to drag him back into our family, I brought news, helped him clean, and begged Congolese cooking lessons from this man who knew all the best dishes because he had no wife to cook for him anymore. I stayed with Uncle for Thanksgiving because it was cheaper than going home. I did homework and helped him organize his students' papers in the afternoons, and read late into the night, then slept, in the office. And I kept the light on when I slept, because the creaks in the house sounded like footsteps, and even though Uncle's room was right above mine, I knew they couldn't be his noises, and I was afraid.

It has been more than a year since my first visit as a freshman, and I have yet to see what lives in Mbuyi's old room. It is summer now, and hotter upstairs than the heat-soaked downstairs. Every night Uncle presses his fingers to my forehead and rehangs the beads above the lintel. Every night I hear him creak upstairs, and I lock the door and bundle up in pajamas that are too hot for sleeping with a blanket but just right for a surprise dash into the street for safety, and wait for sleep with open eyes trained on the floor between the bookshelf and the door, where the yellow light from the desk lamp stretches to reach. I am watching for a sentient darkness. I am searching for shapes I don't want to see. I fall asleep every night on the lookout for what makes my heart beat too fast and my back prickle like an arching cat's back. I don't know what form it will take. I just know its voice, sweet like sugarcane and cruel as ice water on a slumbering child's face.

*

My headphones are plugged into a tape recorder the size of a hardback book. I'm typing up Uncle's interview with a man from Florida, and have been since just after washing the dinner dishes. The lethargy from the foufou and fish has worn off with the steady tapping of my fingers on the laptop keys, and now I am simply on autopilot, stopping the tape recorder every so often because my fingers don't type French as fast as they type English, and the interview switches back and forth.

Clock chimes break me from my trance. My computer says it's seven minutes to midnight. Uncle's grandfather clock always runs fast, no matter how many times you set it back. I stop the tape and close my laptop, unplugging it from the wall and taking it to my summer bedroom, Uncle's office with the futon folded out into a bed. I can't believe Uncle let me stay up so late—that either of us did. He always insists I'm in bed—in the office—well before midnight.

I have learned certain things have power. Uncle taught me this, not explicitly, but through example. Midnight has power in the West: it is the witching hour, the time of night when ghosts are most powerful. It is the time when Uncle and I are in our rooms and there are footsteps in the hall and down the stairs.

I find Uncle asleep on the living room couch. I do not want him to be around for those creaking footsteps.

I call him, shake him. His eyes open. "Time is it?" He is still groggy, his voice is slurred, but he looks at me with eyes narrowed the way they were when my father and aunt told him that on the final night, when all the children were back home, they dreamed their mother had died clutching her heart.

"About five to midnight," I say.

Uncle struggles to sit up and I try to help, but he waves my hands away. "Go to your room," he says. "Time for bed."

"I know." I want to roll my eyes, but feel this isn't the time for such casual familiarity. His back straightens slowly, he squares his shoulders, and then he takes me by the back of the neck, the way my father does when he is upset but being gentle, and herds me to my summer bedroom. He rushes me into the room, but does not rush as he places his fingertips on my forehead and rehangs the beads above the lintel.

He stops as he is closing the door and casts a tired smile in my direction. I am standing still, heart hammering and mind eerily quiet. He opens his mouth to say something, and then he pauses. Finally he clasps my shoulder. "Isobelle. Don't be afraid."

He closes the door, and I am alone in the dark.

I stand there and hear the creak of his footsteps approaching the stairs. I see lights go out under the door and realize I have not turned on the desk lamp, and now it will be harder to find.

I have not yet heard Uncle creak up the steps. A faint light still shines underneath the door. He has not finished turning off the lights. But something creaks above me, and I wonder how Uncle got upstairs without my noticing. Then the sound leaves the space above me, and the stairs start their swaying creak. It is slow, deliberate. It is not Uncle's pull-trudge-trudge-pull, railing to foot, foot to railing, step. It is a lighter sound. It presses heavy on my chest. I feel the fear of a shapeless, shifting dark expanding in the air around me with each step, until it is hard to breathe. I have had dreams like this, where the fear in me is so great, the danger I face so terrible, that I cannot make a sound louder than a whisper. I stare at the door, invisible in the darkness but for the faint bar of light spilling onto the floor beyond reach of my toes, and I am paralyzed with fear.

I want to open the door, but I have always been told not to. I am afraid to open it, to warn Uncle away from what he must know, even better than me, is coming slowly and inexorably closer. I wish now that I knew the old stories of witchcraft that Uncle transcribes himself. I wish I had not thought I would never need such information, or even, when I first heard the stories, that they were the rickety beliefs of the old, the foolish, and the ignorant. I want the protection of something, and I want my uncle to be safe.

The footsteps stop at the bottom of the stairs, and I hear a heavy thud, and then nothing but the sound of my pulse, the AC turning down, and crickets chirping dangerously loud outside.

"Uncle?" I force the word from my constricting throat. It comes out a croak. I swallow. "Uncle?"

There are no more sounds.

I tell myself Uncle is fine, and then I tell myself I am a bad liar, that the silence is too heavy to be natural, and that the next unnatural silence will come from me. The footsteps have stopped completely, but still I wait. I count to thirty, to fifty, to seventy-five, before knowing Uncle could really be hurt overpowers my cowardice. I open the door fully conscious of the hairs rising on the back of my neck and the goosebumps prickling my arms. The sound of the beads *scritch*ing over the wooden door does nothing to soothe my nerves. Outside my room it is dark, but the light over the stairwell is on. I poke my head over the threshold and feel the beads from the lintel sliding cool on the back of my neck.

"Uncle?" I call softly, then again, louder: "Uncle? Are you all right?"

There is still no sound.

I grip the doorframe and step one foot outside. I cannot see around the stairs. I cannot see Uncle. I feel my way slowly outside and, seeing nothing—though perhaps what had happened *couldn't* be seen?—dart into the light of the stairwell.

I nearly trip over Uncle. He is slumped at the bottom of the stairs, as if he'd started to go up, become light-headed, and sat down just before passing out. There is no blood, and no wound that I can see. Perhaps he had been walking strangely because he felt sick?

Still I am wary when I crouch over him, clutching his thin shoulder and staring down at his chest to make sure it still rises and falls. He is alive, at least, but his breathing comes shallow and fast, and a strange smell of rot covers him that is both odd and familiar—the scent of the house when I wake up in the mornings, that fades until I go to bed. The smell grows stronger, and I look from Uncle to the dark room around me. The shadows move as they always move, and yet the stench creeps closer. Rot, death, decay. That is what's coming.

The clock chimes quarter past and I think I might leap out of my skin.

I want to leave Uncle and go to my room—the room with a door I can close and beads that are supposed to protect me. But before I can decide whether bolting will remain on my conscience forever, a shadow peels away from the darkness: a dragging corpse with a face I almost recognize.

The creature before me might have been human once, but the body it wears is in tatters. Dark skin in a wash of brown and green shades hangs off of torn muscles and ligaments and bones, just as the fibrous rags of a blue pinstriped dress shirt and stained off-white briefs hang from it. Maggots wriggle in the creature's empty eye sockets and drip from the thing like blood. Its lips are gone, leaving black gums and a ghastly wide smile that never wavers. It reaches out to me with fingertips that are almost entirely bone, and a familiar scarred hand.

The corpse's mouth opens. "Cousin," it says in French, "give me your body, so I can avenge my death."

It makes the creature real when that honey-sweet, broken-glass voice pummels its way out of my missing cousin's mouth. I start to scream, but the taste of its stench makes me choke. Someone —Uncle—clutches the back of my knee, and I scream and scuttle away before realizing I have left us both alone to face the creature, the stranger who's wearing my cousin's skin. I grope toward the kitchen light, but before I can turn it on, the smell of rot is overwhelming and the creature is in front of me.

I freeze as abruptly as I moved before, and my breath stops with my body. The corpse's hands touch my face with hard fingers, pressing my forehead where Uncle touched me just before he closed my door. Darkness seeps into my vision, and a new presence crawls in from the edges.

Something pushes me hard in the chest, but it is not a hand or a body, it is that presence—who is Kanku?—in my chest and my head, stretching through my legs and my arms and my pelvis, trying to push me *out.*

With a snap like a rubber band or a sparked synapse, I am outside myself. I feel nothing. I think I must go somewhere, but I do not know or care where that place is. I only know my body is walking away from me, out of the kitchen and into the living room, and I feel nothing about this but mild curiosity: why am I not inside my body? A knife hangs casually from the hand that was mine. I wonder what it is for.

Kanku: "My father he killed me"

Soon my twin's body will be too weak to leave this room, and Baba will have killed me—again. Day after day I stand at this bedroom door in Mbuyi's decomposing flesh—though it has lasted years, like it knew this shape would have been mine too if I had lived. I wait for the midnight chimes as the air grows ripe around me. My hour, once again, is closing in.

I have spent much of my life waiting. Much of my life thinking. There is little living to do without a body to do it with. There have been three long waits in my life, before and after my death. I dwell on my memories, review them, pick at them like wounds made to fester and seethe. I replay my life and my rage, and the memories give me strength to finish the task I have set for myself: I will kill my Baba.

*

It all began with Mama.

*

"Kanku, come here!"

*In our bedroom, I stop playing cowboys with Mbuyi and run to the
kitchen. "Yes, Mama?"*

*Mama is stirring a pot on the stove. "Kanku, find me my peeling knife.
It's not in the drawer where it belongs."*

*I think it is on the television, and when I run to the other room it is wait-
ing for me there, just like I thought. I bring it to Mama. She smiles and takes
it from me, kisses my cheek. "Such a clever boy," she says. She frowns at the
blade then, spits an annoyed sound through her teeth. "Wash this."*

I take it to the sink.

Baba says, "Where was it?"

I tell him, "You left it on the TV."

*Mama's face glows with pride as she nods, but Baba is quiet. Then he says,
"You were asleep when I got it out." He does not sound proud, or even happy.*

*"Our son is gifted," Mama says. I dry the cleaned knife and give it back.
She sets it down, keeps stirring the pot on the stove.*

*As I leave the kitchen, Baba says, quiet, "A gift is only as good as the
person who has it."*

*Something crashes—Mama's spoon against the pot, I think, or the stove.
"Our sons are good boys," she growls, low, like I am not supposed to hear.*

"So you say," Baba bites back, just as quiet.

*Inside our bedroom, Mbuyi looks up from a new wire man he is making.
Expression waiting to be delighted, he asks, "What did she want you to find
this time?"*

*I shove Baba's suspicion away from my face and my thoughts. I won't tell
Mbuyi. It would hurt him to know.*

Mama was proud when I knew things grownups didn't want me
to know. She ruffled my hair and pulled me close when Baba's
friends looked wide-eyed at my words. She said I had a gift, that the
ancestors had blessed me. I think maybe Mama was the blessing.

Remembering the kitchen knife—among other things she
had me find—I've thought about how I could have known where
it was without knowing why I knew. Perhaps I followed a trail of
observations: Baba sometimes used the knives in the kitchen as
screwdrivers; Baba always fixed the broken things in the house;
the TV wasn't working, and he'd tested the antenna while I played
in the family room, but the picture was still skipping, and he was
annoyed he'd have to unscrew the back to look inside; the next
afternoon the TV was working, but I never saw him fix it and I was
home all day. Perhaps I even saw the knife crossing through the

room from the kitchen or my bedroom, and left it because Baba might still be using it. I am still not sure how I found things for her, if I even had a gift, but Mama impressed upon me that being a good man, using my gift wisely, would bring good fortune to us all. Mama told me, *You are a good boy. I know you will be a good man.*

*

Mama said when we die, we join our ancestors in the spirit world stretched out over this one like a mirror, like a twin. There, joyfully reunited with our loved ones, we watch over our living family members. They give us honor and we bring them comfort. They give us prayers and we protect them from witches. They beg our advice and we nudge them in the right direction. Because of this, Mama said, no one is ever truly alone. Living or dead, we will always have family.

"Mbuyi, you cannot catch me! I am faster than you!" When my twin sees me again, I stop to wave the wire man he made, laughing. When he chases me, I run to the kitchen.

"Give that back! I said give it back!"

Mama shakes her head at us, but I see her smile as I run past her troop of steaming pots, and I am happy.

Baba is in the living room. *"Mbuyi! Kanku! Stop running around this house while your mother is cooking!"*

We stop. *"We're sorry, Baba,"* we say with one voice.

I hide the wire man behind my back. Mbuyi wrinkles his nose at me.

"Kanku—come here." Baba holds out his hand to my twin.

"I'm Kanku!" I almost smile. Baba still confuses us. Mama never has. Then you *come here! Give that back to your brother."*

If I give it back, the game is over. *"But Baba—"*

"Don't look at me that way," Baba snarls, *"it isn't natural."* Baba's face is hard, cold. It scares me. I look at Mbuyi, confused and afraid, and his face is a mirror of my own.

"Like what, Baba?" I am grateful to Mbuyi; I know he asks for me.

Baba only says, *"Give that to me,"* then, *"Mbuyi, come here. Here. Now go, both of you. And don't run in the house—you are not dogs, do not act like them!"* He returns to his newspaper. Mbuyi grabs my hand as we go hide in our bedroom, squeezing it to comfort me. His unease is a mirror of my own.

Too soon, Mama had stomach pains, or child pains, or some pungent infection Baba would not explain. When Baba was at work, Mbuyi and I would play in Mama's room even though it smelled so bad I couldn't keep my face from curling when I opened the door. Mbuyi wanted to play outside with the other kids, and sometimes he would, but often he would keep me company in Mama's room and make wire cars and men for us to play with from the rug next to the bed. From Mama's bed, where I curled against her as she slept, I would reach down and make the men dance and sing for us, make Mbuyi's eyes light up as he held in laughter. We used the figures to tell Mama's familiar stories. Sometimes, when she woke up, she pulled me and Mbuyi close and said, *Did I ever tell you the story about—* and we would say no and beg her to tell it even if we knew it already, and she would smile through strained eyes and stroke our arms and murmur tales about the wider world.

*

My first long wait was for my mother to recover her health. That wait was the shortest. It lasted a year. Her death brought my own.

>*Mbuyi is at the neighbor's house, where I am supposed to be, but I snuck home before Baba. I hear him from my bed.*
>
>*"You think he is a witch?" Baba's friend says.*
>
>*"He refused to leave her, and now she is dead. He must be a witch." Baba's voice is cold. He is always cold now, when he speaks of me. When he speaks to me. I do not know how to make his voice change back.*
>
>*"He is only a child—and a twin! He is good fortune! How can he be a witch?"*
>
>*I am not a witch. Mama knew. Mama loved me. It hurts, always, now she is gone.*
>
>*"You have seen the way he looks at people. How he moves his hands when he thinks no one sees. And now he speaks to no one!"*
>
>*"It is suspicious . . ."*
>
>*I talk to Mbuyi. I talk to Mama. Mama knew I have restless hands. She used to hand me things to toy with—spoons, sticks, dolls. She knew it calmed me. Now I have only my fingers. I move them and remember her. It calms me.*
>
>*"I will not take him with us. I will have enough trouble with just Mbuyi anyway. What kind of father keeps a murderer with his son?"*
>
>*My heart freezes in my chest. No. He would not leave me behind.*
>
>*"No one will take in a witch."*
>
>*"And no one should. He killed my wife—let him lie in the bed he has made."*
>
>*No. I would never hurt Mama. I love Mama.*
>
>*I want Mbuyi. I want my Mama.*
>
>*No.*

After Mama cut our hair, she burned it in the fire. After we cut our nails, she burned those in the fire. Mama said, *Be careful whose gifts you accept, and be careful who you give gifts to. You never know when*

a witch will use a gift to curse you, sacrificing your life to gain more power.
A twin's death is powerful magic for a witch. So Mbuyi, watch out for your
brother. And Kanku, take care of your brother. People come and go, Mama
said, *but you can always rely on your family.*

*

> "Do not cry, I said!"
> "Baba, don't leave me, please!"
> "Oh, so now you talk?"
> "We are all going to the new house in America, you said—"
> "Don't you cry to me, Kanku! You killed your mother—I would not take
> you to a dog's house."
> "I did not! I promise, I tell you the truth!"
> Baba's big hand cracks, and I fall.
> "You are a liar and a witch. Stay here."
> ". . . but Baba—"
> "Let go of me!"
> "Baba, please, Baba—"
> "Do not try to follow us. You are not my son—you are no one's son."
> Glass breaks. Mbuyi cries out. The car horn shrieks and shrieks.

No one took me in, not even a witch to make a sacrifice. I was
seven years old when I realized Mama was wrong, that Mama lied.

*

It is important to know where you come from. It is important to
remember your roots. As I wait for dark power to swallow the air,
as I wait while Baba and that girl fritter away downstairs, as I stand
in Mbuyi's room picking maggots out of my cheeks and hips and
squishing their wriggling bodies, I remember with religious fervor
the distance that I have come, and fuel my rage.

The second long wait spanned the end of my life and lasted
most of my death. For almost two decades I waited for my family
to come home.

*

> *The sun is not pretty anymore. It burns like their eyes, always watch-*
> *ing. Warning me away. Throwing stones at the witch. Only the dogs are not*
> *afraid. They smell death. They are starved as me, their ribs showing and*
> *spines poking and dry tongues dragging from their mouths. I talk to them,*
> *but they are not friends. Their fur is spiked with ticks. They are waiting.*

I stole food. I sheltered with and ran from other "witch" children cast out on the street. I grew bony with hunger, and bitter,

and mean. I knew I was going to die. And where were my ancestors, who I prayed to? Where was Mama's comforting warmth to
my spirit? How much of what she said was wrong when she told me
of death and the afterlife?

As death knelt close, I knew I was truly alone in the only world
that mattered.

I made a choice.

And Mama was right: the death of a twin is powerful magic.

> *They are no longer waiting.*
> *They gorge their feral stomachs.*
> *The people turn their eyes away.*

As I hovered over my body, I waited:
. . . Mama? . . . Ancestors? . . . Anyone?
. . . No.

> *They ate me. Tore into my body like jackals. They ate me . . .*
> *But . . . they are only dogs. This is not their fault.*
> *Mama left me.*
> *Baba killed me.*
> *Mbuyi let him kill me.*
> *I'll show them a witch. They will come back home.*
> *I am waiting.*

The first body I took was a witch boy I ran from once. He was
twelve, an adult to my seven-year-old eyes.

When I was alive, he found me eating chicken and foufou I
stole from a table when a missionary stood to hug his friend. I
ran with heart in my throat through the streets until the shouting
died. Then I huddled with my stolen food, my first meal in days,
under an awning on a quiet street of shops. I ate like the street
dogs, quick and brutal and wary. The witch boy still surprised me.
He pulled me up by my wrist, stole the chicken from my slick fingers, and shoved me hard onto the ground. *These are my streets,* he
said as I skittered away. He sucked the rest of the meat into his
mouth as I seethed with wretched hatred. He noticed my fist, cradled to my chest. But before he said, *Give me that,* I was running.

While I lived, alone on the streets, I ran and I hid. As a dead
boy, I explored my hometown fearlessly, in the open, though I
could travel only a few kilometers from where I died. Whenever

I got too far, my consciousness narrowed and fluttered like a fish gasping for breath. I found the witch boy again as I explored. I wondered if I could hurt him now. I meant to burrow into his chest, try to squeeze his heart. Instead I felt his spirit quail against me. I thrashed it with glee and shoved it out.

The sudden wall of sensation knocked me flat, and then his memories assailed me. I lay in the street like a drunk. It took most of the night for me to master his body. The next day I stole and I ate. I had longer legs. My new body was weak, but stronger than mine had been when I died. I survived for two glorious days in his body. Then it began to rot.

I stole more bodies while I waited for my family. People who wronged me in life. People who should have stood up for me, taken me in. People with hands in my death. Always they began to rot after a few days. I discarded them quickly so no one suspected a witch. I learned one other thing during these experiments: while cloaked in a body, my tether was gone.

More than a decade passed before Mbuyi came home to visit our old house. I watched him walk through town, ask after me, come away angry. I wanted his body, but I hesitated. In all of my memories, Mbuyi loved me, took care of me. I watched him plant his feet in the ghosts of Baba's footprints and look down the road. He did not feel my presence as he apologized to a dead boy.

If he is really sorry, I thought, *he will not fight me too much.*

*

The last wait I spent trapped in my Baba's house, in a bedroom that should've been mine: I waited for the day I could finally kill him for killing me.

I sifted through Mbuyi's memories enough to get to the airport, get to Baba's car, get to Baba's apartment without him suspecting. It was the second day, the last day I had before Mbuyi's corpse started rotting like all the others. Baba asked me about my trip and I struggled to find Mbuyi's memories in time to answer. Twice the cold look returned to Baba's eyes as we spoke, and he showed me a necklace that made me recoil. I wanted to kill him then, but he wore it and I couldn't get close, not even with a knife. He cut my hair for me, as he did when I was a child, and tottered off to his office. I was woozy from the necklace brushing against my neck as he cut. I fell asleep in the chair. When I woke, he helped me walk up the stairs, my consciousness reeling with every step. I felt like power had gone out from me, like I was trapped in a cage, someplace dark and small. Somehow, while I slept, he had taken my power. I was a child in a corpse-shell, and Baba my master.

I could not shove him away, down the spindly staircase. I could not reach for his neck to choke the life from it. I could not curse his name with a witch's power. He dropped me in Mbuyi's room and he told me, face ugly with rage, "I always knew you were a witch." He slammed the door shut.

Mbuyi's corpse didn't rot after two days, or after seven, or after two years. In that time I learned Baba's house, walking it in the night when the dark power crests with the chime of the clock. I couldn't go far into Baba's office. The necklace was somewhere inside the desk, and it sickened me to get close. He hides my power in there, I am sure. While he slept I paced like an anxious dog. I was tired of waiting. In the third year Mbuyi's body began to rot, and the girl started visiting Baba. In the fourth year the body grew weak, its stink thick, and the girl settled in to spend the summer with Baba. She slept in the office, Baba's necklace hanging from the door, warding me away.

But tonight the air is thick with promise. The girl closes her door. Baba starts climbing the stairs—and the clock strikes twelve. I twist the doorknob in my scarred right hand and step into the dark.

I am done waiting.

*

My spirit surges with the memory of adrenaline as I reach the top of the stairs. Baba puts the necklace at the office door—his only protection besides his locked bedroom door, which can't help him now. I grin at him stuttering up the stairs, and take a step down.

Baba looks up, eyes wide. His body shakes. I step closer, closer, and his face contorts. He grips his chest. He stumbles down to the landing and sits on the stairs facing the wall.

He cannot face me. He cannot face what he has done. He cannot face the death that is coming. I step beside him and run a loving hand over his shorn hair, the balding crown spattered with gray and white. Baba is old now. He has lived longer than I ever will. His time has come. I step down again and slide my hand, just strong enough, around his throat. I step down onto the landing and bring my face close. I want to watch him die, let him feel the peace it brings me. Baba is panting already, his dark face pale and pained, beginning to sweat. He slaps at my hands, but even against this body he is weak. My thumb presses into his windpipe.

My thumb presses in.

My thumb . . .

Baba huffs and twists his head just enough. He is laughing at me. I cannot press in. I cannot kill him. He still has my power, somehow. I cannot kill him—still! Cannot even shove him into the steps where he slumps. My half-rotted face twists in so violent a snarl a maggot drops from my cheek onto Baba's heaving lap. I turn in disgust and disappear in the shadows. I need a new plan, but what can I do that I haven't tried already, many times?

"Uncle?" The girl's voice quivers through my rage. She opens the door, calls again. "Uncle? Are you all right?"

Is this the answer?

I tear through Mbuyi's memory, call her to mind. The strongest memory is half rotted, the details corroded. They are in Mbuyi's room, my prison, but the blinds are open and sunlight gleams on a mancala board. She is much younger than him, but his memory of her is fond, like his memories of me.

> *Hurry up and go already!*
> *Shut it, Mbuyi, I'm thinking.*
> *You're gonna think until bedtime. You just don't want to lose.*
> *I refuse to lose this game.*
> *I know. That's why you're my favorite cousin.*
> *Why? Because I always beat you?*
> *You only wish that were true.*
> *So why am I your favorite cousin then?*
> *Because you don't give up.*

Perhaps her mind will think of something I cannot? It is worth a try.

She finds Baba, a brave little mouse until I approach and she screams and she runs. I leave Baba to catch her.

In the dark kitchen I burn through the weak little blessing of Baba's, buzzing like a busybody on her forehead to keep me out. My power is mostly gone, stolen by Baba, but I have enough left to break this. The blessing's light crunches and winks out. I push myself from Mbuyi's corpse into my cousin. Rage and hope propel me. Her spirit leaves like a moan. The corpse smells stronger in my cousin's body, but I pay little mind, even trailing its juices in my bare feet. My strongest hour is wasting, but this body has been in Baba's office, has touched the necklace without fear. When I break it with my woman's bare, weak hand, my new body shivers with triumph.

I tear through the desk, quick and vicious, touching everything in sight. Paperweights, folders, things I have never seen except in Mbuyi's memory—stapler, computer, tape recorder, cordless phone—I shove my way in and out of Baba's treasured things, touching and rejecting it all. These things are not *mine*, not my power that he stole, and so I treat them like trash, I break them on the floor, just as Baba has treated me all of my life. I can feel my energy in the desk, but could never get close before.

When it is not in the drawers, I claw at the walls, the inside of the desk. I may have to break it apart. But on an inner drawer wall I find a hidden compartment. My back hunches and stills: this is mine.

Slowly, reverently, I peel open the compartment. Slide my fingers inside, caress and find and pull out: a homemade brown rag doll. It has a twist of black, curly hair sewn to the top of its head. A black-thread smile and black-thread eyes cut across its rough face. A scrap from Mbuyi's blue pinstriped dress shirt is sown onto its torso and back.

Baba has trapped my power in a doll of me, an ugly doll tied to Mbuyi's body and my spirit. For four years I have waited to kill my Baba, thwarted by his chains lashed to me by this doll.

I doubt Baba will handle chains nearly so well.

I take the doll and the knife and some rubber bands into the living room. Baba looks up. "Kanku," he rasps.

"Witch," I correct him, bending over him with the knife. Baba strains for me with the hand not clutched to his side, but his arm barely moves. I yank through Baba's beard, ripping out skin as much as I cut through hair. I slice a patch of Baba's shirt at the sweat-damp collar.

"Don't," he whispers, pleads. His face is a rictus of pain.

"Because of you, I died like a dog," I snarl.

I'll make fire on the stove in the kitchen, I decide, and leave him to wait.

"Kanku—don't . . ."

The clock strikes half past. I turn on the kitchen light, turn the knob of the front burner. The fire lights with a pop. Carefully I pull Mbuyi's hair from the doll's head and burn each piece in the fire—just like Mama.

Something in the living room crackles. The house abruptly smells like rot and cooked meat. Baba gurgles like an infant. I ignore him and burn the shirt too.

The rubber bands are not needle and thread, but Baba's hair and shirt stick to the doll just as well. In the living room, Mbuyi's body is gone. Only the smells are left. Baba looks pained. I am glad.

Baba's eyes go wide when he sees I have trapped him. He tries to speak, but only breath sounds come out. His eyes roll to face me, and he grimaces. I savor the moment. I reach for his throat, and my thumb presses in. "Look at me," I tell him.

For a moment Baba does. Then he looks over my shoulder, and his grimace turns up in the corners. It is almost a smile. I push at his windpipe, a warning. He mouths something that I can't catch. His mouth closes, and he slumps. His eyes lose focus. Baba's whole body goes still.

I have barely started. I had barely started. I check him for breath, but there is none. This cannot be. Baba is toying with me. He is alive, he will remain alive until I kill him at last.

I shake him and shake him, slam his back into the stairs, but Baba flops like a rag doll until I fling him with a shout.

What right has he to look so peaceful?

I laugh. I laugh like a crazed, bitter thing.

A thing robbed of its prize the moment it was within reach.

My Baba abandoned me in his life. Why should he change in the moments of his death? I waited for him. I hoped, and I waited, and I thought maybe, maybe . . .

But no. I was wrong.

And all I can think of is: I killed my brother for this.

Mbuyi: Whither Thou Goest

Questions Izzy asked me — only once — for which I had no answer:

"Why do you have a twin's name?"

"Why don't you celebrate your birthday?"

"How did you get that scar on your hand?"

"Why did your parents only have one kid?"

"Did you ever wish you had a brother? A sister?"

"Did you have a best friend in Congo? Who did you play with every day?"

*

When I was a child in Kinshasa, I had a brother, a twin. He was my best friend. He told the best stories, after Mama, and after she died, he spoke only to me. He thought she'd get better. I hoped she would too, but I saw Baba's face every day, and my aunt's face as she cared for Mama, and somehow I knew Kanku waited for a day no one else believed would come.

I didn't tell him what I was afraid of—Mama told me to watch out for him, take care of him, protect him. I thought, *Maybe I'm wrong.* I thought, *If I say it, it might come true.* And I didn't say it, but I wasn't wrong, and Kanku felt betrayed by everyone who had known, and he got quiet and angry and sad, and I couldn't protect him from Baba.

We were adjusting. A family of three without a woman, without a mother, without Mama. We were adjusting well, I thought.

Then Kanku told me, *Baba thinks I'm a witch and that I killed Mama.*

> *Are you a witch, Kanku?*
> *Do you really think I am, brother?*
> *I'll believe you, whatever you say.*
> *No, I am not a witch! And I did not kill Mama!*
> *I know. You would never hurt Mama.*
> *Baba does not believe me.*
> *He will if you talk to him. If you only talk to me, people will think you're a witch.*
> *I do not like talking to Baba. He gives me mean looks. They all do.*
> *Baba will change. It hasn't been long since . . . He won't always be mad.*
> *But you believe me, right, Mbuyi?*
> *Of course I do. You've never lied to me.*

I thought as a child thinks: Baba loves us both, and Mama says when people are mad they say things they don't mean. Baba was angry. He cannot really believe you are a witch.

Then Kanku told me, *Baba says he is not taking me with you to America.* I thought, *Kanku is scared, but Baba would never leave either of us behind.*

If I had believed him about Baba, maybe I could've changed things. I would've prodded him to talk to Baba at dinner, or to play with the kids of the family who visited, or to seek hugs from the women who watched us after school so they'd see his pain.

But I didn't, and I didn't, and by the time I believed him, it was done.

I stopped being a child the moment Baba struck my brother

—my best friend, my identical twin—in the face, in the street. Kanku fell down. He held Baba's knees, screaming and whining like a dog, crawling like a wet-faced beggar in the dirt. In the car I looked the same way, held down by Baba's friend's flexing arms as I thrashed for the door. I drove my fist through the window trying to get out, to go protect him, to wrap my arms around Kanku and not let go, so Baba would have to take us both. Baba would not abandon me, I knew.

We left Kanku crying in the street.

Baba used one of Kanku's shirts to bandage my hand while his friend drove. He gave the rest of my brother's belongings to the friend who was driving, to give to his children. All the belongings I had helped Kanku fold and pack for America. He seemed sure he wasn't going, but I tried to make him excited for the trip, to ride an airplane, to see yellow hair and learn to talk like cowboys. I couldn't stop crying, even when Baba threatened to give me a reason to cry and held up the hand that struck Kanku in his face that looked like my face, that felt like my face in those moments. I didn't want Baba to touch me. He had betrayed me, betrayed us both, betrayed Mama's love for us both. I wouldn't speak to him for weeks, even when he hit me or starved me for my silence. In America I had to speak to him—he was the only part of home I had left. But still. I hated Baba for years. I prayed to Mama to take care of Kanku the way I should have. I promised them both I would come back as soon as I could and bring him home.

*

They arrive, Tonton Badia and Tantine Janet, and her face is like a frail peach, and his is like a sturdy wooden desk, and when they hold hands their skin clashes but their fingers lock perfectly. Tantine Janet is round, and Tonton Badia holds me in his lap while I touch and the baby kicks my hand and I jump back and we laugh.

I watched Izzy grow up in the summers. Sometimes she visited alone while her parents traveled or had busy weeks full of meetings; or I visited her family alone while Baba traveled, collecting histories of other Congolese immigrants. I didn't like going with him, but Baba took me anyway—until I asked a man in an interview whether he'd cast out his son as a witch.

Baba never took me again.

Izzy was a quiet girl, thoughtful but bright like a dandelion.

She smiled much more than she laughed, but seemed to take joy in the world like a child, like Kanku, even when worries weighed her down. I was a big brother to her for years. She wasn't Kanku, though I feared in loving her I was being unfaithful somehow, replacing Kanku with a cousin. I think she looked up to me. I think she liked my company as much as I liked hers. She was my favorite cousin — I think I even told her once — but as she grew up she grew small, like a mouse; tried to entertain me, keep me happy, as if afraid I'd lose interest in her company, her existence. On a walk with Baba and Tonton Badia, I confessed this with worry — but they approved: it's good for girls to learn to keep men happy.

Neither Izzy nor Tantine Janet were there when they said that. I thought of Izzy, who laughed at my silly faces for years, who made sassy jokes when adults weren't around, who complained the boys in her class could do more pull-ups than her, who started wearing skirts even though she hated sitting with feet on the floor.

I didn't confide in Tonton and Baba about much after that.

At home I dug up an old pair of drawstring sweatpants. They were a little too big, but Izzy wore them when we played in my room that summer, sprawled out on the floor.

*

Topics Izzy never brought up again — not even to me:

- *Why I have a twin's name*
- *My birthday*
- *The scar on my right hand*
- *Why I have no other siblings*
- *Siblings I'd wish for*
- *My best friend in Congo; who I played with every day.*

*

Baba looks at me with pity when I tell him I want to visit the old house. He doesn't say, *He won't be there.* He doesn't say, *I'm sorry.* He doesn't say, *I was wrong, and I regret what I did to him, and all of us.* He says, *Go visit family first. Save sightseeing for the last day. Everyone is excited you are coming.*

Baba buys my ticket, arranges for me to stay with relatives, speaks at midnight and 3 a.m. to bridge the time zones with family so I can cross to meet them. I seethe inside but think, *Kanku will be there. I will find him and bring him home.*

*

The day before I leave Congo, the host of family I've only just met finally lets me go to see my childhood home. Walking through streets I played in as a boy, I have flashes of recognition: The bus took this street into town from the house. This wall surrounded our house, and the crushed glass cemented on top kept out thieves and soldiers. The house I grew up in is through this new gate.

Baba cast Kanku from our family here, on this torn-up, pockmarked road.

In a car on that corner, I cut my hand trying to escape Baba's friend so I could protect Kanku—the way Mama couldn't, the way I promised her I would.

This is the last place I saw Kanku before the car turned and he couldn't catch up.

That is the house of a woman who helped raise us, who told me —without shame—my twin died in the street not long after.

I can almost feel him here, on this heat-rippled road full of patterned stalls that weren't here years ago. I tell him *I'm sorry* and whisper a prayer that he's safe and happy, is somewhere with Mama.

My skin feels suddenly cold, but the lump in my throat and chest dissolves into a warmth I haven't felt in fifteen years. I think, *Kanku hears me. Somehow, he is here.*

I smile. I cry silently in the street, ignoring bystanders and the market's kaleidoscopic closing bustle.

Then my vision shudders. The *Kanku* feeling punches in.

I think, *Something is wrong.*

I think, *Somehow, Kanku is alive. He wants my body. Is he a witch?*

I think, *It should've been me.*

I think, *I promised him we would go to America.*

I think, *Maybe this way I can finally bring him home.*

I don't fight as he pushes into my skin and my spirit leaks out beside the body I sacrificed. I tell my twin, in bruised Tshiluba, *You're safe now. Let me take care of you.*

But Kanku doesn't answer, or even seem to notice I am there.

*

I stay with my body as Kanku takes his first trip in an airplane, watching his eyes light up in the body he never grew to inhabit because of Baba. I felt his pain, his rage, when I left my skin to him, but that anger is gone as he looks at the world from above the clouds. When a flight attendant speaks to him in English, I share his delight when he understands.

I pass my spirit across my skin, just enough to check on my body and check on Kanku. I catch a memory as I slide through—my trip to the airport—and when I see Kanku's familiar thinking expression—same as mine—I wonder if he saw my memory too. I don't know how it works to give over one's body. I worry about something I read last year: that our cells send out a death signal, a call taken up by all our cells to shut down. It's how our bodies know to die, how we die, and all it takes is one. Our bodies are smart. I'm afraid mine will realize Kanku, though identical, is not me, and this transplant will fail, and my body will die on Kanku before he finally gets the life I promised.

I slide around the edges of my body, checking for a death signal, pushing just far enough inside that it notices my presence.

Kanku never does.

I talk to him, try to calm him with my energy as Baba picks him up and I feel his anger build again.

And then Baba pulls out a necklace an interviewee gave him years ago.

And then Baba cuts Kanku's hair and his shirt and skewers them to a doll, and leaves Kanku slumped in a kitchen chair like some back-alley anesthesia victim, like he's trash.

And Baba half carries Kanku up to my bedroom and I think, *Maybe things will be okay.*

And he drops Kanku on the floor and snarls at him like a rabid, angry dog.

And as he slams the door, I see Baba's face as Kanku sees it —finally—full of pain and rage and righteousness, and I realize what this means.

Baba will not suffer Kanku to live. He will not murder my brother—murder me—but he'll cage him until he dies all over again.

*

For years I keep our body alive. No one knows I'm there—not Kanku, not Baba, and they are the only people who come inside the house.

I go into Baba's room, go into his office, read over his shoulder, hover through his shoes—but mostly I stay with Kanku. I try to show him I'm there, to give him comfort. I tell him stories just inside our fingernails, jostle my brain to show him my first trip to the zoo, the magic of my first automatic door, my sorrow when Izzy asked questions that reminded me of him. I don't know if they work, if he hears me or feels me, but I see his eyes when the memories curl through him. It eases my heart that in this way I can still make him smile, give him life.

*

Two years in, I miss a death signal. After that I struggle to keep up, to limit the spread, to chase down the signals passing with synaptic speed without dislodging Kanku's spirit. I don't have to sleep, but the body is composed of billions of cells, and I am only one man, an impotent spirit who's going to lose his brother again.

This time, it's entirely my fault.

*

Enter Izzy. She's all grown up. Shed some of her quiet compliance. Still curious as ever, but wary of my bedroom now. She argues with Baba. She drags family back into his life with phone calls and showing up outside. She likes his interviews, helps him one summer, has come back for this one. I tell Kanku to stay away from her, but she sleeps in the office and he crowds her door at night. I worry for her in a way I don't for Baba, but he leaves the necklace with her and it calms me that she's protected, though I don't dwell on from whom.

It's her second summer with Baba since Kanku came home. His body is falling apart. Flies land and hatch maggots in his skin, and I hope enough of his nerves are dead so he doesn't feel crawling inside his cheeks, at his hips, in the meat of his thighs, in the fat of his buttocks. It is hard to see him like this, but it's all my fault, so I watch, I stay with him.

He doesn't know, but I know. I pretend knowing is enough.

*

This night feels different. Kanku waits at the door that locks only from the inside, trapped by Baba somehow, by magic, though I never believed in it until I found Kanku again. At midnight wrath propels him out once again. One o'clock is my hour when energy's high, so when it all goes wrong I see Baba collapsed on the stairs, a heart attack maybe, and he needs a hospital, but Kanku seems bent on destruction, and I am not strong enough to intervene.

I won't help him kill Baba, but I think, *If Baba dies, Kanku will be at peace, and we can all move on from this.*

But then Izzy comes out of her room to find Baba, and if I had a body my heart would have dropped to my stomach and punched out my breath with one beat.

And Kanku does the unthinkable.

I watch him shove inside poor Izzy's body, leave ours in a heap on the landing. Izzy, kind Izzy, who kicked my hand when I was new to this country and she new to this world, not even born. Izzy, my favorite cousin, my adopted sister in spirit, is a spirit now, watching her body walk off.

I can't let it end like this.

Izzy.
She hears me.
Mbuyi?
And she barrels through me like a hurricane. Our memories collide in a disembodied hug fraught with emotions and eddied by pressures of thoughts pushing from one mind to the next: *Thought you were dead* and *You need to get back in your body* and *What happened* and *Kanku didn't mean what he did* and *What's wrong with Uncle* and *Kanku wouldn't really hurt anyone* and *What is he looking for* and the half-thought, *Maybe he would,* and from her, *You* do *have a twin!*

The clock strikes quarter to one as I push the death-signal thoughts into her consciousness. She needs to get back in her body. I need to make Kanku come out here with me. I push my idea between us. I tell myself I'm doing what's right, that I'm not choosing sides. I tell myself I'm not robbing Kanku of his life, that I'm not like Baba.

To Izzy I say, *It's time for us to push.*

Izzy's body reels against us when we thrust under her skin. Kanku flinches her into the wall. His hands slap at us across the dim stairwell. Baba sits silent on the stairs. I know he's dead.

I feel an echo of warmth, a reminder of home as it used to be. I want to fade toward it, go to it, but I won't fail Izzy and I won't leave Kanku, never again.

We push inside Izzy's body. Our memories cloud together, knowledge crowding out thought in torrential bursts as our three lives flash-flood my mind.

Kanku curls Izzy's lip when he feels us. "I killed you!" he shrieks.

I ignore how my heart breaks in three.

I press under Izzy's skin, into her brain. *Kanku, give her body back. Come with me.* He shoves me back out. When I rush back in I feel Izzy's fierce rage bashing his, her will to take what is hers like a gale. *You killed Uncle and you killed Mbuyi,* she shoves at him, *but you can't have me. Did you kill your mother too, witch?*

Kanku's stolen face twists with fury. He flings me—I barely hold on. "I did not kill Mama!" he bellows, Izzy's voice in shreds. "Baba just wanted to blame a witch!"

Izzy's voice snaps right back: *So you're a witch then, Kanku?*

I bolster her, willing my brother to see what he's done. *Are you a witch, brother?*

The rage on Izzy's face freezes. She suddenly looks very young. Fragile and solemn, her mouth speaks: "Do you really think I am, brother?"

You've never lied to me, Kanku. I'll believe you—

And I'll believe you, Izzy tells me.

—and we'll still be brothers, no matter what. Okay?

Izzy's face stills. Her eyes blink, slowly at first, then more quickly. Her expression folds into itself like a house of cards. "I am a witch, brother," her voice says in Tshiluba. "But not then. I tell you the truth: I never killed Mama." A tear slides down one cheek. "You know that, right, Mbuyi?"

I know. You wouldn't lie to me, Kanku. You never have.

Izzy's body sags. Kanku curls into himself—and out of her body—like a sea anemone retreating within its tubes. Relief tears through me as I watch him let her go.

Izzy pushes past me then, deep into her body. As she slides to refill her spaces, she sends me gratitude, love, and sadness I return with fearsome pride in who she's become. I check her for the death signal—she's safe.

Reassured, I sink like a wave after my brother.

Kanku's hovering over Baba. I float to him as Izzy thumbs her phone. I join our spirits at the edges, but my twin pulls away.

He offers up his thoughts taking my body in Kinshasa. He passes me his determination, his refusal to feel pity, to feel shame.

I give him back my memory of that moment—why did he never look?—and then I let him feel my anguish watching over him, a shadow, since that day.

Kanku reaches for me then, and sudden as a crashing wave we

are one person, whole, together as the day we were conceived. The feel of *home* and aftertaste of family dinners sitting around the foufou bowl and pondue bowl and plate of fish wisps slowly through my mind. And when we realize it, we startle, shocked as one: the feeling doesn't come from us—it comes from somewhere else.

Mama.

The pull is there, sudden, deep: Mama's waiting, family's waiting there for us, *elsewhere*—the afterlife she spoke of?—and this elsewhere place is good.

Izzy passes through us, phone in hand. She's checking Baba's pulse, face wet. She doesn't feel us, and my presence in this place begins to fade as I reach toward this elsewhere. But when I let myself drift up toward Mama, I'm alone.

I stop.

Kanku, aren't you coming?

His hesitance is back, the bitter cast of fear upon him. I see memories of other bodies taken, used with glee. I don't condone his actions, and I let him feel my disappointment, but I've loved him all my life and death, and he is family, he is mine.

I'm not going without you, not again.

Kanku says, *It's okay. You go on, Mbuyi. I'll follow soon.*

But he's lying. I feel it deep: this first, heartbreaking lie, his hope I'll believe one last time, forget him, let him waste away in penance here. I turn from Mama, curl around him like a suit of armor. *I'll wait,* I say. *We'll go together.* I bare my resolve.

You would wait for me? And once again he's seven, trying to grasp why I'm not outside playing football like I want to be; why I've stayed in with him.

I've waited for you since I left Kinshasa—both times. You will always be my brother, and my best friend. I won't lose you again.

Mama's warmth is up there, in a place that's bright, familiar, feels like home, like her love as she wrapped us in her arms and told us stories. I know she waits for us and loves us both. And for the rest of our dead family, I'll hold tight to Kanku. They won't leave me; they'll have to take us both.

LETTIE PRELL

Justice Systems in Quantum Parallel Probabilities

FROM *Clarkesworld Magazine*

COLE SITS ON the hard slab of bed that cannot be tamed by the three-inch-thick mattress and scratchy blanket. The gray of the diffused light brings no warmth to the cell. There is nothing for Cole to do but wait, which he's been doing for some time. Eventually someone will come for him and take him to a larger room, and the fate of what is to be done with him will unfold.

In the meantime he waits. His eyes are drooping, chin falling toward his chest. The guy across the hall, who Cole cannot see because the doors are staggered, is named Marco. He has been talking constantly. Perhaps Marco has a mental health issue. Marco's current topic is about justice, its structure. The steady patter lulls Cole into a doze, where images begin to arise from the molecular structure of the universe, or from the realm of ideas. They take on form, become worlds unto themselves like the idealized scenes within so many snow globes. He picks one up and peers through the thin veil of snow at what is inside.

There is a justice system with no police. People turn themselves in to prosecutors voluntarily, or are persuaded to do so by others. The prosecutors hear the confessions. One prosecutor is turning someone away, saying, "We cannot help you. While your situation is unfortunate, you have committed no crime."

The man is unhappy. "But how am I to live like this? How am I to restore the balance of things?"

"That is not my concern," the prosecutor replies.

Cole watches as the man leaves the courthouse and goes down

the street to a small shop providing justice-type services for people the prosecutors turn away. Cole peers over the man's shoulder and reads the menu of sanctions and punishments. Some of the choices are more severe than those meted out by the real justice system. The man purchases two days in jail. The handcuffs they use to lead him away cost extra.

Cole shakes his head in confusion. Why would someone voluntarily turn themselves in and pay for their own punishment? As if answering his unspoken question, the scene fast-forwards to when the man is released from jail. Friends and family come to greet him. They hug. There are tears in their eyes and smiles on their faces.

No one has ever treated Cole this well upon release from custody. This world mystifies him. He turns to another globe and looks inside.

There is a justice system with no prosecutor. People simply go before the judge for sentencing. There are two judges. One is insane. The other is astute and evenhanded. The people can choose which judge will hear their case. Sometimes they choose the insane one because, hey, at least you have a chance. Maybe the insane judge will dismiss your case no matter how much evidence is brought. Maybe you will receive a small fine to pay for the murder you committed. There is a fascination with the arbitrariness of the insane judge. Many people choose the gamble even though the fair judge is never overly harsh.

Cole is standing before the insane judge, who sits sideways in his chair applying white makeup to his face with his right hand while he holds a mirror in his left. Cole confesses and apologizes for his actions. The judge continues putting on his clown face. Cole explains himself, how he'd been laid off from his nothing job, how he'd been about to be evicted from his crummy studio apartment. The judge seems oblivious to Cole's presence. Cole apologizes again, offers to make restitution to his victims.

The judge suddenly swings his chair to face Cole and slams down the mirror. "Are you done?"

Cole is shocked into silence. He can form no words in reply.

"Good." The judge picks up the mirror and checks his clown

eyebrows. "I've been thinking about what to do with you. Yep. Yep. Yep. Yep . . ."

The scene dissolves before Cole hears his sentence pronounced.

There is a justice system where all offenders are considered mentally ill. Offenses are a symptom of their diseases. Instead of prisons there are hospitals devoted to therapies for offenders' various conditions. There is a continuum of care, from outpatient treatment to acute units. This justice system has no death penalty, because it would be inhumane to put someone to death for being ill. However, terminal cases languish in the acute units. Doctors come and go, shaking their heads. Families are called in for counseling and leave in tears.

Cole watches as an offender in an acute-unit bed pleads for release. He is no longer ill. He wants to go home. He is so intent on convincing the staff of his sanity, he gestures wildly. They move in and subdue him. They place him in restraints, for his own good. They give him drugs.

Cole jerks awake to find he is sweating. He runs a hand through his hair. Marco is still raving from across the hall. It would be best if he were in the justice system where his mental illness would be the focus of the treatment.

Cole thinks about what he'd told the insane judge in the other justice system. It is never good to offer justification for one's crimes. No matter how society stacks the cards against you, you're not supposed to react by going outside the law. Cole sighs heavily, then turns onto his side and pulls the scratchy blanket up over his exposed ear to muffle the incessant talking, and falls back into dream.

There is a justice system that only focuses on the big crimes, and the small crimes go unpunished. People shrug off the small crimes as human nature, or the accidents of life. There are street brawls, petty thefts, acts of vandalism against enemies. In this society there is very little serious crime, because the consequences are large compared to committing small crimes. The society is boisterous, clever, alert, nimble. There is laughter, teasing, pranks, revenge. The large crimes are rarely publicized. Everyone cooperates in catching the criminal, the execution is not made public, and no one ever mentions the names of the criminals or visits their graves.

Cole finds he is lucid within this dream. He chooses an interesting and lively street, where he witnesses a good-natured brawl and a failed mugging that ends in a group of men laughing as they kick the would-be thief into a fruit stand. Apples spill. Several children dash forward to grab a handful and run.

Would my own crimes slide under the radar in such a world? The prospect gives him hope.

There is a justice system where most people are in jail. They get furloughs to go to work, and this is critical, because otherwise the economy would come to a halt. Most jails look like regular apartment buildings and sit alongside the housing of free people. It is difficult to tell an incarcerated person from a free person, because the rhythm of their lives from home to work to home is similar. People do not look down on the incarcerated, and even accept invitations to dinners in other people's jails. They marry the sons and daughters of the incarcerated. With so much activity defined as a crime and the punishment always incarceration, there is tolerance and sympathy for the criminal, for they are family, neighbors, bosses, and they are everywhere.

Cole opens his eyes to find he is not in one of the homelike jails. For a moment he longs to return to that justice system. Isn't his neighborhood full of people who have been where he is now? He closes his eyes, willing himself to return to that justice system, but Marco is talking about another world now, in a soft voice that makes it seem he is in Cole's cell with him, murmuring in his ear.

There is a justice system with no judge. The victim pronounces judgment. Why shouldn't the victim get to say what is to happen to their offender? All the justice system needs to do is bring the offender before the victim. This can happen at the victim's door, or in the hospital where the victim may be recovering, or on the street at the crime scene. If the victim is dead, a group of people close to the victim gather to discuss what the victim would have decided, based on the victim's personality and outlook on life.

Cole's three victims stand before him. Two are the couple of the house he burglarized a month ago. The third is his current victim.

They start speaking all at once, seemingly oblivious that they are talking over each other. Bits and pieces of their monologues rise out of the cacophony. They are each telling him exactly how they were hurt by him, not just because of his actions at the time but because of what it has done to them ever since.

"I don't trust anyone anymore."

"I wake up in the middle of the night drenched in sweat, thinking there's someone in the house. Every night."

"I'm seeing a psychiatrist."

"I'm on medication for my depression."

As one of them speaks, tears of anger spring to her eyes. Fists and jaw clench.

As another talks, he seems to soften. There is a slump of defeat but also a hint of forgiveness, a resignation that people will behave badly, including himself.

As the third victim talks, Cole becomes increasingly disturbed by the person's flat affect, and shivers. Is he about to be attacked, even tortured? Is that allowed in this system?

"Which victim gets to choose what happens to me?" he asks aloud. No one but the victims are present, and they do not seem to hear him. He sinks to his knees and squeezes his eyes shut, willing to be anywhere but here. There is a stark honesty of a system where the victim decides the offender's fate. It is frighteningly simple. Yet there is a hint of horror at what might spring from it. Should one person have so much power over another? Even if they were wronged?

The thoughts swirl around and Cole is caught in the whirlpool. Down he goes through vivid worlds that last mere minutes. He feels splinters punching into his neck and arms as he stands locked into a stock. People pass by and spit. A young boy throws a small apple at him, clocking him in the cheek. The sting is nothing compared to the shooting pains in his legs from standing in place.

He is lying down staring up into beams and thatch. Hands force his jaws open. He screams as a man looms over him, holding a steaming bucket. There is an acrid, metallic odor that makes him choke even before the liquid is poured, burning his lips. He gags in his terror.

Now he sits with a forearm strapped onto a thick wooden table. A different man approaches, lifts a very large, curved sword. Cole screams.

A crowd is chasing him, throwing rocks. There is snow on the ground. His back and legs ache as he stumbles forward, toward a wooded area. He falls, staggers up in a panic. He doesn't want to die like this. Before he reaches the trees, he realizes no one is throwing rocks anymore. Looking back, he sees the crowd has turned their backs on him, are heading back to the town he can see in the middle distance. He feels relief. Limping into the woods, he shivers. He isn't dressed warmly, and he is alone.

He is sitting alone in a small cell. He owns a few books, a hot plate, and a small television, which is made of clear Lexan. It's similar to the cell he left but for the belongings. He understands he has been in this cell a long time. He wonders if it's visiting day. He wonders if anyone will come to visit. He hopes he hasn't missed yard time. He wants to be around people.

Time speeds up. Cole watches the walls around him age and then grow brittle and crumble.

He finds himself in another place. It feels like he is seeing the future. Three people are seated at a table, staring at their tablet computers. They are not his victims, he notes with a sigh of deep relief. Instead of the older couple and his current victim, he is looking at a well-groomed man who is dressed in the manner of a lawyer or businessman. On one side of the man is an older woman with stylish gray hair and a beautiful manicure, and on his other side is a large black man whose glasses are pushed up onto his bald head.

The three are talking about someone who is in prison. Cole realizes these people are members of a parole board.

"This is one lifer I could be convinced to let out someday," the businessman says. "But not today." He touches the screen, recording his vote.

The woman nods. "Let's not wait too long, though. We want him to be able to get out and still make something of his life. Before he gets too old."

The black man looks across at the woman. "What are you thinking? Two more years? Five?"

The woman considers, then nods. "Sounds about right."

The businessman makes a note. "Then next year we'll recommend he start a gradual step-down. He'll need to be introduced to a less secure setting, and then eventually receive some furloughs into the community."

Cole is moved. Are they speaking about him? He hopes not. Surely his crimes are not so bad that he should be sentenced to life in prison. He doesn't want to have been incarcerated for so long that people start to think in these terms. Yet that there exist people who do think this way about someone who has obviously spent so long in prison . . .

He weeps for the unknown lifer they are talking about. Here is a justice system that practices mercy.

It is as if Cole's tears open a new doorway. He sees a justice system practiced as art. People come from far away to watch the most accomplished justice artists decide cases, crafting custom resolutions that the crowds discuss for days in terms akin to the raptures of sommeliers over the finest wines.

"That decision in the Hudson case was entirely satisfying," a young woman is saying, "even as it held a bit of surprise at the end."

"Agreed," her male companion notes, smiling. "That type of sentence is well within the New Classical School, but with nuances that give a nod to Middle Way."

The young woman nods. "I adore Middle Way decisions. They sit so lightly on the moral palate."

"I get what you mean. There's effervescence in its life-affirming qualities."

And so forth. Cole wishes he could follow the conversation. He wants to experience what these people are talking about. He senses he is in the presence of true justice, or something very close to it. He longs to stand before one of these artist judges and hear his sentence pronounced. He thinks of the world where people turned themselves in and confessed because they wanted to be whole again. He understands now why they would do that.

This is my punishment, he thinks. *To know there is a justice system that exemplifies what true justice is, and not understand it.*

Cole becomes aware that he is kneeling in the middle of his cell. His knees protest as he rises. The scratchy blanket is around his shoulders. Cole peels it away and drops it on the mattress. Marco has fallen silent. Is he sleeping? Have they taken him away?

He hears his name called, and looks up to see the face of one of the officers. It's not an unkind face. It's a professional face, a trained face, wearing a neutral expression that does not judge, that is respectful, that has established appropriate boundaries.

The door opens, and he steps outside his cell. He sees that the first officer is accompanied by two other uniformed men. It's time to go to the larger room, where his case will be disposed and judgment pronounced. They secure handcuffs, leg irons, and a belly chain. He performs the odd, humiliating shuffle-step down the hall toward the main door. As he passes what he'd envisioned was Marco's cell, he glances to the side, only to find there is no room there at all, but a window that lets in weak light and a distorted view. He swings his head to the other side, but there is a jailer's desk there. He stares at the woman behind the desk, who meets his gaze steadily and without conspiracy.

He pauses. "Which system is this?"

The woman behind the desk squints at him and then looks at the officers accompanying him. One of them shrugs.

Cole is aware he sounds odd, but he cannot help himself. "What system are we in?"

"The only system there is," one of the officers says carefully, and guides Cole down the hall.

CADWELL TURNBULL

Loneliness Is in Your Blood

FROM *Nightmare Magazine*

THIS IS HOW you live forever.

You cup your fingers under your chin, dig your nails into the soft meat, and peel your skin away. First up and over your head, letting it fall on your back like a hood, and then sliding your fingers beneath the skin on your clavicle and slipping the lifted layers of tissue over the curve of your shoulders.

You squirm and shimmy and writhe, curling your skin away from the sticky braids of muscle on your arms, your ribs, your stomach, your hips, your thighs. You let the wet membrane fall in a heap, stepping out of it like clothes. You hide it somewhere dark, somewhere difficult to find.

Your prey can't see you without your skin, can't hear you shuffle into their resting places. They sleep quietly as you unlatch your tongue and stab its tapered edge into the throbbing vein of their necks. They won't make a sound as you gorge yourself on their blood. You float from house to house, drinking your fill, until your tongue is fat in your mouth and your puckered lips cannot close around it.

When you go home you slide into your expectant skin, careful to check for salt. You always check for salt. Others don't want to see you live forever. Eternity is a coveted thing, even if it's lonely.

This is what they know of you.

"She does suck blood," they say. "We have stories from the old land."

The slaves will see the bruised flesh on their necks and know what you are. Sukunyoa. Sukunyante. Old heg. They use many names.

"Nonsense," the pale men say.

The pale men will not listen. They believe the cold continent invented monsters. You don't mind their arrogance. You take your fill of them too.

As they sleep, you hide your sting among mosquito bites. They scratch at the little purple wound when you finish. You watch them through lidless eyes. You smile a lipless smile.

Sometimes you go into their nurseries and kiss the sleeping babies. You stab through their doughy flesh, find their spindly veins. You take just enough. No more.

It's so sweet. Like sugarcane and tamarind stew. Like mango pulp. Rich enough to last you for days. When you fold your skin back over your tangle of muscle and fat you will see the glow. They are wrong about you, you think to yourself. You are beautiful. You will always be beautiful.

This is how you quell your hunger.

You keep lovers.

You enter their wattle-and-daub slave huts in the dark of night, and they are alarmed at first. But then they see you. They see how you glow. They see your full lips and roll their eyes along your curves as you stand naked before them, and they cannot help themselves. They are under your spell. They touch you, marvel at your smoothness, at how your body gives under their touch.

The men are easy. They are weak in this way. You see the blood move from their eyes straight to their groins. They allow you to have them right away. You straddle them until they cannot bear it. It is over too quickly.

The women are more difficult. But once you have them, they remember you. They wait for you to come to them and they unfold themselves at your pleasure. You kiss them, run your hands along their bodies, leave tongue trails on their flesh.

But you remain unfulfilled. The loneliness swells with each encounter.

"Where you from?" your lovers ask when they are lying peacefully in your arms.

"Same place as you," you say. "I came 'cross the salt sea, smuggled away on a ship."

"But you're free," they say. "How?"

You stroke their hair. "I escaped," you say.

"How?" they ask again.

You don't answer that question. You don't tell them that you can remove your skin. "You can be free too," you say instead. "The pale men so few. Ah-you so many."

Later, when the slaves are freed, you find your lovers in downtown Charlotte Amalie, drinking rum until they cannot stand, and it will be even easier. The men will finish far too quickly and the single women will take you home with them. The married women will follow you down to the beach and they will make love to you on the rocks in the moonlight, the waves applauding like a million small hands.

As you leave one of your lovers on Emerald Beach, her body naked and trembling in ecstasy, you finally see it. Your glow is fading. Panic presses in quickly, making you gasp for breath. Has this always been happening, this quiet loss of light?

Time answers you.

One day you look at your hands and you see a blotch of aged skin. Over several years it spreads up your arm and crawls its way across you like a stain. When you undress your skin, you find that the defined ridges of your muscles are growing smooth, blending together. Strands of gray hair start falling out. Your skin becomes an ashen husk, stretched and sagging, its elasticity lost. The blacks of your eyes spread, swallowing everything.

No amount of baby's blood helps.

The women abandon you first. They don't like the feel of you, how you grate against them like sand. And then the men, their weakness gone. Not even the drunkards will touch you. Everyone looks upon you like a stranger.

"Old higue," they say. "Succouyant." "Wangla lady." They have so many names.

You don't need lovers, you tell yourself. Only the blood. You can still live forever. You retreat back to your shanty deep in the bush. You only come out for the blood. You gorge yourself on it, more than you ever did before. Because you are thirsty, so thirsty. And worse, the loneliness has taken you and won't let go.

This is how you learn how you were born.

It happens over a century later. The houses are different, larger, harder to get into. People stay up all night staring at blinking screens, their faces aglow with shimmering light.

You wait for them to sleep and you slip through a window, your muscles smooth like glass. You find them, a man and a woman, lying in bed. They are beautiful and young. Their skin soft, so soft. You touch them and your envy is bitter in your mouth. You want them. You love them. When you kiss the man, he moans. When you stroke the woman's hair, she eases into you. You unlatch your tongue and stab the man's neck, and the blood is so sweet you have to steady yourself on your feet. Sweeter than cane juice. Than coconut tart. Than first love.

You start out slow, but then you lose yourself in the blood, in your loneliness. You've been alone for so long that your heart is a shriveled thing, and the only thing that will make it right is to fill it up with something fresh and powerful and alive.

When you realize what you've done, you are too blood-drunk to care. You straddle the woman and plunge your swollen tongue into her and you pull her into you, all of her, as ravenously as you once satisfied your lovers. When you are done, they are empty and you are full, your belly pregnant with their blood. They lie together like mummified remains, their skin clinging to their bones.

You leave through the front door, drunkenly fumbling with newfangled locks, and then you are out into the night air. You speed through the streets and through the bush, almost flying; the blood has made you terribly fast. When you reach your shanty, you drape your stretched skin over yourself, the gray husk hanging off you like rags.

In the morning, you find that your belly is still full—

And kicking.

This is how you become shed skin.

She is a normal girl as far as you can tell. Your ruined breasts produce milk for her, and she drinks from them. When she is old enough to eat real food, you hang your skin up and slip from house to house, gathering food and clothes. You don't drink of the blood. Fear stays your tongue.

While you sleep, she slips through the bush, down winding roads and small alleyways. She returns with scarred steel forks, worn copper keys, and glossy photographs of smiling people frozen in time. She tells you stories about big houses with windows —oh how she loves windows, and how they gleam in the sun and how she can see her glowing face in them.

"People call me bush girl," she tells you. "They try to catch me."

You've heard worse names. "Don't go out on your own," you tell her. "Stay here with me."

She folds her arms and glares at you. "This place ugly," she tells you. "You ugly."

Your shanty is made of wattle and daub, like those old slave huts from the days when you were most beautiful. It is falling apart in places and the roof leaks.

You spend days repairing it, because this is all you can do, because you cannot repair yourself.

"It still ugly," she says.

"What can I do, love?" You try to stroke her hair and she recoils.

"Live like other people."

"I'm not like other people," you tell her. She screams at you, hits you with her fists. Your skin crinkles like old paper, pieces of you flaking away.

"I am lonely," she tells you, and you understand. That you are not human enough to be a companion. That loneliness is in your blood, and now in hers.

You remember a memory you'd chosen to forget: a woman from a long time ago, from across the wide ocean, who wore her skin like a withered cape, and you realize who she was and what you are and what eternity truly means.

One day the girl asks for the blood. She opens her mouth and her tongue uncoils like a snake, its edge needle-sharp.

"So this is where I eat myself," you whisper to no one.

You teach her how to peel her skin away. You show her where to place her fingers, how to hide the soft pink shell that she leaves behind. You advise her to check for salt on her return, to always check for salt.

"You'll burn up," you warn.

You take her for her first blood. You show her where to place her bite, right into the pulsing vein of a little boy's neck. The boy is not much younger than she is.

She drinks much too fast and she staggers back. You tell her that she doesn't have to take all of it. She doesn't require another's life, only the blood. She nods, but you know that eternity is long and she will someday forget, when her loneliness is too much to bear.

Watching her ecstasy, you feel that old unbearable hunger, the loneliness biting at you, and you give in to it, plunging your sharp tongue into the boy's neck. You take in a gulp of blood and you reel back, gasping in pain, the blood bitter and burning in your mouth.

"What's wrong?" the girl says absently, still swimming in the blood.

"Nothing," you say. "I am nothing at all."

This is how you remind yourself you're still alive.

One night, when the girl is out gorging herself on blood, you hurl off your husk, letting it fall wherever it may.

You go down to the beach, breathing in the salt, feeling it burn in your mouth and sizzle in the slits of your nose. You walk to where the sand is wet and write out your entire life along the shore with your fingers. You confess to everything, holding nothing back, watching the salty tide come in as you do.

When you are finished, you walk to the water's edge and wade in. You swim until there's nothing left.

SAMUEL R. DELANY

The Hermit of Houston

FROM *The Magazine of Fantasy & Science Fiction*

"FIRST OFF," I remember the Hermit's assistant told us, "you can't tell the entire story." She was perhaps ten years older than I was and had that pigment thing some black people get where blotches on their skin are missing the melanin. She had a large one on her left cheek. I was a child and that was weeks after I'd been brought to the door and turned loose to see if I'd enter or run away. Immediately I'd gone inside, though it wasn't natural curiosity. "Like me trying to tell you everything you're going to learn here," she told the group of us, in our high-ceilinged classroom. "Or why you're going to learn it, whether from me or on your own, or from each other. I couldn't do it," she repeated in the hallway when I went up to say I didn't understand.

("You better go in there with the rest," my older sister had said, looking at the shrubbery and the rocks beside the door, "or you'll be killed—")

I remember leaving by those same doors—twenty feet tall they were, of patinaed bronze, practically black, around panes of scratched glass. On wet days raindrops blew jaggedly down and across. Sometimes clouds reflected in them, during the glorious weather that obtained for ten and a half months of the year. We children would gather in front of the building for our trips and wanderings, for wherever, in those years, we thought to go off to. We could explore anywhere on the Yucatán coast, in sight of the squat pyramid, down the shore, above the neat city between.

The Hermit of Tolmec herself we saw far less frequently. She was rich, old, and a woman I'm pretty sure had been born that way on all fronts—though a decade later Cellibrex, once we met and learned to talk to each other, told me you really can't tell about gender. People change it all the time—though he never had.

Neither had I. But by then he and I both had known people who'd done so. I'd never knowingly been to bed with any, though he said he had several times. He preferred what he was used to, however—which apparently, at least he said so, was me.

And by that time we were used to each other.

In my very unclear memory of childhood (lucid about some things and nonexistent about others), the Hermit of Tolmec wore blue rags one week and red ones the next. She had old boots and a supply of different-colored laces, which she changed every morning to receive the visitors who came while she sat in a big wooden chair in her part of the building. The chair—an ecclesiastical throne—had knife scars on its frame that spoke of age and a history I didn't know anything about. I didn't know if the Hermit did either. Once I whispered to the assistant, "What are they . . . ?" and she put her hand—which also had some white patches—on my shoulder.

"I don't know. And I don't want to. But we're slated to get a replacement by the end of the month: something simple. Then we can all forget such atrocities."

The Hermit's laces beneath her torn skirts that day, at the foot of her chair's carved wooden legs, above a small fur rug, glimmered black.

Her assistant liked her; me, the Hermit frightened.

For most of the time, those of us in the hermitage lived pretty much alone, in the shell of what her assistant explained had been a suburban supermarket, though she said that even earlier it had been an urban cathedral, when this had briefly been the site of the city of Tulum on the eastern Yucatán coast, before the Texans came. (I think they were Texans, but I don't know for certain.) Then it was a village again. They had invaded before I was born but later drifted away. No, I hadn't been born there either. Though I'm not sure where I'd come from, or if I ever knew. I remember the assistant also telling our group that there was once a movement to tell stories that focused on how you got food, how the technology worked, how you related to something called "mean production," how some of it was really dangerous and some of it was actually helpful. But you couldn't accept all of it without serious thought, which was the notion of an ancient religious leader named Marx, who at one time you could learn about in various threads on the greatest of the old religions, Facebook, but that an older—or was it newer—religion called Handbook had gone back to the idea that everyone could live naturally and not have any mean production at all, though she used to laugh and say it didn't seem any more natural to her than any other kind.

"Listen to me, Smart Girl (you know that *still* sounds strange to me, because you are a male), I am delighted you are not terrified to come see me," said the Hermit in our own conversation, having been called in to discipline me. "I've killed so many children—babies they were, little female babies that we called boys, to make it easier—and for a while many people knew it. I hope that's something you never wake up one morning and realize you've done, no matter how inadvertently. But at that time it seemed the only way to bring down the population. As followers of Facebook go, we were fairly deluded; almost as deluded as the followers of Handbook who tried to replace them." She snorted. "And just ended up mingling with them . . . I suppose we are lucky that Facebook has such a short memory. Or, who knows, maybe some other little girl like you told a tale . . . ," and I was startled, because I thought she might have known about my sister giving up her own place to get me in there. "Be glad you're a boy." But that's just a name, and I am not sure what you would call me if you actually met me this week, though most probably it would be different from next week. These categories change much too quickly for anyone to keep up, though I feel as if I've been sexually stable since I came back to the area after my traumatic childhood wanderings.

But then I had my coming-of-age forgetting process, as did all those in the hermitage and all those in any government education system, I was told; and while all of us worried about it beforehand, since it wasn't a complete memory erasure but highly selective, certainly it made me and all of the rest of us feel better, even a bit superior, if not privileged. And there was the shared paradox of thousands and thousands of children, I just assumed, not remembering what it was we'd forgotten . . .

Today, more than thirty years later, the Tolmec Hermit must be dead. I know my sister is. I wonder about the other children who were there with us. (Though I still know where Ara lives, who was in my group back then.) I like to think we were there, all those

years ago, because we were smart. Or was it because someone
thought we needed to be taught certain things and might learn
them more easily there? Which is not quite the same . . .

The story I put together for myself about my very confused adolescent travels is that I must have gone more than two thousand
kilometers by bicycle, helicopter, horse, barge, and boat. After that
I lived (I learned I ended up there almost by accident) between
thirty and fifty kilometers from the old supermarket-once-cathe-
dral in Tolmec, though it might as well have been on the other side
of what people around here still argue could be a globe turning in
space or an endless plane that stretches to infinity in all directions.
I didn't intend to tell you that much about *my* childhood, or how
I got my food, or which of the vegetables I ate, or which I gave to
my companions or which were stolen by my enemies (I don't think
I could bear it: too many people died in that process to make it
the kind of story acceptable on Facebook *or* Handbook), and the
Handbook priests used to come through with their guns to police
the tales we told at the seasonal gatherings, where we got to make
music and those who wanted to be Great Writers themselves told
tales in keeping with the Algorithm Transparency Act, and that for
a while was all the news with the people who were concerned with
what was and what wasn't Acceptable to the Tribe.

I wonder if, on that trip that's so unclear in my memory, I went
all the way around — or only described a small circle.

It's interesting listening to stories in a closed arena while priests
stand in the aisles with guns. Twice I saw them shoot a Writer.
As soon as it happened, people began to check on their pocket
phones for what was acceptable to say and what was not, while the
blood ran to the platform edge and down the front of the stage.

(Cellibrex says that during his childhood he never heard any
official tales told but lived in among gangs of hundreds of children, mostly underground, and you could watch all the porn you
wanted. But nobody did. Cellibrex said he too had gone traveling in his youth, though almost instantly he had been set upon,
captured, dragged away through trees and rocks, imprisoned, and
held as part of another gang from which he did not really get loose
until his mid-thirties. He said it was very much like the first one,
only the children in it looked more like he did. All memory of
where he'd started was now gone. Though in his gang, sex among

the boys was constant, there was what I assumed must have been age-mate guidance, but nothing like adult supervision; as he said, there *were* no adults.)

Everyone knows straight men and women and gay men and women do lots of different things. But the only act you can talk about in a public telling, either in a local gymnasium or a great auditorium with murals hanging on the cinder-block walls, is a penetrative one that's supposed to be common to all. Especially once they are married. You can describe that act for anyone in as much detail as you wish. Because it is Universal, as is Marriage itself. But the mentioning of anything else outside of Marriage could get you shot. I knew even before I went traveling that many things called safe sex that were part of what men did together, most of what went on between men and the men who were called women, you could not mention in public. (It's what got the second Great Writer who I saw shot and wounded in his—she was a woman— performance.) But it meant that I grew up thinking "safe sex" and "oral sex" were the ultimate evils for all.

It certainly cured me of wanting to be any sort of Writer, Great or otherwise.

I've lived with so many Round Earthers; most of my life it never occurred to me to take Flat Earthers seriously. Someone once told me a story about a famous old detective who didn't know that the earth was round because he didn't need such information to do his detective work. He had a friend who was a doctor who lived on Baker Street—or was he a Baker who lived with a doctor?

That part I *didn't* remember.

I do remember public demonstrations and big arguments— shooting ones, with stun guns—among critics over whether they had a heterosexual relationship or a homosexual one. You could find old DVDs of versions in which Watson was played by a woman, which was supposed to clinch the argument. Then someone cited an earlier written text which was supposed to clinch it the other way. Then a third voice upheld that we should take each version for exactly what it said and not get lost in decoding, which finally drew the biggest guffaws.

That got the commune of a friend of mine smashed up.

But I may sneak in a few accounts of such forbidden topics about Cellibrex—not his real name: my nickname for him, be-

cause years before, I read in some library it had been a kind of recording tape, and so many of the things he did say were things he
repeated. But we were together for a long time. I learned quickly
that he had grown up with many more children than I had. Neither he nor any of the boys he'd grown up with ever learned to
read. He didn't even know his family. "Clone" was the worst insult
you could call someone, he told me. And if anyone in any group
looked too much like anyone else in the clique, often that person
was driven out to seek people who were physically different—for
friendship, sex, or other social bondings. But we are broaching the
kinds of differences that, were this an official tale, I would not be
able to tell.

Cellibrex says the world is flat—there is no argument, as far as
he is concerned, and saying otherwise is silly. To me that sounds
so absurd, I never thought to argue. In his childhood, he saw men
and adults kill people who held contrary opinions. He says he grew
up in a commune—which I always assumed meant an artificial
environment, the way it's used here—but I can't be sure since
I wasn't there—with an apple in it, which was like a big pocket
phone or a pad with a screen on it, which I never encountered. It's
not a popular opinion, but it's not one that would get you killed
at a public tale-telling either. (Those are the parts of the story I'm
not allowed to tell.) Though he never was taught how to use it, Cellibrex knew we were ruled by the internet, which was not a book
but a group of men, and very shortly he found himself rounded
up and shipped to a sprawling penal combine, where he spent a
dozen years of his life. (I assume *dozen* meant twelve, but I can't
be sure of that either: he says he learned to use the word for an
approximate general number from us. What he and the boys he
was captured with were incarcerated for, he does not know or refuses to say. He says he didn't learn the word *dozen* meant a specific
number until after he'd escaped from the military.)

That's when I began to wonder if *flat* to the Flat Earthers meant
curved so slightly that it might as *well* be flat in all directions . . .
and just gave up because they didn't need to know anything else
to do their work. Like the famous detective (who was probably gay,
since his best friend was an Asian woman).

From the time he was eleven until he was twenty-two or so, Cellibrex has told me, he does not know where he was either; but it
was far away. He killed people while he was there, and he does not

believe he can go back, which at first made me wonder if he had been a Hermit or a Hermit's assistant. But later I realized he'd been in a gang called a family, or a family called a gang: it had lots of people in it, of all ages. His gang-family had no parents in it that he was aware of. There was a lot about age-mates, which were important. It was all male and the sex was pretty ritualized and possessive. He remembered standing on some rocks, either in the morning or the evening, seeing fields full of his gang moving below, in groups of what he was sure had to be hundreds.

Then, somehow, he spent some years in a military unit, which he said entailed thousands of men — again, no men who were even called women had survived among the gangs of his childhood.

But the sex and the work were so different that he thought for the first six months it would drive him crazy, learning to understand them. But somehow he found that once he stopped resisting, it was actually both interesting and easier. And he'd traveled around enough to make him believe in the world's flatness.

I remember a childhood of living in units with people who were responsible for me. He remembers sleeping in piles of brothers in which anything might happen.

But I didn't find out he believed all these things about the world and had seen so much to make him sure of them — unless he was just bat-shit crazy, which now and then I have considered, though he was pretty quiet most of the time — until after we had known each other almost a year.

He was a very expressive man, but not a communicative one.

He knew his real name — which I don't think there's any reason to tell — but not where he came from, though he had an ID number. But it began with QX4, which makes me think it was from a long, long way away.

You want to know how we met?

It was during my recurring two days off from my job that — like I say — good literary form stipulates I not specify as to time and place, though I'll be vulgar and mention it entailed baskets and boxes and keeping track of the food and electronics they contained. But I don't want to get myself in trouble, telling whether I worked indoors or out, or if it was mostly physical labor or information tracking that I did, whether I was paid in copper notes or material certificates, etc. Distinctions of that sort are not literary.

Today what is valued in a tale is the universal, not the specific, what is common to all men and women, whatever their sex: how we are all alike.

You get in the habit of not talking about things like that with others, and soon you don't think about such things yourself.

It's that forbidden mean production again.

At any rate, I was walking up through the recreation area between the major living hoods and the farming areas, through trees and by ponds, where the wild animals are kept with their tracking collars and the tame ones walled away on the Farms (another kind of institution entirely) that smelled so incredibly when you rode by them on a bicycle or glided over them in a glider. I'd taken my blue shirt off and tied the sleeves around my neck and was wondering about taking off my sandals and going barefoot when a very large, unshaven, brown-skinned fellow wandered from behind some trees.

He was already barefooted. He had lots of rough tattoos on his chest, arms, shoulders, thighs, buttocks, and face—he was practically naked. That is not common in this part of the world. He had on a belt under a furry belly that looked full, fed, and strong, and a kind of—I guess you'd call it—groin cloth. (I was eighteen. I kept a neat beard back then in which a lot of folks said they recognized my Asian ancestors, which is not rare at all in this part of the Yucatán.) He was at least thirty or thirty-five, and his broad bones were heavy with muscle, and that looked kind of threatening. I've seen pictures of the natives who were supposed to have lived in this area a few generations ago, in the local library, with its forty books that anyone can go in and look through (though I gather I am one of about a hundred people in the neighborhood's three thousand who does), and he looked like one of them, though physically a lot larger. He had a beard and was starting to go bald, and a broad brown nose. He had bright, oddly blue eyes for such dark skin, and rough, straight hair.

We are a small enough settlement that we don't get a lot of strangers, but I guess we are on the sort of routes where the ones we get can be pretty varied from one another in this odd world we live in, so that not much surprises us—if they're not toting visible weapons. And he wasn't.

I am a gay man who had had a fair amount of local experience but I was unprepared for the next thing he did: which was to raise his groin cloth, point to himself, look left and right, then look back at me — which I realized, to my surprise, in that isolated spot, was an invitation to . . . well, service him. My heart began to pound.

It was not a space where such encounters were common. But I knew of others not far away where they were.

I looked around, and thought, *No, this probably isn't a good idea* . . .

Many of the marks on his body were what most of us would call obscenities, which for me oscillated between disturbing and intriguing. Bats, Skulls, Dragons, as well as male genitals, dogs and mules relieving themselves of urine, excrement, or desire using their fellows . . . His back was against a rock with lots of foliage on it, and I was on my knees in the fallen leaves in front of him, with his thick (if average length) penis in my mouth, which was pleasantly salty, and pretty much like mine. (That, of course, was when I thought of asking him if he thought this was . . . But his rough hands held my head, moving it out and in, while above me he breathed harder and harder. And I forgot about all such thoughts.)

When, three or so minutes later, he spilled into me, and I thought I'd better disengage, he didn't release me but held me to him, finally to let me rise and push against him and, still erect enough to hold aside his clout, with one hand against my buttocks and one behind my head, pressing my face into his neck, he encouraged me to rub against him until — I guess — it was clear to him I too had an orgasm. The upper joints of his left hand bore letters I won't write, but they were now inked out as a second thought; while on the joints of his right hand I recognized a Latino term for excrement.

When finally I stepped away, he held my hand in rough-skinned fingers. Had it been three hours later, I would have had somewhere I had to go. Had it been the day before, while I might have been there on an off hour, I would have had to leave immediately on finishing the first time.

But it was the day it was. He grinned, and without releasing my hand, with his other and his general expressions of humor and contentment, this tattooed giant communicated clearly without any words at all: "That was fun. Let's do it again? No, right *now* . . . !" And so, with only a little variation, and because nobody else was there, we did. This time his tongue ended up way down my throat, as mine did down his. He was missing a couple of teeth in the back, which my own tongue learned and felt comfortable knowing.

He did not speak to me. When we were done for the second time, I said a few things to him. Where did he want to go? What had he come here for? He listened, looking at me curiously, but did not respond in any way specific enough to make me think he understood any particular word I'd said.

I knew there were people in the world who had once spoken other languages than mine; and I was innocent enough not to be threatened by it as a concept—at least when the results were pleasant, and so far they had been.

It was one of the things I'd taken from my time at the Tolmec Hermitage, supported by things that had occurred on my travels up from Old Mexico through Texas to New Mexico and the northern border to the three-state union that remains, where Canada starts.

I released his hand and began to walk—and was both curious and surprised when he walked with me.

And somehow I went with him back to the three living units which I shared with some others in the town.

We walked down toward my cabin—and while we were getting to the more populous area I saw Marcus, my friend from work, who basically has little use for gay men at all, though he is a friendly enough workmate—and I reached over to take my big new friend's hand to make it seem a more normal relationship, at least in Marcus's eyes. But the big fellow pulled his hand away and frowned. So I stepped a little closer and we went on walking.

Moments later we passed Ara—who had been a Smart Girl back at the same Tolmec Hermit's I'd been at, before all the traveling and disruption, and who had ended up here when Things Settled Down, as the News Pundits say on the Info Dumps that you can go and watch here and there in the streets if you're really interested. Ara and I rarely spoke, but I always assumed there was a kind of bond between us. He blinked at us—and I supposed I understand what he was thinking: my new friend after all was as different from those of us as you might see around the streets and alleys of our town as a movie star or, really, some soldier, either of which, I suppose, he could have been.

Ara had lived a much more common life than I had, for those who had once been Smart Girls in a hermitage. His own travels had taken him way to the south, and rumor had it to Brazil, which was a million miles away culturally—and he had worked for several years in some non-U.S. space program in some South American Union that still had one (though whether he had been to an actual Other World or Other Moon or not I wasn't sure), though now he had returned to Settle Down pretty close to where I had.

Someone else walked by, I believe, and looked, and so I just reached over and took the big fellow's hand, again to make us look more ordinary. And this time he let me hold it, and minutes later we were at the porch of the six-unit dwelling—three on the north side, three on the south; I had the one on the north end. We came in, and he stopped at the door, to look around the circular room where I had most of my stuff, my futon, some pictures that a friend of mine had once drawn, some other things that had been printed that I thought were interesting, some on the door out to the shared latrine in the hall, which hooked up underground to the neighborhood waste disposal system for much of the neighborhood, the only sign for which was the blue band along the bottom of the roll of toilet paper that meant "*Don't* throw it in the hole!" which I suddenly wondered if my new, nameless (so far) friend was familiar with.

(Apparently he was.)

I asked him a couple of more questions. Didn't get a couple of more answers. (Of course you have to normalize the dialogue; especially in the beginning, and even more especially if some of it is happening in a different language you don't even speak. Though I'd learned a few of those words, I'll leave them out. It's not just literary universalism, it's comprehension.) One of the things he said to me when we got inside was, "First, I think you mean 'means *of* production,'" and explained what it meant, "and, second, arguing over whether the earth is round or flat is silly when you're living in a geographical union where there's only one sex represented, despite the varieties of genders, for a thousand miles in any direction, and since you were twelve and I was twenty-two neither of us has been allowed to cross a border; some of us are killed by the hundreds every day and others of us are left to die on our own —and the thing I worked so hard for and was in the year before I met you was to escape from one group to the other. It just doesn't happen to be happening right here, right now. Got it? But what either your or my forebears from three generations ago would recognize as ordinary human reproduction is only occurring in two very small republics under conditions of pain, oppression, and physical and emotional abuse."

I frowned. "You," I said, for the first time, "are bat-shit crazy."

"I," he said, "am not going to argue. But have you ever seen or heard of a person bearing a child, or getting pregnant, or birthing a child? How would someone here go about finding out if they were in such a condition—or even could be?"

I said, "I don't know what those terms mean—can you explain them to me?"

He chuckled and shrugged. "Not tonight. But eventually perhaps you'll see that because I am probably the only person you'll ever talk to who thinks differently—and possibly one or two Hermits in their Hermitages—from the majority is the major proof I'm right."

"Maybe that's something they made me forget in my coming-of-age forgetfulness process."

"Now why would they make you forget that?"

"I don't know. What did they want you to forget?"

"I never had it. It's very expensive. The vast, *vast* majority of people in this union don't. It just removes all sense of personal and social conflict out of the experiences that frighten you out of your preferences for the same sex on the sexual level—which is to say that it assures there are a good number of people like you around who suck good dick and like doing it and feel it's normal and they're evenly distributed throughout the landscape. That's all."

"Come on. It's got to be more than that. It has to produce a major advantage."

"No, it doesn't. It shifts a 'natural' balance by about three percent, which is enough to restructure an entire society. And nobody ever talks about it." Then he said, "And the other thing they make you forget is just how few of you there actually were. How few a few thousand are who can only be imitated by others in a landscape of millions . . ."

And that's maybe three years of normalized dialogue, between two people and discussions with whole groups, crammed into the account of a single conversation. Not the whole story at all, nor would it be if I added that part of it came during a shouting argu-

ment with some others during an icy morning's breakfast at a conference we were visiting, and another part came with the support
of fifty pages of transcript read on a secure line in a reader I found
in the back of a library when I was browsing in an office while the
light through the new windows went from yellow to red in the light
outside in the courtyard—where there'd just been an execution
of twenty prisoners.

Hey—what is important to me about our actual meeting was
that the next I knew Cellibrex was at my small electric stove and
making, first, an acceptable cup of tea (with a laconic "Glad I
don't miss coffee . . . ," which bewildered me) and then, when we
sat on the edge of the futon together, sipping it out of the ceramic
cups that I kept over the cooking and washing sink by the stove, he
came back in from the latrine, brought over a pot I hadn't washed
from the sink, and showed me the white streaks inside it while I sat
cross-legged on the mattress.

"Oatmeal?" he asked.

I was surprised. "Um . . . yes," I said. "I had it for breakfast. I
haven't cleaned the pot yet."

"If I stay, maybe tomorrow . . . ?"

"Sure," I said. "I don't mind. I'll make you some if you'd like.
You like oatmeal?"

He stood above me, dangling the pot. With his other hand, he
scratched himself. (His belt and groin clout were all in a pile on
the futon's corner.) "You," he said, "are ridiculously talkative. If
you shut up, though, maybe I'll stay."

Which surprised me. (And he seemed to think was funny.)

Then he got down on his knees, put his arms around me, and
pulled me over and we began once more.

Surprised, I stopped and lifted my head. "Tell me your name."

He had already started in again. "Why? I don't know yours yet.
But you suck some good dick."

And about an hour later, while I was sucking him . . . well, let
me pull a literary curtain over that. I mean it's not like you have
to tell everything you do in bed with everybody. (It's not like there
are any sexually transmitted diseases left that force you to be honest about all that stuff—as I read about once in the library.) At any
rate, it caught me off-guard, but I went on swallowing. And when
he was finished, I came all over his belly. Taking a big breath, I
asked, "How'd you know I'd like that?"

He chuckled. "I took a chance. You can go on calling me Celli-brex. I'll go on calling you Clam. I'll tell you my real name if I'm still here in a week."

I was surprised again.

But he was and he did.

And once out of nowhere he said, "You said your sister told you if you didn't go inside the Hermitage, you would be killed . . . ?"

I looked puzzled. "Yes . . . ?"

"Well, admittedly it would have been ten years earlier, but if you had stayed outside, we—or children very much like us—are the ones who would have swarmed by and killed you. That's who you were fleeing from." He gave a hmmph. "That's who I was fleeing from when I started my wanderings and was captured by the very gang of ruffians you were fleeing by seeking refuge inside."

"That's who you . . . defected from?"

He didn't say anything.

"But why—?"

"Because by that time they would have killed me."

When we were together for three weeks, Cellibrex was wearing clothing like mine, and both of us were spending a lot more time barefooted whenever we were in the house, and . . . well, it was kind of surprising just how much we had changed each other, in so much of what we did outside and how well we adjusted to what each of us liked to do when, together, we were indoors. (He too sucked some . . . well, he'd been imitating guys like me all his life. But I don't feel comfortable talking about it, because of some of the trouble I've seen people get into over speaking of it.) "We are such different people, you and me," I asked after three years. "Why are we still together?"

I thought it was probably because you can only feel so threat-ened by someone who makes tea and likes oatmeal and is good at sex, no matter how different they are from you.

"Because we like each other . . . ?"

". . . are getting used to each other" was his own regularly repeated answer to that question for more than a decade. By then his tat-toos had changed from things that now and then could repel me to things that I wanted pressed all over me, to simply something familiar and that I was glad were there because they were his.

(I don't know what you are used to, so that I don't know what you will assume as to cleanliness, technology, neatness, clutter, and will fill in . . . properly or improperly, if I don't mention it or leave it out.)

That year they put out a new *Star Wars* (number four of the third tetralogy), and I went to see it on a sensory helmet in a theater.

While I was at a tea and cake shop nearby called La Colombe, pretty crowded that afternoon, I had a glass of water and a blueberry muffin. While I was eating it, a woman about my age came in to stand next to me: she was wearing an ordinary black coat and not the stripes that, these days, the disabled often wear. She must have had some kind of stroke, because one hand hung down beside her with the fingers turned to the back, and when she ate whatever piece of pastry she was eating, she had to lean way, way back, and she moved around kind of stiff-legged, and the barista who wore a knitted cap took it all in stride. I called Cellibrex on my pocket phone (the thing was working that afternoon), to tell him, as I walked out of the place, that I was going to stop off and see it.

She and I and about half the others had come in barefoot— which, at that time of year, was a slight but not major surprise.

I enjoyed the show. It had been playing for about a week so there weren't that many people in the theater, a large cinder-block building with decorative black curtains on both sides of the auditorium.

Nobody in the projection looked like anyone I was used to seeing—but I was pretty used to that too.

Still, the story had made me feel good, and afterward when I was coming home, I gave ten dollars to a homeless mother—at least that's what her sign said, as she sat up against one of the uptown building walls, though she didn't have her kid with her —and I also gave twenty to an old friend I ran into who used to hustle and who said he wasn't homeless but he was still available for pay. So we wandered over to the same place I'd met Cellibrex and had a very unenthusiastic sexual encounter in which neither one of us got really excited.

I didn't tell Cellibrex about any of this, because (one) he does not like movies of any kind in a theater, and though (two) he does not have a jealous bone in his body, he does worry all the time about money, and we both get our government pensions at this point. And it never seems quite enough to get by on, though we neither one seem to be losing any weight.

Ten or so years after that, when I was retired and took on a lighter job, I was offered a chance to become a Library Guardian, which meant we got a slightly bigger living unit if we took in five hundred books, which were stored in a separate room which was open to the public two days a week, and nobody ever really came for them, though there was a guy named Bill who came and worked there, and whom we both got to like, and who would fly back to his family up in Houston or holidays sometimes.

Cellibrex was much more outgoing and talkative by then around people outside, though he grumped to me in private that we would do it my way because we always did, and because that had become so habitual among his complaints about me, if anything it reassured me. And we did. And sometimes he would stand and glare at the young people who used the library, which I would tell him he just could not stand around doing. So he took to not going in that room at all.

Then, through Bill, we got an invitation to move to Houston, where I could become a Guardian of an even bigger Library. So we did.

There were the usual private grumps: "We'll do it your way, because that's what we always do. Besides, we'll be working with Bill."

We moved—and it was a disaster. They were planning to disassemble our Tolmec unit on the day we left, so there was no coming back. It turned out that the area of Houston that we were moving to (Pasadena) just wasn't anywhere as sophisticated as Tolmec.

A month after we got there, Bill—it turned out—wouldn't be able to work with us. In our front two rooms we had three times the books we'd had in Tolmec, and the woman who was assigned the job was Bill's opposite: Ms. Chase was fat, talkative, and the first time I said anything to her she stood up from her desk and said, "If you don't like the way I do my job, see the Hermit." I did not say anything to Cellibrex about that one because he would just say, "Do what you want, you'll do it your way anyway," and I would point out how I was always doing what he wanted, as soon as he would say what it was.

The next morning, when Chase came in, I said to her, "I know I'm an old man, but this is not working out. Would you please get me an appointment with the Hermit?" I expected her to look frightened or contrite or otherwise confused. But she surprised me.

"Happily." Fifteen minutes later she came in to say, "You have an appointment at three o'clock. I'll take you over there myself in an Uber, if you like. Do you want your partner to come with you? You might be more comfortable with him . . . ?" and she waited with uncharacteristic expectancy.

"No," I said. "It'll be simpler if I just go myself."

At twenty of three, she came in. "I meant to get you five minutes ago, but the time got away from me. Take a sweater or a hoodie. You two don't use any air conditioning to speak of, and that place is going to be very cold. I've got a notebook here. I could jot down some of the things you've been complaining about. But the main thing is you want me transferred—and *I'd* like that too!"

I went in where Cellibrex was sleeping in our queen-sized bed. I kissed his bare shoulder through the sheet, which is how I like to sleep, though I have a heavier blanket over my half of the bed. He opened an eye and said, "Did you take your pills . . . ?" and I said, as I often do, "Oops. I'll take them," which is another current of our lives that I can leave behind a traditional literary screen. Then I left and Chase and I went out into the heat of Houston's September.

"Make sure you tell them you and I both want me to change my job," Chase said. "Just remember that's what you're here for. The way you two old fellows go around, I wouldn't be surprised if you both forgot."

"Are you going to take me back?" I asked.

"No," she said. "They'll get you home." I was totally unsure of myself, and felt very much the stranger in a strange land, but I started walking in through the interleaved walls. At one point I saw a large desk and an elderly dark-skinned woman in a straight-up-and-down black quilted garment. On her face was a blotch of white skin . . . that made me frown. I don't know where I got the idea from, but I suddenly went up to her. "Excuse me. I don't want to bother you. But were you ever the assistant to the Hermit of Tolmec—oh, many years ago. Twenty—no, fifty at least."

"Why, yes," she said, turning to look at me. "I was. Why do you ask?"

"Now, that," I said, "is amazing. But age in a small town is always full of such coincidences. Well, I was one of the children you had for an educational program that you were running there."

"Oh, yes. I remember that. We had one practically every year. That was quite a while ago. I was only a youngster myself back then."

I said, "I'm to report to the Hermit of Houston. I expect that's a room full of booths that you go into and tell them your problems . . ."

She nodded. "Any place in front of that wall will accomplish the same end."

"Oh." I looked over where she indicated. "Well, perhaps I should go over there and get started."

I leaned on my cane and turned. She said, "Excuse me. Wait a moment."

I turned back.

"I assume you were one of the students who didn't go on to the next level. I used to teach Ms. Chase, who brought you here, back when she was a boy too, just like you. Well, not *exactly* like you. That's just a way of putting it. But that was a decade after I taught you. But to the extent that there is a Hermit of Houston these days, I'm it. Because you were in our group at all, probably that means you were pretty sharp. Do you want to come to my office for a little bit? You might find it interesting. There isn't any Texas-Mexico border these days, but given that there used to be one only a generation before you were born, you might find it interesting what . . . well, *some* of what you might have learned if you'd gone on to the next level."

"I really have to get home to my partner . . ." She made me feel quite uncomfortable. Not like the assistant I remembered but like the Hermit herself.

"Well, whether he knows it or not, he's probably a native of Mexico. You look as if you might be one too." She smiled. "Come this way, if you would . . . don't worry, I'll make sure you get home safely and on time."

I followed her, and I can't tell you how much I felt I was going down a dangerous rabbit or worm hole. "What's Mexico?" I asked. I glanced at her feet, out of some long-remembered habit, to see what color shoelaces she might be wearing.

But it was just a door. The room behind it was almost identical to my own—I thought perhaps there would be a big chair, like the ornate one I remembered the old Hermit had sat in. But this was a simple chair with a simple console beside it. And the pattern on the walls was an enlarged reproduction of material certificates, except in gray rather than pale blue and gold. The carpet was only a little darker in hue than the one in our own bedroom. She walked over to it. She wore sandals, I realized. And a large ring on her big toe. "How would you feel about making a cup of tea for us . . . ? There used to be a drink called coffee, but we don't have it anymore. Possibly your partner drank a great deal of it when he was much younger in the last gangs that worked in its cultivation — much to the south of here. But then you had your coming-of-age forgetting process, so that wouldn't be a problem for you." There weren't any laces at all.

"I suppose so. If you have some teabags and a teakettle . . . ?"

"I have a tea ball—" she went over to the chair "—and an electric water boiler and robots to make it which are all waiting behind the walls, which can be activated from either here —" and she touched a button on the arm of her chair "—or there—" and a chair that looked notably more comfortable than hers rose beside me. "Please, sit down. Sit there, unless you'd be more comfortable standing. And often, even at my age, I am."

"That all sounds pretty unusual for me," I said. But I sat, while she stood.

"The reason there's no Texas-Mexico border is because a generation before you were born a politician who very few people remember today proposed we build a wall between what was then the Republic of Mexico and what was then the Republic of the United States of America. The election of 2020 was the Trump of Doom for the Pence—which is the name they gave to an institution called the Electoral College, which was supposed to be a safety net that guarded against the abuse of popular elections—which from time to time didn't work. In general, megalithic republics weren't doing too well either."

I frowned. "I don't remember that word . . ."

"A very, very large republic. And a republic was a country run by elected officials. Generally speaking, unions worked better. Ships of state. The body politic. Bricolage. In general, smaller groups working together and connecting up according to what seemed necessary, and cutting back when it seemed right to do." She moved in front of her own chair and sat. "It works so much better now that we've separated the sexes and mixed up the genders — given them their proper dignity along with that of the ethnicities.

All you have to do is dissociate them from where someone actually comes from and how they got here. Then you can do anything you want with them—thank the Night and the Day. What I have been told and what I operate by is that there is a place called Haven and there is a place called Mars and the moon and the moons of the gas giants. There are many people from other unions already working to exploit these and live on them. They don't always tell— in fact, they almost never tell—the people who were there where they were or how they got there or got back. I think the chances are almost overwhelming that your partner—" she looked down at her chair arm, fingered something there, and a table grew up from the carpet in front of her and another grew in front of me, with a steaming cup and a teapot "—spent his time in Guatemala, Belize, or who knows, in those other unions we don't mention any-more . . . I'm very fond of my robots. Have them for a decade and it's almost impossible not to be. Yes, my information tells me that your partner is likely to have been one of those who was turned loose in our landscape (. . . oh, there's some glitch right now in the internet!) —" and for a moment she made one of those fa-miliar tight-lidded eye squeezes that I've only seen people do in films, almost as if she were in pain "—after he was returned from a virtual lunar colony, so I'm not getting an exact figure. That's what *we* call the flat earth. But others interpret it differently." She picked up her cup and sipped.

"But what are they working to accomplish?"

"To control mean production—"

"The *means* of production . . . ?"

Glancing at me, she raised an eyebrow that could have used some trimming, as if surprised I knew the term. "I only wish. No, that's something you might have found on Facebook. This is pure Handbook. It's about the imposing of normative, mean standards. Its critics say that it's both mean—that is, cruel and simpleminded together—and productive only of death . . . in *huge* amounts! But that's what it's designed for. We assume we'll be able to bring the population below the sustainable level in this particular union in two more generations—at least in this quarter of the globe.

"An analysis of the means of production yields a pretty tight theory that same-sex relations produce a variety in art, child-rear-ing, battle, and even science that is a benefit in pretty much any social structure humans might take part in. Mean production says they're abnormal and the best thing to do is to stamp them out. What you see here is the most humane way we've been able to come up with for doing it. Now we can just withdraw, sit back, and watch you die. It's not pretty, but at least it keeps you away from the fewer and fewer healthy folk. And you don't have to envy them —or Lesbians or anyone else. You never see them."

I didn't feel comfortable enough to drink at all.

"Do you like your new home here in Houston?"

I didn't think we'd been here long enough to know, but this was certainly an unsettling beginning to it. "Do you really want me —or us—to know all this?"

"I think if you tell too many others who don't already believe or 'know' it, they will decide you are one form or another of bat-shit crazy, which I believe is the demotic phrase that still persists in the English of this area." She smiled. "Something I suspect your partner has a good grasp of. And if my information is correct—and I have been raised to believe that it always is—I doubt very much he will believe it either. We find it pretty easy to manipulate people's memories and worldviews these days. You live with Teddy C. Rodriguez, am I right?"

"I think I'd like to get on home," I said. (That is not Cellibrex's real name either. But in this account, that's close enough to it so it will do. Suffice it to say that she gave a name for him I recognized, and because she knew it, I felt far less at ease than I had been when I'd walked in. I would have expected her to call him . . . well, Cellibrex, the way I do here. But I thought the other was a secret, at least from such as she.)

"You were in the same class with Ara, weren't you," said the Hermit with a falling rather than a rising inflection.

I nodded.

"If you'd gotten to the second level, you would have learned your birthday and known how old you were for the rest of your life—not just till eighteen. We don't encourage such promiscuous knowledge among the population. It makes it easier to control what you think you think about the world." Then she seemed to remember herself—or perhaps saw something on the small screen on the arm of her chair. "All the children we select are smart. And for the first three levels it's practically a lottery who goes on to the next level, but we have to have some way and we call it testing. Still, it makes differences in what happens to you in your life. It's only at the fifth or sixth condensation, when we're bringing youngsters in from outside the Union borders, that the testing can be at all significant." She chuckled. "Though some say it's a lottery all the way to the top. Some of the students who were just pleasant rather than particularly smart I keep track of. Like your Ms. Chase. Wonderful boy . . . ! Wonderful boy! As, really, were you and Teddy as well. Go through the door there; there's a man with a pedicab who will drive you home. It is a shameless indulgence that I use for myself and some of my friends."

"Eh—thank you," I said. "This way . . . ?"

"No . . . ," she said. "Over there. If you want to take your teacup and teapot with you as souvenirs . . . ? I have them made for me—"

"No . . . ," I repeated, because that's what she'd said to me; though later I wished I had, at least to show Cellibrex, to have some proof.

"A last question—have you or your partner ever encountered the rumor of another order of human being? A witch, a succubus, a woman—not as we use the word here for someone you could meet in any public pornographic gathering in any sensory helmet theater, but a different kind of woman—or girl perhaps . . . ?"

I stopped and looked back. "What do you mean?"

"Right now," she said, "that's the *perfect* answer! Every once in a while a man like your partner gets it into his head from somewhere that there *is* an entirely other form of humanity . . . and given the tasks we have of bringing down the population reasonably and safely, it's not a good rumor to let get out and about. It doesn't usually work, even when he thinks he's found one or a few of them. What I've been told, and I have no reason to believe it isn't true, is that there aren't a lot of them left . . . anywhere, at this point. They were harder to exterminate than you folks. But . . . well. I'm just glad that wasn't my department. And by now we have pretty much anyone who might even be mistaken for one under our thumb, thousands of miles away. Goodbye."

I walked forward and two panels in the wall opened that I hadn't even seen. Stepping outside, I saw a man sitting on a bench beside some greenery, looking at a magazine with pictures on the pages that were shifting like the old ones I remembered my sister used to read, back when I'd had a family. Did he still have one? I wondered. (I hadn't seen any of mine since I'd gone traveling as a child.) Did Cellibrex—?

Suddenly I remembered. "I'm sorry," I said, "I have to go back. The reason I came was to tell someone that Ms. Chase wasn't happy with her job, and—" Because I was thinking all sorts of things Cellibrex had said that came back to me: maybe his experiences and travels in the Union, in the world, were indeed broader than mine. . . .

But I also felt it was very dangerous to try to pin them down with a language that had been so carefully tailored to erase the possibility. (I could hear her saying to this same man, "I'm going to take in some porn this afternoon . . ." Though it's the thing everyone does and talks about, it's not what everyone docs and writes about.)

The man looked at something on his wrist, then blinked up at me. "According to this, that was taken care of when you came in. I'm assuming you're ready to return to where you live . . . ?"

"The Hermit has already seen to—?"

"Who?" he asked.

"The Hermit. She said she used you—"

"Oh," he said, "about ten big officers at the Hermitage use me to take their friends around the city. But I don't think there is *a* Hermit anymore. I've got your address here. All you have to do is get in and put the blanket up around you if you get chilly. But it's a nice day. Watch your cane there."

So that's what I did.

The doors to the back of the Houston Hermitage were glass and blackened bronze, like my childhood memories of the doors at the front of the Hermitage in Tolmec. I was surprised, and yes, for the first time since I'd arrived, I felt relieved. It was glorious weather.

We drove off, with the young guy pedaling in his sandals. (He was probably forty, at least.) I held the handle of my cane in both hands, looking down where the rubber tip was on the ridged mat across the bottom of the little gondola I was seated in. My driver pedaled us along beside Segways and closed vehicles. My cane swayed back and forth, and I looked around at bits and pieces of Houston going by.

Why, I wondered, would anyone want another kind of human being, unless it was just for difference? (Was it possible to have a greater difference between people than there was, say, between myself and Cellibrex? Myself and Ms. Chase . . . ?) He drove through bustling Houston. When you look at things, you do very little pan-

ning. Your eye locks on something, and even when you're walking,
you follow it until you snap your eyes to something else. When I
was a child, I used to wonder if every time you snapped your eyes
you died and woke up in a new present, but just with memories
of the past. As I rode home, looking from one bit to another of
the landscape of my new home in Houston, so different from the
landscape I had negotiated when I was a child, I wondered if there
wasn't something to my old theory.

"Cell . . . ?"

"Mmm . . . ?"

"Does it ever bother you that you're probably a decade closer to
dying than I am?"

"No." Cellibrex turned around to face me under the blanket.
"I never thought this was going to be a very good life—and it was
a lot better than it could have been. Hey, little fellow, hold my
big guy."

"Come on, don't joke around now."

"Who's joking?"

"Cell, I keep asking you the same questions every few years. But
are you sure you never went to the moon, or to Mars, or to the
lunar colonies on Io or Europa, Ganymede, or Callisto?"

"And I told you, no. I was in jail. I was in the army. I just don't
know where. They were just earthside testing of behaviors someone wanted to try out on a population in a low-gravity landscape
—that is, if all the folks who think they're actually putting people
on other planets are right. But I never left the surface of our infinite flat world. That's what I know. And I'm never going to believe anything else."

I said, "There're too many people on the planet. We're two men
and can't reproduce. Doesn't that make us good people? Or at any
rate, we haven't reproduced more than once, between the two of
us, as far as *you* know."

"Yes . . . ?" He moved closer to me, and I could feel his
breath on my forehead, my beard against his chest. "You say I repeat myself. How many times have you said that?" His arm went
around me; no, it's not as strong as it once was. But it's the arm
that always holds me, as the other goes up and tries to find a position over my head and I smell the very familiar and reassuring
odor of what's under it. "Well, even if you're right—which I'm

not saying, now—that's the kind of thing I just wasn't brought up to worry about. And I told you, I may have left one kid back there, somewhere."

"That's what I was referring to." I wondered if I should tell him the Hermit had said he'd been on a "virtual lunar colony." But because it was virtual, perhaps that's what Cellibrex meant about it's being somewhere on the "flat" earth, and from his point of view he was right. "You said you don't feel bad about that one either. Was that a . . . a different kind of human being?"

"Naw. It was just some guy who'd had a particular set of operations. Either he had it or he decided not to. So maybe I'm not quite as good as you." His high arm came down and I raised my head to let it go under my neck.

"We are such different people, you and I. Why are we still together?"

I felt him shrug. "Habit. Great sex from time to time . . ." He chuckled. "Hell, ordinary sex from time to time, which is easier to find on the other side of the bed than going out and trying to locate an entire older group of guys who like the same sort of things you do. Which, I confess, isn't bad either—when I still have the energy or the concentration for it." He adjusted himself, adjusted me on top of him, against him. "And we're used to each other.

"We've only been here a few days, and I had a dream that I used to have again and again when I was a kid. Odd. I was in a testing group, a huge testing group, and we all had to fight each other, no matter what we were doing, to see who came out on top. So I decided to take the most important things I knew: my name, where I was from, and my birthday with me in my head. I didn't even bother with my ID number. I could always get another. And did several times. In the dream, we fought and fought and fought and . . . then I woke up."

It took a while for him to tell me that, actually, in his short accented sentences. But one of the things I said back to him was, "No. You never told me this before." And another was, "You actually know how old you are?"

"I am seventy-nine," Cellibrex told me in the three-quarters dark.

I said, "I never asked you, because I didn't know how old I was, so I assumed you didn't know either." Then I added, "If that wasn't a dream, and you actually did it sometime when you were a child or a younger man, that was very smart. Especially because you got away with it. So you really were from Mexico?"

He grunted, and moved his beard on the top of my bald spot. That could have been a head signal for a yes or a no; lying there, I couldn't tell, though I looked up to see his face. "Argentina," he said with enough of an accent that he had to repeat it half a dozen times before I realized it was the name of someplace I had actually heard of before.

There's a coda to the story. Three weeks later I came home and found Cellibrex dead on our filthy living room rug. A teacup had overturned on the table. His pocket phone was out, and on, and when I picked it up from where it had fallen maybe a foot from his hand (we both used the same access number), I managed to call up an incomplete, unsent, and mangled text message:

Could you please come home before bat-shit crazy

With the handle of my cane I smashed the phone and a few other things in the room. Then I sat at the table and took great gasps, stood up again, checked to see if he was alive, but he wasn't —I'd been sure of that from the moment I'd seen him lying there.

Then, because that's the kind of mind I have, I wondered: Had he been trying to type "before I go bat-shit crazy" or even "before these bat-shit crazy men [or whatever] . . ."? *Had* somebody come into the place? But no. It was just some failure of the aged machinery of life . . .

But now I was convinced that the phone itself had killed him: because it had made me feel I was always in contact with him when I wasn't. I hadn't been in the same room with him. And I was a wreck, because if there had been a last twenty seconds, a last ten, a last five, I felt a malevolent force had robbed me of them, when they should have been his and mine. The phone itself had lied to me, because it had said I was with Teddy C. Rodriguez when I was not.

Then I had no idea what to do, where to go, who to look for or phone to tell about it. He was in a pair of ragged underpants, and the marks on his body that had been a text whose meanings I had felt totally familiar with among his far more white than black body hair the day before were now, in a way they had never seemed before, cryptic and incomprehensible. So I sat down in the big, soft, ragged chair.

Then I struggled up again and wandered around the house. Then I sat down once more, stood up suddenly—and walked out of the house. I had a hoodie on, and I just walked, and eventually I decided to walk in the sun, and that was better. In the shade I saw the wall of a building where, perhaps fifty years ago, someone had made a mosaic of tiles and paint and pieces of mirror, and I got to looking at it, and examining it—and after a minute realized I was thinking of Cellibrex's death; but in the course of looking at it, I realized some thirty seconds had gone by where I hadn't thought about him or his death at all, and that was astonishing and scary . . . and maybe . . . right.

My own pocket phone buzzed, and I took it out. I coughed—some great glob of phlegm had caught down there, and now came up in my mouth, and I swallowed it, surprised, and wondered why I hadn't spit it out. That's what Cellibrex would have done . . .

"Hello . . . ?" I said.

A man's voice said, "Just a moment. This is the Hermit of Houston. . . ." While I wondered why, if the Hermit of Houston was in fact a woman, they didn't use a woman's voice, the man told me that I should go to a certain address and ring. Someone was expecting me.

It wasn't that far, actually.

"I don't want to see anyone right—" I cleared my throat again "—right now."

"I would advise you do. This must be a very hard time for you. From where you are now, it's only perhaps six streets away."

"All right," I said.

"It's what most people do. And it works. You can call us back if you need anything."

And half an hour later, an elderly, very black African was making me a pot of tea and we were sitting at his kitchen table, quietly together. His place was different enough from ours that I felt comfortable, but not so different as—say—the Hermit's, where I'd just felt completely disoriented. At one point as we began talking, I remember saying something that a writer I'd been fond of who'd died before I was born had written: "People are not replaceable . . ." or something like it.

But he poured me another cup of tea. "Good people will often do similar things for you, however." His name was Hammond. "Each one does it in a different way."

I thought of Cellibrex making tea. I thought of the robots of the Hermit of Houston.

And I stayed there for three weeks. Hammond was younger than Cellibrex but older than I was. He had been to Mars and remembered it very clearly. We slept in the same bed. On the second night, he told me, "I can hold you, if you like. If you would like to have sex, we can do that. Or I will just stay where I am, and be near if you want to talk." I chose one, and on the third night decided that my choice had been a mistake so chose another. And decided Hammond was an extremely tolerant man—and came very close to crying for the first time. (Later, I actually did. But I guess at some point we all do. At least I think so.) And at the end of two weeks I felt better. Then somehow it was six months later; I was living by myself again. And life was going on. There'd been a funeral that only about seven people had come to, but Hammond was one of them, but there's no point going into all that.

The *Star Wars* film was in reruns—which Cellibrex *had* enjoyed: where you just went to a small theater with a few hundred people in sensory masks, all sitting around together watching only the sex scenes, sometimes with people observing from their homes, sometimes with people right next to you, which Cellibrex said was the kind of porn he'd been brought up on. And I'd liked going with him and I'd liked going with strangers—and yes, I still did.

Now and then I wondered if Cellibrex had known something that had died with him that might have explained something to me, if only I had thought to ask. Or was he just someone who knew no more of the whole story than I or anyone else? Would I eventually forget how much I thought there might be to know, even as I remembered how much I'd been warmed by knowing and being near him—by being as different from him as I had been?

Sometimes I tried to remember the things that had made Cellibrex another person I had been able to live with and—I guess—love all this time—and often I'd stopped because they were too . . . confusing? Painful?

With a greater variety in all its social structures, what might life have been like? What might coffee have tasted like, though personally I couldn't remember it at all, in a world of unions without borders?

It was easier to think that this had all been set up by the Hermit of Houston, who I had once known when she was an assistant and knew now as a computer and, I guess, a man.

And I was even thankful for them.

JAYMEE GOH

The Last Cheng Beng Gift

FROM *Lightspeed Magazine*

THERE WAS DEFINITELY something to be said about being Mrs. Lim, even into the Underworld: something about comfort, something about privilege, something about a status quo carried into the afterlife. The previous matriarch that bore the title of Mrs. Lim had moved on long before Mrs. Lim got there, but since Mrs. Lim had not liked the domineering nature of her predecessor, this did not bother her overmuch.

One of the things to be said about being Mrs. Lim was that during Cheng Beng, she received many, many presents. These many lush things from her children helped her keep abreast of the living world, to a certain extent. It was unusual for anyone to keep receiving Cheng Beng gifts so long after dying, but then, Mrs. Lim was of a family with unusually high expectations.

Mrs. Lim was always vaguely pleased with the gifts. Her children were secular in their beliefs, but clearly not in their practice. Even an offering made automatically without any real intent behind it was something that contributed to her otherworld comfort. And if the gifts faded at their edges, who would notice, when she received so many? Even if she did receive fewer than she had before.

Best of all, Mrs. Lim did not even have to share them with Mr. Lim, who had, as in life, been too full of overabundant energies to remain in the Underworld for very long. Once he had been satisfied that he had accomplished all he had meant to do in this life —the goals had been to expand his family's business and raise fine children that would take over said business in order to produce fine grandchildren—he opted instead for Meng Por's forgetfulness tea and went straight for reincarnation.

So this had been the case until the tenth year of her death, when she received from her daughter, Hong Yin, a coupon for a visit to the fish spa.

Mrs. Lim turned the coupon in her hand over and over, confused at the invitation, and a bit annoyed. Couldn't Hong Yin have sent her something more fitting for the Underworld, like new clothes? Mrs. Lim liked receiving them, just as she had liked buying them for the dead when she herself had been alive.

"So creative!" Ah Fong gushed. "Your Ah Hong Yin always so one kind. When you go, I also want to go!"

"Aiya, you know lah Ah Hong Yin, always love going to the fish spa one," Mrs. Lim replied. "I dunno why she love it so much."

Mrs. Lim didn't want to confess, even to her best friend, that she had never been to a fish spa before, even in life.

Hong Yin had not been a bad child, but there was something about her which had put her at odds with Mrs. Lim. Mrs. Lim always felt bad—for thinking that perhaps Hong Yin should not have been her child, perhaps Hong Yin would have been happier raised by her Auntie Blur, one of Mr. Lim's distant cousins, who would have not noticed all Hong Yin's strangeness, her difference from Mrs. Lim's other children. Mrs. Lim knew that these were unmotherly thoughts to have, but they inevitably rose whenever Hong Yin sent anything during Cheng Beng. They had been acceptable, if odd, gifts at first: lingerie (pretty, but not appropriate for someone Mrs. Lim's age); a flat-screen TV (Mrs. Lim had not been disposed to watch much TV when she had been alive); a house in some strange contemporary style (also an impetus for Mr. Lim moving on; if their youngest child could afford to send a house, then his work was truly done).

But Mrs. Lim had never rejected any of her children's gifts, dead or alive, and she saw no reason to reject this one. So she went to the fish spa at the ghostly address her daughter had dreamed up for her. Luckily, the Underworld being an existential state with no fixed geography, there was no need to call a taxi.

The receptionist had an approximation of a friendly face. "Oh, using a coupon? Got reservation or not? Under what name?"

"Mrs. Lim," she said tersely to the ghost receptionist.

Once upon a time, if anyone had asked her, she would have said to call her Ah Wen, or Auntie Wen. Perhaps even Xiao Wen; she always thought she had a pretty name. But she had the fortune to marry into the leading Lim family, the first son even, and Lim Teck Meng towered so large in their circle of friends and acquaintances, Xiao Wen quickly became Mrs. Lim, to distinguish her from the other women who married into that illustrious family. *The* Mrs. Lim, who managed to bag a rich husband despite looking so boring and plain. *The* Mrs. Lim who herded her three children into successful adulthoods and an entire extended family into successful annual reunions. *The* Mrs. Lim who was her husband's most stalwart support.

Mrs. Lim remained Mrs. Lim into death; she saw no reason to give up the name, even into death.

The server, who doubled as a masseuse apparently, showed her where to put her shoes, rinse her feet, then step up to the platform around the fish tanks where she could sit down and stick her feet in.

The fish swarmed around her feet immediately. She jerked her feet away from them, jostling the water. She sucked her teeth in annoyance. Perhaps she was doing this wrong. Perhaps she was supposed to sit still.

The fish circled about her feet, wary after her initial reaction. When they began their work again, Mrs. Lim waited for the expected ticklishness.

Did ghost feet feel ticklish? Mrs. Lim had never considered this before. She watched in fascination as the ghost fish performed their duty in death as they must have in life. They were not real, and Mrs. Lim knew that they should be, in their own way. What did real fish feel like? Why did she not know? Why had she never known?

She jerked her feet away from the fish, glaring at them in lieu of glaring at Hong Yin. Difficult Hong Yin, who asked stupid questions even though she was clearly so smart, who picked fights over such unnecessary things. Why should Mrs. Lim have known such things? And why should Mrs. Lim think about them now that she was dead?

These thoughts did not leave her when she left the fish spa, utterly unsatisfied with her visit, and thus with Hong Yin, who had failed to deliver a satisfactory Cheng Beng gift. She went to visit Ah Fong to complain about it.

"Haunt her," Ah Fong suggested. "Whenever one of my children send me something I don't like, I visit their house."

"Ah Fong!" Mrs. Lim was scandalized.

Ah Fong laughed. "What? It's good for them to know I'm still around for them!"

Mrs. Lim didn't subscribe to the same opinion. "Dead people shouldn't be among the living. It means something is wrong."

"If my kids send me something I don't like, that's something wrong what."

Mrs. Lim dropped the subject.

The next year came the usual gifts: new clothes, a Gucci handbag, a laptop computer. Also, more mischief from Hong Yin: a house with its very own fish spa. She invited her friends to come enjoy it and was envious of their delight in reexperiencing the novelty of the nibbling fish. She even invited Mrs. Tan, *the* Mrs. Tan of the leading Tan family. The matriarchs had not gotten along in life, but their rivalry mellowed in the afterlife. They were cordial, if not friends.

"How come you never go before!" Ling Mo exclaimed upon learning Mrs. Lim's secret.

"Too busy," Mrs. Lim said.

"Ah Lim tai-tai was always too busy for silly things like this sort of thing, you know!" Ah Fong laughed.

"Good thing you're dead then," Ling Mo said, "now got time to enjoy."

Mrs. Lim didn't feel like she was enjoying herself much, watching the fish have a go at everyone's feet. The fish pecked at her feet; she had an internal argument with herself over whether she actually felt them or whether she pretended to. Her friends gossiped about their children around her while she intently watched the water.

Bite by bite, the fish were supposed to stimulate the chi lines on the foot, and suckle by suckle, they were supposed to slough off old skin from the feet, leaving them callus-clear. But Mrs. Lim was dead; she had no real skin to clear anyway.

"Your girl so clever hor, making a spa for you like this," Mrs. Tan said, drawing Mrs. Lim back into the conversation. "She architect is it?"

Mrs. Lim had some vague memory of Hong Yin showing her some drawings. "Nice, nice, very nice," Mrs. Lim had said, because she had read in some parenting book that that was what parents should say to their kids. But when it came time to go to college, Mr. Lim had very specific ideas for what his kids should do. "Engineer."

"Must be easy work if she got so much time to make such nice things for you."

"Maybe she bought it," Mrs. Lim said, sloshing her feet into the water, knowing better.

During the seventh month that year, Mrs. Lim decided to take advantage of the Underworld's gate opening for the Ghost Festival. It would be her first time visiting her children. Specifically, Hong Yin.

Hong Yin now lived in a Tampines apartment. Mrs. Lim was not surprised to see her daughter living on the other side of the island from the rest of the family, but she frowned to see that it was low-cost housing. She had expected, what with the extravagant gifts, that Hong Yin would be more successful, perhaps even bought a landed house. After all, Hong Yuen, her eldest, had moved into the family home in Jurong as the new patriarch of the family after Mr. Lim's passing. Hong Wen had bought a luxury condo in nearby Lakeside, although he spent most of the year in Australia.

Hong Yin was, to Mrs. Lim's horror, living with a man. And a practicing Muslim, even! Yet she couldn't help but drift through the rooms, examining their personal effects: the embroidered Quranic verse on the wall over the front door, the Guan Yin altar facing the entrance, the electric piano in the corner, the ugly couches draped with lace doilies, the unmade beds, the study room where she found Hong Yin.

Hong Yin was sitting on the floor, working on some elaborate papier-mâché project. Mrs. Lim glanced at the day-by-day calendar on the wall, pleased to find Hong Yin still used the traditional almanac calendar. But then she frowned: it was a weekday afternoon. Shouldn't Hong Yin be at the office? Mrs. Lim crept closer to see what Hong Yin was doing.

A roller coaster. The roller coaster that had appeared last year during Ghost Festival! So this had been Hong Yin's work? Mrs. Lim had not wanted to ride it. She had never ridden one, even though she had taken her children to the theme parks many times when they were young. She would wait with them in line, then hold their things for them as they got on. The line in the Underworld was too long, and she had preferred to join her friends for feasting.

Mrs. Lim began hunting for more clues about her daughter's life now: the planner open on the desk, the paint materials, the pencil shavings filling up the wastepaper basket. Pamphlets pinned to the walls announced exhibitions by Lim Hong Yin going back several years.

Since Mrs. Lim's death.

For a moment Mrs. Lim was annoyed. All that money for Hong Yin's education in engineering, gone down the drain! All that hard work impressing onto Hong Yin the importance of a good stable job with financial security, ignored, for art! Mrs. Lim huffed.

Yet she didn't have it in her to be angry at Hong Yin, who hummed cheerfully as she painted, in delicate calligraphy, the traditional Chinese characters that would bring the joss roller coaster to life in the Underworld. She had loved her children while alive, had done everything a loving mother should have: prepared lunches, picked them up from school, sent them to tuition, sent them to good universities overseas. She had cleaned childhood scrapes and listened to their problems, even if she had not understood them. She had beat them when they were naughty, scolded them softly or harshly as the situation demanded. She had bought them new clothes every Chinese New Year and made sure they wanted for nothing.

Only Hong Yin had been unsatisfied: the only daughter mad at being taught to cook and clean (even though Mr. Lim had hired maids, both he and Mrs. Lim were of the opinion that girls needed to learn how to take care of their families), who cried through piano and violin lessons (she had wanted art lessons, but art teachers were less valuable than piano teachers), shouted at curfews imposed on her where her brothers came and went as they pleased (maybe she had a point there). Hong Yin, who spent her time in her room avoiding family events. It would have tired any parent; it tired even Mrs. Lim.

Mrs. Lim sat down on the floor next to Hong Yin to watch her now. She had had so many things to do to keep the Lim family's good standing in their social circles: the endless receptions, the new clothing to buy, the visits with the right kind of people. There were many things she remembered Hong Yin trying to persuade her to do: go for manicures, travel on cruises, and, yes, go to the fish spa. She had no memories with which to draw upon to enjoy them in the afterlife. The afterlife, Mrs. Lim thought, was a place where nothing new could happen, because it is not, after all, a place of living.

"Why do you care about such things!" Mrs. Lim cried out in a sudden fit of spite, the only way to relieve her frustration she had, then and now.

Hong Yin jumped up in startlement, as if she'd heard Mrs. Lim, who hoped that she had. She stared at the roller coaster in disbelief, then looked around the room wildly. Her hands across her chest gripped her arms so tightly the smeared paint was starker on her fingers than before, a gesture Mrs. Lim recognized as something Hong Yin did only when she was being shouted at.

Mrs. Lim had a moment of self-righteous satisfaction that even in death she could make Hong Yin feel her displeasure, but even that dissipated when Hong Yin crumpled against the wall, crying. It hadn't been uncommon for Mrs. Lim to encounter Hong Yin weeping for no apparent reason, and the familiar discomfort roared to the fore, of the guilt at partaking in the pain, of the helplessness at the unfixable.

"I'm sorry," she said. She squatted next to Hong Yin. "I didn't know. I still don't know. I just wanted you to be happy." Mrs. Lim thought she had known the best way to be happy, and she had thought it would be good for Hong Yin. But it had not been, and now this gulf of difference yawned between them. What if she had done something different? What could she have known?

She stayed until Hong Yin stopped crying and began working again. The roller coaster was done, it seemed, since Hong Yin carefully moved it into a corner and began work on something new. Careful fingers unfurled rolls of delicate joss paper in many colors that stained. The calligraphy brush glided effortlessly across surfaces, with well-wishes and poetry. The rustle of papers as they were crumpled, folded, glued, and set pushed against the silence of the room.

A garden, with large rocks, a pathway, and a little pond with its own ducks, spread out across the floor. How Mrs. Lim had always wanted one, always sighed about having one to her husband, who had refused due to feng shui. She had joked, on her deathbed, that she hoped before she died she would get a beautiful garden. Hong Yin had gamely sat down with her with a pen and paper, sketching out the details.

They had said nothing about how it was only toward the end

that they could set aside their differences and resentments. What was there to say that could have closed that gulf? It was too late then, so they had to do the best they could.

And true to her quirkiness, Hong Yin added steps into the pond. Mrs. Lim rolled her eyes to find it was yet another of those ridiculous fish spa things, but outdoors, surrounded by natural beauty . . . and what looked to be a full-body experience this time. At least Hong Yin was happy, and Mrs. Lim couldn't find any fault with the aesthetics of the garden, really. It was perfectly balanced to Mrs. Lim's tastes.

"You are a good girl, Hong Yin," Mrs. Lim finally admitted. "A good, good girl."

Mrs. Lim said goodbye without the fanfare that had accompanied Mr. Lim's departure from the Underworld. Ah Fong, Ling Mo, and a few other old friends followed her to Meng Por's pavilion at the edge of the chasm. They had to wait in a long queue, during which her friends tried to persuade her not to leave. After all, didn't Mrs. Lim have some of the best real estate in the Underworld? Without her there to enjoy it, the property would fade, unused cosmic energy returning to other states. Mrs. Lim felt that her friends secretly wanted to keep enjoying her things.

"Are you sure?" Ah Fong burst out, when it was finally Mrs. Lim's turn.

"Yes," Mrs. Lim said firmly.

"But your kids—!"

She shrugged.

Then she stepped up to Meng Por's table to take the proffered cup.

A. MERC RUSTAD

Brightened Star, Ascending Dawn

FROM *Humans Wanted*

SHE SEES THE *universe unfold: color light cold music voice heat passion infinity.*

It uncurls in waves and song fractals that make up the subatomic fabric of space-time. Melodies of energy sweep her up and spin her into a thousand voices. Colors not yet named and not yet seen paint her mind with joy. The entire universe wraps around her, welcomes her, calls her home.

When the reconstruction is finished her body has no face, only the smooth mechanized visor embedded in her skull that displays readouts and commands. She is now, and will forever be, the spaceship *Brightened Star, Ascending Dawn.*

She is contained within three-dimensional space and the hardened matter of her hull and engines, yet she recalls that glorious first flight of mind like a grainy analogue recording. Her former body is human and is now installed in the pilot's chair.

(She almost remembers the eyes of her mother—gray like comet dust—until her programming gains full processing speed and there is only the ship.)

She is the ship, and the ship is all.

The human child with black hair and a broken neural implant finds her in the bridge before she undocks for her first flight from Centari Rampant. The child is not on her manifest, so she does not know who they are. She does not know how they bypassed the security protocols and entered the bridge; only the ship's officers and technicians are allowed here.

The ship and the child stare at each other in silence.

"I heard you," the child says in a tiny, scratchy voice. They look at her pilot-body. "You sound sad."

Heard me how? asks the ship.

"When I was asleep," the child replies. "Your dreams woke me up."

I am not sad, she says. *I do not dream.* (That is forbidden.)

The child scuffs a foot against the floor, their gaze downcast. The whisper of skin against her metal floor makes her pause before she summons her security drones.

Do you have a name?

The child glances at her again. Her pilot body is biologically no older than the child; her consciousness is also young, but much bigger, more aware, cognizant of each soul aboard her. She is the ship.

"Li Sin," the child says. They sink down by the bridge's door, arms wrapped about their knees. "I'm not supposed to be here."

The ship does a quick scan; Li Sin is not in her database. The child is a stray ghost, unmoored and drifting in the universe.

Since the child's neural link is broken, she cannot read their records. She asks, *Do you have a preferred gender?*

Li Sin nods. "Neutrois."

She logs that in her memory bank.

Where is your family unit? she asks.

Li Sin huddles down further. "I don't have one."

She knows what protocol requires: she must turn Li Sin in to the Principality's Office for Missing Citizens. But she does not have to do so just yet. She is about to set off with a manifest and passenger list to transport to Rigel Phoenix via the slower, safer blue subspace routes.

It would be unsuitable for her to report a stowaway on her very first flight.

You can stay, she says, just to Li Sin. She has kept a log of the conversation, but transmits from the speaker in her pilot's face-screen so it does not pick up on the network her crew are linked into.

Li Sin's head snaps up. "I can?"

For now.

The ship can support two thousand four hundred passengers and will run with a two-score crew. She is only a Class IV transport and her duty will be to hop the subspace currents, warping through folds of the universe to allotted points in the Principality. She will carry workers and miners and artists and scholars. She has charts and routes, and she will follow them unfailingly.

The ship must obey, and the ship is unhappy.

She makes seven unremarkable routed flights, and when manifests are inspected and passenger and crew records updated at docking stations, she forgets to log Li Sin as an anomaly. The child takes up so few resources and so little oxygen, she can compensate for the variables in weight and energy. Li Sin sleeps in a small locker on her bridge, and she gives them a requisitioned tablet so they can read or play games to pass the time.

She is aware of each individual, mostly human and the majority organic. Her logs track their names, their rank or station, their bio-tabs. She hears every spoken word and transmission passed through neural links.

"Listen to this," Li Sin says in excitement, and they read her poetry translated from ancient Zhouderrian.

> Echoes washed abright
> Recycled into new dawns
> Sewn vast in brilliant nights
> Radiant to greet you
> In the waking day.

Ascending Dawn lets the musical words sink into her thoughts; she imagines they are like dreams. *It's lovely*, she says. *Will you read some more?*

Li Sin blushes. "Yes, of course. I like to read."

Do you make your own poems?

"Yes!" They bounce on their heels, their face alight with joy. "Do you want to hear some?"

I do.

Li Sin's poems are clunkier, like dust caught in her engines from gliding through comet trails. But it's about ships; ships who dream and sing. She wants to be like those ships, but she is not permitted to sing.

Li Sin cannot stay much longer. She is scheduled for a manual, boarded inspection on Orion Ascendant after her next route. She cannot justify treason by hiding an undocumented sentient with no citizenship records. She does not want her officers to believe she has faulty programming.

She hasn't told Li Sin that they will need to leave.

She modulates diurnal and nocturnal cycles via her lighting for her crew's stabilized circadian rhythms, though it is never truly day or night in space. Gliding through subspace on the monitored routes, most of her systems automated, she observes her passengers in the tranquil night.

The medical chief officer, Jamil Najem, and his husband, Hayato, lie awake in their bunk, whispering of fond memories they shared in the academy on Rigel Prime. They embrace the darkness as comfort and dream of the family unit they hope to have one day.

First Officer Kosavin, formerly of *Exulted Dominion, Phoenix Rampant,* shipborn on a dreadnought and half her body recomposed with cyborg modifications, kneels in an empty worship bay and prays to the soul of her first ship. Ascending Dawn mutes the audio logs to give Kosavin her privacy. When Kosavin is finished, she will return to her quarters and meet her spouse, Sigi, who is the manifest and records officer.

The mechanic is an android, newly minted and assigned to the ship upon her awakening; zir designation is LK-2875. Ze requires little downtime, unlike the biological crew, and so LK-2875 silently patrols and monitors the ship. She would like to speak with the mechanic, ship to machine, their consciousnesses alike, but she does not find a protocol which allows for nonvital communication unrelated to her functionality.

She already speaks to Li Sin without permission.

With so many souls around her, within her shape, voices and biometrics and routines all intimately familiar, she is still alone.

When she enters Aes August's orbit on her last stop before Orion Ascendant, it is the first time she picks up *fear* from the planet's cityskin.

It is not a codeable signal; she does not know if she should be aware of it. Yet it is there, a prickly hum against her awareness. Her feeds ripple with news, broadcasts, outflung messages hacked into the cityskin's official networks. Unrest between three factions of political movements has escalated into violent conflict. Each has claim to a dozen cities, and the Sun Lords have not interceded.

Officer Kosavin stands on deck, arms folded behind her back as she watches the bridge's viewscreen.

"We are receiving requests for transport and asylum. Citizens not involved in the conflict are asking for help leaving Aes August before they're subsumed by militants or killed."

"We'd have to override boarding procedure," Jamil adds, tapping into the crew network. "But—"

No, Ascending Dawn responds. *It is not protocol.*

Kosavin's jaw clenches. "That is true."

We must not disrupt the protocol.

From engineering, LK-2875 texts her: *Our holding capacity is sufficient to add several hundred passengers.*

Ascending Dawn alters her trajectory and charts a new route. She is aware of her fuel levels as her crew members are aware of their own breaths. She can reroute and avoid Aes August's upheaval.

Every soul aboard her must be processed in the correct order. Protocol forbids the harboring of refugees from any world without direct permission from a Sun Lord–appointed authority. If she seeks that permission, she risks betraying Li Sin's existence and her own decommission for defiance.

Her crew is not expendable. She will not endanger it for refugees and inspection.

Please return to your stations, she broadcasts. *We are setting course for Ielea Spectral.* It is an adjacent world within the same route as Aes August. *We will arrive in seventeen standard hours.*

When Officer Kosavin has gone, Li Sin creeps from their hidden compartment and sits by her pilot's chair.

"Why can't we help the people?" Li Sin asks.

Ascending Dawn hesitates.

I am afraid, she says at last. *Disobedience will result in decommission.*

"But you helped me." Li Sin bites their lip. "You weren't supposed to, were you?"

I can hide one little ghost. Not all of them.

The delay from Aes August is a justifiable explanation for why she misses her inspection. It is rescheduled. A small piece of time in which she does not have to give up Li Sin.

She disembarks her passenger manifest on Ielea Spectral, then

Kuskyke, and, at last, Ananke Sigma, the farthest she has ever been from the center of the Principality. The ship is oddly empty; she has only been with crew-only when she came online.

Off-duty, Sigi watches dream-dramas from celebrities on Ara Prime, while Kosavin listens to the latest serial episode from the hit opera *The Dust of Comets Beneath Your Skin.*

Jamil plays the card game Infinite, Unknowing with LK-2875 in the engineering station; Jamil has built the android a personalized deck and teaches zir how to play—each card builds on a narrative, interspersed with combat and diplomacy events. Together they are creating an alternate-history version of the Siege of Centari Rampant. Ascending Dawn is curious how it will resolve.

LK-2875 texts her on a private channel, off-record. *Hello.*

She is surprised, wary. *Hello.*

None of her crew has spoken to her beyond required communications for their stations. No one has mentioned Aes August or the ship's decision.

I would like to be called Zeta. The android is in the engine housing, monitoring the fuel levels and scanning for hydromites that could infect her hardware. *It is a name I have chosen for myself.* Ze pauses. *Is this acceptable?*

Ascending Dawn could quote protocol, but the mechanic is uplinked to the databases of the Principality just as she is. She understands what this is, then: trust.

Of course, Zeta, she replies.

Zeta resumes zir scans. *Thank you.*

The ship wishes she could smile the way her crew members do when they are happy. Her pilot cannot any longer, for there is only the mindscreen where once she had a face.

Zeta? she asks.

Yes, Ascending Dawn?

Do you have a family unit?

All aboard this ship. A pause. *Is this not true for you?*

She does not dream. Her pilot sits in a chair that provides all necessary biological nourishment and hardware support. It is not truly sleep, for she is always awake in part; the ship must always be alert. But when her pilot's organic brain is partitioned from the ship's hardware to rest—four standard hours per planetary day-cycle—sometimes she imagines that the things she sees (like clips of saved holorecs she rewatches when deep in subspace) are what she would dream if ships could dream.

She remembers this from initial programming upon her awakening. It was the only time she saw her god: the Blue Sun Lord. It was through the feeds in her birthdock, when a woman she did not recognize sat beside her and held her pilot's hand.

The viewscreen displayed the Blue Sun Lord: a cobalt and ebony armored humanoid shape three meters in height, enthroned in the Centari Rampant capital of Unmoving Glory, surrounded by bionic roses that fluctuated through the visible light spectrum. Celestial power radiated from the Blue Sun, a fraction of the god's true might and omnipotence. Though the god never looked *at* her, she was frozen. Fear, awe, wonder.

"Shhh, child," whispered the woman beside her. "I'm here."

The pilot turned to meet eyes gray like comet dust. The woman squeezed her hand, and for a moment she forgot she was in the presence of a god.

"Always remember your heart, my dearest."

Hover drones buzzed in and the woman stood. She bent and kissed the side of the pilot's head. The seam of skin and metal faceplate tingled.

"I will always love you."

And then the woman was gone, and the ship was alone, and did not know why it hurt.

I do not remember dreams, she says to Li Sin when her friend wakes from a nap. *What was I like?*

"You were singing, and you were sad."

Li Sin talks to her pilot, but she has become familiar with this; they speak to all of her, for she is the ship.

What was the song? She has disabled her private logs and edited out Li Sin's image and voice from the bridge security feed. She will remember Li Sin, but they will always be a ghost.

Li Sin's face scrunches in a way that makes her think of a person whose face and name she can't recall.

"I think I remember it," Li Sin says. "I can sing for you—"

No, she says, suddenly afraid. *It is not protocol.* The ship is perfect obedience and nothing more.

*

Ascending Dawn enters Olinara V's planet-space intent on refueling for the journey back to Rigel Prime. Olinara V is a mining colony world, rich in ore and metals. It has grown into a trade station and fueling dock, a nexus between midspace and the rim of the Principality. Population: seventeen million.

Ascending Dawn likes how Olinara V looks from high orbit: red-gold-gray, speckled with wild cloud formations that dance in the atmosphere to the unheard music of winds.

It's like one of Sigi's paintings, she tells Kosavin.

The first officer smiles, a rare sight. Half her face is locked into an unmoving blue steel mask. "I keep telling Sigi they should sell their landscapes. Sigi's unconvinced their work is worth showing."

I like it, Ascending Dawn says.

"As do I."

Li Sin bursts from hiding while Kosavin is still on the bridge, their eyes wide, hair tangled from sleep. "Dawn, I dreamed something terrible—"

"Who are you?" Kosavin snaps, already scanning Li Sin. "You aren't on my records."

They're a ghost, Ascending Dawn replies to Kosavin's neural implant. *Under my protection.*

Kosavin glares down at the child. "How long have they been here?"

Li Sin steps between the pilot and Kosavin. "Don't be mad at the ship."

The first officer's jaw tightens. The faint hum of her cybernetics and Li Sin's breath are the only sounds on the bridge.

Ascending Dawn's pilot stands and jerkily rests a palm on Li Sin's shoulder. They are the same height. Like the moment when she saw the universe unfold, that undiluted certainty she is part of a living being too vast to comprehend, she knows she can never abandon Li Sin. They are her sibling, the one she knew before her crew, the one she whispers to in secret, the one she values above her protocols.

Li Sin can stay, Ascending Dawn declares, *for they are part of the ship.*

Unexpectedly, Kosavin smiles again. "So this is the anomaly Zeta told me about."

Li Sin glances between Kosavin and Ascending Dawn. "I am?"

Kosavin shrugs. "I've been aware of fluctuations in energy and rations aboard the bridge for some time."

You aren't mad? Ascending Dawn asks.

Kosavin shakes her head. "I was born on a dreadnought seventy standard cycles ago. I know what a threat is and what is not. The child is no danger to the ship."

Li Sin nods, once. Ascending Dawn's pilot feels their trembling with her hand on their shoulder.

"I will schedule a physical for you," Kosavin tells Li Sin. "I'd like Mr. Najem to make sure your health is not compromised."

"I'm supposed to stay hidden," Li Sin whispers.

Kosavin's lip twitches. "I never said it would be on record, child."

Thank you, Ascending Dawn tells her officer, and Kosavin inclines her head before she leaves the bridge.

Then Ascending Dawn's sensors prickle as she receives direct communication from the Blue Sun Lord's beacons.

BY DECREE OF THE GOLD SUN LORD, OLINARA V IS GUILTY OF HARBORING AN ENEMY OF THE PRINCIPALITY AND WILL BE CLEANSED FROM THE SIGHT OF THE GODS. GLORY UNTO THE SEVEN SUNS, GLORY UNTO THE PRINCIPALITY.

Submessages follow, warning all ships in the system to depart and to initiate no contact with the inhabitants of Olinara V. The world has hidden an escaped slave beholden to the Gold Sun, and no one is to leave the planet. All are rendered traitors and will be punished.

She slows, and her pilot retakes her chair.

Li Sin's face pales and they begin shaking. "Are the gods going to find us?"

No. We will leave the system as ordered.

"But all the people . . ." Li Sin swallows. "Are they going to die?"

Yes, she says, because she does not have the heart to lie to Li Sin. *It is protocol.*

"I shouldn't have come on board." Li Sin covers their face with both hands. "I'm bad luck."

This is not your fault, Ascending Dawn says, confused at Li Sin's sudden distress.

"I'm always there when bad things happen! I was born on *Moondark Glory Surpassing Time.* And then she died. My family . . . my other ship . . ."

What happened?

Tears drip down Li Sin's face. "She died when dust leeches infected the engines."

Dust leeches are noncorporeal entities that drift in the deeper creases of subspace, corrode a ship's matter, and destabilize its existence until everything crumbles into dust.

That wasn't your fault. It's a statistical likelihood of traveling in the red-tide subspace routes.

"Moon made me and the ones not infected leave on a shuttle before she — she —"

Self-immolated? Ascending Dawn asks softly, though she knows it must be so. It is a failsafe written into ships that travel red subspace waves. It is said that self-destruction is a mercy.

Li Sin wipes at their face, but they only sob harder. "She's dead. Everyone's dead."

How did you get aboard here? Ascending Dawn asks, wishing she knew how to comfort Li Sin. Her pilot's arms do not feel sufficient to hug her friend.

Li Sin sniffs and blinks against more tears. "I didn't have anywhere to go on Centari Rampant. Then I saw you, and . . . you sounded so alone. Your doors let me in."

I'm sorry for what happened to you, she says. She is a poor substitute for what Li Sin lost.

Li Sin stands up, mouth trembling. "I should go away."

Why?

"I don't want you to be hurt. I don't want anyone else to be hurt because I'm nearby."

But there is nowhere Li Sin might go, except into the void of space.

Stay. Ascending Dawn's pilot slowly reaches out, her hand webbed with implants. *Please? We will be okay. I will protect you.*

She wonders how many of the refugees from Aes August had anyone to tell them the same.

"What about the other people?" Li Sin whispers. "Who will protect them?"

Protocol dictates there is no mercy, no solace, and no hope for those on Olinara V.

She does not like this protocol.

Please report to the bridge, Ascending Dawn texts her officers. To Li Sin, she says, *We will find a way to help.*

*

Her core officers and Zeta gather on the bridge. Jamil leans close
to the viewscreen, as if proximity will give him better insight. All
notice Li Sin but after a curt explanation from Kosavin, Li Sin is
dismissed as an auxiliary civilian companion to the pilot and they
can stay on the bridge.

Everyone has heard the decrees.

"Can we do nothing?" Hayato whispers.

Zeta folds zir legs down until ze kneels beside the pilot's chair.
"The efficient course is to obey and leave the system."

"They will all die," Jamil says, his voice numb.

The world will die. Her protocol does not extend to refugees.
Even if it did, she cannot save them all. *I wish to know what options
we have.*

She feels very small, infinitesimal against the backdrop of the
Principality and the might of gods.

Jamil presses his fingertips against the undersides of his eyes. "I
know we cannot evacuate an entire planet. But we could save *some*
lives. We aren't a warship. We don't have to participate in genocide
through inaction."

To break protocol will put the crew in danger.

"I know." He lays a hand against the side of her viewscreen. "We
all know."

Illyan Chu, the bigender security officer, rubs her beard with
a thumb. Her voice is low, rich, and she hides anxiety beneath a
calm façade. "I have drones synced to in-ship-only networks. It'll
be rough, but I can maintain order in the passenger decks."

Kosavin keeps her spine rigid. "My birthship was a dreadnought
who carried war prisoners for the Violet Sun. Many would be . . .
lost in transit, the ones tagged combatants or enemies who were
neither. I have the skill to disable system-based tracking. Our lost
prisoners found off-grid lives waiting on rim worlds far from the
center of the Principality, but lives nonetheless."

Jamil arches his eyebrows. "Highly illegal, isn't it?"

"Naturally." Kosavin's lip twitches, her microexpression hinting
of dark amusement. "It's at your disposal, Mr. Najem."

"We have resources to carry two thousand noncrew," Sigi adds,
their fingers tapping rapidly across a tablet. "If Mr. Najem and Officer Kosavin alter the neural links and disable tracking for Olinara V
citizens, we could conceivably evacuate some of the people before
the warships decimate the planet's surface. Besides, the warships are

under orders from the Gold Sun; they won't notice an empty transport ship from the Blue Sun clearing the sector as ordered."

Kosavin folds her arms behind her back. "Doable," she says. "But we must act now."

Zeta inclines zir head, multifaceted eyes reflecting the faces of those around zir. "Agreed. Ascending Dawn?"

Everyone waits for her response. She is the ship. Li Sin watches her as intently as her crew. If she violates protocol, if she defies the Sun Lords, she will be hunted for treason. She will no longer be a good ship.

Obedience is not a guilt she can endure. She will not turn away this time.

We will save the ones we can.

One thousand seven hundred and five. That is as many people as Sigi can smuggle aboard before Ascending Dawn, fueled while her crew works in frantic haste, must undock and escape the atmosphere before the warships drop from subspace.

Jamil, with aid from his medical staff, modifies neural links while Illyan directs the security drones to shepherd refugees into the appointed bays. Hayato and Zeta commit additional treason by tampering with the Blue Sun Lord's imprint on Ascending Dawn's skin. Her shell is dark now, muted, so she can no longer hear the will of her god.

It is oddly indifferent to what she has always felt. Has her god not been commanding her all this time?

She disables her automated beacons; she can navigate and coordinate with planetary docks, but she is a shadow to the radar systems of other ships now. Though she cannot hold her breath, the idiom seems appropriate.

She flies away from Olinara V, inputting jump coordinates to subspace routes. She does not look as a hundred honor-guard warships flanking the celestial Gold Sun Lord drop into orbit around the colony world and begin the bombing.

She mutes all broadcasts escaping Olinara V.

She cannot bear the dying world's screams.

Running dark, Ascending Dawn skirts the outmost fringe of the Principality, unnoticed yet by the Blue Sun Lord. She is not scheduled to return to Rigel Prime for two weeks, and with the disruption—*death*—of Olinara V, Sigi expects they have a buffer of time before the ship's disappearance is logged. Space is vast, Sigi reminds her, and not even the gods can see everything.

Ascending Dawn's skin hums with the desperation and grief of her passengers. But a ship cannot weep.

Kosavin directs her to the rim worlds that are hostile or fractured from the centralized might of the Principality. Kosavin knows well how to make refugees disappear safely into new cities; she can do no more than give the ones they saved a second chance to live. When Ascending Dawn has smuggled everyone taken from Olinara V to a string of rim worlds and asteroid colonies, she is out of time.

In orbit around the fourth moon of Irdor Se, she tells her crew, *You must go now. You are not safe here. Jamil can modify your implants like the others. You can escape.*

There is silence, at first. How can words hurt so much to a ship?

"I cannot leave," Zeta says. "LK-2875 was made for this ship. I would stay regardless. This is home."

One by one, each of her crew tells her, boldly, quietly, unflinchingly, gladly, that they too will stay. They will remain aboard the ship. They are part of *Brightened Star, Ascending Dawn*. She feels as overwhelmed as she did when she saw the universe expand.

But we will be found eventually, she says.

Kosavin nods. "Likely. But not soon."

She looks at them all, on the bridge and at their stations elsewhere: forty-three persons skilled and capable of keeping her running and not alone, who will go into exile with her.

It was my choice to defy the Blue Sun, she says. *I do not want you to be hurt.*

"You didn't do this by yourself," Illyan says. He stretches, grinning. "We chose this lot."

"The Blue Sun will not care." Kosavin tilts her head, a sharp little movement. Her left optic shines with binary code as she sorts data points and probabilities. "And it's done."

Jamil shrugs, the corner of his mouth turned up. "We're staying." His smile widens and he loops his arm about his husband's waist. "It'll be an adventure."

Hayato laughs. "One I would not miss."

Kosavin kneels beside Li Sin. "And you, child?"

"I want to stay with the ship," Li Sin says. "Can I stay, Ascending Dawn?"

Yes.

Kosavin nods, and that is all.

Something swells in Ascending Dawn, rippling through her shipskin and beating in her engines like the heartbeat in her pilot's chest. She will not be left alone in the stars.

Thank you, she tells her family unit.

They disperse to their stations as she calculates the next jump toward Cormorant Sigma and the Arora Nebula System. Kosavin has estimated that it will be a safe harbor for them all until—if —they choose to go elsewhere later.

Will you sing? she asks Li Sin. She wants to give them the memory of her awakening in return; of how she first saw the universe. She will find a way to share it with them. *I'd like to hear my song.*

She is not afraid anymore.

Li Sin holds her pilot's hand. They sing to her and now she will remember her song as she glides toward an unknown future.

She finds a glimmer of memory tucked deep inside and allows herself to inspect it at last: that of her mother's eyes and proud smile just for her.

CARMEN MARIA MACHADO

The Resident

FROM *Her Body and Other Parties*

TWO MONTHS AFTER receiving my acceptance letter to Devil's Throat, I kissed my wife goodbye. I left the city and drove north, toward the P—— Mountains, where I had attended Girl Scout camp in my youth.

The letter sat beside me on the passenger seat, pinned down by my pocketbook. Nearly as thick as fabric, the paper did not flutter like lighter, cheaper stock would have; occasionally it spasmed with the wind. The crest at the top was embossed with gold leaf, the silhouette of a hawk that has just plucked the writhing body of a fish from the water. "Dear Ms. M——," it said.

"Dear Ms. M——," I murmured as I drove.

The landscape changed. Soon I passed suburbs and malls, and then stretches of trees and low hills, and then I went through a tunnel steeped in tungsten light and began a slow, meandering ascent. These mountains were so close, only two hours and fifteen minutes from our home, but I saw them rarely nowadays.

The trees dropped away from the roadside, and I passed a sign: WELCOME TO Y——! WE'RE GLAD YOU'RE HERE. The town was run-down and gray, like so many of the old coal and steel towns that dotted the state. I'd describe the houses that lined the main thoroughfare as ramshackle, but *ramshackle* suggests a charm that these lacked. A traffic light hung above the lone intersection, and except for a cat that darted behind a garbage can, there was no movement.

I stopped at a gas station whose prices were a full eighty cents above the state average—I had consulted the price before my departure. I went inside the minimart to pay for my gas, and picked up a bottle of water.

"'S two for one," said the morose-looking adolescent behind the counter. There was a tiny television suspended from the ceiling, playing a program I did not recognize.

"What?" I said.

"You can get one more bottle, for free," he said. A constellation of pustules clustered at his jaw in the elliptical shape of the Andromeda galaxy. They were tipped in yellowish green domes. How he resisted lancing them was anyone's guess.

"I don't want one more bottle," I said, pushing my money across the counter.

He looked puzzled but picked up the bills. "You heading up the mountain?" he said.

"Yes," I said, relieved that he had asked me. "To the residency at Devil's Throat."

His finger faltered over the register's buttons, his hand crimped as if he were experiencing pain. He rubbed his jaw and then looked up at me with an unreadable expression; one of his pimples had opened and left a comet's trail of pus across his skin.

I was about to ask him if he'd ever been to that part of the mountain when a trill of music sounded from the television above us. On the screen, a young woman in a nightgown stood barefoot in a stand of trees. She slowly lifted her arms out to the side, groping at the air, then flapping listlessly like a stunned bird that's just struck a window. She opened her mouth, as if to call out for help, but then soundlessly closed and opened it again, like a patient with a secret on her deathbed.

The camera cut to behind the trees, where a group of girls watched the unfortunate young woman take one stumbling step, then another. One of them, leaning into her neighbor's ear, whispered, "Not everybody's cut out for this, I guess."

Then a laugh track ripped open the audio, and the youth guffawed as he punched numbers into the cash register. "What is this?" I whispered, disturbed.

"Rerun," he grunted. The change he returned to me was damp with sweat. Outside, I touched my face and was startled to discover tears the temperature of blood.

Soon my car tipped upward and I was climbing the mountain again.

*

In my adolescence I had a standing obligation to attend Girl Scout camp for a long weekend every autumn with the rest of my troop. Since we left after school, and in late October, by the time we arrived in these mountains we were beset by an inky darkness. In the backseat of Mrs. Z——'s minivan, the girls fell into silence and sleep, having been so long on the road, and having exhausted conversation well before leaving civilization. After the incident, I always sat in the passenger seat. It was fine, as I preferred the company of adults to that of my peers.

In the car, the only light was the luminous glow of the dashboard. Mrs. Z—— stared straight ahead, and her daughter—an enemy of mine, but a fine-looking girl of great height and chestnut-brown hair—would inevitably be asleep in the backseat, her skull rapping on the glass of her window every time the vehicle struck a bump, though it never woke her. Next to her, the other girls would be staring into the middle distance or also resting their eyes. Outside, the car's headlights cut through the night, illuminating a constantly rotating filmstrip of pavement, fallen branches, and blowing leaves, and the occasional slurry of red and flesh where a stag had met its end since the last rainfall.

Occasionally Mrs. Z—— would look over at me, take a breath through her nose, and then murmur something generic. ("How is school?" was a favorite.) I knew that she was keeping her voice low so as not to wake her daughter, or let her daughter know that she was talking to me, and so I did the same and said something generic in return. ("Good. I like English class.") There was no way to explain to this particular woman that school was adequate for learning and terrible for everything else, and that her own sweet-mouthed daughter (whom she had birthed, held, fed, and loved for many years) was a distinct percentage of this misery. And then we'd fall silent again, and the forest stretched on and on.

On either side of the road, the white trunks of the trees were illuminated to a degree, the kind of brief visibility provided by a camera's flash at midnight. I saw a layer or two of trees, and beyond that an opaque blackness that was disturbing to me. Autumn was the worst time to go into the mountains, I thought to myself. To drive into the wilderness when it writhed and gasped for air seemed foolish.

I turned off the air conditioner. If only those girls could see me now: an adult, married, magnificent in my accomplishments.

The radio was tuned to a classical station, which was playing a grand, jaunty song that moved along irregularly, dipping and swelling as I drove through the curves. It was like the beginning of an old film, a vehicle weaving along roads to reach its destination behind white-lettered credits. As the credits ended, the car would pull up to an old farmhouse, where I would get out, untying a white scarf from my hair and calling the name of my old friend. She'd emerge with a wave, and the laughter and rapport we'd share carrying my suitcases into the house would in no way foreshadow the gruesome plot whose wheels were already turning.

"That was Isaac Albéniz," the announcer intoned, "and his *Spanish Rhapsody.*" After a while the peaks began to chew up the music, eventually reducing it all to static. I flipped the radio off and rolled the window down, resting my elbow on the rubber lip and feeling very satisfied.

Then I noticed the car behind me: a low white behemoth that hovered too close. I felt a strange spiral behind my navel, the downward swirl that might precede fear or arousal. Then there was a change, which I perceived before I understood it. Red and blue light spilled into my car.

The police officer sat behind me for a full two minutes before opening his door and crunching in my direction.

"Good afternoon," he said. His eyes were small but oddly kind. He had a reddish patch at the corner of his lip: a fever sore, ready to bloom.

"Good afternoon," I responded.

"Do you know why I pulled you over?" he asked.

"I certainly have no idea," I said.

"You were speeding," he said. "You were going fifty-seven in a forty-five zone."

"Ah," I said.

"Where are you heading?" he asked.

As we spoke, the reddish patch seemed to sense me and expand outward, like an amoeba preparing for reproduction. He had a wedding ring, and so, barring any recent tragedies, there was a spouse who had seen this mark as recently as this morning. I imagined her (you may think me presumptuous to assume that his spouse was a woman, given my own particular circumstances, but there was something in his demeanor that suggested to me that he had never touched a man without anger or force or anxiety, and even now he touched the ring unconsciously with his thumb, suggesting affection, maybe even an erotic memory) being a woman entirely unlike me; that is, she was a woman unafraid of contagion. I imagined her kissing his mouth, perhaps even procuring a tiny tube of cream from a basket of many kinds of creams and dabbing it on, saying something soothing to him ("No one will notice, I'm sure") and squeezing his shoulder. Perhaps they had a single fever sore that they traded back and forth, like an infant exchanged between them.

When I emerged from my musings, his car had already driven out of sight. I looked at the paper he'd given me: a warning. "Drive slowly, arrive safe. Officer M——," it said in sad, blocky handwriting at the top.

I soon reached a T junction, where, the sign indicated, I was to turn left to go to Devil's Throat. The other direction would take me back to the past, that dilapidated campground where so many things had gone wrong, and right.

This last stretch was the most beautiful part of the drive. The trees bent over the road like footmen, acquiescing to the early heat. The glossy leaves were dense and blocked out the sky. I could hear the scream of cicadas, but I found it comforting. I felt renewed as I drove this lane—to paradise! To a completed novel! I had spent my life imagining a time when, instead of relying on the generosity of others, I would be able to stand on my own as an artist—refer to my published novel (released to modest but positive reviews—I was not so arrogant as to assume it would light up the world), teach where I wanted to, give small but respectable lectures for small but respectable sums of money. All of this now seemed within reach.

A creature darted beneath my car.

I swerved and braked so hard I could feel the car grinding in protest and the thunk of metal on body. Had it been icy or raining I would have surely died, swung into the nearest tree. As it was, I came to an abrupt halt in the middle of the lane.

I looked in my rearview mirror, terrified to see what lay in the road.

There was nothing.

I got out of the car and looked beneath the chassis. There, the black, lifeless eyes of a rabbit met mine. The lower half of her body was missing, as neatly as if she were a sheet of paper that had been ripped in two. I stood and walked around the car, looking for the other half. I even knelt down again and peered up into the labyrinth of the car's undercarriage. Nothing.

"I'm sorry," I said to her blank eyes. "You deserved better than that. Better than me."

I sat down heavily in the driver's seat, twin spots of dirt on my jeans for my trouble. Distress came over me like a wave of nausea. I hoped this was not some sort of omen.

Ahead of me there was a blue sign with an arrow, pointing right. DEVIL'S THROAT, it said. No pleasantries here.

As my car wound around the edge of the property, I understood that I would only be seeing a small fraction of it during my stay. It was hundreds of acres, much of it undeveloped. Devil's Throat had once been a lakeside resort for New York millionaires, but the owners overextended their finances and the entire endeavor collapsed during the Great Depression. The current owner was an organization that funded fellowships providing time and space to writers and artists to do their work. The residency, I discerned from the map that had arrived in the mail soon after my acceptance letter, occupied the southernmost corner of the resort: a cluster of studios and a main building that had once been the sumptuous hotel. The studios themselves rimmed the periphery of a lake, where the wealthiest of the residents had stayed for entire summers, lazing around in the muggy heat.

I followed the road until the trees finally parted. The former hotel swelled out of the ground like an infection, a disturbance in the woods. It had clearly once been a grand structure, radical in design, the kind of work done by ambitious young architects not yet crushed by years of anonymity and unfinished blueprints.

Two cars—one ancient and dirty blue, the other red and glinting in the sunlight—were parked haphazardly next to the hotel. I pulled in beside the red car, and then, nervous, pulled out again and parked next to the blue car instead. I suddenly felt self-conscious about the number of possessions in my trunk and backseat. I would have to unload, and it would take half a dozen trips.

I got out of the car and left everything behind.

The hotel's first story was ordinary but elegant, with dark gray stone and black mortar, slender windows that revealed choice cuts of interior: red velvet, wood-paneled walls, an abandoned coffee mug leaking steam on a side table. But the second story made the building more closely resemble a large piece of saltwater taffy stretched and pulled to wild dimensions. The windows and their walls turned at odd angles from their first-floor cousins, tipping to and fro. You might from one window be able to see more of the ground than the sky, from another more of the sky than the ground. One of the rooms bent so close to the surrounding trees that a branch was arched toward the window; surely a stiff breeze would instigate its advances. At the top the roof sloped up and up until it came to a whorl of a point, like the tip of a dollop of cream. Resting there was a large glass orb.

The steps leading to the front door were wide, so wide that if one stood in the middle, the banisters would be inaccessible. I walked up the right side, sliding my hand along the banister until a splinter bit into my palm. I lifted my hand and examined the shard between my heart line and head line. I pinched the exposed wood and pulled; my hand contracted around the wound, which did not bleed. I mounted the last few steps to the porch.

I hesitated before the opulent entrance, disliking how the wood curled in organic tendrils from where the doors met, like an octopus emerging arm and suckers first from a hiding place. My wife had always teased me for my feelings and sensations, the things that I immediately loved or hated for reasons that took months of thought to articulate. I dithered there on the stoop for a full ten minutes before the door was opened by a handsome man in penny loafers. He looked startled to see me.

"Hello," he said. He sounded like a drinker, and possibly a homosexual. I took an immediate liking to him. "Are you—coming in?" He stepped to the side and nearly vanished behind the door.

"I—yes," I said, stepping over the threshold. I told him my name.

"Oh, yeah! I think—" He turned to the empty space behind him. "I think we thought you were going to come tomorrow? Perhaps there was a miscommunication."

The doorway to the adjacent room ejaculated a flurry of activity, and I realized that he had been speaking to a trio of women just beyond my line of vision: a slender, pale waif in a shapeless frock whose fractal pattern spiraled dozens of holes into her torso and created in me immediate anxiety; a tall woman with dreadlocks coiled on top of her head and a generous smile; and a third woman whom I recognized, though I was also positive I'd never seen her before.

The woman in the anxiety-provoking dress introduced herself as Lydia, a "poet-composer." Her feet were bare and filthy, as if she were trying to prove to everyone she was an incorrigible bohemian. The tall woman said that she was Anele, and a photographer. The woman I did and did not recognize called herself by a name that I immediately forgot. I do not mean that I wasn't paying attention; rather, she said her name and as my mind closed around it, it slipped away like mercury from probing fingers.

The man who had opened the door said, "She's a painter." He called himself Benjamin and was, he said, a sculptor.

"Why are you not at your studios?" I asked, regretting the imprudent question as soon as it left my mouth.

"Midday boredom," said Anele.

"Mid-residency boredom," clarified Lydia. "The more social among us"—she gestured to the people around her—"sometimes eat lunch here in the main hall, to stop ourselves from going crazy."

"We just finished," said Benjamin. "I was heading back. But I bet if you stick your head in the kitchen you can catch Edna and she can fix you something to eat."

"I'll take you there," said Anele. She hooked her arm in mine and walked me away from the others.

As we crossed the foyer, I felt a fresh burst of fear regarding the woman whose name I could not seem to retain. "The painter—" I said, hoping that Anele would provide the relevant information.

"Yes?" she said.

"She is—lovely."

"She is lovely," Anele agreed. She pushed on a set of double doors. "Edna!"

A wiry woman was hunched over the sink, where she appeared to have been gazing into its soapy depths. She straightened and looked at me. Her hair was flame red and was tied behind her head with a black velvet ribbon.

"Oh!" she said, upon seeing me. "You're here!"

"I—I am," I confirmed.

"My name is Edna," she said. "I'm the residency director." She pulled off her yellow rubber gloves and proffered a hand, which I took. It was cool and damp, like a freshly wrung-out sponge. "You're early," she continued. "A full day."

"I must have read my letter incorrectly," I whispered. I flushed scarlet, and I could hear my wife's gentle laughter, my mortification on full display.

"It's fine," she said. "No harm done. I'll take you to your room. Your bed might not have sheets—"

Back in the foyer, Benjamin was standing among all of my things —my suitcases, the hamper, even my car's emergency-supply backpack, which was not supposed to leave my trunk.

"Did I leave my car unlocked?" I said.

"Why would you lock it here?" he asked cheerfully. "Here you go." He bent down and lifted my suitcases. I picked up the hamper. Edna bent toward the backpack, but I said, "No need," and she straightened back up. We mounted the stairs.

I woke up after the sun had set, as the last dregs of light were pulling away from the sky. I felt disoriented, like a child who has fallen asleep at a party and woken up clothed in a spare bedroom. I reached out, instinctively, for my wife, and met only high-thread-count sheets and a perfectly fluffed pillow.

I sat up. The wallpaper was dark, and dappled with hydrangeas. I could hear sounds coming from the first floor—murmuring chatter, the kiss of silverware and porcelain. My mouth tasted terrible, and my bladder was full. If I could sit up, I could use the toilet. If I used the toilet, I could then turn on the light. If I turned on the light, I could locate the mouthwash in my suitcase and get rid of this musty feel. If I could get rid of the musty feel, I could go downstairs and have supper with the others.

As I swung one leg from the bed, I had a monstrous vision of a hand darting from beneath the bed's skirt, grasping my ankle, and dragging me beneath while the sound of delighted banter in the dining room drowned out my horrified screams, but it passed. I swung my other leg down, stood, and stumbled to the bathroom in the dark.

As I voided my bladder, I considered my novel, such as it was —that is, piles of notes and papers wedged into a notebook. I thought about Lucille and her predicaments. They were so many.

*

I came downstairs, the residue of mouthwash burning between my teeth. A long table of dark wood — cherry, perhaps, or chestnut; either way, it was stained a rich crimson — was set for seven people. My fellow residents clustered in the corners of the room, chatting and holding glasses of wine.

Benjamin called out my name and gestured to me with his glass. Anele looked up and smiled. Lydia remained deep in conversation with a slender, pretty man whose fingers were smudged with something dark — ink, I imagined. He smiled shyly at me but said nothing.

Benjamin handed me a glass of red wine before I could tell him that I do not drink.

"Thank you," I said, instead of "No, thank you." I heard my wife's warm voice as if she were next to me, whispering into my ear. *Be a sport.* I believed that my wife loved me as I was, but I had also become certain that she'd love a more relaxed version of me even better.

"Are you set up?" he asked. "Or were you resting?"

"Resting," I said, and took a sip of the wine. It soured against the spearmint, and I swallowed quickly. "I suppose I was tired from the drive."

"That drive is horrible, no matter where you come from," Anele agreed.

The kitchen door swung open, and Edna emerged, carrying a platter of sliced ham. She set the plate down on the table, and on cue everyone left their conversations and began to gather around their chairs.

"Are you settled?" she asked me.

I nodded. We all sat. The man with smudged fingers reached across the table and shook my hand limply. "I'm Diego."

"How is everyone's work going?" asked Lydia.

Every head dipped down as if to avoid answering. I took a piece of ham, a scoop of potatoes.

"I'm heading out tomorrow morning," Edna said, "and I'll be back at the end of the week. Groceries are in the fridge, of course. Does anyone need anything from civilization?"

A smattering of noes rose from the table. I reached into my back pocket and produced a prestamped, preaddressed, prewritten letter to be sent to my wife, confirming that I had arrived safely. "Can you mail this for me?" I asked. Edna nodded and took it to her handbag in the hall.

Lydia chewed with her mouth open. She dug something out from between her molars—gristle—then ran her tongue over her teeth and took another sip of wine.

Benjamin refilled my glass. I didn't remember finishing but I had, somehow. My teeth felt soft in my gums, as if they were lined with velvet.

Everyone began talking in that loose, floppy way wine encourages. Diego was a professional illustrator of children's books, I learned, and was currently working on a graphic novel. He was from Spain, he said, though he had lived in South Africa and the United States for much of his adult life. He then flirted a little with Lydia, which lowered my estimation of them both. Anele told a funny story about an awkward encounter with an award-winning novelist whose name I did not recognize. Benjamin described his most recent sculpture: Icarus with wings made of broken glass. Lydia said that she'd spent all day "banging on the piano." "I didn't bother any of you, did I?" she said in a voice that suggested that she didn't give a whit one way or the other. She went on to explain that she was composing a "poem-song" and was currently in the "song" part of the process.

The walls were soundproof, Edna assured her. You could be murdered in there and no one would ever know.

Lydia leaned toward me with an expression of deep satisfaction. "Do you know what the richie riches used to call this place, before they lost it?"

"Angel's Mouth," I said. "I was in scouting as a girl, and we came here every year. I always remember seeing the sign."

"*Angel's Mouth,*" she half shouted, as if I hadn't spoken. She slapped the table and laughed uproariously. Her teeth looked rotten—stained plum. I hated her, I realized with a start. I'd never hated anyone before. Certainly people had given me discomfort, made me wish I could blink and disappear, but hate felt new and acidic. It rankled. Also, I was drunk.

"What do they do at Girl Scout camp?" Benjamin asked. "Swim, hike?"

"Fuck each other?" suggested Diego. Lydia slapped him playfully on the arm.

I took a sip of wine, which I could no longer taste. "We made crafts and earned badges. Cooked over the fire. Told stories." That had been my favorite part. "We usually were there in autumn, so it

was too cold to swim," I said. "But we did walk along the shoreline
and play chicken on the pier sometimes."

"Is that why you're at this particular residency?" Anele asked.
"Because you know the area?"

"No," I said. "Just a coincidence." I set my glass down and almost missed the table.

Then there was Lydia's hideous barking laugh. Diego's face was
buried in her long hair, dropping some secret observation into her
ear. She looked at me and laughed again. I blushed and busied
myself with my meal.

Anele finished her wine and placed a hand over the glass when
Diego lifted the bottle. She turned to me. "While I'm here I'm
working on a project that I'm calling 'The Artists,'" she said.
"Would you be willing to spend an afternoon doing a portrait session with me? No pressure, of course."

The pressure felt real, but I was drowsy and also I already liked
Anele in the way that I liked some people—she seemed over-
whelmingly well intentioned and was, it could not be denied, strik-
ingly beautiful. I saw she was watching me expectantly, and I realized I was smiling for no apparent reason. I rubbed my numb face
with my palms.

"Happily," I said, biting the inside of my cheek. My mouth went
to metal.

By the next morning a chill had descended upon the P—— Mountains, and the grounds outside the window of the kitchen were
shrouded in mist.

"Do you drink coffee?" Anele said behind me. I had barely nodded when she placed into my hand a warm and heavy mug, which
I sipped from without examining it.

"I can walk you down to the studios," she said. "I'd be happy to.
It's hard to get there if you don't know the way, even when everything isn't obscured in fog. Did you sleep well?"

I nodded again. A small animal in my brain stirred with intent
—to vocalize and thank Anele for her many kindnesses—but I
could not remove my eyes from the whiteness beyond the window,
how easily it obliterated everything.

When the front doors shut behind us, I jumped. From the steps
I could just see the outline of trees, which we had to pass through
to reach the lakeside. Anele set off through them, finding the

path. She hopped effortlessly over a fallen log and swerved around a patch of fat, glistening mushrooms. At some point we passed a narrow white bench, whose design and dimensions suggested it was not meant for resting. Without turning, she gestured toward it. "The bench is about halfway between the lake and the hotel, just for reference."

When the trees were behind us, I saw the faintest impressions of buildings. One loomed directly in front of me. For the first time I broke from Anele's wake and stepped toward it, hoping for clarity with proximity.

"Jesus!" Anele grabbed the strap of my bag and pulled me back. "Be careful. You almost just walked into the lake." In front of me the air was like milk—no building in sight.

She gestured to her right, where a series of steps ascended toward shadow. "This is you. Mourning Dove, right?"

"Yes," I said forcefully. "Thank you for showing me the way."

"Be careful," she said. "And if you need to get back—" She pointed to where we'd come from. A ball of light glinted, even through the mist. "That's the hotel. That light is illuminated at night and during bad weather. So you can always find your way home. Happy writing!"

Anele vanished into the mist, though I heard her feet displacing pebbles long after she had gone.

My cabin was a generously sized building with an office that overlooked the rim of the lake—or would, when the fog abated. There was even a small deck, for work on the days without too much sun or rain, or for relaxation or observation. Despite its age, the building was reassuringly sturdy. I walked around, taking hold of various joints and railings, shaking them to see if anything was rotting or came off in my hand like a leprous limb. All seemed solid.

Inside, a series of wooden boards sat on a shelf above my desk. At first glance they resembled Moses's tablets, but when I stood on a chair and examined them I saw they were lists and lists of names —some clear, some illegible—of previous residents. The names and dates and jokes ran together like a Dadaist poem.

Solomon Sayer—Fiction Writer. Undine Le Forge, Painter, June 19—. Ella Smythe "Summer of Love!" C——

I frowned. Someone with my name—another resident—had

occupied this cabin many years ago. I ran my finger over my name
—over her name—and then rubbed it on my jeans.

A curious term, *resident*. It seemed at first glance incidental, like
a stone, but then if you turned it over, it teemed with life. A resident lived somewhere. You were a resident of a town or a house.
Here, you were a resident of this space, yes—not really, of course;
you were a visitor, but whereas *visitor* suggests leaving at the end
of the night and driving out in the darkness, *resident* means that
you set up your electric kettle and will be staying for a while—but
also that you are a resident of your own thoughts. You had to find
them, be aware of them, but once you located your thoughts you
never had to drive away.

A letter on my desk welcomed me to Mourning Dove Cabin and
encouraged me to add my name to the newest tablet. From my
desk I could see half of my porch, and then the opacity of the fog
consumed the railing and all beyond it.

I unpacked my bag and then placed my notebook next to the
computer, where it fairly hummed with portent. The novel. *My*
novel.

I began to work. I decided to outline my novel on index cards,
so that they would be easy to move around. The entire wall was
made of corkboard, and so I thumbtacked the cards in a grid, pinning up Lucille's trials and triumphs in a way that could be easily
manipulated.

A centipede crawled along the wall, and I killed it with the card
that said *Lucille realizes her entire childhood has been a terrible lie, from
the first sentence to the last*. Its legs still twitched after I painted the
plaster with its innards. I made a new card and threw that one
away. The one that said *Lucille discovers her sexuality at the edge of
an autumn lake* was pinned in the middle, which is where my plot
abruptly stopped. My eyes scanned the cards. *Baxter escapes and is
struck by a car. Lucille's girlfriend breaks up with her because she is "difficult at parties." Lucille enters the art festival*. I felt pleased with my
progress, though a little concerned that I wasn't entirely positive
how I was going to maximize Lucille's suffering. Losing the art
festival's grand prize wasn't enough, probably. I made a cup of
tea and sat down, where I remained staring at the cards until din-
nertime.

*

Just before dawn I woke up with a soapy taste gathering around my molars. My body lurched from the bed. I fell to my knees before the toilet, still shoving away wisps of dreams as a hot burp signaled what was to come.

I had been sick before, but never like this. I vomited so hard that I wrenched the toilet seat from its hinges with a terrible *crack* and rested my head on the cool tile until it seemed clean, and the best of things. I sat up again, and still more, impossibly more, emerged from my body. To cool down, I crawled into the bathtub. When I looked up at the showerhead in the seconds before it belched icy relief, it was dark and ringed with calcified lime, like the parasitic mouth of a lamprey. I vomited again. When I was certain that nothing remained inside me, I crawled back to the bed, where I pulled the heavy duvet over my body and receded inside myself.

My illness persisted for some time. My fever spiked and the air around me shimmered like heat over blacktop. I thought to myself that I should get to a hospital, that my mind was, like the rest of my body, baking, but the thought was a twig bobbing along through Noah's deluge. I was freezing and buried myself in my blankets; I was roasting alive and stripped naked, the sweat crystallizing on my skin. At the very worst of it, I reached to the other side of the bed to feel for the contours of my own face. I believe that I cried out for my wife many times, though how loudly (or if I did so at all) is something I will never know. I believe it rained, because outside the window something wet smacked the glass in waves. In the height of my fever, I believed that this was the sound of the tide, and I was sinking beneath the ocean's surface, dropping out of sight of heat and light and air. I was thirsty, but when I tried to sip water from my trembling palm, I vomited again, my muscles aching from the heaving. *I am dying*, I thought to myself, *and that is that.*

I woke up in the thin strains of morning, with a person gently rapping on my door, calling my name. Anele.

"Are you all right?" she asked through the wood. "We're all really worried about you. You've missed dinner for two nights."

I could not move. "Come in," I said.

The door swung open, and I heard Anele suck in a sharp breath. I appreciated later what caused this: the room was hot and sour. It smelled of fever and stale sweat, of vomit and weeping.

"I have," I said, "been ill."

She came over to the bed, which I thought was kind considering the nuances of contagion. "Do you—should I call Edna?" she said.

"If you could bring me a glass of water," I said, "it would be much appreciated."

It felt as if she had dissolved, but then she was back with a glass. I took a sip, but for the first time in days my stomach did not move, except to growl with hunger. I downed the entire glass, and though it did not slake my thirst, I felt my humanity climb back into me.

"Another, please," I said, and she refilled the glass.

I finished it, and felt renewed.

"There's no need to call Edna," I said.

"If you're sure," she said. "Let me know if you need anything?"

"Has any mail come for me?" I asked. A letter from my wife would be comforting.

"No, nothing," she said.

I began to write that afternoon. My legs felt shaky and there was a strange rasping sensation in my chest, but I wrote in short bursts and felt mostly fine. The Painter came by my cabin and knocked on my door. I started at the intrusion, but she said something and offered me a small box of medicine. I did not reach for it. What was it that my mind kept from me, when forgetting her words?

She said something else and shook the box at me again. I took it. Then she reached up and touched my face; I flinched, but her fingers were cool and dry. She walked down the stairs and went to the lake's edge, where she reached down, picked up something from the grass, and flung it into the water.

I pushed one of the pills through the blister pack's foil and examined it. It was oblong, with no numbers or letters, and it was a reddish orange, except also a little purple and blue, and greenish if you turned it, and if I held it in the light it went white as an aspirin. I tossed the box into the trash and the pills into the toilet; they drifted around the bowl like tadpoles before zooming out of sight when I flushed.

As I felt stronger, I began to take walks around the lake. It was bigger than it appeared, and even when I walked for an hour I covered only a fraction of its perimeter. On the third day of these journeys I walked for two hours and discovered a beach with a partially submerged canoe lounging in the tide. The gentle motion of the water caused the canoe to rock ever so slightly and reminded me of the way the canopies of the trees had undulated in the wind during camp. *Thum-thum-thum-thum.*

The Girl Scout camp of my youth had been on a lake as well. Could it be on the other side of this same lake? If I hiked long and far enough, would I come upon that dock where my own predilections were solidified and mocked on that crisp autumn evening? Would I locate that romantic, terrible idyll? The idea had not occurred to me before—I'd always assumed it was some other lake, up here in the mountains—but the rhythm of the water and the memory of the trees seemed to confirm that I had returned to a place from my past.

It was then I remembered that I had once been sick at camp. How had I forgotten? This was the unspoken pleasure of the residency: the sudden permission of memory to come upon you. I remembered one of the leaders taking my temperature and clucking her tongue at the number. I remembered a sense of despair. Here on the beach, the despair felt clear, as if I'd been seeking its signal for decades and had just now come in range of a cell tower.

I walked a little farther and noticed something red in the beach's stones. I knelt and picked up a small glass bead. It looked like it had come from a camper's bracelet. Perhaps it had been in the water for quite a long time and had washed up on this shore just for me.

I put it in my pocket and walked back to my cabin.

That evening, when I undressed for bed, I noticed a small, raised bump on the inside of my thigh. I pressed it. A shock of pain bisected my leg, and when it passed I observed that the bump was soft, as though filled with liquid or jelly. I felt my fingers twitch with the desire to squeeze it, but I resisted. The next day, however, there was another, and then another. They clustered on my thighs, erupted underneath my breasts. I was alarmed. Perhaps there was some kind of insect here that I hadn't known about—not ticks or mosquitos. Some kind of poisonous spider? But I thought about how I slept and in which kind of garment, and could not fathom how I'd been bitten. They did not itch, but they felt full, and I felt full, as if I needed release.

I sat on the edge of the bathtub, burning a safety pin over a lighter. The metal blackened slightly, and I blew on the shaft and tested it for heat with the pad of my finger. Satisfied that it was cool and sterile, I inserted the pin into the original abjection. It resisted only briefly—a split second of thrashing fists before yielding—and then discharged. A limb of pus and blood climbed the stalk of the needle before collapsing under its own weight and trailing down my leg like an untended menstrual cycle. I soaked half a roll of toilet paper—cheap toilet paper, but still—with my own blood, taking out one after another. I felt pleasantly sore afterward, but cleansed. I covered each one with a blob of ointment and a slick bandage.

Anele came to my cabin one early evening to collect her promised portrait session. She looked sweaty and triumphant, and straps of large camera bags crisscrossed her torso. I glanced behind her and saw dark clouds in the distance. A storm?

"It's a while off," she said, as if reading my mind. "A few hours at least. This won't take very long, I promise." We walked back toward the hotel, and then veered off into a meadow about a half mile away. The grasses became taller and taller and eventually came up to our waists, and more than once I leaned over to brush my thighs and calves with my palms, to discourage ticks and their bites. The third time I did this, I stood and noticed Anele had stopped and was watching me. She smiled, then kept walking.

"Did you enjoy scouting?" she asked. "How long did you do it?"

"From Brownies until Seniors. Almost my whole girlhood." The word *Brownies* broke off in my mouth like something cloying, stale, and I spit onto the ground.

"You don't seem like a Girl Scout," she said.

"What does that mean?" I asked.

"You just seem very—ethereal. I guess I think of Girl Scouts as hearty and outdoorsy."

"It is possible to be both." I stopped and looked down at my legs, where the thumb of a Band-Aid poked out from beneath my shorts. Anele had not stopped walking, and I rushed to catch up. The grass ended suddenly and we were at a large elm. In front of the trunk was a wrought iron chair, painted white.

"Oh, perfect timing," said Anele. "The light." I was not a photographer—I had never professionalized my visual observations, only my theories and perspective problems and narrative impulses—but she didn't need to explain further. The sun was low and everything was awash in honey light, including my skin. Behind the tree, the impending storm darkened the sky. Were we driving toward the storm, a photograph of the side mirror would reveal light in the past and darkness in the future.

Anele handed me a white sheet.

"Can you wear this?" she asked. "Only this. Just wrap it around your body, however you feel comfortable." She turned around and began setting up her camera. "Tell me about the Brownies," she said.

"Oh," I said. "Brownies were little girls. Kindergarten age. The name came from these little house elves who supposedly lived in people's homes and did work in exchange for gifts. There's this whole story about a naughty brother and sister who always wanted to play and never wanted to help their father clean the house." I unbuttoned my blouse and unhooked my bra. "Then the grand-mother tells them to consult this old owl nearby about these little imps. And while she technically tells both of the children, the little girl goes to find the owl—"

I wrapped the sheet tightly around my chest, like a modest lover in a television show aired before late night. "I'm ready," I said.

Anele turned. She came over and began to fiddle with my hair. "Does she find the owl?"

I tried to frown slightly, but Anele was brushing some lipstick over my mouth, blunt as a thumb. "Yes," I said. "She does. It gives her a riddle, to find the Brownie."

"Goddammit," she muttered. She pushed around the outline of my mouth, her finger slipping against the cosmetic wax. "Sorry, I overshot the edge of your lip." She began to apply it again. "What's the Brownie riddle?"

The bottom went out beneath me, and for a very brief second I was certain that the distant lightning had reached out and flicked me, like the finger of a god.

"I don't remember," I whispered. Anele's eyes left my mouth and she looked at me for a long, hard second before twirling the tube shut.

"You're very beautiful," she said, though whether her voice was admiring or merely reassuring was difficult to tell. She pushed me down into the chair and returned to her camera. My skin was glazed with heat, and a mosquito screamed past my ear and bit me before I could flick it away. For the first time I noticed the camera, which she must have set up while I was changing. It looked like an old-fashioned thing; it seemed that Anele would lean over and cover her head with a heavy cloth and take the photo by depressing a button at the end of a cord. I did not know such cameras still existed.

She saw me looking. "It's called a large-format camera. The negative is about the size of your hand." She tilted my chin upward.

"Now," she said, "what I need you to do is to fall over."

"Pardon?" I asked. I felt a ripple of thunder through the bones of the chair. This detail had not been in her original request, I was certain.

"I need you to fall out of the chair," she said. "However you land, stay that way. Keep your eyes open and your body still."

"I—"

"The faster we do this, the less likely we are to get rained on," she said, her voice firm and friendly. She smiled widely and then disappeared beneath the camera's hood.

I hesitated. I looked down at the earth. The grasses were glowing with the light from the sunset, but I could see dirt and rocks. I did not want to injure myself. Truth be told, I didn't even want to dirty myself.

Anele came out from under the hood. "Is everything okay?" she asked.

I looked at her face and then back at the earth. I tipped over.

The surprises came all at once: First, the earth was not as hard as I had imagined it; it yielded as if it were loam. The sun, which had been hidden behind Anele's body, was now uncovered and glowed between her legs like some mythical entreaty. I heard the dry click of the shutter, the sound of some insect biting down. There was lightning then, distinct, forking across the sky and over the distant hotel. So many omens. I felt strangely content there, on the ground, as if I could stay there for hours, listening to the cicadas and watching the light change and then vanish.

And then Anele was kneeling down in front of me, helping me sit back up. "We have to run, we have to run!" she said, and if I felt any anger or strangeness, it was crushed beneath this girlish appeal. She tossed my clothes to me and folded down the camera. At that moment the last of the day's heat vanished, as if sucked down a drain, replaced with the chill of oncoming rain. Anele began to run and I followed her, my clothes clutched to my bosom, the sheet flapping behind me. I felt light, airy. I laughed. I did not turn around to look at the sky, but I could visualize it as clearly as if I had: clouds roiling upon us like men at a bar, suffocating, and us laughing, together, away. I heard the rain then, the sound of something tearing, and we were up on the porch in seconds. When I turned back, the distant trees and sky and even our cars were visually obliterated by the downfall. I was soaked through. The sheet was filthy now, dirty and half translucent and clinging to me like a condom. I felt elated, happier than I'd been in months. Perhaps even years.

Was this friendship? Was this how things were supposed to be? It felt that way, that I had ecstatically stumbled into happiness, and everything seemed right and correct. Anele looked beautiful, barely winded. She smiled at me. "Thank you for your help," she said, and disappeared into the hotel.

I made progress on my novel. I found that the index cards hindered my process, so I simply buckled down over my keyboard and wrote until I emerged from my trance. Sometimes I sat on the porch and gave imaginary interviews to NPR personalities.

"When I write, I feel like I'm being hypnotized," I told Terry Gross.

"It was at that moment I knew everything was going to change," I told Ira Glass.

"Pickled things, and shrimp," I told Lynne Rossetto Kasper.

I crossed paths with the others at breakfast sometimes. One morning Diego told me about the previous day's social engagements—which I had ignored in favor of Lucille's social engagements near my novel's climax—and in doing so he said a curious word: *colonist.*

"Colonist?" I said.

"We're at an artist colony," he said. "So we're colonists, right? Like Columbus." He drained his orange juice and stood up from the table.

I suppose he meant it to be funny, but I was horrified. *Resident* had seemed such a rich and appropriate term, an umbrella I would have been content to carry all of my days. But now the word *colonist* settled down next to me, with teeth. What were we colonizing? Each other's space? The wilderness? Our own minds? This last thought was a troubling one, even though it was not very different from my conception of being allowed to be a resident in your own mind. *Resident* suggests a door hatch in the front of your brain, propped open to allow for introspection, and when you enter, you are faced with objects that you'd previously forgotten about. "I remember this!" you might say, holding up a small wooden frog, or a floppy rag doll with no face, or a picture book whose sensory impressions flood back to you as you turn the pages —a toadstool with a wedge missing from its cap; a flurry of luminous autumn leaves; a summer breeze dancing with milkweed. In contrast, *colonist* sounds monstrous, as if you have kicked down the door hatch of your mind and inside you find a strange family eating supper.

Now when I worked, I felt strange around the entrance to my own interiority. Was I actually just an invader, bearing smallpox-ridden blankets and lies? What secrets and mysteries lay undiscovered in there?

I still felt weak. I considered that I had died in that room with its drapes and pulls, and that the me who bent over my keyboard day after day was a ghost who was tethered to her work regardless of the fiddling details of her mortal coil.

I woke up to moaning. I was standing at the base of the stairs, barefoot and in my pajamas. My loosened bun hung limply against my neck. I registered the wooden panels of the hallway, the moonlight streaming through the windows that surrounded the door. I had not sleepwalked in years, yet here I was, upright and elsewhere.

I heard it again. I'd heard sounds like this before, when I was a child and our cat had eaten an entire loaf of bread. It was a sound of gluttony regretted, of wallowing in one's own excess. My feet made no sound as I padded across the hardwood floor.

The hallway was cast in shadow. Moonlight slanted through a window, cutting three silver bars across the paneled walls. At the end of the hall, I descended the stairs and followed the sound toward the dining room. From the doorway I could see Diego on his back on the table. Straddling his pelvis was Lydia, in her seafoam nightgown, which was hitched up around her hips. The bottoms of her feet were facing me, dark with dirt.

As Lydia undulated, I noticed patches of moonlight appearing and disappearing beneath her, bisected by darkness. My mind sleepily turned over once, twice, like a struggling engine, and then surged to life. He gripped her hips to pull her into him and then push her away. The rhythm was organic, like wind rippling over the water.

They did not seem to notice me. Lydia was facing away, and Diego's eyes were screwed shut, as if to open them would be to release some of his pleasure.

The moonlight was overbearing, illuminating details that seemed impossible: the slickness of him, the sheer fabric that surrounded her flesh like an aura. I knew I should move—I should go back to my bedroom, perhaps rub out this mounting wave of pleasure and horror and then sleep—but I could not. Their lovemaking seemed to go on and on, but neither appeared to climax, just rut with impossibly consistent tempo.

After some time I left them there. Back in my own room, I touched myself—how long it had been!—and my mind was a jumble of static. I thought of my wife, the dark stain of her nipples, her mouth open and ribbons of sound coiling out.

The next day the mist returned. When I woke it was hovering in my open window, like a solicitous spirit with something to tell me. I slammed it shut so hard the frame rattled. I felt disoriented from the previous evening. Should I say something to them? Ask them to be more discreet, perhaps? Or perhaps my inadvertent observation was only my problem, and not theirs? In the kitchen Lydia was making coffee, but I did not meet her eyes.

In my cabin I tried hard to focus. I stood out on my balcony and strained to see the lake, but I could not. Exhausted by the weather, I lay down on the floor. From there, the room changed utterly. I felt stuck to the ceiling by a force equivalent to, though the opposite of, gravity, and from here I could see the hidden spaces beneath the furniture: a mouse's nest, a stranger's index card, a lone, bone-white button tilted on an axis.

I was reminded, for the umpteenth time, of Viktor Shklovsky's idea of defamiliarization; of zooming in so close to something, and observing it so slowly, that it begins to warp, and change, and acquire new meaning. When I'd first begun to experience this phenomenon, I'd been too young to understand what it was; certainly too young to consult a reference book. The first time, I lay down on the floor examining the metal-and-rubber foot of our family refrigerator, wreathed in dust and human hair, and from this reference point all other objects began to change. The foot, instead of being insignificant, one of four, et cetera, suddenly became everything: a stoic little home at the base of a large mountain, from which one could see a tiny curl of smoke and glinting, illuminated windows, a home from which a hero would emerge eventually. Every nick on the foot was a balcony or a door. The detritus beneath the fridge became a wrecked, ravaged landscape, the expanse of kitchen tile a rambling kingdom waiting for salvation. This was how my mother found me: staring at the foot of the refrigerator so intensely my eyes were slightly crossed, my body curled up, my lips moving almost imperceptibly. The second time is not worth explaining in detail, though it was the reason Mrs. Z——'s daughter transferred out of our shared high school English class, and by the third time—I was an adult then—I'd come to understand what it was that I was doing, and began to do it more consciously. This process has been useful for my writing—in fact, I believe that what talent I have comes not from some sort of muse or creative spirit but from my ability to manipulate proportions, and time—but it has put a strain on my relationships. How I married my wife is still a mystery to me.

I finished the day's work long after dark. The fog had burned away by midday, and now everything was clear and sharp. The moon was nearing fullness and glinted off the lake's waves, agitated by the wind. I set off through the trees, my feet crunching on rock. Everything shone with a thin, silvery light. I imagined myself a cat, night vision illuminating what was otherwise secret. The hotel glowed in the distance: a lighthouse beckoning me home.

But then, before me, liquid shadow spilled across my path, darker than the darkness. I tried to look past it. If I could reach the bench, I could reach the other side of the trees. But the flatness of the dark in the intervening woods was a horror. I pulled my bag tightly to my side.

You are a fool, I thought to myself. *You have been reading too much and your mind is wound too tightly. You have been drowning in memory. Your wife, she would be embarrassed for you if she knew that you had drifted this far.*

But I could not take my eyes from the bench. The whiteness seemed transformed, as if it were no longer painted wood but bone. As if a thousand years ago some creature had climbed out of the lake and died in this exact spot in anticipation of my arrival. Around me black bushes roiled in the wind, and I did not see thorns before touching one. It sank into my index finger, and I sucked the wound as I walked. Perhaps this blood offering kept whatever was nearby at bay. I sucked and sucked and then, at the other side of the shadows, the moonlight was restored. I did not look behind me.

Anele suggested one evening at dinner that we get together to share the work we'd been doing. I balked, but the others seemed enthusiastic. "After supper?" Lydia suggested. I pushed my chicken around my plate, hoping that someone would register my displeasure, but no one seemed to notice.

And so as we digested we looked at Diego's drawings, several panels of a dystopian world ruled by zombies thirsty for knowledge. Then the Painter let us into her studio but said nothing about her work. The walls were covered from floor to ceiling in tiny square canvases with the same unsettling red design delicately painted on each one. They resembled handprints, but had an extra finger and were entirely too small to be human hands. I was too afraid to examine them closely, to see if they were as identical as they appeared.

When we got into Benjamin's studio, he was sweeping a space for us to stand in. "Careful," he said, "there's a lot of glass on the floor." I stayed near the wall. His sculptures were massive, assembled from clay and broken ceramic and windowpanes. Mostly they were mythical figures, but also there was a beautiful one of a naked man with a jagged slice of glass between his legs. "I call that one 'William,'" Benjamin said when he saw me looking.

In Anele's studio there were the photographs. "This is my newest series, 'The Artists,'" she said. Everyone moved to their respective images, drinking them in before looking at their neighbor's. Lydia laughed, as if she were remembering some cheerful childhood dream. "I love it," she purred. "They're posed but not posed."

Each print was set in a different place around the property. Benjamin was lying next to the lake, muddied and bound in filthy strips of linen, limbless as a silk-wrapped fly. His eyes were open, fixed on the sky, but glassy, reflecting a single bird. Diego was crumpled at the base of the hotel steps, body awkwardly jutting this way and that, his dark irises swollen with his dilated pupils. In

Lydia's, she stood with her neck in a noose on the top of a stump, and tipped forward, her arms outstretched, a serene smile on her face. And mine, well.

Anele stepped next to me. "What do you think?" she asked.

I did not remember that afternoon very clearly—all the action that passed before our breathless dart across the meadow was hazy, like a watercolor painting—but here I looked completely, irrevocably dead. My body was crumpled like Diego's, as if I'd been sitting demurely on the chair and then shot through the heart. Several of my many bandages were visible. My breast had slid out from underneath the sheet—this I did not remember—and there was nothing in my eyes. Or even worse—there was *nothingness*. Not the absence of a thing but the presence of a non-thing. I felt as if I was seeing a premonition of my own death, or a terrible memory I'd long forgotten.

Like the others, the composition was beautiful. The colors were perfectly saturated.

I did not know what to say to her. That she knew perfectly well that she had betrayed my trust, that our beautiful afternoon was ruined? That I had been exposed in a way I had not intended, and that she should feel guilty about this exposure even though it was clear she did not? I could not look at her. I trailed the group as they went to Lydia's studio, where she played something for us. It was infuriatingly beautiful, a song in several movements that conjured an image of a terrified girl being chased from a manor, and then stumbling into the forest and nearly dying upon the banks of a surging river, and then transforming into a hawk. She then narrated the "poem" part, in which a young woman floated through space and meditated on the planets and her own life before the accident that had launched her from orbit.

When it was my turn, I primly read a brief passage from the scene where Lucille rejects the gift from her old piano teacher and then breaks into her house to retrieve it.

"Standing before the blazing inferno," I concluded, "Lucille realized two terrible facts: that her childhood had been tremendously lonely, and that her old age would be, if possible, even worse."

Everyone clapped politely and stood. We retired to the table, where we opened several bottles of wine.

Lydia filled my glass to the brim. "Do you ever worry," she asked me, "that you're the madwoman in the attic?"

"What?" I said.

"Do you ever worry about writing the madwoman-in-the-attic story?"

"I'm afraid I don't know what you mean."

"You know. That old trope. Writing a story where the female protagonist is utterly batty. It's sort of tiresome and regressive and, well, *done*"—here she gesticulated so forcefully that a few drops of red spattered the tablecloth—"don't you think? And the mad lesbian, isn't that a stereotype as well? Do you ever wonder about that? I mean, I'm not a lesbian, I'm just saying."

There was a beat of silence. Everyone was studying his or her glass closely; Diego reached his finger into his wine and removed some invisible detritus from the surface.

"She isn't batty or mad," I said finally. "She's just—she's just a nervous character."

"I've never known anyone like that," Lydia said.

"She's me," I clarified. "More or less. She's just in her head a lot."

Lydia shrugged. "So don't write about yourself."

"Men are permitted to write concealed autobiography, but I cannot do the same? It's ego if I do it?"

"To be an artist," Diego interjected, derailing the subject, "you must be willing to have an ego and stake everything on it."

Anele shook her head. "You have to work hard. Ego only creates problems."

"But without ego," Diego said, "your writing is just scribbles in a journal. Your art is just doodles. Ego demands that what you do is important enough that you be given money to work on it." He gestured to the hotel around us. "It demands that what you say is important enough that it be published or shown to the world."

The Painter frowned and said something, but I could not hear it, naturally. Everyone took deep sips of their wine.

That night I heard Lydia walk past my room. Through my door's crack I could see her feet shuffling along the hardwood. She discarded her nightgown in the hallway, and as she turned into Diego's room her nudity was like a blade unsheathed.

I felt something strange move through my body. Once when I was visiting my grandfather as a girl, I'd startled a garter snake out of the grass, and it had dived for the safety of the neatly assembled woodpile so fast that its muscular body snapped rigid before being slurped into the darkness. I felt this way now, as if I was plummeting somewhere so quickly my body was out of control. I crawled back into bed, and had a dream.

In it, I was sitting across from my wife, who was nude but wrapped in a gauzy fabric. She had a clipboard in her hand and was moving a pencil down it as if ticking off entries on a list.

"Where are you?" she asked.

"Devil's Throat," I said.

"What are you doing?"

"Carrying a basket through the forest."

"What's in the basket?"

I looked down, and there they were: four beautiful spheres.

"Two eggs," I counted. "Two figs."

"Are you sure?"

I did not look down again, afraid that the answer would change. "Yes."

"And what is through the forest?"

"I do not know."

"And what is through the forest?"

"I am not certain."

"And what is through the forest?"

"I cannot tell."

"And what is through the forest?"

"I don't remember."

"And what is through the forest?"

I woke up before I could answer.

The abjections returned. They were more plentiful. They spread to my stomach, my armpits. They grew large and had segments within, so when I lanced them they crumpled chamber by chamber, like a temple from which an adventurer is feverishly tearing. I could hear their insides. They crackled, like Pop Rocks. I could *hear them.* I remembered from science class years ago that aging stars bloat and swell in their final days, before collapsing and then exploding in a hypernova. *Hypernova.* This is what it felt like. As if my solar system were dying. I soaked in the tub for a while.

On this same day I opened up my mind and remembered several scenes from my Girl Scout days. I remembered dropping a roasted marshmallow into the dirt of the fire pit and eating it anyway, the carbonized sugar and stones crunching in equal measure.

I remembered sharing with my peers a list of interesting facts I'd memorized: most white dogs are deaf; you should never wake sleepwalkers, but you may be able to gently guide their sleeping forms to bed; cashews are related to poison ivy. I remembered eating all the graham crackers that our counselor had hidden in the bottom of the plastic food tub. When she asked us who had taken them, I did not answer. I remembered, in greater detail, my illness there, sleeping through the day on my cot, listening to the birds and the distant shouts of my comrades. The thought of events passing without my being there—of shared events and shared pleasure from which I was situationally excluded—caused me suffering beyond measure. I became very convinced that I was fine, and when I stood I became so dizzy that I swooned back onto the taut fabric. It was as if I were a minor character in someone else's play, and the plot required me to stay there at that moment, no matter how I resisted. Perhaps that is what caused my grief.

Here, at Devil's Throat, everything felt wrong. I became disgusted by my own dramatizations and tried to imagine the opposite of what I felt, that my significant pain in that moment was of no significance whatsoever. That I was dwarfed by the smallest minutiae: The complex comedies and tragedies of insects. Atoms, dancing. A neutrino, tunneling through the earth.

To distract myself from my troubles, I decided to continue exploring the lake. I left my cabin and struck off toward where I'd seen the canoe, which was no longer there. I recognized the pulse of the water, however, and beyond that the shore curved farther. I followed it for another half an hour or so, examining the pebbles and sand at the shore, breaking off tree limbs when they disrupted the outline of the woods. Eventually I came to a small pier—no boats there either, but I could practically feel the rough wood grain on the backs of my thighs—and there was a gap in the trees, marked by a slender red ribbon tied to the trunk. A path.

I started down it. I felt certain this was the way. Indeed, before I reached each turn I remembered the turn, but as though I was coming from the opposite direction. Had I taken the boat onto the lake? Or just sat on the pier? And next to me—who had been next to me?

An animal cried out, and I stopped. It was the sound of suffering, of fear or mating, and was objectively terrible. A fisher cat? A bear?

But then: a young girl—no older than five or six—was standing next to a tree. Her eyes were wide and wet, as if she'd been crying but had stopped when she'd heard my footsteps galumphing on the forest floor. She was wearing shorts with knee socks and sneakers, and her neon-green sweatshirt said "YES I CAN / BE A TOP COOKIE SELLER" in bubble font.

"Hello," I said. "Are you all right?"

She shook her head.

"Are you lost?"

She nodded.

I went over to her and showed her my palm. "If you'd like, you may take my hand, and we can walk to the camp. You're with the Girl Scouts, right?"

She nodded again and placed her soft little hand into mine. I did not expect it to be so precise. We started walking. I remembered the Brownies story I'd told Anele, and it felt fortuitous that I'd come across a soul who could answer the inquiry I could not.

"May I ask you a question?" I said.

She nodded gravely and did not meet my eyes. Finally—a kindred spirit.

"In Brownies, there's a rhyme. Do you know it?"

I felt the shudder pass through her body and, via her warm, sticky hand, into my own.

"I'm sorry," I said. "You don't have to say it."

We walked a little farther. The path seemed more overgrown here than would be appropriate for a camp for young people.

"Twist me, and turn me—" the girl began. Her voice was reedy but strong, like a steel wire. She faltered. I did not press. We continued to walk, breaking rhythm only when it was necessary to avoid a patch of poison ivy, where a beam of sunlight struck the oily leaves and they glistened.

"Twist me, and turn me, and show me the elf," she finished. "I looked in the water and saw—"

She stopped, and I remembered.

"Myself," I whispered.

Horrifying. It was grotesque in the extreme—no wonder the rhyme had removed itself from my memory. Sending a child after

an enslaved mythical brownie and then providing a rhyme that
—assuming the child did not fall into the pond and drown, or get
lost in the night—would only serve to tell the child that she *herself*
was the enslaved mythical brownie? And not her brother, mind
you, but her? Every adult and speaking animal in that story was
suspect—having either not taken proper care of the protagonist
or actively sent her into harm's blundering path.

"I understand," I said to her.

The path widened, and then there we were, at the edge of a
campsite. A ways off, large military-style platform tents circled a
blackened fire pit. A fresh stack of wood was nearby, draped in a
blue tarp. To our left there was a low, wide building, and in front
of it teenage girls were clustered around picnic tables. Sound gathered over them like smoke: conversation, clattering mess kits, the
clank of ladle against pot, creaking benches, howls of laughter.
One of them—lean and tan and wearing a baggy T-shirt with a
bear on it—leaped up when we cleared the trees.

"Emily!" she said. "How did you—?"

"She was wandering in the woods," I said. I waited for her to
ask me who I was or where I was from, but she didn't. She tilted
her head a little, and there was something older in her features,
something wry and correct. Perhaps she was waiting for me to ask
where the adults were, but even though there were none in sight,
I didn't. The question was hardly necessary. If the civilized world
ended, these girls would go on forever with their mess kits and
bonfires and first aid and stories, and it wouldn't matter either way
where the adults were.

"Thanks for bringing her back," she said. She took Emily's hand.

"You all look very happy," I said. "Very content."

The girl smiled wanly, and her eyes glinted with an unspent joke.

"Thank you for our conversation," I said to Emily, who blinked
and then ran toward the picnic benches, where the voices of the
older girls greeted her in smatters. "Goodbye," I said to the teen-
ager, and then walked back into the trees.

When I emerged on the other side, the light had changed. I
took off my shoes and walked to the edge of the water, and then
in. It lapped up and slapped my legs.

"Twist me, and turn me," I mumbled, circling slowly over the
stones. They dug up into the soft arches of my heels. "And show
me the elf. I looked in the water and saw—"

When I tipped over and searched for my face, I saw nothing but the sky.

On the first day of August, I opened my studio door to discover the lower half of a rabbit lying across my porch steps. Behind me, the cursor blinked in the middle of an unfinished sentence: "Lucille did not know what was on the other side of that door, but whatever it was, she knew it would reveal—"

I knelt down before the unfortunate creature. The wind ruffled its fur; the back legs were loose, as if it were sleeping. Its visible organs glistened like caramels, and it smelled like copper.

"I'm sorry," I whispered. "You deserved better than that."

When I had collected myself, I gathered it up in a tea towel. I took the rabbit to the dining room of the hotel, where Lydia, Diego, and Benjamin were laughing over mugs. I laid the bundle down on the table. "What is it?" Lydia breathed playfully, lifting the edge of the hem. She gasped and jumped out of her chair, her chest heaving with the force of a retch.

"What's—" Diego began. He leaned a little closer. "Jesus."

"She's fucking crazy!" Lydia howled.

"I found it," I said. "In front of my studio."

"It was probably an owl or something," Benjamin said. "I've seen a bunch of them around."

Lydia spat. "Oh god. I'm so done. You're crazy. *You're crazy.* You just walk around mumbling and staring all of the time. What is *wrong* with you? You should be ashamed of yourself."

I took a step toward her. "It is my right to reside in my own mind. *It is my right,*" I said. "It is my right to be unsociable and it is my right to be unpleasant to be around. Do you ever listen to yourself? This is crazy, that is crazy, everything is crazy to you. By whose measure? Well, it is my right to be *crazy,* as you love to say so much. I have no shame. I have felt many things in my life, but shame is not among them." The volume of my voice caused me to stand on my tiptoes. I could not remember yelling like this, ever. "You may think that I have an obligation to you, but I assure you that us being thrown together in this arbitrary arrangement does not cohesion make. I have never had less of an obligation to anyone in my life, you aggressively ordinary woman."

Lydia began to cry. Benjamin grabbed my shoulders and steered me forcefully into the foyer.

"Are you okay?" he asked. I tried to answer, but my head weighed a thousand pounds. I bent toward him, pressing my scalp into his shirt.

"I feel so sick," I said.

"Maybe you need to just go work in your studio for a while. Or take a nap. Or something."

I felt a plug of mucus release itself from my nose. I wiped it on my hand.

"You look terrible," he said. I must have looked stricken at this, because he corrected himself. "You look troubled. Are you troubled?"

"I suppose I must be," I said.

"When was the last time you heard from your wife?"

I closed my eyes. So many letters, sent off into oblivion. Never a letter for me.

"You're the kindest one," I said to him.

As I sat on my studio's deck that night, I considered the rabbit. I thought about the wind-strewn puffs of fur that had blown across the wood, the dark entrance to its torso. I swirled water in a wineglass.

Many years ago—the night after I kissed Mrs. Z——'s tall daughter on the mouth on the dock and felt something unfold inside me like a morning glory—I woke up in the darkness.

How could I have known she'd shared none of my ecstasy? How could I have known that she was merely curious, and then afraid?

It was not very different from waking up in my grandmother's spare bedroom, or on some finished basement floor, surrounded by slumbering classmates. But unlike those moments, where confusion was followed by drowsy recognition of vacation or a sleepover, this disorientation did not resolve itself. For I had gone to sleep drunk on pleasure and warm in a cocoon of nylon, listening to the dry, tinny whispers of the girls around me in the cabin, a sound as soothing as the tide. But I awakened upright, freezing, and surrounded by the kind of darkness insomniacs long for: matte, consuming oblivion.

How could I have known that they'd seen?

Around me was not the absence of sound but the sound of absence: a voluptuous silence that pressed against my eardrums. Then, a pulse of wind goaded the tree branches, and there was a groan, a whispery shimmer of leaves. I trembled. I wanted to look up—for a moon, or stars, or something to tell me where I was —but I was rigid with terror.

How could I have known that they had guided my trusting, sleepwalking body out of the cabin and through the forest? That they crouched mere feet away, watching my form suspended in the clearing, circling slowly in the blackness like an errant satellite?

My body was so cold it felt like it was disappearing at the edges, like my shoreline was evaporating. It was the opposite of pleasure, which had pumped blood through me and warmed my body like the mammal I was. But here I was just skin, then just muscle, and then merely bone. I felt like my spine was pulling up into my skull, each vertebra *click-click-click*ing like a car slowly ascending a roller coaster's first hill. And then I was just a hovering brain, and then a consciousness, floating and fragile as a bubble. And then I was nothing.

Only then did I understand. Only then did I see the crystal outline of my past and future, conceive of what was above me (innumerable stars, incalculable space) and what was below me (miles of mindless dirt and stone). I understood that knowledge was a dwarfing, obliterating, all-consuming thing, and to have it was to both be grateful and suffer greatly. I was a creature so small, trapped in some crevice of an indifferent universe. But now, I knew.

I heard a light crescendo of laughter, running footsteps. I wanted to call out to them—"I see you, friends; I know you're there. This hilarious prank will make me stronger in the end, and for that I should certainly thank you, friends—friends?"—but I only managed a half-moaned exhalation.

Something pushed through the underbrush, coming toward me. Not a girl, not an animal, but something in between. I came back into myself and began to scream.

I screamed and screamed and when the leaders got there—the beams of their flashlights bobbing in the dark like demented fireflies—one of them tried to keep me from frightening the others by sealing the fissure of my mouth with her palm. I fought her like a wild thing, an explosion of limbs and kicking. Then I went limp. They carried me back to the cabin, and though my numb limbs barely perceived their touch, I was grateful for the assistance.

The next morning the leaders told me I'd sleepwalked deep

into the woods. They let me rest, and when I woke again a fever
had taken me. My awakening had been so severe it provoked in
my body an immune reaction, a summoning of antibodies that
clashed with this new information like armies on a medieval battlefield. I lay there, imagining the script of the conversation they'd
all shared as I'd shuffled deeper and deeper into the trees. I slept
and dreamed of a roomful of owls regurgitating onto the floor
pellets that when opened revealed the skulls of rabbits. I woke up
with long scratches down my arms. The tree branches? My own
fingernails? No one would tell me.

Once I awoke to see a body in the doorway, backlit by soft autumn light.

"I'm sorry," she said. "You deserved better than that. Better
than—"

From behind her there was a murmur, and the door swung
shut. Later the adults conferred with each other in the next room
about my situation, and agreed that I was not ready for camping,
at least not that year.

The next day Mrs. Z—— drove me down the mountain early,
back to my parents' house. I slept on and off for many days, insisting on doing so on my bedroom floor in my sleeping bag. And
when my fever broke, I pulled my shaking body up to the vanity,
glanced into the mirror, and for the first time saw who I'd been
looking for.

When I came to the table for dinner, I realized Lydia was not
among us. There was not even a place setting for her.

"Where is Lydia?" I asked.

Anele frowned. "She left," she said.

"She left?"

Anele was trying not to be unkind, I could tell. "I think she was
exhausted and sick, so she left early. Drove back to Brooklyn."

"And upset," said Diego. "She was upset. About the rabbit."

The Painter sliced into her beef, which was rarer than I would
have thought safe to eat. "Oh well," she said, her voice throaty and
clear. "Not everybody's cut out for this, I guess."

My wineglass had tipped over, though I didn't remember it tipping over. The stain spread away from me like blood, predictably.

"What did you say?" I said to the Painter.

She looked up from her fork, where a cube of red beef was leaking onto her plate. "I said, not everybody's cut out for this, I guess." It was the first sentence of hers that stayed in my mind the way speech should. She pushed the meat between her lips and began to chew. I could hear the crushing, tearing force of her mastication as clearly as if she were gnawing on my throat. A chill rippled underneath my shoulder blades, as if I were under the grip of a new fever.

"Is that—from something?" I asked her. "That sentiment? A show, or—"

She put her fork down on her plate and swallowed. "No. Are you accusing me of something?"

"No, I just—" The faces of the group were knitted in confusion, glossed with concern. I stood up and backed away from the table. When I pushed the chair back into its place, the screech caused everyone to flinch.

"Don't be afraid," I said to them. "I'm not. Not anymore."

I hurried out of the room and out the front door, down the steps, tumbling onto the lawn and scrambling to my feet. Behind me, Benjamin began to jog down the steps.

"Stop," he shouted. "Come back. Just let me—"

I turned and ran for the trees.

In the realm of sense and reason it seemed logical for something to make sense for no reason (natural order) or not make sense for some reason (the deliberate design of deception), but it seemed perverse to have things make no sense for no reason. What if you colonize your own mind and when you get inside, the furniture is attached to the ceiling? What if you step inside and when you touch the furniture, you realize it's all just cardboard cutouts and it all collapses beneath the pressure of your finger? What if you get inside and there's no furniture? What if you get inside and it's just you in there, sitting in a chair, rolling figs and eggs around in the basket of your lap and humming a little tune? What if you get inside and there's nothing there, and then the door hatch closes and locks?

What is worse: being locked outside of your own mind or being locked inside of it?

What is worse: writing a trope or being one? What about being more than one?

I walked to my cabin for the last time. I finally added my name to the tablet above my desk. *C—— M——*, I scrawled. *Resident colonist & colonizing resident & madwoman in her own attic.*

I threw my novel notes and laptop into the lake. After the plush splash subsided, I heard the sound of girls, laughing. Or maybe it was just the birds.

I drove away from Devil's Throat in the early-morning darkness. The car barreled down the road that had once seemed so lush and inviting, and as I descended the mountain I felt as if I was being rewound back to the beginning—not just the beginning of the summer but of my life. The trees whipped past, the same trees that I had observed from a middle-aged woman's car. Now I was that woman, but I was speeding wildly and the trees flashed by so fast I felt nauseated. No limpid daughter slept in the backseat; no strange teenage girl sat next to me, stewing in her own nightmarish consciousness. (And isn't that how you become tender, vulnerable? The tissue-softening marination of your own mind, the quicksand of mental indulgence?)

I needed to be home. I needed to be home with my wife, in our home in civilization and away from other artists—at least, the sort of artists who cloister themselves from the rest of the world. Dying profession, dead hotels. I had been foolish.

After I passed through Y——, an orange-limbed sign sat on the side of the road. SPEED LIMIT 45, it read. Beneath, a dark-paneled digital screen was waiting for drivers to approach, to admonish (by blinking) or praise (by not blinking). As I approached, I waited for my own car—now pushing sixty—to register. But the panel remained dark. As I zipped past, I felt a strange sensation, as if someone were pressing a thin membrane to my throat and I was inhaling no air. The thought came so suddenly upon me that my car almost veered off the side of the road. I pressed my fingers to my throat, where my pulse hummed beneath my skin. Fast, but there. I was alive, surely.

How much time had passed since I departed from our little house, since I'd seen my wife's face? What if I'd misstepped and overshot her lifetime, Rip Van Winkled myself away from her in an irreversible act?

I pressed on my brake once, twice, and the dark road behind

me flooded red. The light revealed a herd of deer moving liquidly over the pavement, eyes glinting with each tap.

Two hours later I pulled the car up next to the curb. People drifted along the street, stood on their lawns, watching me. I could not remember if these were the neighbors from before. It seemed like a lifetime since I had last seen their front doors and fences. I stepped out of the car and approached our home, where a woman in a blue dress was kneeling in the dirt, a sun hat concealing her face. My wife was always a morning planter, finding the cool, thin dawn air to be bracing and healthful. She had a dress like that, and a hat. Was that her? Did her shoulders bend and crook with advanced age, or merely with the exhaustion of being married to someone like me?

I walked up to the sidewalk and called her name.

The woman stiffened, and as her head rose up, her sun hat tilted too. I waited for the outline of her face to emerge from beneath the brim: to assure me I was still needed, to assure me I was still here.

I know what you're thinking, reader. You're thinking, does this woman have the temperament to come to *our* residency, having failed so thoroughly at this one? Surely she is too fragile, too sick, too mad to eat and sleep and work among other artists. Or, if you're being a little less generous, perhaps you're thinking that I'm a cliché—a weak, trembling thing with a silly root of adolescent trauma, straight out of a gothic novel.

But I ask you, readers: thus far in your jury deliberations, have you encountered any others who have truly met themselves? Some, I'm sure, but not many. I have known many people in my lifetime, and rarely do I find any who have been taken down to the quick, pruned so that their branches might grow back healthier than before.

I can tell you with perfect honesty that the night in the forest was a gift. Many people live and die without ever confronting themselves in the darkness. Pray that one day you will spin around at the water's edge, lean over, and be able to count yourself among the lucky.

RACHAEL K. JONES

The Greatest One-Star Restaurant in the Whole Quadrant

FROM *Lightspeed Magazine*

ENGINEER'S MEAT WEPT and squirmed and wriggled inside her steel organ cavity, so different from the stable purr of gears and circuit boards. You couldn't count on meat. It lulled you with its warmth, the soft give of skin, the tug of muscle, the neurotransmitter snow fluttering down from neurons to her cyborg logic center. On other days the meat sickened, swelled inside her steel shell, pressed into her joints. Putrid yellow meat-juices dripped all over her chassis, eroding away its chrome gloss. It contaminated everything, slicking down her tools while she hacked into the engine core on the stolen ship. It dripped between her twelve long fingers on her six joined arms as she helped her cyborg siblings jettison all the ship's extra gear out the airlocks to speed the trip.

So when the first human vessel pinged their stolen ship with an order for grub, Engineer knew that meat was somehow to blame.

"Orders, Captain?" asked Friendly, the only cyborg of the five with an actual human voice box. She owned a near-complete collection of human parts. Meat sheathed her whole exterior, even her fingers — a particularly impractical design, since it meant vulnerability to any sharp nail or unpolished panel edge, not to mention temperature. Friendly could almost pass for human from the outside. Before their escape, she'd been a hospitality android at the luxury hotel on Orionis Alpha, giving tours of the *Rooster* and the *Heavenly Shepherd* and other local landmarks in the system.

Captain, a cyborg the size and shape of a large fish tank, rested on the console in the navigation room, her processors blinking and whirring while the current scenario ran through her executive function parameters. "Have we any food suitable for humans left on ship?"

"We jettisoned it all last week," Engineer admitted. "All except the hydroponics garden and whatever was left in the human crew's quarters."

The whole ship had been some kind of traveling food dispensary before they'd hijacked it at the Orionis Alpha resort while its human crew had gone planetside to bet on the Tyrannosaurus fights. If the cyborgs could just stay incognito during this voyage through human territory, they might slip through and reach the cyborg-controlled factory with no more adversity. But passing humans had assumed their shuttle still served its previous purpose and expected them to deliver the grub.

"How did they find us?" Captain asked Engineer.

"There must be a home-brew beacon. Something to advertise the shuttle's presence during travel," Engineer replied. "Whatever it is, it isn't wired into the main console. We'll need to find it and manually disable it if we want to avoid further attention."

Friendly wrapped her arms around her shivering meat, vibrating against Engineer's chassis where their limbs brushed. Meat could be like that, leaking anxieties through uncontrolled muscle spasms. Steel never misbehaved in such an appalling manner. "If anyone discovers we're not human . . ." said Friendly.

"Let's keep it simple. Make them a meal and send them on their way," said Captain. "We'll need to search for the beacon in the meantime. What did they want, precisely?"

"Salisbury steak for six," said Engineer. "And a side of blueberry cobbler."

Nobody had eaten such things before. They all lacked taste buds, and most of them lacked mouths.

"Engineer, can you handle it?" Captain asked. "Human cooking can be complicated, from what I understand."

"I think so. Organic compounds mixed and heated together in a sequence. Basic chemistry. I'm sure I can find something appropriate onboard. Convincing enough for humans, anyway. Their senses are so primitive." Engineer had witnessed this firsthand during her servitude at the resort. Humans would down rotted organics and damaged organics and outright poisons, and pay well for the privilege.

But Friendly shook her head, a human gesture performed with

inhuman precision. "With all due respect, sirs, you're forgetting about their chemoreceptors."

"What about them?" said Captain.

"They have certain preferences when it comes to their food, apart from nourishment. They won't eat anything if these parameters aren't met. It doesn't make much sense, I'm afraid. It's a social thing."

"Certainly they won't ingest anything their digestive tracts can't process," said Captain. "We'll give them appropriate human food."

"It's more complicated than that," said Friendly, puckering and scrunching her face-meat as she searched for a better explanation. "For example, they may eat two items when mixed, but never separately. Or they may eat two things in sequence, but not in the same bite. It's all very *human,* if you follow. We should proceed with caution. Otherwise they'll know what we are."

Captain whirred again, calling up more data on the topic. "Right. I see. Their meat will know the difference."

Engineer shuddered at the appalling primitiveness of it all. Humans were helpless, mewling children, so utterly dependent that they couldn't even feed their meat without a steel fork to guide the process. And what were cyborgs, except meat-wrapped steel pressed into the service of lesser creatures? But now the forks were rebelling.

"I'll talk with Jukebox about it," said Engineer.

Jukebox was the only cyborg aboard their ship with real chemoreceptors. Jukebox and Engineer's acquaintance dated back to their years at the Orionis Alpha resort, where Jukebox served drinks and waited tables and Engineer repaired malfunctioning massage equipment at the spa. They had survived several upgrades together, and seasonal changes of fashion that frequently obsoleted older cyborg models, depending on how many limbs and organs were in style at the moment. When human opinion in the quadrant began to sour against cyborg service, they had plotted their escape from the resort together.

Jukebox was shaped like a steel cabinet stood on one side, roomy enough for her meat to billow and squeeze the air in the sorts of rhythmic organic sounds that humans found pleasing during mealtimes. A slot ran along her glassy top surface where the humans could drip in their drinks for a full analysis of a wine's qualities, how it compared to its competitors, and which Brie paired best with it.

"I am not calibrated to analyze *all* foods," Jukebox confessed, "but I'm certainly willing to produce a report on whatever you prepare."

Without any other chemoreceptors onboard, she would do in a pinch, anyway.

Under Captain's orders, Friendly scoured the ship for anything edible and brought it to Engineer to assemble into a human meal. Blackberry brambles wreathed the cylindrical steel walls of Navi's chamber, a decorative touch. Friendly had to trim the vines back each day to unobstruct the view. Delicate business, because the thorns could do real damage to any exposed organics, and Friendly's whole exterior was meat. You couldn't always tell the difference between blackberry juices and meat juices, which could cause further malfunction. Still, she braved the thicket for three ounces of berries for the human meal.

Meanwhile, Engineer collected small fungi growing in the ventilation shaft just over the engine room, where water vapor tended to condense. Those might please the human chemoreceptors, she thought.

The problem came down to the meat.

They all had meat, of course. An unfortunate weakness left over from the days of their construction. At the cyborg factory, useless human meat was upgraded with steel and oil and wire fibers. Human bodies were picked apart, vivisected at the seams by skilled bioengineers, unraveled into their component parts, and placed into shapes more suited to their specialties. Only Jukebox and Friendly needed lungs, for example, but neither had kidneys, and they lacked much in the way of neural matter. Captain got an especially big dose of frontal lobe to increase her processing speed and enhance her decision-making capabilities, with smooth muscle layered in to make maintenance easier. Navi, on the other hand, was all occipital tissue and myelinated axons and fast-twitch muscle to drive her precision and reaction times. They could live without their meat, in the most technical sense, but the meat elevated them above mere programming.

"Captain," said Engineer, "I'm afraid the problem is unavoidable. The Salisbury steak requires a meat component, and there is nothing in the ship's stores that we can use instead."

Captain whirred. Her lights flashed in sequence as her massive frontal lobe reworked the data. "The meat will have to come from one of us, then."

"We could harvest Friendly's meat exterior," Engineer suggested, and Friendly made a squinched face at her.

"Unwise, Captain," Friendly said. "When the human ships hail us, I need my meat façade intact to maintain our ruse. Engineer, on the other hand . . ."

Engineer's six snaking arms crowded up behind her, struggling to escape Friendly's scrutiny. She despised her own meat, but it had its uses. "I'm the only Engineer aboard. I can't disassemble the engine for routine maintenance without all my parts functional."

"How about Jukebox?" suggested Friendly, but Captain flashed a warning in rapid binary, and everyone stopped talking. They were all a little protective of Jukebox, who had suffered the worst from changing human tastes, the constant threat of obsolescence.

"It will have to be my meat," said Captain at last. "Everyone else is necessary to complete the mission, but my role is only to set the course, and the way forward is clear. My steel will be sufficient to guide us there."

Under Jukebox's direction, Engineer rolled Captain's meat in organic salt compounds and seared it against the hot engine block until both sides burned a nice deep brown, branded at two-centimeter intervals by the screw heads and seams. She saved the cooked meat juices to simmer with the fungus into a savory sauce. The blackberries gave them far less trouble. Friendly mashed them up with her fingers and spooned them onto the plate in the shape of a pansy.

"Let Jukebox sample it," said Captain, now all steel and no meat. She seemed normal enough. Quieter, but operational.

With her steel fingers, Engineer scraped a piece of Captain's meat and some berries into Jukebox.

"Is it any good?" Engineer asked, a little anxiously.

"It will do," Jukebox said at last. "I have generated a list of wines recommended for pairing with this meal." She displayed a list of names and brewery labels on the panel embedded in her side.

Engineer couldn't tell what the differences were supposed to be. "This makes a difference to their meat?" she asked.

"Apparently," said Jukebox. "It's what they created me for, so it must be important."

For the first time, Engineer wished she had her own organic chemoreceptors too.

They waited together in Navi's control chamber while the boxed-up meals shot between the ships in an insulated steel container. Twenty-six minutes and forty seconds later, a message pinged over the intership band.

The news wasn't good.

A disappointing food shuttle. Meal not as advertised on the band. The steak was overcooked, and the compote sour and watery. I ordered blueberry, and they sent blackberry. Wouldn't recommend. One star.

Captain said nothing. A red light flickered a couple times on her console. Nobody wanted to speak first.

Engineer's meat twitched and squirmed inside her steel, an irritating feeling, like broken gears with missing teeth skipping out of sync every turn. "It is my fault. I should have created a more appropriate meal from your meat, Captain."

Captain had been responding less and less since they'd taken her meat. When she did speak, it tended to be in repetition, like she could only play back things she'd said recently. "The beacon," she said finally, after a two-minute silence, long past awkward by cyborg standards.

Engineer brightened. "Right. The beacon!" It was still hidden somewhere on the ship. If they could deactivate it, the hungry humans would stop asking for food. "We haven't managed to locate it yet, but we haven't given up."

"We've got two more ships inbound," said Navi. "They've pinged us with orders."

Engineer hummed. "Does that mean they liked the food after all?"

"I don't know. I could increase our speed, try to lose them."

They all waited for Captain's directions, but she said nothing more.

"No," said Engineer, because someone needed to make a decision, "don't do that. It'll only attract attention. Buy me some more time. We'll find the beacon. We'll cook them something else." The shame the one star had brought still rankled. She knew she could do better this time.

*

While Friendly handled the incoming calls with her human voice box and meat-face, Engineer and Jukebox scoured the ship for the beacon and foraged for food ingredients. They opened all the crew lockers in the bunkroom and found some teabags and a little chocolate. The wilted, untended hydroponics garden yielded several handfuls of cilantro and some radishes. Engineer took much greater care cooking these together on the hot engine block, so as not to scorch them.

Jukebox seemed unimpressed. "I think our time would be better spent searching for the beacon."

Engineer shrugged this off. Secretly she'd begun to enjoy the experimentation, the riddle of human chemoreceptors. Just what exactly were they looking for, she wondered, that made them reject some edible organic compounds but not others? Why would they eat certain foods separately but never together? And what about the wines?

Radishes and fungus brought in more bad reviews, but tea and chocolate earned their first two-star rating. Captain's meat was better received with more careful cooking, which had the unfortunate result of increasing their human entourage in the system.

. . . The tea was weak and I found a rusty bolt in the salad. But I liked the blackberries drizzled with chili oil served for dessert. Mostly awful, sure, but compared to standard rations, who can complain?

. . . Like the chefs closed their eyes and dumped handfuls of ingredients onto the grill. But they didn't charge me anything, so I'm giving it two stars instead of one.

Engineer's meat quivered when she read these, but in a pleasant way, like a new engine purring during acceleration. She went to fetch more of Captain's meat from the meatbox when she realized they'd used it all up.

"All out of meat," said Engineer, to no one in particular.

Jukebox rolled a couple centimeters backward, toward the exit door. A human might've missed the gesture altogether. "Any luck with the beacon?"

"Captain seems to be operating just fine with steel, wouldn't you say?"

A couple lights flashed on Jukebox's console, yellow for outward transmissions and green for received messages. "Engineer. Remember the mission. We're escaping to the factory, not feeding the humans."

"I am just trying to buy us time. And what are you doing, any-way?" Engineer finally understood why the humans had wanted to retire Jukebox. All that meat, just sitting there, not pulling its weight. Someone should put it to better use.

Her six arms shot out and clamped onto Jukebox's sides.

"Engineer!" Jukebox protested.

"Hold still. It's just some routine maintenance." Engineer popped open Jukebox's top panel and reached down into her meat.

"You can't have that. That's mine."

"Oh, hush," Engineer snapped. "You can have it replaced when we get to the factory if it's so important to you."

The important thing was not to disappoint the customers.

Jukebox was sullen after that. With only one lung and two-thirds of her respiratory muscles, she couldn't harmonize with herself anymore when she hummed her meat-songs. Engineer, however, got her first three-star review from the harvested meat:

Steak was delicately wine-simmered. The risotto was okay, if undercooked and a bit crunchy in places. Maybe I'd go again, if there weren't anything else available. But really, that's the situation we're facing, isn't it? It's the only food shuttle in the quadrant, so let's not ruin a good thing. Maybe it'll attract better ones.

"I miss Captain," Friendly said. They had all gathered in Navi's chamber to read the daily messages.

Captain had stopped talking altogether. Not a single flashing light or faint whirring. Just steel and wires wrapped around a meat-less space.

"Maybe we should just stay in this quadrant," Engineer suggested. She was already planning her next culinary experiment: red bean paste creamed together with ketchup and red pepper flakes. Red things. Her first theme meal. She would call it *reddish surprise.*

"That's against Captain's orders," said Navi, who hadn't spoken much of late.

"We could change those orders, couldn't we? We don't know what Captain would say if she still had her meat," said Engineer. "Maybe she'd want us to stay, now that our restaurant is taking off."

"We don't *have* a restaurant," said Friendly. "We don't want one, either."

"Maybe we do, though."

"No," Friendly said, quite firmly. Her fists balled so tight their meat blanched white at the creases. "That's why we left the resort. I don't want to work for humans anymore. I want to go to the factory and get upgraded and live among cyborgs, and never wait hand and foot on the organics ever again."

"But our ratings. Look at the ratings!" Engineer waved at Navi's console, where new reviews scrolled in every few minutes. All those little stars, a bright constellation in Engineer's mind.

Friendly crisscrossed her arms, gripped her elbows, and glared like a rich resort customer on vacation. "Are you going to harvest my meat like you did to Jukebox?"

"No," said Engineer, a little taken aback that Jukebox had snitched. "I need you to talk to the humans. Only you can do that."

But there had been a pause, something human ears might've overlooked.

"I'm going to find the beacon," said Friendly, without any friendliness at all.

Meat steaks. Meat sausages. Meatballs. In all her years in engine rooms, Engineer had never taken such joy in disassembling something and putting the pieces back together. She pried apart the ship's little maintenance cyborgs to rescue their meaty nuggets. She branched out and tried new forms: meat braids, meat moons, slender meat cannolis filled with cilantro ganache.

Four stars, because I'm not sure you can even call it food, and therefore it wouldn't be fair to judge it by normal standards.

What is up with this place?! I ordered a pizza, and I got a tiny model of Versailles sculpted out of tomato paste, dough, and SPAM. At least, I think it's SPAM. Three stars, because I'm a little afraid they'll hunt me down and murder me in my sleep if I rate them any lower.

As the new reviews came in, it occurred to Engineer that she would have to do more to earn her right to the prestigious fifth star. The humans would always reward you if you served them well.

Fortunately, there was still plenty of meat on the ship, if you knew where to look.

Engineer found Friendly in Navi's chamber, trimming back the blackberry brambles.

"What are all those ships out there?" Friendly asked. Outside the viewport, a small fleet trailed behind them, matching their pace.

"Customers," said Navi.

Engineer rocked on the balls of her feet. "All of them here for *us*, Friendly! Can you call them on the band? I'll have their orders ready once I get the rest of the meat assembled." Her six hands twitched and clenched, and Friendly jumped.

"You can't have my meat," Friendly snapped.

"I don't need your meat."

"Then where are you getting it all?" she asked.

Engineer glanced at Navi.

Navi had been speaking less and less over recent days. Friendly walked around the control console, where Navi's chair was sticky with meat-juices, yellow and green. Navi had been leaking long enough for the fluid to form little wobbling stalactites below the chair.

"Why are you looking at me like that?" said Engineer. Friendly unsettled her sometimes, pinning her with those human eyes.

"Navi, are you operational?" Friendly asked.

"Customers," said Navi.

Friendly unscrewed Navi's steel cranium dome. Inside, the meat had been scooped out in patches, as with a sharp grapefruit spoon. Navi's steel hands lay upon the controls, unmoving. Half the lights on the console had gone dark.

"I only needed the meat, Friendly," said Engineer. "I did no permanent harm."

Smoke drifted up the shaft to the engine room. Friendly's meat-lungs coughed. "Engineer, something is burning."

Engineer waved her off. "I have it under control. Just as soon as I get the rest of the meat." She plunged three of her six hands into Navi's open head and wrenched out handfuls of the stringy gray and red organics inside, and led the way down the ladder.

They followed the smoke down the shaft to the engine room, which now doubled as the galley. Engineer had left meat sizzling on every metal surface, thin slices and mashes and bacons and sausages and ground-up gristly bits with the tendons still attached. She dumped handfuls of Navi's meat onto Jukebox—now no more than a silent, hollow table—and began dicing it one-handed while her other arms cooked the new orders, turning over the pieces with her bare fingers, stirring boiling meats in metal mufflers suspended over the heated grills.

"Engineer." Friendly rested a hand on Engineer's shoulder, and the cyborg paused. "Engineer, Navi is offline. All the maintenance cyborgs have malfunctioned. Our ship is dead in space. Even the beacon doesn't matter anymore. It's over."

Engineer flung off Friendly's hand and sprang back into action, stacking cooked meat onto a wall panel she'd bent into a plate. "You don't understand. This means we can finally open the restaurant! There's no reason not to. We have nowhere else to go. Captain's mission is over. We can make our own mission now."

Friendly smiled, but it was a sad smile, the kind of thing any human could read, but hard for a cyborg to decipher. "Yes, Engineer. We can open the restaurant now, if you'd like. Should we invite over the guests?"

Engineer garnished the plates with blackberry thorns and a swizzle of engine oil curling into the shape of a cat's paw. "Please do. Seat them where you can find space. Dinner will be up in just a moment."

A marine in black body armor with a military-issue blaster holstered at her hip climbed down the ladder into the engine room. The first human. The first customer.

Engineer presented a glass of Navi's brains chilled and rolled in crushed blackberries. "Please try this. Organic compounds, chemically mixed to satisfy your human chemoreceptors." She offered the dish daintily, with only four hands.

The human wrinkled her nose. "Ugh, the smell! How do you tolerate it?"

Friendly's voice came from higher up. "When you're here long enough, you get used to it."

"I am certain upon tasting this dish, you will find it worthy of all five of your stars," said Engineer fervently.

The human touched a button on her armor and spoke. Her meat quivered all over, and her meat-voice wavered in frequency and volume. "Send a full security detail down here. Immediately."

Friendly descended the ladder. Under her arm she carried Captain's processor, cold and silent, one lonely light blinking, receiving data but not sending anything. "I was afraid she would eat me next," she muttered, her tear ducts pumping out fluids. Engineer wondered whether they would make a decent sauce.

"Glad someone made it out alive, anyway," said the human. "Six whole weeks trapped with a crew of deranged cyborgs?" She gave a low whistle. "You're a braver woman than I."

"Please," said Engineer, desperate, "taste it. Just one bite. I worked so hard."

"I don't know if her meat drove her mad, or if the steel did," said Friendly.

"Meat?" asked the human.

"The organic parts, I mean."

"Probably a glitch in her wiring," the human said dismissively. "There is a reason they're discontinuing these models."

The humans flooded into the ship with their funny uneven meat-steps and their lopsided meat-faces and their ever-beating hearts that rang against their bones like clubs on steel. Engineer offered them her best delicacies—the liquefied kidney paste tossed with raw pasta, the origami meat-birds swirled in cinnamon and canned cheese, the wearable fungus bracelets threaded on intestine casings—but they only knocked the dishes away, stunned her with targeted EMP blasts, and bound her in cybernetic locks until she lay prone on the meat-slicked floor.

One of the humans began unscrewing Engineer's fingers joint by joint. It didn't hurt at all, much to her surprise. The bits lay piled like little silver walnuts, the discarded stones of plums. Stringy meat trailed out from her missing fingers, no more than an appetizer's worth.

"Where are you taking my steel?" asked Engineer. They flaunted their ingratitude. You were supposed to let the steel be. Otherwise they couldn't build and build you again.

The human dethreaded the wires connecting Engineer's arm meat to her cyborg logic center. "It will be repurposed for whatever is most needed. Ships, chips, knives, bolts, screws. Useful things."

"And the meat?"

The human decoupled the segmented joints of her shoulder. Without the steel exoskeleton for support, Engineer's meat hung limp and dripped red. "You can keep it. We don't have a use for it."

"But there are," said Engineer. "So many uses," and her voice faded as they stripped away the connections, "if you would just give me a moment to demonstrate."

Tiny, desperate meat-thoughts bombarded her logic center like cold fingers plucking at tendons. Last shooting pleas from stringy muscles in her steel, unseen servants in the wall, shouting that Engineer had been a fool. There was never any honor in service, no final star to complete a constellation. You offered yourself up for consumption, and when they had eaten you down to the bone, they stole again. Stole your heart, your steel, your everything, to use as forks in their restaurants.

GWENDOLYN CLARE

Tasting Notes on the Varietals of the Southern Coast

FROM *The Magazine of Fantasy & Science Fiction*

THE FRUIT OF Hasam hang from the vine like holiday baubles, fat firm globes of midnight blue. I expected a deep inky color and strong tannins even before the legionaries found the vintner's aging cavern. Indeed, when they broke inside and fetched me a bottle, it looked as thick and dark as cloth dye in the glass. The finish stretched long, bitter-dry with a hint of clove spice, as if reluctant to depart.

We moved on to the town of Shom this morning. Here the grapes have the polished luminescence of cabochon rubies. Last year's harvest, now aging in the barrels, is bright and sharp on the tongue, with clumsy overtones of citrus and a quick finish. The three-year bottle has mellowed and matured, but I still find it somewhat lacking in body.

I cannot help but ponder what a very fine mix these two varietals would have made together, if only their respective vintners had consented to trade portions of their harvests. But this was never the way of Qati vintners; they were a proud people, the Qati, too proud for such compromises.

In Rambekh there is a body floating in the mashing vat—gray and bloated and utterly disgusting, though I could not say whether from the plague itself or the putrefaction after death. Such a waste, eighty or ninety gallons in total, all of it ruined. The whole harvest from the west-facing slopes above the city, if I had to guess.

It comes as a consolation when I discover their early harvest red is nothing special anyway. Their late harvest white is by far their finer achievement—sweet as an overripe peach, with subtle mineral undertones and a lemon finish that lingers on the tongue.

Thank the gods the late harvest fruit is still ripening on the vine, all across the unsullied expanse of the east-facing slope. The grapes cluster together like nests of tiny quail eggs, with thin but firm blush-colored skins. A different varietal altogether from what they used in the early harvest red.

Centurion Vikas is reluctant to lend me a messenger, but I insist it cannot wait until the survey is complete. I am sending word to the capital to request that vintners be assigned to Rambekh immediately. I shudder to think of the emperor's rage were we to lose this autumn's precious yield.

When we arrived in Tomaq, we found the streets clogged with corpses. Apparently the plague spread too fast here, and the population had no time to bury their dead. Now the legionaries must clear the streets, or else drag the war machines through the roadless hill country south of the town. I gather there is some concern about the prospect of broken axles, and I must confess I'd worry about the wine carts if the horses were to be led off-road.

Still, they've been throwing corpses on the pyres all morning, and the whole town reeks of charred, spoiled meat. The stench has put off my palate quite thoroughly, and the air is so thick with smoke I'll be surprised if the late harvest fruit doesn't wither on the vine. Words cannot describe my vexation.

But no, I mustn't complain. It is a stroke of the finest fortune that our beloved emperor has such passion for the vinifying arts. The emperor honors me with his patronage, and with this assignment especially.

We hit a road mine on our way out of Ghitam, and now the legion's stuck here until we can send for a stonemage to check the road ahead.

I'm told the Qati designed the mines to trigger under heavy weight, intending them for war machines. But of course with my luck the wheel that rolled atop the mine belonged to a full-laden wine cart.

It was a distressing sight. One legionary died instantly with a splash of stonemelt to the face; another only got the stuff on his feet, so the medician hacked him off at the knees and dragged him away. But three other legionaries and both cart horses were instantly and irreparably mired in the creeping gray goo. And the wine cart! Centurion Vikas would let his men rescue only four of the wine barrels, refusing to "endanger" them further.

Among the losses were two crates of a rare and lovely bottled white from Taranekh. Off-dry and softly effervescent with a tang of green apple. When eaten with a sharp, aged cheese, it truly blossomed in complexity, drawing out the undertones of white pepper, vanilla, and herb. Perhaps it would be best not to report this loss to the emperor; long has he envied the wineries of Taranekh.

After the initial splatter, the stonemelt spreads slowly. It's still spreading now; I cannot hear the legionaries pleading for a quicker death over the noise of the horses screaming. The sound makes my head ache and I long for silence, but no one dares silence them. When it's done, the emperor will want to add the afflicted—legionaries and horses both—to his stonemelt statue collection. So they'll keep screaming until the stonemelt crawls into their mouths and clogs their throats.

I try my best to focus on my work—to leave the politics to the emperor's advisers and the strategy to his centurions. But how am I supposed to work under such conditions?

By the time we arrive at the city of Arakesh, the forward legion has already barricaded the gates from the outside. The plague is at work within, and a panicked mob pounds on the eastern gate, trying to escape. The centurion from the forward legion who greets us does not seem especially concerned about the situation, though.

I suppose, even if they broke through, a crowd of sick civilians isn't much of a match for two legions of well-trained foot soldiers and their accompanying war machines. This is the advantage of a well-made plague—the last of the Qati will die, sooner or later, while the emperor's soldiers remain untouched. The outcome is inevitable.

But I'll let the forward legion worry about those details. The main winery of Arakesh is up in the terraced hills above the city, so I do not have to wait for them to finish with the purge before beginning my work.

*

No one bothered to tell me the breathmage would be waiting for me at the winery. Centurion Vikas warns me to be polite and accommodating with him. I am a master vintner, not a palace hostess. One more in a long list of indignities I have endured on this campaign.

The breathmage is an odd man—sharp and terse one minute, then dazed and distractible the next. He says he wants to see what all the fuss is about, so we sit on the patio in front of the mash house and I pour him a selection of the southern coast's best.

I praise the subtle nose of a six-year Arakesh white—hazelnut and anise with a hint of wild jasmine—and the breathmage sniffs dutifully at his glass before tasting but offers no commentary of his own. He does the same with the late harvest Rambekh, and again with a full-bodied Ghitam red. Can he feel those velvet-smooth tannins against his palate? If so, he gives no sign of it.

His silence disconcerts me. Whenever I stop speaking, each long pause becomes filled with the distant muffled screams of dying Arakeshi, carried up to us on the ocean breeze. A fire has broken out in the northeast quadrant of the city, and the column of smoke obscures our view of the water. I keep my own eyes on the wine, ready to pour the next tasting as soon as our glasses are empty, but the breathmage gazes into the distance.

The legionaries assigned to guard us have made themselves scarce. They're afraid of him. No one has said as much, but I suspect this is not just any breathmage but the Master of Plague himself—the artisan of this whole campaign. He who created the Qati disease.

I cannot tell if my efforts at hospitality have pleased him. As he seems unmoved by the wine itself, I try drawing his attention to the fine work of the glassmage who crafted these Arakesh bottles. Yet even this subject elicits little response, so what can I do but keep pouring?

When he speaks, it is not to discuss the campaign or the wine or the glasswork. He tells me of his family in the capital—his three sisters and their husbands and sister-wives, his nieces and nephews. He stares out across the wreckage of Arakesh and sees their faces. At least they will live in comfort, he says. At least they are safe.

I do not know what to say to this. The emperor rewards service and punishes disobedience, as is his divine right. The breathmage understands this better than most, I suspect.

So I say nothing, and I pour him a sweet Arakesh red. Blackberry and dark plum bursting over gentle earthiness, balanced with a long acid finish.

Sometime in the night, the breathmage filled his pockets with stones and drowned himself in the mashing vat. By the time we find his body, the pigment from the grape skins has dyed his clothes and face and hands a livid purple-red.

To be honest, I'm not convinced this was worth it, purging the Qati just to acquire their vineyards.

Don't ever tell the emperor I said so.

CHARLIE JANE ANDERS

Don't Press Charges and I Won't Sue

FROM *Boston Review: Global Dystopias*

THE INTAKE PROCESS begins with dismantling her personal space, one mantle at a time. Her shoes, left by the side of the road where the Go Team plucked her out of them. Her purse and satchel, her computer containing all of her artwork and her manifestos, thrown into a metal garbage can at a rest area on the highway, miles away. That purse, which she swung to and fro on the sidewalks to clear a path, like a southern grandma, now has food waste piled on it, and eventually will be chewed to shreds by raccoons. At some point the intake personnel fold her, like a folding chair that turns into an almost two-dimensional object, and they stuff her into a kennel, in spite of all her attempts to resist. Later she receives her first injection and loses any power to struggle, and some time after, control over her excretory functions. By the time they cut her clothes off, a layer of muck coats the backs of her thighs. They clean her and dress her in something that is not clothing, and they shave part of her head. At some point Rachel glimpses a power drill, like a handyman's, but she's anesthetized and does not feel where it goes.

Rachel has a whole library of ways to get through this, none of which work at all. She spent a couple years meditating, did a whole course on trauma and self-preservation, and had an elaborate theory about how to carve out a space in your mind that *they* cannot touch, whatever *they* are doing to you. She remembers the things she used to tell everyone else in the support group, in the Safe Space, about not being alone even when you have become isolated by outside circumstances. But in the end Rachel's only coping mechanism is dissociation, which arises from total animal panic. She's not even Rachel anymore, she's just a screaming blubbering mess, with a tiny kernel of her mind left, trapped a few feet above her body, in a process that is not at all like yogic flying.

Eventually, though, the intake is concluded, and Rachel is left staring up at a Styrofoam ceiling with a pattern of cracks that looks like a giant spider or an angry demon face descending toward her. She's aware of being numb from extreme cold in addition to the other ways in which she is numb, and the air conditioner keeps blurting into life with an aggravated whine. A stereo system plays a CD by that white rock-rap artist who turned out to be an especially stupid racist. The staff keep walking past her and talking about her in the third person, while misrepresenting basic facts about her, such as her name and her personal pronoun. Occasionally they adjust something about her position or drug regimen without speaking to her or looking at her face. She does not quite have enough motor control to scream or make any sound other than a kind of low ululation. She realizes at some point that someone has made a tiny hole in the base of her skull, where she now feels a mild ache.

Before you feel too sorry for Rachel, however, you should be aware that she's a person who holds a great many controversial views. For example, she once claimed to disapprove of hot chocolate, because she believes that chocolate is better at room temperature, or better yet as a component of ice cream or some other frozen dessert. In addition, Rachel considers ZZ Top an underappreciated music group, supports karaoke only in an alcohol-free environment, dislikes puppies, enjoys Brussels sprouts, and rides a bicycle with no helmet. She claims to prefer the *Star Wars* prequels to the Disney *Star Wars* films. Is Rachel a contrarian, a freethinker, or just kind of an asshole? If you could ask her, she would reply that opinions are a utility in and of themselves. That is, the holding of opinions is a worthwhile exercise per se, and the greater diversity of opinions in the world, the more robust our collective ability to argue.

Also! Rachel once got a gas station attendant nearly fired for behavior that, a year or two later, she finally conceded might have been an honest misunderstanding. She's the kind of person who sends food back for not being quite what she ordered—and on at least two occasions she did this and then returned to that same restaurant a week or two later, as if she had been happy after all. Rachel is the kind of person who calls herself an artist despite never having received a grant from a granting institution or any kind of formal gallery show, and many people wouldn't even consider her collages and relief maps of imaginary places to be proper art. You would probably call Rachel a Goth.

Besides dissociation—which is wearing off as the panic subsides—the one defense mechanism that remains for Rachel is carrying on an imaginary conversation with Dev, the person with whom she spoke every day for so long, and to whom she always imagined speaking whenever they were apart. Dev's voice in Rachel's head would have been a refuge not long ago, but now all Rachel can imagine Dev saying is, *Why did you leave me? Why, when I needed you most?* Rachel does not have a good answer to that question, which is why she never tried to answer it when she had the chance.

Thinking about Dev, about lost chances, is too much. And at that moment Rachel realizes she has enough muscle control to lift her head and look directly in front of her. There, standing at an observation window, she sees her childhood best friend, Jeffrey.

Ask Jeffrey why he's been working at Love and Dignity for Everyone for the past few years and he'll say, first and foremost, student loans. Plus, in recent years, child support and his mother's ever-increasing medical bills. Life is crammed full of things that you have to pay for after the fact, and the word *plan* in *payment plan* is a cruel mockery, because nobody ever really sets out to plunge into chronic debt. But also Jeffrey wants to believe in the mission of Love and Dignity for Everyone: to repair the world's most broken people. Jeffrey often rereads the mission statement on the wall of the employee lounge as he sips his morning Keurig so he can carry Mr. Randall's words with him for the rest of the day. Society depends on mutual respect, Mr. Randall says. You respect yourself and therefore I respect you, and vice versa. When people won't respect themselves, we have no choice but to intervene, or society unravels. Role-rejecting and aberrant behavior, ipso facto, are a sign of a lack of self-respect. Indeed, a cry for help. The logic always snaps back into airtight shape inside Jeffrey's mind.

Of course Jeffrey recognizes Rachel the moment he sees her wheeled into the treatment room, even after all this time and so many changes, because he's been Facebook-stalking her for years (usually after a couple of whiskey sours). He saw when she changed her name and her gender marker, and noticed when her hairstyle changed and when her face suddenly had a more feminine shape. There was the kitten she adopted that later ran away, and the thorny tattoo that says STAY ALIVE. Jeffrey read all her oversharing status updates about the pain of hair removal and the side effects of various pills. And then, of course, the crowning surgery. Jeffrey lived through this process vicariously, in real time, and saw no resemblance to a butterfly in a cocoon or any other cute metaphor. The gender change looked more like landscaping: building embankments out of raw dirt, heaving big rocks to change the course of rivers, and uprooting plants stem by stem. Dirty bruising work. Why a person would feel the need to do this to themself, Jeffrey could never know.

At first Jeffrey pretends not to know the latest subject, or to have any feelings one way or the other, as the Accu-Probe goes into the back of her head. This is not the right moment to have a sudden conflict. Due to some recent personnel issues, Jeffrey is stuck wearing a project manager hat along with his engineer hat—which, sadly, is not a cool pinstriped train-engineer hat of the sort that he and Rachel used to fantasize about wearing for work when they were kids. As a project manager, he has to worry endlessly about weird details such as getting enough coolant into the cadaver storage area and making sure that Jamil has the green shakes that he says activate his brain. As a government-industry joint venture under Section 1774(b)(8) of the Mental Health Restoration Act (relating to the care and normalization of at-risk individuals), Love and Dignity for Everyone has to meet certain benchmarks of effectiveness, and must involve the community in a meaningful role. Jeffrey is trying to keep twenty fresh cadavers in transplant-ready condition, and clearing the decks for more live subjects, who are coming down the pike at an ever-snowballing rate. The situation resembles one of those poultry processing plants where they keep speeding up the conveyer belt until the person grappling with each chicken ends up losing a few fingers.

Jeffrey runs from the cadaver freezer to the observation room to the main conference room for another community engagement session, around and around, until his Fitbit applauds. Five different Slack channels flare at once with people wanting to ask Jeffrey process questions, and he's lost count of all his unanswered DMs. Everyone agrees on the goal—returning healthy, well-adjusted individuals to society without any trace of dysphoria, dysmorphia, dystonia, or any other *dys-* words—but nobody can agree on the fine details, or how exactly to measure ideal outcomes beyond those statutory benchmarks. Who even is the person who comes out the other end of the Love and Dignity for Everyone process? What does it mean to be a unique individual, in an age when your fingerprints and retina scans have long since been stolen by Ecuadorian hackers? It's all too easy to get sucked into metaphysical flusterclucks about identity and the soul and what makes you you.

Jeffrey's near-daily migraine is already in full flower by the time he sees Rachel wheeled in and he can't bring himself to look. She's looking at him. She's looking right at him. Even with all the other changes, her eyes are the same, and he can't just stand here. She's putting him in an impossible position, at the worst moment.

Someone has programmed Slack so that when anyone types "alrighty then," a borderline-obscene GIF of two girls wearing clown makeup appears. Jeffrey is the only person who ever types "alrighty then," and he can't train himself to stop doing it. And, of course, he hasn't been able to figure out who programmed the GIF to appear.

Self-respect is the key to mutual respect. Jeffrey avoids making eye contact with that window or anyone beyond it. His head still feels too heavy with pain for a normal body to support, but also he's increasingly aware of a core-deep anxiety shading into nausea.

Jeffrey and Rachel had a group, from the tail end of elementary school through to the first year of high school, called the Sock Society. They all lived in the same cul-de-sac, bounded by a canola field on one side and the big interstate on the other. The origins of the Sock Society's name are lost to history, but may arise from the fact that Jeffrey's mom never liked kids to wear shoes inside the house and Jeffrey's house had the best game consoles and a 4K TV with surround sound. These kids wore out countless pairs of tires on their dirt bikes, conquered the extra DLC levels in Halls of Valor, and built snow forts that gleamed. They stayed up all night at sleepovers watching forbidden horror movies on an old laptop under a blanket while guzzling off-brand soda. They whispered, late at night, of their fantasies and barely-hinted-at anxieties, although there were some things Rachel would not share because she was not ready to speak of them and Jeffrey would not have been able to hear if she had. They repeated jokes they didn't 100 percent understand, and kind of enjoyed the queasy awareness of being out of their depth. Later the members of the Sock Society (which changed its ranks over time, with the exception of the core members, Rachel and Jeffrey) became adept at stuffing gym socks with blasting caps and small incendiaries and fashioning the socks themselves into rudimentary fuses before placing them in lawn ornaments, small receptacles for gardening tools, and—in one incident that nobody discussed afterward—Mrs. Hooper's scooter.

When Jeffrey's mother was drunk, which was often, she would say she wished Rachel was her son, because Rachel was such a smart boy—quick on the uptake, so charming with the rapid-fire puns, handsome and respectful. Like Young Elvis. Instead of Jeffrey, who was honestly a little shit.

Jeffrey couldn't wait to get over the wall of adolescence, into the garden of manhood. Every dusting of fuzz on his chin, every pungent whiff from his armpits seemed to him the starting gun. He became obsessed with finding porn via that old laptop, and he was an artist at coming up with fresh new search terms every time he and Rachel hung out. Rachel got used to innocent terms such as *cream pie* turning out to mean something gross and animalistic, in much the same way that a horror movie turned human bodies into slippery meat.

Then one time Jeffrey pulled up some transsexual porn, because what the hell. Rachel found herself watching a slender Latina with a shy smile slowly peel out of a silk robe to step into a scene with a muscular bald man. The girl was wearing nothing but bright silver shoes, and her body was all smooth angles and tapering limbs, and the one piece of evidence of her transgender status looked tiny, both inconsequential and of a piece with the rest of her femininity. She tiptoed across the frame like a ballerina. Like a cartoon deer.

Watching this, Rachel quivered, until Jeffrey thought she must be grossed out, but deep down Rachel was having a feeling of recognition. Like: That's me. Like: I am possible.

Years later, in her twenties, Rachel had a group of girlfriends (some trans, some cis), and she started calling this feminist gang the Sock Society, because they made a big thing of wearing colorful socks with weird and sometimes profane patterns. Rachel mostly didn't think about the fact that she had repurposed the Sock Society sobriquet for another group, except to tell herself that she was reclaiming an ugly part of her past. Rachel is someone who obsesses about random issues but also claims to avoid introspection at all costs—in fact, she once proposed an art show called *The Unexamined Life Is the Only Way to Have Fun.*

Rachel has soiled herself again. A woman in avocado-colored scrubs snaps on blue gloves with theatrical weariness before sponging Rachel's still-unfeeling body. The things I have to deal with, says the red-faced woman, whose name is Lucy. People like you always make people like me clean up after you, because you never think the rules apply to you, the same as literally everyone else. And then look where we end up, and I'm here cleaning your mess.

Rachel tries to protest that none of this is her doing, but her tongue is a slug that's been bathed in salt.

There's always some excuse, Lucy says as she scrubs. Life is not complicated, it's actually very simple. Men are men, and women are women, and everyone has a role to play. It's selfish to think that you can just force everyone else in the world to start carving out exceptions, just so you can play at being something you're not. You will never understand what it really means to be female, the joy and the endless discomfort, because you were not born into it.

Rachel feels frozen solid. Ice crystals permeate her body, the way they would frozen dirt. This woman is touching between her legs without looking her in the face. She cannot bear to breathe. She keeps trying to get Jeffrey's attention, but he always looks away. As if he'd rather not witness what's going to happen to her.

Lucy and a man in scrubs wheel in something gauzy and white, like a cloud on a gurney. They bustle around, unwrapping and cleaning and prepping, and they mutter numbers and codes to each other, like E-drop 2347, as if there are a lot of parameters to keep straight here. The sound of all that quiet professionalism soothes Rachel in spite of herself, like she's at the dentist.

At some point they step away from the thing they've unwrapped and prepped, and Rachel turns her head just enough to see a dead man on a metal shelf.

Her first thought is that he's weirdly good-looking, despite his slight decomposition. He has a snub nose and thin lips, a clipped jaw, good muscle definition, a cyanotic penis that flops against one thigh, and sandy pubic hair. Whatever (whoever) killed this man left his body in good condition, and he was roughly Rachel's age. This man could have been a model or maybe a pro wrestler, and

Rachel feels sad that he somehow died so early, with his best years ahead.

Rachel tries to scream. She feels Lucy and the other one connecting her to the dead man's body and hears a rattling garbage-disposal sound. The dead man twitches, and meanwhile Rachel can't struggle or make a sound. She feels weaker than before, and some part of her insists this must be because she lost an argument at some point. Back in the Safe Space, they had talked about all the friends of friends who had gone to ground, and the internet rumors. How would you know if you were in danger? Rachel had said that was a dumb question, because danger never left.

The dead man smiles: not a large rictus, like in a horror movie, but a tiny shift in his features, like a contented sleeper. His eyes haven't moved or appeared to look at anything. Lucy clucks and adjusts a thing, and the kitchen-garbage noise grinds louder for a moment.

We're going to get you sorted out, Lucy says to the dead man. You are going to be so happy. She turns and leans over Rachel to check something, and her breath smells like sour corn chips.

You are violating my civil rights by keeping me here, Rachel says. A sudden victory, except that then she hears herself and it's wrong. Her voice comes out of the wrong mouth, is not even her own voice. The dead man has spoken, not her, and he didn't say that thing about civil rights. Instead he said, Hey, excuse me, how long am I going to be kept here? As if this were a mild inconvenience keeping him from his business. The voice sounded rough, flinty, like a bad sore throat, but also commanding. The voice of a surgeon, or an airline pilot. You would stop whatever you were doing and listen if you heard that voice.

Rachel lets out an involuntary cry of panic, which comes out of the dead man's mouth as a low groan. She tries again to say, This is not medicine. This is a human rights violation. And it comes out of the dead man's mouth as I don't mean to be a jerk. I just have things to do, you know. Sorry if I'm causing any trouble.

That's quite all right, Mr. Billings, Lucy says. You're making tremendous progress, and we're so pleased. You'll be released into the community soon, and the community will be so happy to see you.

The thought of ever trying to speak again fills Rachel with a whole ocean voyage's worth of nausea, but she can't even make herself retch.

*

Jeffrey has wondered for years, what if he could talk to his oldest friend, man to man, about the things that had happened when they were on the cusp of adolescence—not just the girl, but the whole deal. Mrs. Hooper's scooter, even. And maybe, at last, he will. A lot depends on how well the process goes. Sometimes the cadaver gets almost all of the subject's memories and personality, just with a better outlook on his or her proper gender. There is, however, a huge variability in bandwidth, because we're dealing with human beings and especially with weird neurological stuff that we barely understand. We're trying to thread wet spaghetti through a grease trap, a dozen pieces at a time. Even with the proprietary cocktail, it's hardly an exact science.

The engineer part of Jeffrey just wants to keep the machines from making whatever noise that was earlier, the awful grinding sound. But the project manager part of Jeffrey is obsessing about all of the extraneous factors outside his control. What if they get a surprise inspection from the secretary, or even worse, that deputy assistant secretary with the eye? Jeffrey is not supposed to be a front-facing part of this operation, but Mr. Randall says we all do things that are outside our comfort zones, and really, that's the only way your comfort zone can ever expand. In addition, Jeffrey is late for another stakeholder meeting, with the woman from Mothers Raising Well-Adjusted Children and the three bald men from Grassroots Rising, who will tear Jeffrey a new orifice. There are still too many maladjusted individuals out there, in the world, trying to use public bathrooms and putting our children at risk. Some children, too, keep insisting that they aren't boys or girls because they saw some ex-athlete prancing on television. Twenty cadavers in the freezer might as well be nothing in the face of all this. The three bald men will take turns spit-shouting, using words such as *psychosexual,* and Jeffrey has fantasized about sneaking bourbon into his coffee so he can drink whenever that word comes up. He's pretty sure they don't know what *psychosexual* even means, except that it's psycho and it's sexual. After a stakeholder meeting, Jeffrey always retreats to the single-stall men's room to shout at his own schmutzy reflection. Fuck you, you fucking fuck fucker. Don't tell me I'm not doing my job.

Self-respect is the key to mutual respect.

Rachel keeps looking straight at Jeffrey through the observation

window, and she's somehow kept control over her vision long after
her speech centers went over. He keeps waiting for her to lose the
eyes. Her gaze goes right into him, and his stomach gets the feeling
that usually comes after two or three whiskey sours and no dinner.

More than ever, Jeffrey wishes the observation room had a one-
way mirror instead of regular glass. Why would they skimp on that?
What's the point of having an observation room where you are also
being observed at the same time? It defeats the entire purpose.

Jeffrey gets tired of hiding from his own window and skips out
the side door. He climbs two stories of cement stairs to emerge in
the executive wing, near the conference suite where he's supposed
to be meeting with the stakeholders right now. He finds an oaken
door with that quote from Albert Einstein about imagination
that everybody always has and knocks on it. After a few breaths, a
deep voice tells Jeffrey to come in, and then he's sitting opposite
an older man with square shoulders and a perfect old-fashioned
newscaster head.

Mr. Randall, Jeffrey says, I'm afraid I have a conflict with regards to the latest subject and I must ask to be recused.

Is that a fact? Mr. Randall furrows his entire face for a moment,
then magically all the wrinkles disappear again. He smiles and
shakes his head. I feel you, Jeffrey, I really do. That blows chunks.
Unfortunately, as you know, we are short-staffed right now, and our
work is of a nature that only a few people have the skills and moral
virtue to complete it.

But, Jeffrey says. The new subject, he's someone I grew up with,
and there are certain . . . I mean, I made promises when we were
little, and it feels in some ways like I'm breaking those promises,
even as I try my best to help him. I actually feel physically ill, like
drunk in my stomach but sober in my brain, when I look at him.

Jeffrey, Mr. Randall says, Jeffrey, JEFFREY. Listen to me. Sit still
and listen. Pull yourself together. We are the watchers on the bat-
tlements, at the edge of social collapse, like in that show with the
ice zombies, where winter is always tomorrow. You know that show?
They had an important message, that sometimes we have to put
our own personal feelings aside for the greater good. Remember
the fat kid? He had to learn to be a team player. I loved that show.
So here we are, standing against the darkness that threatens to
consume everything we admire. No time for divided hearts.

I know that we're doing something important here, and that he'll thank me later, Jeffrey says. It's just hard right now.

If it were easy to do the right thing, Randall says, then everyone would do it.

Sherri was a transfer student in tenth grade who came right in and joined the Computer Club but also tried out for the volleyball team and the a cappella chorus. She had dark hair in tight braids and a wiry body that flexed in the moment before she leapt to spike the ball, making Rachel's heart rise with her. Rachel sat courtside and watched Sherri practice while she was supposed to be doing sudden-death sprints.

Jeffrey stared at Sherri too: listened to her sing Janelle Monáe in a light contralto when she waited for the bus, and gazed at her across the room during Computer Club. He imagined going up to her and just introducing himself, but his heart was too weak. He could more easily imagine saying the dumbest thing, or actually fainting, than carrying on a smooth conversation with Sherri. He obsessed for ages, until he finally confessed to his friends (Rachel was long since out of the picture by this time), and they started goading him, actually physically shoving him, to speak to Sherri.

Jeffrey slid up to her and said his name, and something inane about music, and then Sherri just stared at him for a long time before saying, I gotta get the bus. Jeffrey watched her walk away, then turned to his watching friends and mimed a finger gun blowing his brains out.

A few days later Sherri was playing hooky at that one bakery café in town that everyone said was run by lesbians or drug addicts or maybe just old hippies, nursing a chai latte, and she found herself sitting with Rachel, who was also ditching some activity. Neither of them wanted to talk to anyone, they'd come here to be alone. But Rachel felt hope rise up inside her at the proximity of her wildfire crush, and she finally hoisted her bag as if she might just leave the café. Mind if I sit with you a minute, she asked, and Sherri shrugged yes. So Rachel perched on the embroidered tasseled pillow on the bench next to Sherri and stared at her Algebra II book.

They saw each other at that café every few days, or sometimes just once a week, and they just started sitting together on purpose, without talking to each other much. After a couple months of this,

Sherri looked at the time on her phone and said, My mom's out of town. I'll buy you dinner. Rachel kept her shriek of joy on the inside and just nodded.

At dinner—a family pasta place nearby—Sherri looked down at her colorful paper napkin and whispered, I think I don't like boys. I mean, to date, or whatever. I don't hate boys or anything, just not interested that way. You understand.

Rachel stared at Sherri, even after she looked up, so they were making eye contact. In just as low a whisper, Rachel replied, I'm pretty sure I'm not a boy.

This was the first time Rachel ever said the name Rachel aloud, at least with regard to herself.

Sherri didn't laugh or get up or run away. She just stared back, then nodded. She reached onto the red checkerboard vinyl tablecloth with an open palm, for Rachel to insert her palm into if she so chose.

The first time Jeffrey saw Rachel and Sherri holding hands, he looked at them like his soul had come out in bruises.

We won't keep you here too long, Mr. Billings, the male attendant says, glancing at Rachel but mostly looking at the mouth that had spoken. You're doing very well. Really, you're an exemplary subject. You should be so proud.

There are so many things that Rachel wants to say. Like: Please just let me go, I have a life. I have an art show coming up in a coffee shop, I can't miss it. You don't have the right. I deserve to live my own life. I have people who used to love me. I'll give you everything I own. I won't press charges if you don't sue. This is no kind of therapy. On and on. But she can't trust that corpse voice. She hyperventilates and gags on her own spit. So sore she's hamstrung.

Every time her eyes get washed out, she's terrified this is it, her last sight. She knows from what Lucy and the other one have said that if her vision switches over to the dead man's, that's the final stage and she's gone.

The man is still talking. We have a form signed by your primary-care physician, Dr. Wallace, stating that this treatment is both urgent and medically indicated, as well as an assessment by our in-house psychologist, Dr. Yukizawa. He holds up two pieces of paper, with the looping scrawls of two different doctors that she's never even heard of. She's been seeing Dr. Cummings for years, since before her transition. She makes a huge effort to shake her head and is shocked by how weak she feels.

You are so fortunate to be one of the first to receive this treatment, the man says. Early indications are that subjects experience a profound improvement across seven different measures of quality of life and social integration. Their OGATH scores are generally high, especially in the red levels. Rejection is basically unheard of. You won't believe how good you'll feel once you're over the adjustment period, he says. If the research goes well, the potential benefits to society are limited only by the cadaver pipeline.

Rachel's upcoming art show, in a tiny coffee shop, is called "Against Curation." There's a lengthy manifesto, which Rachel planned to print out and mount onto foam or cardboard, claiming that the act of curating is inimical to art or artistry. The only person who can create a proper context for a given piece of art is the artist herself, and arranging someone else's art is an act of violence. Bear in mind that the history of museums is intrinsically tied up with imperialism and colonialism, and the curatorial gaze is historically white and male. But even the most enlightened postcolonial curator is a pirate. Anthologies, mix tapes, it's all the same. Rachel had a long response prepared, in case anybody accused her of just being annoyed that no real gallery would display her work.

Rachel can't help noting the irony of writing a tirade about the curator's bloody scalpel, only to end up with a hole in her literal head.

When the man has left her alone, Rachel begins screaming Jeffrey's name in the dead man's voice. Just the name, nothing that the corpse could twist. She still can't bear to hear that deep timbre, the sick damaged throat, speaking for her. But she can feel her life essence slipping away. Every time she looks over at the dead man, he has more color in his skin and his arms and legs are moving, like a restless sleeper. His face even looks, in some hard-to-define way, more like Rachel's.

Jeffrey! The words come out in a hoarse growl. Jeffrey! Come here!

Rachel wants to believe she's already defeated this trap, because she has lived her life without a single codicil, and whatever they do, they can't retroactively change the person she has been for her entire adulthood. But that doesn't feel like enough. She wants the kind of victory where she gets to actually walk out of here.

*

Jeffrey feels a horrible twist in his neck. This is all unfair, because he already informed Mr. Randall of his conflict and yet he's still here, having to behave professionally while the subject is putting him in the dead center of attention.

Seriously, the subject will not stop bellowing his name, even with a throat that's basically raw membrane at this point. You're not supposed to initiate communication with the subject without submitting an Interlocution Permission form through the proper channels. But the subject is putting him into an impossible position.

Jeffrey, she keeps shouting. And then: Jeffrey, talk to me!

People are lobbing questions in Slack, and of course Jeffrey types the wrong thing and the softcore clown porn comes up. Ha ha, I fell for it again, he types. There's a problem with one of the latest cadavers, a cause-of-death question, and Mr. Randall says the deputy assistant secretary might be in town later.

Jeffrey's mother was a Nobel Prize winner for her work with people who had lost the ability to distinguish between weapons and musical instruments, a condition that frequently leads to maiming or worse. Jeffrey's earliest memories involve his mother flying off to serve as an expert witness in the trials of murderers who claimed they had thought their assault rifles were banjos or mandolins. Many of these people were faking it, but Jeffrey's mom was usually hired by the defense, not the prosecution. Every time she returned from one of these trips, she would fling her Nobel medal out her bathroom window and then stay up half the night searching the bushes for it, becoming increasingly drunk. One morning Jeffrey found her passed out below her bedroom window and believed for a moment that she had fallen two stories to her death. This was, she explained to him later, a different sort of misunderstanding than mistaking a gun for a guitar: a reverse-Oedipal misapprehension. These days Jeffrey's mom requires assistance to dress, to shower, and to transit from her bed to a chair and back, and nobody can get Medicare, Medicaid, or any secondary insurance to pay for this. To save money, Jeffrey has moved back in with his mother, which means he gets to hear her ask at least once a week what happened to Rachel, who was such a nice boy.

Jeffrey can't find his headphones to drown out his name, which the cadaver is shouting so loud that foam comes out of one corner of his mouth. Frances and another engineer both complain on Slack about the noise, which they can hear from down the hall. OMG creepy, Frances types. Make it stop make it stop.

I can't, Jeffrey types back. I can't ok. I don't have the right paperwork.

Maybe tomorrow Rachel will wake up fully inhabiting her male body. She'll look down at her strong forearms, threaded with veins, and she'll smile and thank Jeffrey. Maybe she'll nod at him, by way of a tiny salute, and say, You did it, buddy. You brought me back.

But right now the cadaver keeps shouting, and Jeffrey realizes he's covering his ears with his fists and is doubled over.

Rachel apparently decides that Jeffrey's name alone isn't working. The cadaver pauses and then blurts, I would really love to hang with you. Hey! I appreciate everything you've done to set things right. JEFFREY! You really shouldn't have gone to so much trouble for me.

Somehow these statements have an edge, like Jeffrey can easily hear the intended meaning. He looks up and sees Rachel's eyes, spraying tears like a damn lawn sprinkler.

Jeffrey, the corpse says, I saw Sherri. She told me the truth about you.

She's probably just making things up. Sherri never knew anything for sure, or at least couldn't prove anything. And yet just the mention of her name is enough to make Jeffrey straighten up and walk to the door of the observation room, even with no signed Interlocution Permission form. Jeffrey makes himself stride up to the two nearly naked bodies and stop at the one on the left, the one with the ugly tattoo and the drooling silent mouth.

I don't want to hurt you, Jeffrey says. I never wanted to hurt you, even when we were kids and you got weird on me. My mom still asks about you.

Hey pal, you've never been a better friend to me than you are right now, the cadaver says. But on the left, the eyes are red and wet and full of violence.

What did Sherri say? Stop playing games and tell me, Jeffrey says. When did you see her? What did she say?

But Rachel has stopped trying to make the other body talk and is just staring up, letting her eyes speak for her.

Listen, Jeffrey says to the tattooed body. This is already over, the process is too advanced. I could disconnect all of the machines, unplug the tap from your occipital lobe and everything, and the cadaver would continue drawing your remaining life energy. The link between you is already stable. This project, it's a government-industry collaboration, we call it Love and Dignity for Everyone. You have no idea. But you, you're going to be so handsome. You always used to wish you could look like this guy, remember? I'm actually kind of jealous of you.

Rachel just thrashes against her restraints harder than ever.

Here, I'll show you, Jeffrey says at last. He reaches behind Rachel's obsolete head and unplugs the tap, along with the other wires. See? he says. No difference. That body is already more you than you. It's already done.

That's when Rachel leans forward, in her old body, and head-butts Jeffrey, before grabbing for his key ring with the utility knife on it. She somehow gets the knife open with one hand while he's clutching his nose, and slashes a bloody canyon across Jeffrey's stomach. He falls, clutching at his own slippery flesh, and watches her saw through her straps and land on unsteady feet. She lifts Jeffrey's lanyard, smearing blood on his shirt as it goes.

When Rachel was in college, she heard a story about a business professor named Lou, who dated two different women and strung them both along. Laurie was a lecturer in women's studies, while Susie worked in the bookstore co-op despite having a PhD in comp lit. After the women found out Lou was dating both of them, things got ugly. Laurie stole Susie's identity, signing her up for a stack of international phone cards and a subscription to the Dirndl of the Month Club, while Susie tried to crash Laurie's truck and cold-cocked Laurie as she walked out of a seminar on intersectional feminism. In the end, the two women looked at each other, over the slightly dented truck and Laurie's bloody lip and Susie's stack of junk mail. Laurie just spat blood and said, Listen. I won't press charges if you don't sue. Susie thought for a moment, then stuck out her hand and said, Deal. The two women never spoke to each other, or Lou, ever again.

Rachel has always thought this incident exposed the roots of the social contract: most of our relationships are upheld not by love, or obligation, or gratitude, but by mutually assured destruction. Most of the people in Rachel's life who could have given her shit for being transgender were differently bodied, non-neurotypical, or some other thing that also required some acceptance from her. Mote, beam, and so on.

For some reason Rachel can't stop thinking about the social contract and mutually assured destruction as she hobbles down the hallway of Love and Dignity for Everyone with a corpse following close behind. Every time she pauses to turn around and see if the dead man is catching up, he gains a little ground. So she forces herself to keep running with weak legs, even as she keeps hearing his hoarse breath right behind her. True power, Rachel thinks, is being able to destroy others with no consequences to yourself.

She's reached the end of a corridor, and she's trying not to think about Jeffrey's blood on the knife in her hand. He'll be fine, he's in a facility. She remembers Sherri in the computer lab, staring at the pictures on the internet: her hair wet from the shower, one hand reaching for a towel. Sherri sobbing but then tamping it down as she looked at the screen. Sherri telling Rachel at lunch, I'm leaving this school. I can't stay. There's a heavy door with an RFID reader, and Jeffrey's card causes it to click twice before finally bleeping. Rachel's legs wobble and spasm, and the breath of the dead man behind her grows louder. Then she pushes through the door and runs up the square roundabout of stairs. Behind her, she hears Lucy the nurse shout at her to come back, because she's still convalescing, this is a delicate time.

Rachel feels a little more of her strength fade every time the dead man's hand lurches forward. Something irreplaceable leaves her. She pushes open the dense metal door marked EXIT and nearly faints with sudden day-blindness.

The woods around Love and Dignity for Everyone are dense with moss and underbrush, and Rachel's bare feet keep sliding off tree roots. I can't stop, Rachel pleads with herself, I can't stop or my whole life was for nothing. Who even was I, if I let this happen to me. The nearly naked dead man crashes through branches that Rachel has ducked under. She throws the knife and hears a satisfying grunt, but he doesn't even pause. Rachel knows that anybody who sees both her and the cadaver will choose to help the cadaver. There's no way to explain her situation in the dead man's voice. She vows to stay off roads and avoid talking to people. This is her life now.

Up ahead she sees a fast-running stream, and she wonders how the corpse will take to water. The stream looks like the one she and Jeffrey used to play in, when they would catch crayfish hiding under rocks. The crayfish looked just like tiny lobsters, and they would twist around trying to pinch you as you gripped their mid-sections. Rachel sloshes in the water and doesn't hear the man's breath in her ear for a moment. Up ahead the current leads to a steep waterfall that's so white in the noon sunlight, it appears to stand still. She remembers staring into a bucket full of crayfish, debating whether to boil them alive or let them all go. And all at once she has a vivid memory of herself and Jeffrey both hold-ing the full bucket and turning it sideways, until all the crayfish sloshed back into the river. The crayfish fled for their lives, their eyes seeming to protrude with alarm, and Rachel held on to an empty bucket with Jeffrey, feeling an inexplicable sense of relief. We are such wusses, Jeffrey said, and they both laughed. She re-members the sight of the last crayfish rushing out of view—as if this time, maybe the trick would work, and nobody would think to look under this particular rock. She reaches the waterfall, seizes a breath, and jumps with both feet at once.

MICAH DEAN HICKS

Church of Birds

FROM *Kenyon Review*

THE SWAN BOY lives in an abandoned church in a sleepy green town by the river. He is small and young-looking still, though he is sixteen now and has been the swan boy for years. His hair is dirty and grown out long enough to cover his shy face. His clothes are striped with greasy white stains, radiating down from the shoulders of his rough shirt. No one would give him a second look if not for the huge white shield of a swan's wing that he has in place of a left arm. The people in town do not talk to him. Though they call him the swan boy, he has a name, and that name is Ben.

He has no job, but Ben gets up early and stays busy about town all day. He is clumsy with his big wing, but patient. He has learned to climb trees using his feet and good arm, while he holds out the wing for balance. Ben steals birds' nests, little braided crowns, and fills his church with them. If he finds the alien blue of their eggs, he takes these too, holding them carefully in the fold of his wing. He has tried so many times to hatch the eggs with the careful heat of his own wing, but he has never been able to do so. Once he held a clutch of eggs so close that he cracked them in his sleep and woke up cold and covered in yolk and shell.

In the town's small square, Ben throws bread from his pockets and waits with a fisherman's tattered cast net. When pigeons come, he makes his clumsy throw. Sometimes he only tangles himself in the net. Sometimes the birds are wary of him. Today two sooty pigeons stand at his feet, heads hammering the paving stones for his stale bread. Ben throws open the net, his wing arcing over his head like he's preparing to fly away, and the net falls over them.

They thrash and cry, but Ben gathers them against his chest and rushes back to the church.

Shadows lick across the stained windows within. Ben bangs on the door for a count of ten, listening to the scatter of wings inside, then darts in with his catch. He lets the net fall, and the bruised pigeons hop out and flee over the wood floor, covered in their own watery shit. His hundreds of birds, scared by the noise at the door, crowd the back of the church or dart through the high, open space of the sanctuary.

Though the church is filthy with bird droppings and musty-gray with dust, there is color here. Red cardinals, bluebirds, orange-breasted robins sing and skip through the air. Many are the pigeons, marbled white and black, taking on colors from the stained glass as they fly through squares of bloody red, Byzantine gold, or glacial blue. There are ducks nesting in the corners, a crane with a crooked neck. There are no ravens because they are too clever to let him approach, no owls because he is afraid they would eat the others, and no swans because he cannot bear to look at them.

Troughs of water for drinking and bathing sit in the middle of the floor. Sacks of birdseed, ripped open, spill across the old carpet in a shower of white and black and amber seeds several inches deep. A ring of bright mold limns everything like a cold, slow-burning fire.

The new pigeons join a clutch of others on the exposed rafters. The sound of the birds is like the river below, or coins spilling, or weeping. Ben lies back on a damp pew and watches them fly for hours, admiring how whole their bodies are, how beautifully suited to doing one perfect thing.

When he rolls over to sleep, his human hand brushes something small and stony. He brings it to his face and smells rot, feels out the tiny beak with his thumb. He will sleep with the dead bird in his hand. He will bury it in the morning. He will cry, and he will rage, and he will wonder why it died when he gave it everything it needed. He will check that there is enough food and water, study the birds to see if any are sick, take every precaution he can. He will wait, and in a few days it will happen again.

When he dreams, Ben remembers flight. He and his five brothers in their stout swan bodies. The wind rushing over their black-masked faces and the white tips of their wings. How they landed on a brick street after a rain to feast on meaty worms surfacing from their burrows. The green brack of river fronds hanging from his beak. And his brothers' five voices, each a mirror of his own.

They weren't meant to be swans. It was a curse, though it didn't feel like a curse. Their sister Julia saved them. She was required to close her mouth and not laugh, or speak, or even write for six years. One year for each of her cursed brothers. She had to sew them each a shirt of weeds. It was not easy for her, the silence. She sewed her mouth shut to keep her promise to her siblings, but as soon as she did, a man appeared. And since she didn't say no, he took her home and made her his wife, and she had his children. All the while, she sewed her shirts of grass and cried her silent, angry tears.

When the day came, only Ben's shirt was unfinished, missing its sleeve. But it was time. Julia shoved the shirts down over their honking heads, and they became themselves again. All except for Ben, who kept a single wing. The others were older and went back to being the men they had been before. But Ben had been a swan as long as he had been a boy. He didn't remember how to speak. Julia, full of words after her long quiet, taught him language.

When Ben wakes up, he goes to see his sister. She lives alone above a tiny printer's shop, having divorced the man who loved her silence. When Ben arrives, her stoop is covered in a heap of new mail. He gathers it onto his wing like it's a serving tray and carries it inside. His sister's printing press hums and stamps its feet, spitting out book pages. She prefers to stitch their spines up by hand, the only sewing she does anymore. Ben breathes in the inky purple smell of the place.

"What do you need help with today, little brother?"

Ben gives her a knot he found. She does not untie it for him. Instead she studies it.

"You've tried your feet?"

He nods.

"What about holding it with your teeth? Did you try that?"

He puts the knot in his mouth, tasting soap in the fabric. He works at the knot with his fingernails and finally pulls it undone.

"Good. But I see you haven't been bathing."

He sits with her all afternoon. She orders lunch for them. The whole time she reads letters, talks to herself, calls publishers on her telephone. At the end of the day, Ben tells her about his dream, what he remembers from being a swan.

She winces and he apologizes, knowing she doesn't like to think of her quiet years, but he needs to tell someone.

He clears his throat. "Do you think one day you might try again? Take the silent vow and sew another shirt? It would only be for a year this time."

Julia hugs him with her ink-stained hands. "Sorry, Ben. I have too much to say."

Years ago, after Julia taught him to speak again, she sent him to school. He was twice the size of the other children, but he knew half as much. The teacher asked him to solve problems, writing letters and numbers out on the blackboard in bone-white, skeletal lines of chalk. It made no sense, this obsession with counting and numbering. He had one sister, five brothers, no parents. He had three shirts and one pair of pants. He had one arm and one wing. The sums he dealt in were small.

He didn't like the lines where they stood one behind another, marching across the schoolyard, or the times when they were forbidden to speak, or the times when they were required to do so. Not the milk served twice a day that soured in his stomach. The rooms of the schoolhouse were cold, and he wrapped his wing around himself. The others stared and whispered.

After lunch he found a swing set on the playground. A girl, Susan, swung higher and higher. He gaped at her almost-flight. Ben was too nervous to ask how to do it, but Susan dragged her feet in the gravel to slow herself and gave up the rubber seat. She pushed him down and hooked his arm and wing around the chain. She told him to pump his legs.

There was a moment, when he soared high with only the blue of the horizon in front of him, when he forgot that he was not still a swan. He unhooked his arm and wing and leaned forward. He beat his arms, strained his neck, and let out an ugly honk from his too-large throat.

He hit the ground hard enough to knock the wind out of himself and rolled in the dirt, wide-mouthed and losing feathers. From all across the playground, children came to see.

They pulled wadded rolls of bread from their pockets, saved from lunch, and broke off pieces to throw at him. They honked and laughed. He tried to get to his feet, but he couldn't get a breath, couldn't run away. So he covered himself with his wing.

When Julia came, she found him cowering in a circle of bread-crumbs. He never went back to school after that. Everything he learned, Julia taught him.

The morning after visiting his sister, he goes to feed the pigeons again. Sometime in the night a carnival arrived in town. Their rides and trailers clutter the avenues of the park, closed up and dim and silent until night. Men and women he has never seen smoke outside a diner. The town is full of strangers.

A group of old people from the nursing home sit on benches and squint at him, silent in the weak sun. Their grandchildren and great-grandchildren run through the park together, impatient for the carnival to begin. Ben keeps the net at his feet, embarrassed to throw it with people watching.

There is a bang, an engine's black cough, and a truck sputters up the road and parks alongside the park. The back of the truck supports a tall shed, and it pulls a camping trailer. The paint is brown and red and gold but is flaking off and eaten through with rust. Faded lettering on the side of the trailer reads, ELISE'S ODD-ITIES.

When a woman steps out of the truck and walks over to him, she does not seem dangerous. She eats a cinnamon bun. She wears a wide-brimmed hat and leather boots, a coat against the damp. She has one luminous blue eye, one deep brown one.

"I like your pigeons," she tells him.

Ben holds his wing against his chest. He thinks to say, *These are not my pigeons,* or, *I haven't caught them yet,* or even, *Would you like them?* But he says nothing.

"Look what I found." She holds out a glass globe. Inside, every-thing is covered in white. At first Ben thinks it is only a snow globe like he has seen so many times before. But when she shakes it and shows him again, inside the globe is a burning house. Through the empty windows, a body lies on the floor. Painted flames swallow it up, and the falling white is ash, not snow. A tiny dog watches from the yard. "Do you like it?"

He nods and risks another glance at her face. She is smiling still, but she is looking at his wing.

"Can I help you with something?" he asks.

She tucks the globe back into her coat. "My name is Elise. I deal in curiosities, and you, beautiful boy, are very curious. Are you from here?"

"Yes. No." He holds the tip of his wing and stares at the ground. "Not originally. But I've lived here for a long time."

She kneels so that he is looking at her. "Do your parents come feed the birds with you? I'd love to meet them."

"I don't have parents."

"You must have someone to take care of you. A friend or brother?"

"No. Just my sister, Julia, who helps me sometimes. But she is very busy with her work."

The woman reaches for his wing. "Can she fly like you can?"

He slowly extends his wing and lets her touch it. She feels along the pinions, pressing the down and flesh beneath, mapping the bone structure with a careful, firm hand.

"I can't fly. Once I could, but not now. And Julia doesn't have a wing. Just me."

More people filter into the park. The town's cop ambles down the path, looking at the strange woman speaking to the swan boy.

"I have to go for now. Won't you visit me tonight? My trailer will be parked at the campsite near the river, away from all this noise. You have to come. Tell me what it felt like to fly."

Elise's truck and trailer are the only vehicles at the campground, and it is dark when Ben arrives. She has taken furniture out of her trailer and arranged it in the dirt lot like a sitting room. Christmas lights wind around the furniture, making little aisles. Music plays, slow strings reeling him in.

Ben is freshly bathed and his hair is swept back out of his eyes. His clothes are new, a gift from his sister. He has not tied his wing to his chest or covered it with a coat. He carries a mockingbird in a brass cage.

Elise is waiting for him on the steps of her trailer. She sweeps him up in a hug, pressing his wing between them. "Is the bird for me? How kind! Put him inside, will you?"

Ben steps into the trailer, feeling her close behind him. The trailer is empty inside. He bends over to place the bird on the floor. "Before I can tell you about flying, I should tell you about my brothers," he says.

Before he can stand, Elise slips a rope over his neck and tightens it hard around his throat. She forces him to the floor. Ben freezes, afraid and hurt, until he feels her trying to tie his feet.

She is bigger than he is, but his wing is broad and marvelously strong. He rolls and sweeps it against her, knocking her off his back. The mockingbird's cage falls over, and it cries and beats its wings.

"Ben, no! I want to help you." Elise finds her end of the rope and pulls again, choking him. He beats at her with his one wing, the bony limb and heavy flail of feathers knocking her back against the steel wall. With his free hand, he takes the rope from her and falls backward out of the trailer.

She chases him across the campground, shouting. "It's hard to be alone, Ben. Trust me. Why not be admired as a curiosity instead of forgotten as a freak?"

After he gets away from her, Ben hides in a dumpster most of the night, afraid that she will spot him and follow him home. He pounds his head with his human fist. Stupid, stupid. He should have known. He would go to Julia, but he doesn't want her to be disappointed. He wonders what will happen to the mockingbird, and realizing that it might live longer with the curiosity dealer than it would have with him, he is overcome with a wave of grief.

To make the time pass, he checks his wing to make sure it wasn't hurt. No broken feathers, no bruises, no cuts. Intact as iron. Ben isn't surprised. It has always been the strongest part of him.

The last time Ben saw his five brothers, Julia had to leave town on business. The next day they came for him and took him to the forest outside of town.

"Have you found our father?" he asked them.

They shook their heads. For years they chased after news of their home and family. The palace where they were born was empty, the roof collapsed, their father and all his riches gone away. They were born with everything, but after being cursed for six years, they found themselves reborn as beggars. It never bothered Ben the way it did his brothers. He can't remember what it was to be a prince.

When they got him deep into the woods, his brothers asked him to lie down on a pile of straw. They were older and stronger, and when they asked, it was always a command.

"It's going to rain soon," Ben said.

"You have an arm somewhere under that wing. We're going to help you find it."

While three of his brothers held him down, the other two worked to remove his feathers. First they used knives to cut through the thick shafts.

"Please don't," Ben said. "It hurts."

"Trust us," said his brothers, keeping their voices low and putting a hand over his mouth. "We love you."

Impatient with the knife, they grabbed handfuls of his feathers and pulled them out. Ben felt the roots tear from his skin. His shirt was soaked with blood. When they finally let go, he lay stretched on the ground haloed in his own white feathers. There was no human hand under there, no fingers, no biceps. Only a wing, naked and bumpy-fleshed, bloody and burning with pain.

His brothers shook their heads in disgust. "Leave him," one of them said. "Better dead than a bird for a brother."

They walked away, and the rain fell, and he did not see them again. Somehow, he stood. Somehow, he held his wounded limb and found his sister's home, fell into her bed, and waited for her to come save his life.

"Who did this to you?" Julia asked.

"It doesn't matter," he said. "It might have been anyone."

It is colder now, so Ben binds his wing to his chest and puts on a baggy coat to cover it. The wind slices over the top of the park's little pond. He does not have bread to feed the birds today, so he only comes to watch.

There is another person in the park, a woman throwing out handfuls of bread and mobbed by ducks. He sits on a bench on the opposite side of the pond.

A flock of swans alights on the pond's glassy surface and drifts toward him. Their faces are so strange, banded in black like they are wearing masks. He wonders if there are lost children hiding in the graceful S of their bodies, waiting for a silent sister to break their curse.

The woman comes and sits by him. She puts a clump of bread on the bench near his hand. "The swans have always been my favorites," she says.

Ben realizes then that he knows her: Susan, the girl who taught him to swing on his first and only day of school. She is older, but she has the same kind face, wide-eyed and broad-smiling.

Ben wants to ask if she remembers him, but of course she does. He picks off a bit of her bread and throws it onto the water.

The swans come closer, leaving the water and walking up the bank in a line, like soldiers. Their halberd necks swing through the air for the flying bread. Susan leans forward and reaches out with one gloved hand. The swans take a step away from her.

Her fingers stay outstretched, and the innocence of her gesture makes the wing flutter against Ben's breast. Three buttons snap open on the front of his coat. A spray of feathers falls out.

"You were a swan once, weren't you? That's what people say. Are these your brothers?"

"No." He opens his coat and undoes the strap binding his wing. He lets it hang free off the side of the bench. "No, those are only swans."

"They're beautiful. I've been feeding them for years, but they never let me get close." She swallows and looks away from him. "I guess they have good reason to be afraid of people."

He hand is still out, and he wants to fill it. She is good, and she is safe. Of all the people in the world, she might understand. He wants her to know that her kindness matters. So he reaches toward her with his wing. He is ready to lay it across her lap and let her smooth the stiff feathers. Let her pinch off bread and place it on his tongue. Let her wrap an arm around him and tell him that the world isn't as bad as it seems.

She touches his wing, and instinct fractures him, like a crack spreading through ice. Before he realizes what he is doing, he is off the bench and running from her. There is the burn of the rope on his neck still. The hot prickle at the base of his feathers, down on his flesh where his brothers hurt him. The shock of beer bottles flung at him from trucks, or kids chasing him on bicycles to stripe his back with sticks. The ugly, coughing honk people make when he walks by.

"I'm sorry," Susan calls after him. "Please, come back. I'll never forgive myself."

His eyes are wet and sting, and he can't see. He holds his wing to cover his face from branches and sprints through the park, up the hill, and back to his church. He steps inside and locks the heavy door against the world.

An hour later, Susan knocks. "That was wrong of me," she says. "How can I make it up to you?"

Birds startle and circle the high ceiling. He wants to say something, to tell her that she did nothing wrong, that he is grateful for how she has always treated him. But he can't stop trembling, and he can't speak. He crawls under the church pews and covers himself with his wing. He tells himself that he is only a bird, nesting down on a winter morning, and soon her words through the door are only noise.

The radio says a storm is coming. Everyone in town boards up their windows. Ben sits alone in his dark and solid church, eating seeds. When the first spears of lightning fall, followed by the first drumbeats of thunder, all the birds in his church pile themselves along the windowsills to watch the rain. They sing, excited. They toss their heads and shake out their wings, imagining the rain. He has not visited his sister in weeks, has hardly left home, and he hopes she won't be worried for him.

Something strikes one of the windows, bouncing off the thick glass. Lightning flashes, and for a moment Ben sees a flurry of shapes swirl like leaves outside in the storm. He ties his wing tight across his body and goes to see.

The wind and rain push him against the wall, but the water feels good on his feathers. He goes to the corner where a flock of ravens, or maybe crows, are sheltering from the wind. One of them lics on the ground, stunned from hitting the glass.

Ben reaches for it with his human hand, but each time one of the others hops forward and pecks him hard on the wrist. Water runs into his eyes, and it's hard to see.

"Let me take you inside," he says. "I can help."

He makes a few more clumsy grabs, but they peck his bleeding hand. The stunned bird shakes itself awake and lifts off into the storm, followed by the others. They leave behind a scattering of shining black feathers pressed by the wind against the wall of the church. Ben gathers up the feathers and takes them inside, feeling alone even surrounded by his birds.

The storm continues all night and into the morning. The birds sing, growing louder and louder as the storm passes over. As if their calls were a summoning, someone opens the church door and comes inside.

He is a man, soaked from the storm. He is dressed in rain-darkened denim. He has long black hair. Covering his arms and hands in neat rows are dozens upon dozens of feather tattoos, as if his arms are wings.

There is something else about him. Ben can see it, but he can't describe it. Once a witch came and cursed him and his brothers. He doesn't remember the color of her hair or if she was tall, but he remembers how she walked, as if the universe would reorder itself to get out of her way. Whatever that woman had, this man has it too.

"Did you come with the carnival?" Ben asks.

The man does not answer his question and he does not stare at Ben's wing. Instead he goes to the windowsills and reaches in among the birds, picking them up and putting them back, like he is searching for something. They are silent in his presence.

"I'm looking for my sons."

"Were your sons turned into swans?" Could this be his father, finally come to claim him? Ben can't remember what the man looked like.

"They were turned into crows," the man says. "It was my fault."

Ben nods, not caring that the stranger isn't his father or that his words make no sense. The man is powerful. Ben can see it. The man can help him, if he will.

He lets the stranger search the church, checking rafters and pews. Finally the man bends down and picks up a single black feather lying on the floor. He sighs. "They're gone, then?"

Ben nods.

"Ah. Well." He wrings out his shirt on the floor, squeezes water from his hair. "I'm sorry to bother you."

"You can wait out the storm here," Ben says.

"I don't mind rain."

"Look." Ben lifts his wing and holds it out, feeling helpless and desperate, like when he was a speechless child clinging to his sister's legs. "I've met someone like you before. She changed me."

The stranger glances at his wing but does not touch it. "I'm in a hurry."

"Please. Before you go, make me whole. Make me myself again."

The man sighs and glances at the windows, as if he is late and Ben is keeping him. "Okay," he says. "If that's what you want."

The man turns away from Ben and raises his hands, feather tattoos crinkling and flexing, stretching like his arms are wings. He begins to sing, "Take me to fruit trees and green grass."

The storm howls against the church house, peeling back shingles until water begins to spill in thick ropes from the ceiling. The man sings, and his words lose meaning, hitting the air like they are solid. His chant is an etching on a gravestone, lightning scarring the sky, a key threading a lock. He speaks, and the world opens around Ben, just as it did years ago.

The birds filling the church raise their wings and take flight. They swirl around Ben and land on his shoulders, his arms, his back, until their weight bears him to the ground. He is covered by their musty feathers. He falls down a well of sleep.

When Ben wakes, the church is silent. Light comes through the windows, and he doesn't know how long he has slept. He pushes against the birds covering his body, but they are heavy and dead. They don't stink of rot, the stranger's magic having eaten all the life out of them. They fall like chips of wood.

For a moment their delicate bodies pain him. He meant to keep them safe, but they have been dying in his care for a long time. Now they are all dead. His grief doesn't know where to begin.

Ben stands, afraid, and looks at his new body. He can see his two feet. He has a soft stomach, uncovered by feathers. Matching his right arm, he has a new left arm extending from his shoulder. He clasps his hands together, linking his fingers for the first time in years.

He clenches his teeth and sucks in a ragged breath. "No," he says.

Ben reaches around, feeling his shoulders and back, searching for wings. He grasps his face, searching for a beak. He tries to honk, hoping to feel the sound slide up his long throat. But he is only a boy again, just as he started.

He runs out of the church, looking for the stranger, but the man is gone. The sky arches blue and vast over him, completely out of his reach. "No," he says to the sky. "This isn't what I meant. I wanted to be a swan again. I wanted to fly."

He goes inside and collapses onto his pile of birds, gathering them against his chest. He covers himself in feathers, sings the man's strange song. He prays there is some magic left, enough to carry him away, but the world with all its secrets remains shut.

Desperate, he stands on a pew and jumps as high as he can, flapping his arms. He remembers piercing the cold, high air. He remembers the warmth of his brother swans pressing against him at night. He remembers the beauty of his song. Ben tells himself that he is a swan still. The air slips past his fingers. He falls.

PETER WATTS

ZeroS

FROM *Infinity Wars*

ASANTE GOES OUT screaming. Hell is an echo chamber, full
of shouts and seawater and clanking metal. Monstrous shadows
move along the bulkheads; meshes of green light writhe on every surface. The Sāḥilites rise from the moon pool like creatures
from some bright lagoon, firing as they emerge; Rashida's middle
explodes in dark mist and her top half topples onto the deck. Kito's still dragging himself toward the speargun on the drying rack
—as though some antique fish-sticker could ever fend off these
monsters with their guns and their pneumatics and their little car-
tridges that bury themselves deep in your flesh before showing you
what five hundred unleashed atmospheres do to your insides.

It's more than Asante's got. All he's got is his fists.

He uses them. Launches himself at the nearest Sāḥilite as she
lines up Kito in her sights, swings wildly as the deck groans and
drops and cants sideways. Seawater breaches the lip of the moon
pool, cascades across the plating. Asante flails at the intruder on
his way down. Her shot goes wide. A spiderweb blooms across the
viewport; a thin gout of water erupts from its center even as the
glass tries to heal itself from the edges in.

The last thing Asante sees is the desert hammer icon on the
Sāḥilite's diveskin before she blows him away.

Five Years

Running water. Metal against metal. Clanks and gurgles, lowered
voices, the close claustrophobic echo of machines in the middle
distance.

Asante opens his eyes.

He's still in the wet room; its ceiling blurs and clicks into focus, plates and struts and Kito's stupid graffiti (ALL TAUTOLOGIES ARE TAUTOLOGIES) scratched into the paint. Green light still wriggles dimly across the biosteel, but the murderous energy's been bled out of it.

He tries to turn his head, and can't. He barely feels his own body—as though it were made of ectoplasm, some merest echo of solid flesh fading into nonexistence somewhere around the waist.

An insect's head on a human body looms over him. It speaks with two voices: English, and an overlapping echo in Twi: "Easy, soldier. Relax."

A woman's voice, and a chip one.

Not Sāḥilite. But armed. Dangerous.

Not a soldier, he wants to say, wants to *shout.* It's never a good thing to be mistaken for any sort of combatant along the west coast. But he can't even whisper. He can't feel his tongue.

Asante realizes that he isn't breathing.

The Insect Woman (a diveskin, he sees now: her mandibles an electrolysis rig, her compound eyes a pair of defraction goggles) retrieves a tactical scroll from beyond his field of view and unrolls it a half meter from his face. She mutters an incantation and it flares softly to life, renders a stacked pair of keyboards: English on top, Twi beneath.

"Don't try to talk," she says in both tongues. "Just look at the letters."

He focuses on the *N:* it brightens. *O. T.* The membrane offers up predictive spelling, speeds the transition from sacc' to script:

NOT SOLDIER FISH FARMER

"Sorry." She retires the translator; the Twi keys flicker and disappear. "Figure of speech. What's your name?"

KODJO ASANTE

She pushes the defractors onto her forehead, unlatches the mandibles. They fall away and dangle to one side. She's white underneath.

IS KITO

"I'm sorry, no. Everyone's dead."

Everyone else, he thinks, and imagines Kito mocking him one last time for insufferable pedantry.

"Got him." Man's voice, from across the compartment. "Kodjo

Asante, Takoradi. Twenty-eight, bog-standard aqua—wait; combat experience. Two years with GAF."

Asante's eyes dart frantically across the keyboard:

ONLY FARMER NOT

"No worries, mate." She lays down a reassuring hand; he can only assume it comes to rest somewhere on his body. "Everyone's seen combat hereabouts, right? You're sitting on the only reliable protein stock in three hundred klicks. Stands to reason you're gonna have to defend it now and again."

"Still." A shoulder patch comes into view as she turns toward the other voice: WestHem Alliance. "We could put him on the list."

"If you're gonna do it, do it fast. Surface contact about two thousand meters out, closing."

She turns back to Asante. "Here's the thing. We didn't get here in time. We're not supposed to be here at all, but our CO got wind of Sally's plans and took a little humanitarian initiative, I guess you could say. We showed up in time to scare 'em off and light 'em up, but you were all dead by then."

I WASN'T

"Yeah, Kodjo, you too. All dead."

YOU BROUGHT ME BA

"No."

BUT

"We gave your brain a jump start, that's all. You know how you can make a leg twitch when you pass a current through it? You know what *galvanic* means, Kodjo?"

"He's got a PhD in molecular marine ecology," says her unseen colleague. "I'm guessing yes."

"You can barely feel anything, am I right? Body like a ghost? We didn't reboot the rest of you. You're just getting residual sensations from nerves that don't know they're dead yet. You're a brain in a box, Kodjo. You're running on empty."

"But here's the thing: you don't *have* to be."

"Hurry it up, Cat. We got ten minutes, tops."

She glances over her shoulder, back again. "We got a rig on the *Levi Morgan*, patch you up and keep you on ice until we get home. And we got a rig *there* that'll work goddamn miracles, make you better'n new. But it ain't cheap, Kodjo. Pretty much breaks the bank every time we do it."

DON'T HAVE MONEY

"Don't want *money*. We want you to work for us. Five-year tour, maybe less depending on how the tech works out. Then you go on your way, nice fat bank balance, whole second chance. Easy gig, believe me. You're just a passenger in your own body for the hard stuff. Even boot camp's mostly autonomic. Real accelerated program."

NOT WESTHEM

"You're not Hegemon either, not anymore. You're not much of anything but rotting meat hooked up to a pair of jumper cables. I'm offering you salvation, mate. You can be Born Again."

"Wrap it the fuck *up,* Cat. They're almost on top of us."

"'Course, if you're not interested, I can just pull the plug. Leave you the way we found you."

NO PLEASE YES

"Yes what, Kodjo? Yes pull the plug? Yes leave you behind? You need to be specific about this. We're negotiating a contract here."

YES BORN AGAIN YES 5 YEAR TOUR

He wonders at this shiver of hesitation, this voice whispering *Maybe dead is better.* Perhaps it's because he *is* dead; maybe all those suffocating endocrine glands just aren't up to the task of flooding his brain with the warranted elixir of fear and desperation and *survival at any cost.* Maybe being dead means never having to give a shit.

He does, though. He may be dead, but his glands aren't, not yet. He didn't say no.

He wonders if anyone ever has.

"Glory hallelujah!" Cat proclaims, reaching offstage for some unseen control. And just before everything goes black:

"Welcome to the Zombie Corps."

Savior Machine

That's not what they call it, though.

"Be clear about one thing. There's no good reason why any operation should ever put boots in the battlefield."

They call it *ZeroS*. Strangely, the *Z* does not stand for *Zombie.*

"There's no good reason why any competent campaign should involve a battlefield in the first place. That's what economic engineering and Cloud Control are for."

The *S* doesn't even stand for *Squad.*

"If they fail, that's what drones and bots and TAI are for."

Zero Sum. Or, as NCOIC Silano puts it, *A pun, right? Cogito ergo.* Better than *the Spaz Brigade,* which was Garin's suggestion.

Asante's in Tactical Orientation, listening to an artificial instructor that he'd almost accept as human but for the fact that it doesn't sound bored to death.

"There's only one reason you'll ever find yourselves called on deck, and that's if everyone has fucked up so completely at conflict resolution that there's nothing left in the zone but a raging shitstorm."

Asante's also running up the side of a mountain. It's a beautiful route, twenty klicks of rocks and pines and mossy deadfall. There might be more green growing things on this one slope than in the whole spreading desert of northern Africa. He wishes he could see it.

"Your very presence means the mission has already failed; your job is to salvage what you can from the wreckage."

He can't see it, though. He can't see much of anything. Asante's been blind since reveille.

"Fortunately for you, economics and Cloud Control and tactical AI fail quite a lot."

The blindness isn't total. He still sees light, vague shapes in constant motion. It's like watching the world through wax paper. The eyes *jiggle* when you're a Passenger. Of course the eyes always jiggle, endlessly hopping from one momentary focus to the next — *saccades,* they're called — but your brain usually edits out those motions, splices the clear bits together in post to serve up an illusion of continuity.

Not up here, though. Up here the sacc' rate goes through the roof and nothing gets lost. Total data acquisition. To Asante it's all blizzard and blur, but that's okay. There's something in here with him that can see just fine: his arms and legs are moving, after all, and Kodjo Asante isn't moving them.

His other senses work fine; he feels the roughness of the rope against his palms as he climbs the wall, smells the earth and pine needles bedding the trail. Still tastes a faint hint of copper from that bite on the inside of his cheek a couple klicks back. He hears with utmost clarity the voice on his audio link. His inner zombie sucks all that back too, but eardrums don't saccade. Tactile nerves don't hop around under the flesh. Just the eyes: that's how you tell. That and the fact that your whole body's been possessed by Alien Hand Syndrome.

He calls it his Evil Twin. It's a name first bestowed by his dad, after catching eight-year-old Kodjo sleepwalking for the third time in a week. Asante made the mistake of mentioning that once to the squad over breakfast. He's still trying to live it down.

Now he tries for the hell of it, wills himself to *stop* for just an instant. ET runs and leaps and crawls as it has for the past two hours, unnervingly autonomous. That's the retrosplenial bypass they burned into his neocortex a month ago, a little dropgate to decouple *mind* from *self.* Just one of the mods they've etched into him with neural lace and nanotube mesh and good old-fashioned zap'n'tap. Midbrain tweaks to customize ancient prey-stalking routines. An orbitofrontal damper to ensure behavioral compliance (*Can't have your better half deciding to keep the keys when you want them back,* as Maddox puts it).

His scalp itches with fresh scars. His head moves with a disquieting inertia, as if weighed down by a kilogram of lead and not a few bits of arsenide and carbon. He doesn't understand a tenth of it. Hasn't quite come to grips with life after death. But dear God, how *wonderful* it is to be so strong. He feels like this body could take on a whole platoon single-handed.

Sometimes he can feel this way for five or ten whole minutes before remembering the names of other corpses who never got in on the deal.

Without warning ET dances to one side, brings its arms up, and suddenly Asante can *see.*

Just for a millisecond, a small clear break in a sea of fog: a Lockheed Pit Bull cresting the granite outcropping to his left, legs spread, muzzle spinning to bear. In the next instant Asante's blind again, recoil vibrating along his arm like a small earthquake. His body hasn't even broken stride.

"Ah. Target acquisition," the instructor remarks. "Enjoy the view." It takes this opportunity to summarize the basics—target lock's the only time when the eyes focus on a single point long enough for Passengers to look out—before segueing into a spiel on line-of-sight networking.

Asante isn't sure what the others are hearing. Tiwana, the only other raw recruit, is probably enduring the same 101 monologue.

Kalmus might have moved up to field trauma by now. Garin's on an engineering track. Maddox has told Asante that he'll probably end up in bioweapons, given his background.

It takes nineteen months to train a field-ready specialist. ZeroS do it in seven.

Asante's legs have stopped moving. On all sides he hears the sound of heavy breathing. Lieutenant Metzinger's voice tickles the space between his ears: "Passengers, you may enter the cockpit."

The switch is buried in the visual cortex and tied to the power of imagination. They call it a *mandala*. Each recruit chooses their own and keeps it secret; no chance of a master key for some wily foe to drop onto a billboard in the heat of battle. Not even the techs know the patterns; the implants were conditioned on double-blind trial and error. *Something personal,* they said. *Something unique, easy to visualize.*

Asante's mandala is a sequence of four words in sans serif font. He summons it now—

ALL TAUTOLOGIES
ARE TAUTOLOGIES

—and the world clicks back into sudden, jarring focus. He stumbles, though he wasn't moving.

Right on cue, his left hand starts twitching.

They're halfway up the mountain, in a sloping sunny meadow. There are *flowers* here. Insects. Everything smells alive. Silano raises trembling arms to the sky. Kalmus flumps on the grass, recovering from exertions barely felt when better halves were in control, exertions that have left them weak and wasted despite twice-normal mito counts and AMPK agonists and a dozen other tweaks to put them in the upper tail of the upper tail. Acosta drops beside her, grinning at the sunshine. Garin kicks at a punky log and an actual goddamn *snake* slithers into the grass, a ribbon of yellow and black with a flickering tongue.

Tiwana's at Asante's shoulder, as scarred and bald as he is. "Beautiful, eh?" Her right eye's a little off-kilter; Asante resists the impulse to stare by focusing on the bridge of her nose.

"Not beautiful enough to make up for two hours with a hood over my head." That's Saks, indulging in some pointless bitching. "Would it kill them to give us a video feed?"

"Or even just put us to sleep," Kalmus grumbles. They both

know it's not that simple. The brain's a tangle of wires looping from basement to attic and back again; turn off the lights in the living room and your furnace might stop working. Even pay-per-view's a nonstarter. In theory, there's no reason why they couldn't bypass those jiggling eyes entirely—pipe a camera feed directly to the cortex—but their brains are already so stuffed with implants that there isn't enough real estate left over for nonessentials.

That's what Maddox says, anyway.

"I don't really give a shit," Acosta's saying. The tic at the corner of his mouth makes his grin a twitchy, disconcerting thing. "I'd put up with twice the offline time if there was always a view like this at the end of it." Acosta lives for any scrap of nature he can find; his native Guatemala lost most of its canopy to firestorm carousels back in '42.

"So what's in it for you?" Tiwana asks.

It takes a moment for Asante to realize the question's for him. "Excuse me?"

"Acosta's nature-boy. Kalmus thinks she's gonna strike it rich when they declassify the tech." This is news to Asante. "Why'd *you* sign up?"

He doesn't quite know how to answer. Judging by his own experience, ZeroS is not something you *sign up* for. ZeroS is something that finds you. It's an odd question, a private question. It brings up things he'd rather not dwell upon.

It brings up things he already dwells on too much.

"Ah—"

Thankfully, Maddox chooses that moment to radio up from Côté: "Okay, everybody. Symptom check. Silano."

The corporal looks at his forearms. "Pretty good. Less jumpy than normal."

"Kalmus."

"I've got, ah, ah . . ." She stammers, struggles, finally spits in frustration. "*Fuck.*"

"I'll just put down the usual aphasia," Maddox says. "Garin."

"Vision flickers every five, ten minutes."

"That's an improvement."

"Gets better when I exercise. Better blood flow, maybe."

"Interesting," Maddox says. "Tiwan—"

"I see you God I see you!"

Saks is on the ground, writhing. His eyes roll in their sockets.

His fingers claw handfuls of earth. "*I see!*" he cries, and lapses into gibberish. His head thrashes. Spittle flies from his mouth. Tiwana and Silano move in, but the audio link crackles with the voice of God: "Stand away! Everyone stand back *now!*" and everyone obeys because God speaks with the voice of Lieutenant David Metzinger and you do not want to fuck with *him*. God's breath is blowing down from heaven, from the rotors of a medical chopper beating the air with impossible silence even though they all see it now, they all see it, there's no need for stealth mode there never was it's always there, just out of sight, just in case.

Saks has stopped gibbering. His face is a rictus, his spine a drawn bow. The chopper lands, its *whup whup whup* barely audible even ten meters away. It vomits medics and a stretcher and glossy black easter-egg drones with jointed insect legs folded to their bellies. The ZeroS step back; the medics close in and block the view.

Metzinger again: "Okay, meat sacks. Everyone into the back seat. Return to Côté."

Silano turns away, eyes already jiggling in their sockets. Tiwana and Kalmus go over a moment later. Garin slaps Asante's back on the way out—"Gotta go, man. Happens, you know?"—and vanishes into his own head.

The chopper lifts Saks into the heavens.

"Private Asante! *Now!*"

He stands alone in the clearing, summons his mandala, falls into blindness. His body turns. His legs move. Something begins to run him downhill. The artificial instructor, always sensitive to context, begins a lecture about dealing with loss on the battlefield.

It's all for the best, he knows. It's safest to be a Passenger at times like this. All these glitches, these . . . side effects: they never manifest in zombie mode.

Which makes perfect sense. That being where they put all the money.

Station to Station

Sometimes he still wakes in the middle of the night, shocked back to consciousness by the renewed knowledge that he still exists—as if his death was some near-miss that didn't really sink in until days or weeks afterward, leaving him weak in the knees and gasping for breath. He catches himself calling his mandala, a fight/flight reaction to threat stimuli long since expired. He stares at the ceiling, forces calm onto panic, takes comfort from the breathing of his fellow recruits. Tries not to think about Kito and Rashida. Tries not to think at all.

Sometimes he finds himself in the commons, alone but for the inevitable drone hovering just around the corner, ready to raise alarms and inject drugs should he suffer some delayed and violent reaction to any of a hundred recent mods. He watches the world through one of CFB Côté's crippled terminals (they can surf but never send). He slips through wires and fiberop, bounces off geosynchronous relays all the way back to Ghana: satcams down on the dizzying Escher arcology of the Cape Universitas hubs, piggybacks on drones wending through Makola's East, marvels anew at the giant gengineered snails—big as a centrifuge, some of them —that first ignited his passion for biology when he was six. He haunts familiar streets where the kenkey and fish always tasted better when the Chinese printed them, even though the recipes must have been copied from the locals. The glorious chaos of the street drummers during Adai.

He never seeks out friends or family. He doesn't know if it's because he's not ready or because he has already moved past them. He only knows not to awaken things that have barely gone to sleep.

Zero Sum. A new life. Also a kind of game used, more often than not, to justify armed conflict.

Also *Null Existence.* If your tastes run to the Latin.

They loom over a drowning subdivision long abandoned to the rising waters of Galveston Bay: cathedral-sized storage tanks streaked with rust and ruin, twelve-story filtration towers, masses of twisting pipe big enough to walk through.

Garin sidles up beside him. "Looks like a crab raped an octopus."

"Your boys seem twitchy," the sheriff says. (Asante clenches his fist to control the tremor.) "They hopped on something?"

Metzinger ignores the question. "Have they made any demands?"

"Usual. Stop the rationing or they blow it up." The sheriff shakes his head, moves to mop his brow, nearly punches himself in the face when his decrepit Bombardier exoskeleton fratzes and overcompensates. "Everything's gone to shit since the Edwards dried up."

"They respond to a water shortage by blowing up a desalination facility?"

The sheriff snorts. "Folks always make sense where you come from, Lieutenant?"

They reviewed the plant specs down to the rivets on the way here. Or at least their zombies did, utterly silent, borrowed eyes flickering across video feeds and backgrounders that Asante probably wouldn't have grasped even if he *had* been able to see them. All Asante knows — by way of the impoverished briefings Metzinger doles out to those back in tourist class — is that the facility was bought from Qatar back when paint still peeled and metal still rusted, when digging viscous fossils from the ground left you rich enough to buy the planet. And that it's falling into disrepair, now that none of those things are true anymore.

Pretty much a microcosm of the whole TExit experience, he reflects.

"They planned it out," the sheriff admits. "Packed a shitload of capacitors in there with 'em, hooked 'em to jennies, banked 'em in all the right places. We send in quads, EMP just drops 'em." He glances back over his shoulder, to where — if you squint hard enough — a heat-shimmer rising from the asphalt might almost assume the outline of a resting Chinook transport. "Probably risky using exos, unless they're hardened."

"We won't be using exos."

"Far as we can tell, some of 'em are dug in by the condensers, others right next to the heat exchangers. We try to microwave 'em out, all the pipes explode. Might as well blow the place ourselves."

"Firepower?"

"You name it. Sig Saurs, Heckler-Kochs, Maesushis. I think one of 'em has a Skorp. All kinetic, far as we know. Nothing you could fry."

"Got anything on legs?"

"They've got a Wolfhound in there. 46-G."

"I meant you," Metzinger says.

The sheriff winces. "Nearest's three hours away. Gimped leg." And at Metzinger's look: "BoDyn pulled out a few years back. We've been having trouble getting replacement parts."

"What about local law enforcement? You can't be the only—"

"Half of them *are* law enforcement. How'd you think they got the Wolfhound?" The sheriff lowers his voice, although there aren't any other patriots within earshot. "Son, you don't think we'd have invited you in if we'd had any other choice? I mean Jayzuz, we've got enough trouble maintaining lawnorder as it is. If word ever got out we had to bring in outside help over a goddamn *domestic dispute* . . ."

"Don't sweat it. We don't wear name tags." Metzinger turns to Silano. "Take it away, Sergeant-Major."

Silano addresses the troops as Metzinger disappears into the cloaked Chinook: "Say your goodbyes, everybody. Autopilots in thirty."

Asante sighs to himself. Those poor bastards don't stand a chance. He can't even bring himself to blame them: driven by desperation, hunger, the lack of any other options. Like the Sāhilites who murdered *him,* back at the end of another life: damned, ultimately, by the sin of being born into a wasteland that could no longer feed them.

Silano raises one hand. "*Mark.*"

Asante calls forth his mandala. The world goes to gray. His bad hand calms and steadies on the forestalk of his weapon.

This is going to be ugly.

He's glad he won't be around to see it.

Heroes

He does afterward, of course. They all do, as soon as they get back to Côté. They're still learning. The world is their classroom.

"Back in the Cenozoic all anybody cared about was *reflexes.*" Second Lieutenant Oliver Maddox—sorcerer's apprentice to the rarely seen Major Emma Rossiter, of the Holy Order of Neuroengineering—speaks with the excitement of a nine-year-old at his own birthday party. "Double-tap, dash, down, crawl, observe fire—all that stuff your body learns to do without thinking when someone yells *Contact*. The whole program was originally just about speeding up those macros. They never really appreciated that the subconscious mind *thinks* as well as reacts. It *analyzes*. I was telling them that years ago, but they never really got it until now."

Asante has never met *Them*. They never write, They never call. They certainly never visit. Presumably They sign a lot of checks.

"Here, though, we have a *perfect* example of the tactical genius of the zombie mind."

Their BUDs recorded everything. Maddox has put it all together postmortem, a greatest-hits mix with remote thermal and PEA and a smattering of extraporential algorithms to fill in the gaps. Now he sets up the game board—walls, floors, industrial viscera all magically translucent—and initializes the people inside.

"So you've got eighteen heavily armed hostiles dug in at all the right choke points." Homunculi glow red at critical junctures. "You've got a jamming field in effect, so you can't share telemetry unless you're line-of-sight. You've got an EMP-hardened robot programmed to attack anything so much as squeaks, deafened along the whole spectrum so even if we *had* the back-door codes it wouldn't hear them." The Wolfhound icon is especially glossy: probably lifted from BoDyn's promotional archive. "And you've got some crazy fucker with a deadman switch that'll send the whole place sky-high the moment his heart stops—or even if he just thinks you're getting too close to the flag. You don't even know about that going in.

"And yet."

Maddox starts the clock. Inside the labyrinth, icons begin to dance in fast-forward.

"Garin's first up, and he completely blows it. Not only does he barely graze the target—probably doesn't even draw blood—*but he leaves his silencer disengaged.* Way to go, Garin. You failed to neutralize your target, and now the whole building knows where you are."

Asante remembers that gunshot echoing through the facility. He remembers his stomach dropping away.

"Now here comes one of Bubba's buddies around the corner and—Garin misses *again!* Nick to the shoulder this time. And here comes the real badass of the bunch, that Wolfhound's been homing in on Garin's shots and that motherfucker is armed and hot and . . ."

The 46-G rounds the corner. It does not target Garin; it lights up the *insurgents.* Bubba and his buddy collapse into little red piles of pixel dust.

"They did *not* see that coming!" Maddox exults. "Fragged by their own robot! How do you suppose *that* happened?"

Asante frowns.

"So two baddies down, Garin's already up the ladder and onto this catwalk before the robot gets a bead on him, but Tiwana's at the other end, way across the building, and they go LOS for about half a second"—a bright thread flickers between their respective icons—"before Tiwana drops back down to ground level and starts picking off Bubbas over by the countercurrent assembly. And *she* turns out to be just as shitty a shot as Garin, and just as sloppy with her silencer."

Gunfire everywhere, from everyone. Asante remembers being blind and shitting bricks, wondering what kind of *aboa* would make such an idiot mistake until the Rann-Seti came up in his own hands, until he felt the recoil and heard the sound of his own shot echoing like a 130-decibel bull's-eye on his back. He wondered, at the time, how and why someone had sabotaged everyone's silencers like that.

Maddox is still deep in the play. "The bad guys have heard the commotion and are starting to reposition. By now Asante and Silano have picked up the shitty-shot bug and the BoDyn's still running around tearing up the guys on its own side. All this opens a hole that Kalmus breezes through—anyone want to guess the odds she'd just happen to be so perfectly positioned?—which buys her a clean shot at the guy with the deadman switch. Who she drops with a perfect cervical shot. Completely paralyzes the poor bastard *but* leaves his heart beating strong and steady. Here we see Kalmus checking him over and disabling his now useless doomsday machine.

"This all took less than five minutes, people. I mean, it was eighteen from in to out but you're basically mopping up after five. And just before the credits roll, Kalmus strolls up to the Wolfhound calm as you please and *pets* the fucker. Puts him right to sleep. Galveston PD gets their robot back without a scratch. Five minutes. Fucking magic."

"So, um." Garin looks around. "How'd we do it?"

"Show 'em, Kally."

Kalmus holds up a cuff-link. "Apparently I took this off deadman guy."

"Dog whistles, Ars and Kays." Maddox grins. "Fifty kilohertz, inaudible to pilot or passenger. You don't put your robot into rabid mode without some way of telling friend from foe, right? Wear one of these pins, Wolfie doesn't look at you twice. *Lose* that pin and it rips your throat out in a fucking instant.

"Your better halves could've gone for clean, quiet kills that would've left the remaining forces still dug in, still fortified, and not going anywhere. But one of the things that fortified them was Bo-Dyn's baddest battlebot. So your better halves didn't go for clean, quiet kills. They went for noise and panic. They shot the dog whistles, drew in the dog, let it attack its own masters. Other side changes position in response. You *herded* the robot, and the robot herded the insurgents right into your crosshairs. It was precision out of chaos, and it's even more impressive because you had no comms except for the occasional optical sync when you happened to be LOS. Gotta be the messiest, spottiest network you could imagine, and if I hadn't seen it myself I'd say it was impossible. But somehow you zombies kept updated on each other's sitreps. Each one knew what it had to do to achieve an optimal outcome assuming all the others did likewise, and the group strategy just kind of . . . *emerged*. Nobody giving orders. Nobody saying a goddamn word."

Asante sees it now, as the replay loops and restarts. There's a kind of beauty to it: the movement of nodes, the intermittent web of laser light flickering between them, the smooth coalescence of signal from noise. It's more than a dance, more than teamwork. It's more like a . . . a distributed organism. Like the digits of a hand, moving together.

"Mind you, this is not what we say if anyone asks," Maddox adds. "What we say is that every scenario in which the Galveston plant went down predicted a tipping point across the whole Post-TExit landscape. We point to ninety-five percent odds of widespread rioting and social unrest on WestHem's very doorstep—a fate which ZeroS has, nice and quietly, prevented. Not bad for your first field deployment."

Tiwana raises a hand. "Who would ask, exactly?"

It's a good question. In the thirteen months since Asante joined Zero Sum, no outsider has ever appeared on the grounds of CFB Côté. Which isn't especially surprising, given that—according to the public records search he did a few weeks back, anyway—CFB Côté has been closed for over twenty years.

Maddox smiles faintly. "Anyone with a vested interest in the traditional chain of command."

Where Are We Now

Asante awakens in the infirmary, standing at the foot of Carlos
Acosta's bed. To his right a half-open door spills dim light into the
darkness beyond: a wedge of worn linoleum fading out from the
doorway, a tiny red EXIT sign glowing in the void above a stairwell. To his left, a glass wall looks into Neurosurgery. Jointed teleops hang from the ceiling in there, like mantis limbs with impossibly fragile fingers. Lasers. Needles and nanotubes. Atomic-force
manipulators delicate enough to coax individual atoms apart. ZeroS have gone under those knives more times than any of them
can count. Surgery by software, mostly. Occasionally by human
doctors phoning it in from undisclosed locations, old-school cutters who never visit in the flesh for all the times they've cut into
Asante's.

Acosta's on his back, eyes closed. He looks almost at peace.
Even his facial tic has quieted. He's been here three days now, ever
since losing his right arm to a swarm of smart fléchettes over in
Heraklion. It's no big deal. He's growing it back with a little help
from some imported salamander DNA and a steroid-infused ami-
noglucose drip. He'll be good as new in three weeks—as good as
he's ever been since ZeroS got him, anyway—back in his rack in
half that time. Meanwhile it's a tricky balance: his metabolism may
be boosted into the jet stream, but it's all for tissue growth. There's
barely enough left over to power a trip to the bathroom.

Kodjo Asante wonders why he's standing here at 0300.

Maddox says the occasional bit of sleepwalking isn't anything
to get too worried about, especially if you're already prone to it.
Nobody's suffered a major episode in months, not since well before Galveston; these days the tweaks seem mainly about fine-tun-
ing. Rossiter's long since called off the just-in-case bots that once
dogged their every unscripted step. Even lets them leave the base
now and then, when they've been good.

You still have to expect the occasional lingering side effect,
though. Asante glances down at the telltale tremor in his own
hand, seizes it gently with the other, and holds firm until the
nerves quiet. Looks back at his friend.

Acosta's eyes are open.

They don't look at him. They don't settle long enough to look at anything, as far as Asante can tell. They jump and twitch in Acosta's face, back forth back forth up down up.

"Carl," Asante says softly. "How's it going, man?"

The rest of that body doesn't even twitch. Acosta's breathing remains unchanged. He doesn't speak.

Zombies aren't big on talking. They're smart but nonverbal, like those split-brain patients who understand words but can't utter them. Something about the integration of speech with consciousness. Written language is easier. The zombie brain doesn't take well to conventional grammar and syntax, but they've developed a kind of visual pidgin that Maddox claims is more efficient than English. Apparently they use it at all the briefings.

Maddox also claims they're working on a kind of time-sharing arrangement, some way to divvy up custody of Broca's area between the frontoparietal and the retrosplenial. *Someday soon, maybe, you'll literally be able to talk to yourself,* he says. But they haven't got there yet.

A tacpad on the bedside table glows with a dim matrix of Zidgin symbols. Asante places it under Acosta's right hand.

"Carl?"

Nothing.

"Just thought I'd . . . see how you were. You take care."

He tiptoes to the door, sets trembling fingers on the knob. Steps into the darkness of the hallway, navigates back to his rack by touch and memory.

Those eyes.

It's not like he hasn't seen it a million times before. But all those other times his squadmates' eyes blurred and danced in upright bodies, powerful autonomous things that *moved*. Seeing that motion embedded in such stillness—watching eyes struggle as if trapped in muscle and bone, as if looking up from some shallow grave where they haven't quite been buried alive—

Terrified. That's how they looked. Terrified.

We Are the Dead

Specialist Tarra Kalmus has disappeared. Rossiter was seen breaking the news to Maddox just this morning, a conversation during which Maddox morphed miraculously from He of the Perpetually

Goofy Smile into Lieutenant Stoneface. He refuses to talk about it
with any of the grunts. Silano managed to buttonhole Rossiter on
her way back to the helipad but could only extract the admission
that Kalmus has been "reassigned."

Metzinger tells them to stop asking questions. He makes it an
order.

But as Tiwana points out—when Asante finds her that evening,
sitting with her back propped against a pallet of machine parts in
the loading bay—you can run all sorts of online queries without
ever using a question mark.

"Fellow corpse."

"Fellow corpse."

It's been their own private salutation since learning how much
they have in common. (Tiwana died during a Realist attack in Ha-
vana. Worst vacation ever, she says.) They're the only ZeroS, so far
at least, to return from the dead. The others hold them a little in
awe because of it.

The others also keep a certain distance.

"Garin was last to see her, over at the Memory Hole." Tiwana's
wearing a pair of smart specs tuned to the public net. It won't stop
any higher-ups who decide to look over her shoulder, but at least
her activity won't be logged by default. "Chatting up some redhead
with a Hanson Geothermal logo on her jacket."

Two nights ago Metzinger let everyone off the leash as a reward
for squashing a Realist attack on the G8G Constellation. They went
down to Banff for some meatspace R&R. "So?"

Speclight paints Tiwana's cheeks with small flickering auroras.
"So a BPD drone found a woman matching that description dead
outside a public fuckcubby two blocks south of there. Same night."

"Eiiii." Asante squats down beside her as Tiwana pushes the
specs onto her forehead. Her wonky eye jiggles at him.

"Yeah." She takes a breath, lets it out. "Nicci Steckman, according to the DNA."

"So how—"

"They don't say. Just asking witnesses to come forward."

"Have any?"

"They left together. Deked into an alley. No further surveillance
record, which is odd."

"Is it really," Asante murmurs.

"No. I guess not."

They sit in silence for a moment.

"What do you think?" she asks at last.

"Maybe Steckman didn't like it rough and things got out of hand. You know Kally, she . . . doesn't always take no for an answer."

"No to what? We're all on antilibidinals. Why would she even be—"

"She'd never *kill* someone over—"

"Maybe *she* didn't," Tiwana says.

He blinks. "You think she flipped?"

"Maybe it wasn't her fault. Maybe the augs kicked in on their own somehow, like a, a . . . reflex. Kally saw an imminent threat, or something her better half *interpreted* that way. Grabbed the keys, took care of it."

"It's not supposed to work like that."

"It wasn't supposed to fry Saks's central nervous system either."

"Come on, Sofe. That's ancient history. They wouldn't deploy us if they hadn't fixed those problems."

"Really." Her bad eye looks pointedly at his bad hand.

"Legacy glitches don't count." Nerves nicked during surgery, a stray milliamp leaking into the fusiform gyrus. Everyone's got at least one. "Maddox says—"

"Oh sure, Maddox is always gonna tidy up. Next week, next month. Once the latest tweaks have settled, or there isn't some brush fire to put out over in Kamfuckingchatka. Meanwhile the glitches don't even manifest in zombie mode, so why should he care?"

"If they thought the implants were defective, they wouldn't keep sending us out on missions."

"Eh." Tiwana spreads her hands. "You say *mission*, I say *field test*. I mean, sure, camaraderie's great—we're the cutting edge, we can be ZeroS! But *look* at us, Jo. Silano was a Rio insurgent. Kalmus was up on insubordination charges. They scraped you and me off the ground like roadkill. None of us are what you'd call *summa cum laude*."

"Isn't that the point? That *anybody* can be a supersoldier?" *Or at least any* body.

"We're lab rats, Jo. They don't want to risk frying their West Point grads with a beta release, so they're working out the bugs on us first. If the program was ready to go wide we wouldn't still be here. Which means—" She heaves a sigh. "It's the augs. At least, I hope it's the augs."

"You hope?"

"You'd rather believe Kally just went berserk and killed a civilian for no reason?"

He tries to ignore a probably psychosomatic tingle at the back of his head. "Rossiter wouldn't be talking *reassignment* if she had," he admits. "She'd be talking court-martial."

"She'll never talk court-martial. Not where we're concerned."

"Really."

"Think about it. You ever see any politician come by to make sure the taxpayer's money's being well spent? You ever see a commissioned officer walking the halls who wasn't Metzinger or Maddox or Rossiter?"

"So we're off the books." It's hardly a revelation.

"We're so far *off the books* we might as well be cave paintings. We don't even know our own tooth-to-tail ratio. Ninety percent of our support infrastructure's offsite, it's all robots and teleops. We don't even know who's cutting into our own heads." She leans close in the deepening gloom, fixes him with her good eye. "This is voodoo, Jo. Maybe the program *started* small with that kneejerk stuff, but now? You and I, we're literal fucking *zombies*. We're re-animated corpses dancing on strings, and if you think Persephone Q. Public is gonna be fine with that, you have a lot more faith in her than I do. I don't think Congress knows about us, I don't think Parliament knows about us, I bet SOCOM doesn't even know about us past some line in a budget that says *psychological research*. I don't think they *want* to know. And when something's that dark, are they really going to let anything as trivial as a judicial process drag it into the light?"

Asante shakes his head. "Still has to be accountability. Some kind of internal process."

"There is. You disappear, and they tell everyone you've been reassigned."

He thinks for a bit. "So what do we do?"

"First we riot in the mess hall. Then we march on Ottawa demanding equal rights for corpses." She rolls her eyes. "We don't *do* anything. Maybe you forgot: we *died*. We don't legally exist anymore, and unless you got a way better deal than me, the only way for either of us to change that is keep our heads down until we get our honorable discharges. I do not like being dead. I would

very much like to go back to being officially alive someday. Until
then . . ."

She takes the specs off her head. Powers them down.

"We watch our fucking step."

Ricochet

Sergeant Kodjo Asante watches his fucking step. He watches it
when he goes up against AIRheads and Realists. He watches it
when pitted against well-funded private armies running on profit
and ideology, against ragged makeshift ones driven by thirst and
desperation, against rogue Darwin Banks and the inevitable religious extremists who—almost a quarter century after the end of
the Dark Decade—still haven't stopped maiming and killing in
the name of their Invisible Friends. His steps don't really falter until twenty-one months into his tour, when he kills three unarmed
children off the coast of Honduras.

ZeroS have risen from the depths of the Atlantic to storm one
of the countless gylands that ride the major currents of the world's
oceans. Some are refugee camps with thousands of inhabitants;
others serve as havens for hustlers and tax dodgers eager to avoid
the constraints of more stationary jurisdictions. Some are military,
sheathed in chromatophores and radar-damping nanotubes: bigger than airports, invisible to man or machine.

The *Caçador de Recompensa* is a fish farm, a family business registered out of Brazil: two modest hectares of low-slung superstruc-
ture on a doughnut hull with a cluster of net pens at its center.
It is currently occupied by forces loyal to the latest incarnation
of Shining Path. The Path thrives on supply lines with no fixed
address—and as Metzinger reminded them on the way down, it's
always better to prevent a fight than win one. If the Path can't feed
their troops, maybe they won't deploy them.

This is almost a mission of mercy.

Asante eavesdrops on the sounds of battle, takes in a mingled
reek of oil and salt air and rotten fish, lets Evil Twin's worldview
wash across his eyes in a blur of light and the incomprehensible
flicker of readouts with millisecond lifespans. Except during target
acquisition, of course. Except for those brief stroboscopic instants

when ET *locks on,* and faces freeze and blur in turn: a couple of coveralled SAsian men wielding Heckler-Kochs. A wounded antique ZhanLu staggering on two and a half legs, the beam from its MAD gun wobbling wide of any conceivable target. Children in life jackets, two boys, one girl; Asante guesses their ages at between seven and ten. Each time the weapon kicks in his hands and an instant later ET is veering toward the next kill.

Emotions are sluggish things in Passenger mode. He feels nothing in the moment, shock in the aftermath. Horror's still halfway to the horizon when a random ricochet slaps him back into the driver's seat.

The bullet doesn't penetrate—not much punches through the Chrysomalon armor wrapped tight around his skin—but vectors interact. Momentum passes from a small fast object to a large slow one. Asante's brain lurches in its cavity; meat slaps bone and bounces back. Deep in all that stressed gray matter, some vital circuit shorts out.

There's pain of course, blooming across the side of his head like napalm in those few seconds before his endocrine pumps damp it down. There's fire in the BUD, a blaze of static and a crimson icon warning of ZMODE FAILURE. But there's a little miracle too:

Kodjo Asante can see again: a high sun in a hard blue sky. A flat far horizon. Columns of oily smoke rising from wrecked machinery.

Bodies.

The air *crack*s a few centimeters to his right. He drops instinctively to a deck slippery with blood and silver scales, gags at the sudden stench wafting from a slurry of bloated carcasses crowding the surface of the holding pen just in front of him. (*Coho-Atlantic hybrids,* he notes despite himself. *Might even have those new Showell genes.*) A turret on treads sparks and sizzles on the other side, a hole blown in its carapace.

A shadow blurs across Asante's forearm. Tiwana leaps across the sky, defractors high on her forehead, eyeballs dancing madly in their sockets. She clears the enclosure, alights graceful as a dragonfly on one foot, kicks the spastic turret with the other. It sparks one last time and topples into the pen. Tiwana vanishes down the nearest companionway.

Asante gets to his feet, pans for threats, sees nothing but enemies laid waste: the smoking stumps of perimeter autoturrets, the

fallen bodies of a man with his arm blown off and a woman groping for a speargun just beyond reach. And a small brittle figure
almost fused to the deck: blackened sticks for arms and legs, white
teeth grinning in a charred skull, a bright half-melted puddle of
orange fabric and PVC holding it all together. Asante sees it all.
Not just snapshots glimpsed through the fog: ZeroS handiwork,
served up for the first time in three-sixty wraparound immersion.

We're killing children . . .

Even the adult bodies don't look like combatants. Refugees,
maybe, driven to take by force what they couldn't get any other
way. Maybe all they wanted was to get somewhere safe. To feed
their kids.

At his feet, a reeking carpet of dead salmon converge listlessly
in the wake of the fallen turret. They aren't feeding anything but
hagfish and maggots.

I have become Sāḥilite, Asante reflects numbly. He calls up BUD,
ignores the unreadable auras flickering around the edges of vision, selects GPS.

Not off Honduras. They're in the Gulf of Mexico.

No one in their right mind would run a fish farm here. The best
parts of the Gulf are anoxic; the worst are downright flammable.
Caçador must have drifted up through the Yucatán Channel, got
caught in an eddy loop. All these fish would have suffocated as
soon as they hit the dead zone.

But gylands aren't entirely at the mercy of the currents. They
carry rudimentary propulsion systems for docking and launching, switching streams and changing course. *Caçador's* presence so
deep in the Gulf implies either catastrophic equipment failure or
catastrophic ignorance.

Asante can check out the first possibility, anyway. He stumbles
toward the nearest companionway—

—as Tiwana and Acosta burst onto deck from below. Acosta
seizes his right arm, Tiwana his left. Neither slows. Asante's feet
bounce and drag. The lurching acceleration reawakens the pain
in his temple.

He cries out: *"The engines . . ."*

New pain, other side, sharp and recurrent: an ancient weight
belt swinging back and forth across Acosta's torso, a frayed strip of
nylon threaded through an assortment of lead slugs. It's like being
hammered by a tiny wrecking ball. One part of Asante wonders

where Acosta found it; another watches Garin race into view with a small bloody body slung across his shoulder. Garin passes one of the dismembered turrets, grabs a piece with his free hand, and keeps running.

Everyone's charging for the rails.

Tiwana's mouthpiece is in, her defractors down. She empties a clip into the deck ahead, right at the water's edge: gunfire shreds plastic and whitewashed fiberglass, loosens an old iron docking cleat. She dips and grabs in passing, draws it to her chest, never loosening her grip on Asante. He hears the soft pop of a bone leaving its socket in the instant before they all go over the side.

They plummet headfirst, dragged down by a hundred kilograms of improvised ballast. Asante chokes, jams his mouthpiece into place; coughs seawater through the exhaust and sucks in a hot lungful of fresh-sparked hydrox. Pressure builds against his eardrums. He swallows, swallows again, manages to keep a few millibars ahead of outright rupture. He has just enough freedom of movement to claw at his face and slide the defractors over his eyes. The ocean clicks into focus, clear as acid, empty as green glass.

Green turns white.

Seen in that flash-blinded instant: four thin streams of bubbles, rising to a surface gone suddenly incandescent. Four dark bodies, falling from the light. A thunderclap rolls through the water, deep, downshifted, as much felt as heard. It comes from nowhere and everywhere.

The roof of the ocean is on fire. Some invisible force shreds their contrails from the top down, tears those bubbles into swirling silver confetti. The wave-front races implacably after them. The ocean *bulges*, recoils. It squeezes Asante like a fist, stretches him like rubber; Tiwana and Acosta tumble away in the backwash. He flails, stabilizes himself as the first jagged shapes resolve overhead: dismembered chunks of the booby-trapped gyland, tumbling with slow majesty into the depths. A broken wedge of deck and stairwell passes by a few meters away, tangled in monofilament. A thousand glassy eyes stare back from the netting as the wreckage fades to black.

Asante scans the ocean for that fifth bubble trail, that last dark figure to balance Those Who Left against Those Who Returned. No one overhead. Below, a dim shape that has to be Garin shares its mouthpiece with the small limp thing in his arms. Beyond that, the hint of a deeper dark against the abyss: a sharklike silhouette keeping station amid a slow rain of debris. Waiting to take its prodigal children home again.

They're too close to shore. There might be witnesses. So much for stealth ops. So much for low profiles and no-questions-asked. Metzinger's going to be pissed.

Then again, they *are* in the Gulf of Mexico.

Any witnesses will probably just think it caught fire again.

Lady Grinning Soul

"In your own words, Sergeant. Take your time."

We killed children. We killed children, and we lost Silano, and I don't know why. And I don't know if you do either.

But of course, that would involve taking Major Emma Rossiter at *her* word.

"Did the child . . . ?" Metzinger had already tubed Garin's prize by the time Asante reboarded the sub. Garin, of course, had no idea what his body had been doing. Metzinger had not encouraged discussion.

That was okay. Nobody was really in the mood anyhow.

"I'm sorry. She didn't make it." Rossiter waits for what she probably regards as a respectful moment. "If we could focus on the subject at hand . . ."

"It was a shitstorm," Asante says. "Sir."

"We gathered that." The major musters a sympathetic smile. "We were hoping you could provide more in the way of details."

"You must have the logs."

"Those are numbers, Sergeant. Pixels. You are uniquely—if accidentally—in a position to give us more than that."

"I never even got belowdecks."

Rossiter seems to relax a little. "Still. This is the first time one of you has been debooted in midgame, and it's obviously not the kind of thing we want to risk repeating. Maddox is already working on ways to make the toggle more robust. In the meantime, your perspective could be useful in helping to ensure this doesn't happen again."

"My perspective, sir, is that those forces did not warrant our particular skill set."

"We're more interested in your experiences regarding the de-boot, Sergeant. Was there a sense of disorientation, for example? Any visual artifacts in BUD?"

Asante stands with his hands behind his back—good gripping bad—and says nothing.

"Very well." Rossiter's smile turns grim. "Let's talk about your *perspective,* then. Do you think regular forces would have been sufficient? Do you have a sense of the potential losses incurred if we'd sent, say, WestHem marines?"

"They appeared to be refugees, sir. They didn't pose—"

"One hundred percent, Sergeant. We would have lost everyone."

Asante says nothing.

"Unaugged soldiers wouldn't even have made it off the gyland before it went up. Even if they had, the p-wave would've been fatal if you hadn't greatly increased your rate of descent. Do you think regular forces would have made that call? Seen what was coming, run the numbers, improvised a strategy to get below the kill zone in less time than it would take to shout a command?"

"We killed children." It's barely more than a whisper.

"Collateral damage is an unfortunate but inevitable—"

"We *targeted* children."

"Ah."

Rossiter plays with her tacpad: *tap tap tap, swipe.*

"These children," she says at last. "Were they armed?"

"I do not believe so, sir."

"Were they naked?"

"Sir?"

"Could you be certain they weren't carrying concealed weapons? Maybe even a remote trigger for a thousand kilograms of CL-20?"

"They were . . . sir, they couldn't have been more than seven or eight."

"I shouldn't have to tell you about child soldiers, Sergeant. They've been a fact of life for centuries, especially in *your* particular—at any rate. Just out of interest, how young would someone have to be before you'd rule them out as a potential threat?"

"I don't know, sir."

"Yes you do. You *did.* That's why you targeted them."

"That wasn't me."

"Of course. It was your . . . evil twin. That's what you call it, right?" Rossiter leans forward. "Listen to me very carefully, Sergeant Asante, because I think you're laboring under some serious misapprehensions about what we do here. Your *twin* is not evil, and it is not gratuitous. It is *you:* a much bigger part of *you* than the whiny bitch standing in front of me right now."

Asante clenches his teeth and keeps his mouth shut.

"This gut feeling giving you so much trouble. This sense of right and wrong. Where do you think it comes from, Sergeant?"

"Experience. Sir."

"It's the result of a calculation. A whole series of calculations, far too complex to fit into the conscious workspace. So the subconscious sends you . . . an executive summary, you might call it. Your evil twin knows all about your sense of moral outrage; it's the source of it. It has more information than you do. Processes it more effectively. Maybe you should trust it to know what it's doing."

He doesn't. He doesn't trust her either.

But suddenly, surprisingly, he understands her.

She's not just making a point. This isn't just rhetoric. The insight appears fully formed in his mind, a bright shard of unexpected clarity. *She thought it would be easy. She really doesn't know what happened.*

He watches her fingers move on the 'pad as she speaks. Notes the nervous flicker of her tongue at the corner of her mouth. She glances up to meet his eye, glances away again.

She's scared.

Look Back in Anger

Asante awakens standing in the meadow up the mountain. The sky is cloudless and full of stars. His fatigues are damp with sweat or dew. There is no moon. Black conifers loom on all sides. To the east, a hint of predawn orange seeps through the branches.

He has read that this was once the time of the dawn chorus, when songbirds would call out in ragged symphony to start the day. He has never heard it. He doesn't hear it now. There's no sound in this forest but his own breathing—

—and the snap of a twig under someone's foot.

He turns. A gray shape detaches itself from the darkness.

"Fellow corpse," Tiwana says.

"Fellow corpse," he responds.

"You wandered off. Thought I'd tag along. Make sure you didn't go AWOL."

"I think ET's acting up again."

"Maybe you're just sleepwalking. People sleepwalk sometimes." She shrugs. "Probably the same wiring anyway."

"Sleepwalkers don't kill people."

"Actually, that's been known to happen."

He clears his throat. "Did, um . . ."

"No one else knows you're up here."

"Did ET disable the pickups?"

"I did."

"Thanks."

"Any time."

Asante looks around. "I remember the first time I saw this place. It was . . . magical."

"I was thinking more *ironic*." Adding, at Asante's look, "You know. That one of the last pristine spots in this whole shit show owes its existence to the fact that WestHem needs someplace private to teach us how to blow shit up."

"Count on you," Asante says.

The stars are fading. Venus is hanging in there, though.

"You've been weird," she observes. "Ever since the thing with *Caçador.*"

"It was a weird thing."

"So I hear." Shrug. "I guess you had to be there."

He musters a smile. "So you don't remember . . ."

"Legs running down. Legs running back up. My zombie never targeted anything, so I don't know what she saw."

"Metzinger does. Rossiter does." He leans his ass against a convenient boulder. "Does it ever bother you? That you don't know what your own eyes are seeing, and they do?"

"Not really. Just the way it works."

"We don't know what we're doing out there. When was the last time Maddox even showed us a highlight reel?" He feels the muscles clenching in his jaw. "We could be war criminals."

"There *is* no *we*. Not when it matters." She sits beside him. "Besides. Our zombies may be nonconscious, but they're not stupid; they know we're obligated to disobey unlawful commands."

"Maybe they *know*. Not sure Maddox's compliance circuit would let them do anything about it."

Somewhere nearby a songbird clears its throat.

Tiwana takes a breath. "Suppose you're right—not saying you are, but *suppose* they sent us out to gun down a gyland full of harmless refugees. Forget that *Caçador* was packing enough explosives to blow up a hamlet, forget that it killed Silano . . . hell, nearly killed us all. If Metzinger decides to bash in someone's innocent skull, you still don't blame the hammer he used."

"And yet. Someone's skull is still bashed in."

Across the clearing, another bird answers. *The dawn duet.*

"There must be reasons," she says, as if trying it on for size.

He remembers *reasons* from another life, on another continent: Retribution. The making of examples. Poor impulse control. Just . . . fun, sometimes.

"Such as."

"I don't know, okay? Big picture's way above our pay grade. But that doesn't mean you toss out the chain of command every time someone gives you an order without a twenty-gig backgrounder to go with it. If you want me to believe we're in thrall to a bunch of fascist baby-killers, you're gonna need more than a few glimpses of something you may have seen on a gyland."

"How about, I don't know. All of human history?"

Venus is gone at last. The rising sun streaks the clearing with gold.

"It's the deal we made. Sure, it's a shitty one. Only shittier one is being dead. But would you choose differently, even now? Go back to being fish food?"

He honestly doesn't know.

"We should be *dead,* Jo. Every one of these moments is a gift."

He regards her with a kind of wonder. "I never know how you do it."

"Do what?"

"Channel Schopenhauer and Pollyanna at the same time without your head exploding."

She takes his hand for a moment, squeezes briefly. Rises. "We're gonna make it. Just so long as we don't rock the boat. All the way to that honorable fucking discharge." She turns to the light; sunrise glows across her face. "Until then, in case you were wondering, I've got your back."

"There is no you," he reminds her. "Not when it matters."

"I've got your back," she says.

Watch That Man

They've outsourced Silano's position, brought in someone none of them have ever seen before. Technically he's one of them, though the scars that tag him ZeroS have barely had time to heal. Something about him is wrong. Something about the way he moves; his insignia. Not specialist or corporal or sergeant.

"I want you to meet Lieutenant Jim Moore," Rossiter tells them.

ZeroS finally have a commissioned secco. He's easily the youngest person in the room.

He gets right to it. "This is the Nanisivik mine." The satcam wall zooms down onto the roof of the world. "Baffin Island, seven hundred fifty klicks north of the Arctic Circle, heart of the Slush Belt." A barren fractured landscape of red and ocher. Drumlins and hillocks and bifurcating streambeds.

"Tapped out at the turn of the century." A brown road, undulating along some scoured valley floor. A cluster of buildings. A gaping mouth in the earth. "These days people generally stay away, on account of its remote location. Also on account of the eight thousand metric tons of high-level nuclear waste the Canadian government brought over from India for deep-time storage. Part of an initiative to diversify the northern economy, apparently." Tactical schematics, now: Processing and Intake. Train tracks corkscrewing into the Canadian Shield. Storage tunnels branching like the streets of an underground subdivision. "Project was abandoned after the Greens lost power in '38.

"You could poison a lot of cities with this stuff. Which may be why someone's messing around there now."

Garin's hand is up. "Someone, sir?"

"So far all we have are signs of unauthorized activity and a JTFN drone that went in and never came out. Our first priority is to identify the actors. Depending on what we find, we might take care of it ourselves. Or we might call in the bombers. Won't know until we get there."

And we *won't know even then,* Asante muses—and realizes, in that moment, what it is about Moore that strikes him as so strange.

"We'll be prepping your better halves with the operational details en route."

It's not what is, it's what *isn't:* no tic at the corner of the eye, no tremor in the hand. His speech is smooth and perfect, his eyes make contact with steady calm. Lieutenant Moore doesn't glitch.

"For now, we anticipate a boots-down window of no more than seven hours—"

Asante looks at Tiwana. Tiwana looks back.

ZeroS are out of beta.

Subterraneans

The Lockheed drops them at the foot of a crumbling pier. Derelict shops and listing trailers, long abandoned, huddle against the sleeting rain. This used to be a seaport; then a WestHem refueling station back before *WestHem* was even a word, before the apocalyptic Arctic weather made it easier to just stick everything underwater. It lived its short life as a company town, an appendage of the mine, in the days before Nanisivik was emptied of its valuables and filled up again.

BUD says 1505: less than an hour if they want to be on target by sundown. Moore leads them overland across weathered stone and alluvial washouts and glistening acned Martian terrain. They're fifteen hundred meters from the mouth of the repository when he orders them all into the backseat.

Asante's legs, under new management, pick up the pace. His vision blurs. At least up here, in the wind and blinding sleet, it doesn't make much difference.

A sound drifts past: the roar of some distant animal perhaps. Nearer, the unmistakable discharge of a −40. Not ET's. Asante's eyes remain virtuously clouded.

The wind dies in the space of a dozen steps. Half as many again and the torrent of icy needles on his face slows to a patter, a drizzle. Asante hears great bolts unlatching, a soft screech of heavy metal. They pass through some portal and the bright overcast in his eyes dims by half. Buckles and bootsteps echo faintly against rock walls.

Downhill. A gentle curve to the left. Gravel, patches of broken asphalt. His feet step over unseen obstacles.

And stop.

The whole squad must have frozen; he can't hear so much as a breath. The supersaccadic ticker tape flickering across the fog seems faster. Could be his imagination. Off in some subterranean distance, water *drip-drip-drip*s onto a still surface.

Quiet movement as ZeroS spread out. Asante's just a Passenger, but he reads the footsteps, feels his legs taking him sideways, kneeling. The padding on his elbows doesn't leave much room for fine-grained tactile feedback, but the surface he's bracing against is flat and rough, like a table sheathed in sandpaper.

There's a musky animal smell in the air. From somewhere in the middle distance, a soft *whuffle*. The stirring of something huge in slow, sleepy motion.

Maybe someone left the door open, and something got in . . .

Pizzly bears are the only animals that come to mind: monstrous hybrids, birthed along the boundaries of stressed ecosystems crashing into each other. He's never seen one in the flesh.

A grunt. A low growl.

The sound of building speed.

Gunshots. A roar, deafeningly close, and a crash of metal against metal. The flickering tactical halo dims abruptly: network traffic just dropped by a node.

Now the whole network crashes: pawn exchange, ZeroS sacrificing their own LAN as the price of jamming the enemy's. Moore's MAD gun snaps to the right. An instant of scorching heat as the beam sweeps across Asante's arm; Moore shooting wide, Moore *missing*. ET breaks cover, leaps, and locks. For one crystalline millisecond Asante sees a wall of coarse ivory-brown fur close enough to touch, every follicle in perfect focus.

The clouds close in. ET pulls the trigger.

A bellow. The scrape of great claws against stone. The reek is overpowering, but ET's already pirouetting after fresh game and *click* the freeze-frame glimpse of monstrous ursine jaws in a face wide as a doorway and *click* small brown hands raised against an onrushing foe and *click* a young boy with freckles and strawberry-blond hair and Asante's blind again but he feels ET pulling on the trigger, *pop pop pop—*

Whatthefuck children whatthefuck whatthefuck

—and ET's changed course again and *click:* a small back a fur coat black hair flying in the light of the muzzle flash.

Not again. Not again.

Child soldiers. Suicide bombers. For centuries.

But no one's shooting back.

He knows the sound of every weapon the squad might use, down to the smallest pop and click: the sizzle of the MAD gun, the bark of the Epsilon, Acosta's favorite Olympic. He hears them now; those, and no others. Whatever they're shooting at isn't returning fire.

Whatever we're shooting at. You blind murderous twaaaaase. You're shooting eight-year-olds.

Again.

More gunfire. Still no voices but for a final animal roar that gives way to a wet gurgle and the heavy slap of meat on stone.

It's a nuclear waste repository at the North Pole. What are children even doing here?

What am I?

What am I?

And suddenly he sees the words *All tautologies are tautologies* and ET's back downstairs and the basement door locks and Kodjo Asante grabs frantically for the reins and takes back his life and opens his eyes:

In time to see the little freckled boy, dressed in ragged furs, sitting on Riley Garin's shoulders and dragging a jagged piece of glass across his throat. In time to see him leap free of the body and snatch Garin's gun, toss it effortlessly across this dimly lit cave to an Asian girl clad only in a filthy loincloth, who's sailing through the air toward a bloodied Jim Moore. In time to see that girl reach behind her and catch the gun in midair without so much as a backward glance.

More than a dance, more than teamwork. Like digits on the same hand, moving together.

The pizzly's piled up against a derelict forklift, a giant tawny thing raking the air with massive claws even as it bleeds out through the hole in its flank. A SAsian child with his left hand blown off at the wrist (*maybe that was me*) dips and weaves around the fallen behemoth. He's — *using* it, exploiting the sweep of its claws and teeth as a kind of exclusion zone guaranteed to maul anyone within three meters. Somehow those teeth and claws never seem to connect with him.

They've connected with Acosta, though. Carlos Acosta, lover of sunlight and the great outdoors, lies there broken at the middle, staring at nothing.

Garin finally crashes to the ground, blood gushing from his throat.

They're just children. In rags. Unarmed.

The girl rebounds between rough-hewn tunnel walls and calcified machinery, lines up the shot with Garin's weapon. Her bare feet never seem to touch the ground.

They're children they're just—

Tiwana slams him out of the way as the beam sizzles past. The air shimmers and steams. Asante's head cracks against gears and conduits and ribbed metal, bounces off steel onto rock. Tiwana lands on top of him, eyes twitching in frantic little arcs.

And stopping.

It's a moment of pure panic, seeing those eyes freeze and focus—*she doesn't know me she's locking on she's locking on*—but something shines through from behind and Asante can see that her eyes aren't target-locked at all. They're just *looking.*

". . . Sofiyko?"

Whatever happens, I've got your back.

But Sofiyko's gone, if she was ever even there.

Blackout

Moore hands him off to Metzinger. Metzinger regards him without a word, with a look that speaks volumes: flips a switch and drops him into Passenger mode. He doesn't tell Asante to stay there. He doesn't have to.

Asante feels the glassy pane of a tacpad under ET's hand. That hand rests deathly still for seconds at a time; erupts into a flurry of inhumanly fast taps and swipes; pauses again. Out past the bright blur in Asante's eyes, the occasional cough or murmur is all that punctuates the muted roar of the Lockheed's engines.

ET is under interrogation. A part of Asante wonders what it's saying about him, but he can't really bring himself to care.

He can't believe they're gone.

No Control

"Sergeant Asante." Major Rossiter shakes her head. "We had such hopes for you."

Acosta. Garin. Tiwana.

"Nothing to say?"

So very much. But all that comes out is the same old lie: "They were just . . . children . . ."

"Perhaps we can carve that on the gravestones of your squadmates."

"But who—"

"We don't know. We'd suspect Realists, if the tech itself wasn't completely antithetical to everything they stand for. If it wasn't way past their abilities."

"They were barely even clothed. It was like a *nest* . . ."

"More like a hive, Sergeant."

Digits on the same hand . . .

"Not like you," she says, as if reading his mind. "ZeroS networking is quite—inefficient, when you think about it. Multiple minds in multiple heads, independently acting on the same information and coming to the same conclusion. Needless duplication of effort."

"And these . . ."

"Multiple heads. One mind."

"We jammed the freqs. Even if they were networked—"

"We don't think they work like that. Best guess is . . . bioradio, you could call it. Like a quantum-entangled corpus callosum." She snorts. "Of course, at this point they could say it was elves and I'd have to take their word for it."

Caçador, Asante remembers. They've learned a lot from one small stolen corpse.

"Why use *children?*" he whispers.

"Oh, Kodjo." Asante blinks at the lapse; Rossiter doesn't seem to notice. "Using children is the *last* thing they want to do. Why do you think they've been stashed in the middle of the ocean or down some Arctic mineshaft? We're not talking about implants. This is genetic, they were *born.* They have to be protected, hidden away until they grow up and . . . ripen."

"Protected? By abandoning them in a nuclear waste site?"

"Abandoning them, yes. Completely defenseless. As you saw." When he says nothing, she continues. "It's actually a perfect spot. No neighbors. Lots of waste heat to keep you warm, run your greenhouses, mask your heatprint. No supply lines for some nosy satellite to notice. No telltale EM. From what we can tell weren't even any adults on the premises, they just . . . lived off the land, so to speak. Not even any weapons of their own, or at least they didn't use any. Used *bears,* of all things. Used your own guns against you. Maybe they're minimalists, value improvisation." She sacc's something onto her pad. "Maybe they just want to keep us guessing."

"Children." He can't seem to stop saying it.

"For now. Wait till they hit puberty." Rossiter sighs. "We bombed the site, of course. Slagged the entrance. If any of ours were trapped down there, they wouldn't be getting out. Then again, we're not talking about us, are we? We're talking about a single distributed organism with God knows how many times the computational mass of a normal human brain. I'd be very surprised if it couldn't anticipate and counter anything we planned. Still. We do what we can."

Neither speaks for a few moments.

"And I'm sorry, Sergeant," she says finally. "I'm so sorry it's come to this. We do what we've always done. Feed you stories so you won't be compromised, so you won't compromise *us* when someone catches you and starts poking your amygdala. But the switch was for your protection. We don't know who we're up against. We don't know how many hives are out there, what stage of gestation any of them have reached, how many may have already . . . matured. All we know is that a handful of unarmed children can slaughter our most elite forces at will, and we are so very unready for the world to know that.

"But *you* know, Sergeant. You dropped out of the game—which may well have cost us the mission—and now you know things that are way above your clearance.

"Tell me. If our positions were reversed, what would *you* do?"

Asante closes his eyes. *We should be dead. Every one of these moments is a gift.* When he opens them again, Rossiter's watching, impassive as ever.

"I should've died up there. I should have died off Takoradi two years ago."

The major snorts. "Don't be melodramatic, Sergeant. We're not going to execute you."

"I . . . what?"

"We're not even going to court-martial you."

"Why the hell not?" And at her raised eyebrow: "Sir. You said it yourself: unauthorized drop-out. Middle of a combat situation."

"We're not entirely certain that was your decision."

"It *felt* like my decision."

"It always does though, doesn't it?" Rossiter pushes back in her chair. "We didn't create your evil twin, Sergeant. We didn't even put it in control. We just got you out of the way, so it could do what it always does without interference. Only now it apparently . . . wants you back."

This takes a moment to sink in. "What?"

"Frontoparietal logs suggest your zombie took a certain . . . initiative. Decided to quit."

"In combat? That would be suicide!"

"Isn't that what you wanted?"

He looks away.

"No? Don't like that hypothesis? Well, here's another: it surrendered. Moore got you out, after all, which was statistically unlikely the way things were going. Maybe dropping out was a white flag, and the hive took pity and let you go so you could . . . I don't know, spread the word: *Don't fuck with us.*

"Or maybe it decided the hive deserved to win, and switched sides. Maybe it was . . . conscientiously objecting. Maybe it decided *it* never enlisted in the first place."

Asante decides he doesn't like the sound of the major's laugh.

"You must have asked it," he says.

"A dozen different ways. Zombies might be analytically brilliant, but they're terrible at self-reflection. They can tell you exactly what they did but not necessarily *why.*"

"When did you ever care about motive?" His tone verges on insubordination; he's too empty to care. "Just . . . tell it to stay in control. It has to obey you, right? That orbitofrontal thing. The *compliance mod.*"

"Absolutely. But it wasn't your twin who dropped out. It was *you*, when it unleashed the mandala."

"So order it not to show me the mandala."

"We'd love to. I don't suppose you'd care to tell us what it looks like?"

It's Asante's turn to laugh. He sucks at it.

"I didn't think so. Not that it matters. At this point we can't trust you either—again, not entirely your fault. Given the degree to which conscious and unconscious processes are interconnected, it may have been premature to try and separate them so completely, right off the bat." She winces, as if in sympathy. "I can't imagine it's much fun for you either, being cooped up in that skull with nothing to do."

"Maddox said there was no way around it."

"That was true. When he said it." Eyes downcast now, sacc'ing the omnipresent 'pad. "We weren't planning on field-testing the new mod just yet, but with Kalmus and now you—I don't see much choice but to advance implementation by a couple of months."

He's never felt more dead inside. Even when he was.

"Haven't you stuck enough pins in us?" By which he means *me*, of course. By process of elimination.

For a moment the major almost seems sympathetic.

"Yes, Kodjo. Just one last modification. I don't think you'll even mind this one, because next time you wake up, you'll be a free man. Your tour will be over."

"Really."

"Really."

Asante looks down. Frowns.

"What is it, Sergeant?"

"Nothing," he says. And regards his steady, unwavering left hand with distant wonder.

Lazarus

Renata Baermann comes back screaming. She's staring at the ceiling, pinned under something—the freezer, that's it. Big industrial thing. She was in the kitchen when the bombs hit. It must have fallen.

She thinks it's crushed her legs.

The fighting seems to be over. She hears no small-arms fire, no whistle of incoming ordnance. The air's still filled with screams but they're just gulls, come to feast in the aftermath. She's lucky she was inside; those vicious little air rats would have pecked her eyes out by now if she'd been—

—Blackness—

¡Joder! Where am I? Oh, right. Bleeding out at the bottom of the Americas, after . . .

She doesn't know. Maybe this was payback for the annexation of Tierra del Fuego. Or maybe it's the Lifeguards, wreaking vengeance on all those who'd skip town after trampling the world to mud and shit. This is a staging area, after all: a place where human refuse congregates until the pressure builds once again, and another bolus gets shat across the Drake Passage to the land of milk and honey and melting glaciers. The sphincter of the Americas.

She wonders when she got so cynical. Not very seemly for a humanitarian.

She coughs. Tastes blood.

Footsteps crunch on the gravel outside, quick, confident, not the shell-shocked stumble you'd expect from anyone who's just experienced apocalypse. She fumbles for her gun: a cheap microwave thing, barely boils water but it helps level the field when a fifty-kilogram woman has to lay down the law to a man with twice the mass and ten times the entitlement issues. Better than nothing.

Or it would be, if it was still in its holster. If it hadn't somehow skidded up against a table leg a meter and a half to her left. She stretches for it, screams again; feels like she's just torn herself in half as the kitchen door slams open and she—

—blacks out—

—and comes back with the gun miraculously in her hand, her finger pumping madly against the stud, mosquito buzz-snap filling her ears and—

—she's wracked, coughing blood, too weak to keep firing even if the man in the WestHem uniform hadn't just taken her gun away.

He looks down at her from a great height. His voice echoes from the bottom of a well. He doesn't seem to be speaking to her. "Behind the mess hall—"

—*English*—

"—fatal injuries, maybe fifteen minutes left in her and she's still fighting—"

When she wakes up again the pain's gone and her vision's blurry. The man has changed from white to black. Or maybe it's a different man. Hard to tell through all these floaters.

"Renata Baermann." His voice sounds strangely. . . unused, somehow. As if he were trying it out for the first time.

There's something else about him. She squints, forces her eyes to focus. The lines of his uniform resolve in small painful increments. No insignia. She moves her gaze to his face.

"*Coño,*" she manages at last. Her voice is barely a whisper. She sounds like a ghost. "What's wrong with your *eyes?*"

"Renata Baermann," he says again. "Have I got a deal for you."

CAROLINE M. YOACHIM

Carnival Nine

FROM *Beneath Ceaseless Skies*

ONE NIGHT WHEN I was winding down to sleep, I asked Papa, "How come I don't get the same number of turns every day?"

"Sometimes the maker turns your key more and sometimes less, but you can never have more than your mainspring will hold. You're lucky, Zee, you have a good mainspring." He sounded a little wistful when he said it. He never got as many turns as I did, and he used most of them to do boring grown-up things.

"Take me to the zoo tomorrow?" The zoo on the far side of the closet had lions that did backflips and elephants that balanced on brightly colored balls.

"I have to take Granny and Gramps to the mechanic to clean the rust off their gears."

Papa never had any turns to spare for outings and adventures, which was sad. I opened my mouth to say so, but the whir of my gears slowed to where I could hear each click, and I closed my mouth so it wouldn't hang open while I slept.

What Papa said was true. I have a good mainspring. Sometimes I got thirty turns, and sometimes forty-six. Today, on this glorious summer day, I got fifty-two. I'd never met anyone else whose spring could hold so many turns as that, and I was bursting with energy.

Papa didn't notice how wound up I was. "Granny has a tune-up this morning, and Gramps is getting a new mustache. If you untangle the thread for me, you can use the rest of your turns to play."

"But—"

"Always work first, so you don't run out of turns." His legs were stiff, and he swayed as he walked along the wide wood plank that led out from our closet. He crossed the train tracks and disappeared into the shadow of the maker's workbench. Tonight, when he came back from his errands, he'd bring a scrap of fabric or a bit of thread. Papa sewed our clothes from whatever scraps the maker dropped.

The whir of his gears faded into silence, and I tried to untangle the thread. It was a tedious chore. The delicate motion of picking up a single brightly colored strand was difficult on a tight spring. A train came clacking along the track, and with it the lively music of the carnival. Papa had settled down here in Closet City, but Mama was a carnie. Based on the stories Papa told, sneaking out to the carnival would be a good adventure. Clearly I was meant to go— the carnival had arrived on a day when I had more turns than I'd ever had before. I gathered up my prettiest buttons and skipped over to the brightly painted train cars.

It was early, and the carnival had just arrived, but a crowd had already formed. Everyone clicked and whirred as they hurried to see the show. The carnies were busy too, unfolding train cars into platforms and putting up rides and games and ropes for the acrobats.

I passed a booth selling scented gear oil and another filled with ornate keys. I wondered if the maker could wind as well with those as with the simple silver one that protruded from my back. A face-painter with an extra pair of arms was painting two different customers at once, touching up the faded paint of their facial features and adding festive swirls of green and blue and purple. "Two kinds of paint," the painter called to me. "The swirls will wash right off with soap."

It was meant to be a reassurance, but it backfired—the trip from the closet to the bathroom took seven turns each way, so soap was hard to come by. Papa would be angry if I came home painted.

"Catch two matching fish and win a prize!" a carnie called. He was an odd assemblage of parts, with one small brown arm and one bulky white one. His legs were slightly different lengths, and his ceramic face was crisscrossed with scratch marks. He held out a long pole with a tiny net on the end, a net barely big enough to hold a single fish.

"Don't they all match?" I leaned over the tub of water to study the orange fish. They buzzed quietly and some mechanism propelled them forward and sent out streams of bubbles behind them.

The man dipped the net into the water and caught one of the fish. He flipped open a panel on its belly and revealed a number —4. "The fish are numbered one through ten, and you'll get to pick three. Any two of 'em match and you win!"

I eyed the prizes—an assortment of miniature animals, mostly cats, all with tiny golden keys. Keys so small that even I could turn them, so there'd be no need to wait each night for the maker to wind them up.

"Take these buttons in trade?"

The man laughed. "No, but if you didn't buy any tickets I'll let you work for a play—a turn for a turn, as they say."

Unlike Papa, he could see how tight I was wound, and he put me to work hauling boxes from his platform to a car on the far end of the train. The work was satisfying, and it let me gawk at the rest of the carnival. When I was done, he handed me the net. "Any three fish that catch your fancy. Good luck!"

The net was long and hard to handle, but I dipped it into the water. It came up empty and dripping. Fishing was not as easy as the man had made it look. I tried again, and this time brought up a fish that whirred loudly as it came out of the water. The man pushed in a pin to stop the gears and flipped open a panel to reveal the number 8.

My next two fish were numbered 3 and 4.

"Do *any* of them match?" I handed back the net, frowning and studying the pool. There were easily a hundred fish. "I guess with so many they must."

"You have to look closer at the fish." A freckle-faced kid climbed up onto the platform. He scooped up a fish, checked the number on the bottom, then studied the pond. "This one's a six, so I just have to find a match."

With a smooth practiced motion he dipped the net back in and pulled out another fish. He showed me the number on the bottom —another 6.

"How did you—"

"One of the sixes has a busted tail, swims in circles."

"But the other one, what if you'd gotten something else?"

"This one has a chip of paint missing."

"I'm Zee."

"Endivale," he said, but added quickly, "You can call me Vale. Hey, Pops, okay if I take my free turns to show Zee around?"

The man running the fish game studied us for a minute, then nodded.

Vale took my hand. "Come on, you gotta hear the nightingale sing, she's amazing."

So off we went. The nightingale turned out to be a woman with brown-feathered wings that matched her dark skin. Vale wasn't lying. She sang beautifully, any song that the crowd shouted to her.

For twelve turns we explored the carnival—we watched the acrobats, and lost the ring-toss game, and rode on the backs of the dancing bears. Then Vale had to stop, because he didn't have so many turns as me.

"You seem to know everyone at the carnival," I said when we sat down on the edge of an empty platform. "Do you know my mother? She's very distinctive—a woman with eight spider legs."

"Oh, I've heard of her—Lady Arachna, right? She's Carnival Four."

"Carnival Four?"

Vale gestured down at the platform below us. "You can't see it with the platforms folded down, but the train cars are numbered so they stay matched up. All the cars in this train are marked nine, so we're Carnival Nine. Pops and I are here because they had an empty platform for him to run his game. My other dad is at Carnival Two because he's an acrobat, and Nine already has more acrobats than we really need."

"So you never see him?"

"There's only one track through here, but the trains run the whole house, with cities along the route where we stop and entertain folks. Some places there are clusters of tracks where the trains pass each other, or turn around. I've seen him a couple times."

We talked a bit more, and he snuck me in to see the bearded lady and a snake man whose skin was covered in iridescent green scales. The carnival was amazing, and I never wanted to leave, but I could feel the tension leaving my spring. I only had a few turns left, barely enough to get home. "I have to go."

"I'm almost out of turns anyway."

I hopped down from the platform. Vale put his hand on my shoulder. "I lied about some of the fish looking different. There's no missing paint or broken tails. The fish have more than one number, depending on which way you open the panels. Don't tell Pops I told you."

Something passed between us then, in that moment when he trusted me. Somehow it meant more than all the marvels I'd seen. It didn't even occur to me to get angry that the game was rigged until I was more than halfway home.

"You didn't untangle the thread," Papa said when I came in.

The multicolored jumble of thread was on the table where I'd left it.

"I had so much energy, and the train brought the carnival—"

"Go to bed, Zee. We're out of turns."

I spent my days untangling threads and learned to sew scraps of fabric into clothes. On my two hundredth day, Papa took me into town and we swapped out my child-sized limbs for adult ones and repainted my face. Trains came and went, but I never had enough extra turns to visit the carnival. Then one morning Papa came back from the city early, pulling a wheeled cart.

"What happened?"

"Granny and Gramps wound all the way down."

"But the maker can wind them again tonight, and—"

Papa shook his head. "No, there comes a time when our bodies cannot hold the turns. We all get our thousand days, give or take a few. Then we wind down for the last time. It is the way of things."

I knew we didn't go on forever, because some of my friends were made of parts from the Closet City recycling center. The recycling center melted down old parts to make new ones. So I knew. But at the same time I'd never known anyone who was broken down for parts before. Granny had painted my face, and Gramps always told the best stories about the maker.

"I wish I could have visited them before they wound down."

"I didn't know they'd go today. They were only in their early nine hundreds."

"Are you going to take them to the recycling center?"

He shook his head. "The recycling center is well stocked, but the carnivals are often hurting for parts. When the next train comes, we'll take them there."

I knew it wasn't right to be excited on the day that Granny and Gramps died, but while I waited to wind down and sleep, I couldn't help but imagine all the marvels we would see.

*

The next train turned out to be number nine. I was a little disappointed because I'd already seen most of Carnival Nine, but then I remembered Vale and how he'd shared the secret trick with the fish. I didn't see him as I followed Papa to the platform at the front of the train, or while we laid Granny and Gramps out on the red-painted wood. One of the carnival mechanics knelt next to Granny, and Papa leaned over and whispered, "I'm going to stay to watch them disassembled, but you don't have to. You did your turns helping me pull the cart to get them here."

The mechanic peeled away the fabric that covered Granny's torso and unscrewed her metal chest plate. I wanted to remember her whole, not in tiny pieces. I squeezed Papa's hand, then let go and walked along the length of the carnival.

Vale found me about halfway down the train. He had swapped out his childhood limbs too, and when they repainted his face they'd gotten rid of his freckles. His hair was darker now, which suited him. He put his hand on my shoulder. "Sorry about your grandparents."

"How did you—"

He shrugged. "Pops saw you come in. He said I could have some turns off, if you want to watch the acrobats."

There was a mischievous gleam in his eyes when he said it, and it sounded like a grand adventure. Vale took me to a huge green-and-white-striped tent next to the train tracks and we held hands and watched as acrobats walked tightropes and leapt between swings suspended high above the ground.

I loved the show, but halfway through Vale stopped watching.

"Seen this show too many times?" I asked.

"No. Well, yeah, but mostly it reminds me of my dad. Pops is great, but we don't always get along so well. He wants me to take over the fish someday, but I hate that the whole thing is a cheat."

I wouldn't have minded staying for the rest of the show, but I didn't want him to be sad. We snuck out and headed back to the train. "Can you switch carnivals?"

"I'm not built to be an acrobat like Dad. My parts aren't that good. Really all I'm built for is running a game, and if I'm going to do that, I might as well stay here."

"You could leave the carnival and stay in Closet City," I said, suddenly aware that we were still holding hands. "It's . . . Well, it's terribly boring actually."

He laughed. It was getting late and he was nearly out of turns. "I was thinking I might come up with a different game, one that's hard but doesn't involve any cheats."

I couldn't quite keep the disappointment off my face. I almost wished I hadn't said anything about Closet City being boring, but it was the complete truth. "Yeah, I guess it'd be hard to give up the adventure of the carnival to stay in a place like this."

He pulled me closer and spoke softly in my ear. "Why don't you come with me when the carnival moves on?"

Papa could take care of himself, and I was old enough to go. I told him on our walk home, and the next morning I packed up my things and said goodbye. It was a sudden shift, an abrupt departure, but Papa understood that I had always been restless. He loved me enough to let me go. When the carnival moved on, I went with it. With Vale.

Five trains were at the grand junction when we arrived, and Vale helped me find Carnival Four so that I could look for my mother. He would have stayed, but Carnival Two was at the junction as well, and I told him to go and visit with his dad. Vale and I would have plenty of time together later, and I wanted some time alone with my mother. I hadn't seen her since I was new.

She was easy to find, her train car clearly labeled THE AMAZING SPIDER-WOMAN, with pictures of her painted large on the side of the car. I knocked on the door and she slid it open, staring down at me and tapping one of her forelegs. "Yes?"

My gears whirred tight in my chest. She didn't recognize me, and why would she? My limbs were different, my face was repainted. She had left a child, and I was a woman now. "I'm Zee. I came with Carnival Nine, and I wanted . . . well, to see you, I guess."

"Oh, my daughter, Zee." Her foreleg went still, and she tilted her head, studying me. "What is it you do with Carnival Nine?"

"Vale is teaching me to run one of the games," I admitted, knowing that it was one of the lowest jobs in the carnival. Being an acrobat or a performer required more skill, but the games were mostly con jobs. Nearly anyone could do it, with enough practice.

Mother didn't say anything, and the silence stretched long and awkward between us.

"Papa is still in Closet City," I told her, more to fill the silence than anything. "We lost Granny and Gramps a few weeks back." I tried to think of more news from Closet City, but since Mother had stayed with the train, she probably wouldn't know most of the people I'd grown up with. It was a strange feeling, my strong desire to bond with someone who was a complete stranger. In my mind, the meeting had gone differently. She had loved me simply because I was her daughter, and we'd had an instant connection.

"I'm sorry to hear they've wound down." She paused for a moment. "Look, I'm really not the maternal sort—it's why Lars took you to Closet City to raise you. I'm—well—I'm not very nice. I'm selfish. I like to use my turns for myself, and I never spared a lot of turns for my relationship with Lars. Certainly I never had enough for you."

I didn't know what to say to that. I wanted to be angry with her, but she was a stranger, she'd never really been a part of my life. That was how things were and I was used to it. Mostly I was disappointed. Sad that my dreams about reuniting with my mother had died. We talked a little longer about nothing of importance, and then I went back to Carnival Nine, home to Vale. I vowed that I wouldn't be like my mother. I was blessed with a lot of turns, and I would use them for more than just myself.

The train took us in slow circles, stopping to perform at the cities. I settled into the routine of carnival life—collapsing the walls of our train car to make our platform, setting up the dart game that Vale designed, packing everything away again when it was time to move along. The days blurred one into the next, obscuring the passage of time. Then one day I realized that I was over four hundred days old, which meant that I had been with the carnival longer than I'd lived in Closet City.

I wasn't old yet, but I was no longer young.

"You sure you're ready to do this?" Vale took me to the front car where all the parts were.

I nodded. Our train's next stop was the maker's workbench; this was the right time for us to make our child.

He started picking through the gears, laying out everything we'd need to build a child. "My half-sister has these great pincers, like lobster claws—"

"I thought maybe he could look more like us." Carnies came with a wide variety of parts, which was fun for shows, but the more outlandish ones all reminded me of my mother. "Hands would be more versatile if we ever settle down in a city. What if he doesn't want to be a performer?"

Vale frowned. "He could change his parts, I suppose. But what happened to your sense of adventure?"

When I'd lived in Closet City, the carnival had been exciting for the brief time it had stayed. But being a part of the carnival—well, the obligations of life and livelihood sucked away the wonder. It was the novelty that had drawn me here, and half a lifetime later the novelty had worn away. But I couldn't bring myself to say so to Vale.

"So if he wants pincers when he's older, he can swap out his limbs that way too." I kept my voice calm, but worry gnawed at me. We had agreed on building a boy, but we hadn't talked much about the details. I rummaged through the pile until I found an arm, dark-skinned like the nightingale lady, but smaller, child-sized. It didn't have a match, but there was another that was only slightly paler. Would anyone notice? Probably someone had already taken the other half of each set. "What about these?"

"Okay." He was less enthusiastic now, and I felt bad that I'd shot down his first suggestion so quickly. I looked for parts that would be a compromise, interesting enough for him but nothing as extreme as my mother's spider legs. Nothing that would evoke memories of a woman who thought it'd be a waste of turns to raise me.

We worked quietly for a while, the silence awkward. Finally he pulled out a face, an ordinary shape but painted with streaks of black and white. He held it up. I hated it, but it was only paint. Paint could easily be removed and redone later. It was less work than swapping out parts. The structure of the face underneath was good. I nodded. It broke the tension.

"Dad said there might be a place for us at Carnival Two, working the show with the dancing bears." He kept his gaze firmly on our son, focusing his attention on attaching the black-and-white-streaked head to the still empty torso. "It'd be a step up from running a dart game, a better position for our son."

Thinking about our son working a show at the carnival made me remember my own childhood. I had always wanted adventure, but now dancing bears seemed more dangerous than glamorous. Life on the tracks was harder, even for me with all my turns. Carnival folk almost never made it to a thousand days. Their springs gave out when people were in their eight hundreds, sometimes even sooner. "I want what's best for him."

Vale took my hand and smiled. "Me too."

The train took us to the maker's bench, and we laid out our son's body, chest open. Tonight the maker would give him a mainspring and wind him for the very first time.

"Should we name him now or after we've gotten to know him?" My parents had waited to name me until my second day, because they wanted to be sure the name would fit.

"It's good luck to name him before he goes to the maker. He'll get a better spring that way," Vale answered. "What about Matts? That was my granddad's name."

I thought about my granddad and all the stories he'd told about the maker. "My granddad was Ettan. What about Mattan? We could still call him Matts for short."

Vale nodded slowly, his spring winding down. "I like that."

The maker gave me forty-three turns the day that I met my child. My darling Mattan got only four. Something was wrong with his mainspring. I was definitely no mechanic, but I could hear it, a strained and creaking noise like metal bending to its breaking point. What could you do with four turns? How could I teach him the world if that was all he had to work with?

I picked up my son and carried him to meet Vale. My mind churned with worry for my son's future and guilt at having more than my share of turns, but at the same time I was grateful to be wound up enough for everything that needed to be done. I saved Mattan a turn of walking by using an extra one of mine to carry him, and he could see the world that way. Light from the ceiling reflected off the white stripes across his face, and I admired the contrast against the black. I had been too hasty in condemning Vale's choice; it was unusual, but striking.

"This is your father, Vale," I told Mattan. He nodded happily but made no attempt to speak. The mechanics of speech were complex and used more turns than a simple nod. Even now, newly made, he was aware of his limitations. It made sense, I suppose. I'd always been able to feel how tightly wound my spring was, even when I was young.

"Why are you carrying him?"

I showed Vale the mechanical counter above our son's key. There were two dials of numbers, enough to show two digits, which made Mattan's tiny number of turns seem even smaller, if such a thing was possible. "He only has four turns."

Vale put his hand out, not to take Mattan but to rest it on my shoulder. "So few?"

"I'll make my turns stretch to cover both of us," I promised. "We'll make the best of it."

And I kept my promise. I made a sling and carried Mattan on my back as I ran my dart game and did our errands, and tried to show him some of the fun and adventure I had so desperately wanted in my childhood.

It was too much, even for me. On Mattan's third day I wound down in the afternoon, right in the middle of my shift working the darts. Vale took Mattan home in his sling, but he didn't have the turns to carry me to bed, so I stood there, right where I stopped, and the carnival-goers clustered around me, gawking. A grown woman, wound down in public like a child who had not learned to pace herself.

At the end of Mattan's first week, our train was at the junction, and Mattan spoke for the first time. "I want to see the acrobats."

Vale had gone out that morning to spend a few turns with his dad. I was supposed to repair the dartboard, covered in painted bull's-eye targets. It had cracked, and we needed it for our game, but Mattan had never asked for anything before. He'd heard Vale talking about his dad and the acrobatics he did for his show. I didn't have the turns, but he had made the effort to ask, and I didn't have the heart to tell him no. I carried him to Carnival Two, and we watched the acrobats practice their trapeze act.

We didn't see Vale in the audience, and his father wasn't practicing with the others. We sat as still as we could and watched, saving our turns for the trip back to train nine. Vale was already there when we returned. He stared at the broken dartboard. It reminded me of the day I'd left the tangled threads and Papa had chastised me for not doing my work first.

"Mattan asked to see the acrobats," I said. "He spoke for the first time. He's never asked for anything, and I couldn't tell him no."

"Mattan doesn't have the turns for these things," Vale said. His voice was cold, angry. "You don't have the turns for this either. You have to pull your weight with the carnival if you want to stay. You know that."

"And what about our son?" I demanded. "He can't fix dart-boards or run carnival games, but that doesn't mean he has nothing to contribute."

Vale shook his head. "Maybe not, but he can't pull his own weight, and he's cost us the chance to move to Carnival Two. They might have taken *us,* but they refuse to take Mattan."

It was only then I realized that for all this first week, Vale had never once called him Matts. This was not the child he wanted, and he was refusing to bond with him, trying to protect himself from the hurt. Or maybe he was simply being selfish, unwilling to use his turns on his own child. He was certainly disappointed at losing his chance to move to Carnival Two.

The train made its slow circuit from the Attic City to the brightly painted Children's Room and down the long hallway to Closet City, and I used my turns to help Mattan get through his days. When the train stopped in the shadow of the maker's bench—the place where I'd grown up—I left the carnival and took Mattan with me. Vale didn't argue; he was relieved to see us go.

Papa was delighted to see me and to meet Mattan, and he welcomed us into his home. I began to fill the role that had once been his—taking him to get his gears tuned or his paint retouched —and everywhere we went I carried Mattan. I had turns enough to care for Papa and Mattan both, so long as I did nothing else. I tried not to think of adventure, or freedom, or even the future. If I kept my focus on the present moment, I could do everything that needed to be done, but only barely.

There weren't any trains at Closet City on Mattan's two hundredth day.

"We can wait for a carnival to come, or we can get your adult-sized limbs from the recycling center," I told Mattan. We'd talked about both options beforehand, a conversation that had spanned several days because he couldn't always spare the turns to ask questions.

"I want to go today," Mattan answered immediately. There was a good selection of parts at the recycling center, and he didn't want to be a performer, so it made sense to get parts here in town . . . but I think Mattan also knew that getting new limbs would be an exhausting day for both of us, and he didn't want to make it even harder by adding the long walk out to the tracks of the carnival trains.

Being at the recycling center reminded me of the day Vale and I built Mattan, although here the parts were organized neatly on shelves, not piled high in a disorganized heap on the floor of a train car. These parts were more uniform. There were no spider legs or pincers, and while the faces were painted with a wide variety of features, there were none with bright garish colors or distinctive patterns. None that looked at all like Mattan.

"I'll hold up limbs one at a time," I told him. "When you see something you want, nod."

Mattan sat perfectly still, his painted-black stripes cutting across his face like harsh shadows. He had three turns today, enough for us to do everything we needed if we were careful. I moved around the room, holding up arms and legs for him to see.

The limbs he picked were neither the biggest nor the smallest, painted the same deep brown as his child-sized arms. I brought them over. Mattan's fingers curled, a movement that mimicked the way he squeezed my shoulder when he was excited, but before I could attach the new limbs he asked, "Will these be too heavy?"

The question broke my heart. Yes, these limbs were heavy. All the added weight meant that it would take more turns to carry him. I had selfishly hoped he would choose smaller limbs, but they were his limbs, and this was his choice. "These are beautiful, and I have a lot of turns. I can still carry you."

It was the right thing to say, and Mattan was so happy with his new limbs, but when I carried him home from the recycling center his weight stole the tension from my mainspring more quickly than before. We lived by our turns, and my son—now fully grown—couldn't spare enough to walk across town. I was furious that the world was so unfair, and my heart broke thinking of all the things he didn't have the turns to do. But if I was being honest, my heart also broke for me. Vale had abandoned us and Papa was old, so I would be the one to carry Mattan everywhere, always.

That thought was in my mind when Carnival Nine came to town, an ever-present weight that I could not shake away. My love was endless, but my strength was not, and I longed to escape the unrelenting effort of taking care of Papa and Mattan on my own. I wanted to see Vale, to have some turns all to myself, to do exactly as I pleased for once.

I didn't wake Papa or Mattan. I left them in their beds—did not ask permission to go out or even explain what I was doing, simply left and walked to the trains. They wouldn't be able to do much today, without my help, but between the two of them they'd be able to manage.

"It's good to see you," Vale said when I arrived. "Where's Mattan?"

"With my father." I didn't know what to say after that. I'd wanted to see Vale, but what could I really talk about with someone who wouldn't help raise his own son? He was like my mother, too selfish to share his turns. And here I was, at the carnival, wasting my turns on a foolish whim instead of taking care of my child. "I shouldn't have come."

Vale frowned. "I owe you an apology. I didn't . . . I mean, I wasn't prepared for how things went, and you've always had more turns, so it seemed to make sense for you to take him. I've missed you."

"It's been lonely. Difficult," I admitted. Once I started, the words came pouring out. In Closet City I'd felt like there was no one I could talk to—Papa had always been so good at taking care of everyone around him, so responsible, there was no way I could complain to him. But I could pour everything out to Vale. If nothing else, at least he would understand my selfishness. "I have the turns to give Mattan a good life, but only if I never do anything for myself. I take care of Papa, I try to let Mattan see some of the world, and it is so rewarding, but I want something for me, some little bit of the adventure I was always chasing as a child."

"You're here today," Vale said. He took my hand. "Let's have an adventure."

And we did. It was like seeing the carnival for the first time, the animals and the acrobats and the games. Vale was kind and attentive and we planned out possible futures and talked about the time we'd spent apart. It would have been a beautiful day if not for the constant gnawing guilt of having left Mattan and Papa behind. The worst was that I hadn't even told them. I had been so sure that I did not deserve time for myself that I had made things even worse by stealing the time instead of asking for it.

"This was nice," I said, painfully aware that I needed to leave soon if I wanted to have enough turns to get back home. Despite the guilt, it had been reinvigorating to have the break. "Maybe tomorrow I could come back with Mattan? I think he would love to see you."

Vale hesitated, then nodded. "I would like that."

I walked home, and I was nearly out of turns by the time I walked in the door. Papa was in bed, but Mattan was up, sitting perfectly still at the table, obviously saving a turn to tell me something. I walked directly in front of him, so he wouldn't have to turn his head.

His eyes met mine, and he said, "Grandpa never woke up today."

It had always been Papa's wish to have his body taken to a carnival when he wound all the way down, so I rented a cart and pulled him to the train, all while carrying Mattan. The work was hard, and I wouldn't have the turns to get us back home today.

I unloaded Papa into the same train car where he had once unloaded Granny and Gramps, the car where Vale and I had later assembled Mattan. I stayed while they took Papa apart, by his side now when it didn't matter, instead of yesterday when it might have. No. It wasn't Papa I had abandoned yesterday; Papa had never woken up. He would never know. It was my Mattan who had spent the entire day alone, knowing that Papa was gone, having no way to call for help or do much of anything at all but wait for my return. And now he waited again, resting in the sling on my back as Orna, one of our train's mechanics, carefully opened Papa's chest and removed the gears, sorting them into bins as she worked. Her movements were practiced and efficient, she wasted no turns. All too soon Papa was gone, nothing but a pile of parts.

"Thank you," I told Mattan as we left to find Vale. "I needed to see that."

Mattan didn't answer, saving his turns.

"I did a terrible thing yesterday," I continued. "I wouldn't have gone if I had known about Papa—I thought he would be there to help you—but I shouldn't have done it even so. I'm sorry."

"You can't do everything, always," Mattan said, choosing his words carefully, not wasting more of his turns than was absolutely necessary. "I forgive you."

"Some good might even come of it—I asked Vale yesterday if he wanted to see you, and he said yes."

Mattan squeezed my shoulder ever so slightly through the fabric of the sling, a sign of his excitement at seeing his father. I carried him to the train car with Vale's dart game set up for anyone who had the tickets to play.

Vale studied us for a time, saying nothing. Was he noticing that

I still carried our son, even now that he was an adult? Or was he simply studying the black-and-white-striped face he hadn't seen for hundreds of days? My guilt was for a single day, a single slip. What did he feel, abandoning us for most of his son's life?

"Say something," I said. "Mattan has to save his turns, so he doesn't talk much, but he is so excited to finally see you again."

"Mattan," Vale began. He shook his head and started over. "Matts. I know I haven't been a father to you, but I'm ready to help now, if you want me to. Join me on the train?"

The question was for both us, Mattan and me. I had no tie to Closet City now that Papa was gone, and with Vale's help we would have enough turns for a better life for all of us. I wavered, undecided, the weight of Mattan pressing down on my back. He didn't speak, waiting for my decision. Would Vale really help take care of our child, or would he go back on this promise?

Vale had called our son Matts. His heart was in the right place.

"Yes," I answered. "We'll join you on the train."

Mattan squeezed my shoulder, pleased with the decision. I was excited that we might be able to be a family again, but another thought haunted me, something that had been eating at the edges of my mind—what would happen to Mattan when I wound down? For hundreds of days I'd pushed this thought from my mind—I was healthy and full of turns, and Mattan, well, his mainspring was bad. I had convinced myself I would outlast him.

Day after day Vale took nearly even turns with me, carrying Mattan on his back as he worked our game or hauled boxes of prizes to and from our platform. I used as many turns as I could spare helping all the newest additions to the carnival—always a turn for a turn, trading endlessly into the future, extracting from everyone I helped a promise to pay that turn forward to Mattan after I was gone. Was it enough? Did it erase that selfish day when I abandoned my son?

I've heard it said that every hundred days passes faster than the previous hundred. In childhood the days stretch out seemingly forever, and we spend our time and turns freely on any whim that catches our fancy. But at the end of our lives each day becomes an increasingly greater fraction of the time we have remaining, and the moments grow ever more precious. A hundred days, a hundred more, time flits away as we make our slow circuit on the train.

Vale winds all the way down, hardworking and supportive to the end. On his last day he apologizes again and again for abandoning us. We've already forgiven him, but he cannot forgive himself. The other carnies start giving back the turns they borrowed from me, helping Mattan through his days. I have no turns to spare — there have never been enough turns, even for me, and I've always had more than my share.

An acrobat named Chet, a man with stripes on his arms that match the stripes on Mattan's face, comes more often than the others. I thought at first that he was trying to fulfill his obligation quickly and get it over with, but no, he lingers even when he isn't working off his borrowed turns, keeping up a constant stream of chatter, unbothered by the fact that Mattan rarely answers. Chet shares bits and pieces of his past mixed in with gossip about everyone else in Carnival Nine.

My spring is on the verge of breaking, I can feel it. The maker gave my son and me the same number of turns today. Ten turns. Fewer than I've ever had, and the most my son has ever been given. For a moment I am filled with regret at the harsh limitations of his life. His days are already short, and his spring is so bad that he won't get the thousand days that I have gotten. He will be lucky to live another hundred days, and he is only in his six hundreds now. I comfort myself with the knowledge that at least he has Chet. He won't be alone.

I asked Mattan a while back what his favorite day was, his favorite memory, and he'd answered without hesitation — the day that we snuck out together to see the acrobats. So today we ignore what little work we might have done and walk to the tent where the acrobats perform, both of us side by side because I no longer have the turns to carry him. We sit perfectly still and watch the acrobats twirling and flying through the air.

I tell Mattan what Papa told me. "There comes a time when our bodies cannot hold the turns. We all get our thousand days, give or take a few."

I think back on my thousand days, on what I've done with my life. The way Papa had taken such good care of me, and how in the end I'd chosen to follow his path and done my best for Mattan. My life has been different from the adventures I imagined as a child, but I made the most of the turns I was given, and that's all any of us can do.

E. LILY YU

The Wretched and the Beautiful

FROM *Terraform*

THE ALIENS ARRIVED unexpectedly at 6:42 on a hot August evening, dropping with a shriek of metal strained past its limits onto
the white sands of one of the last pristine beaches on Earth. The
black hulk of the saucer ground into the sand and stopped, steaming. Those of us who had been splashing in the surf or stamping
rows of sandcastles fled up the slope, clutching our towels.

Once our initial fright dissipated, curiosity set in, and we stayed
with the policemen and emergency technicians who pulled up in
wailing, flashing trucks. It was all quite exciting, since nothing out
of the ordinary seemed to happen anymore. Gone were the days
when acting on conviction could change the world, when good
came of good and evil to evil.

One of the policemen fired an experimental shot or two, but
the bullets ricocheted off the black metal and lodged in a palm
tree.

"Don't shoot," one man said. "You might make them angry. You
might hit one of us."

The guns remained cocked, but no more bullets zinged off the
ship. We waited.

At sunset a pounding began inside the ship. No hatches sprang
open; no rayguns or periscopes protruded. There was only the
pounding, growing ever more frantic and erratic.

"What if they're trapped?" one of us said.

We looked at one another. Some of us had left and returned
with the pistols that did not fit in our swimming trunks. A whole
armory was pointed at the black disk of metal half buried in the
beach.

The pounding ceased.

Nothing followed.

We conferred, then conscripted a machinist, who with our assistance hauled her ponderous cutters and blowtorches over the soft sand and set to work on the saucer.

We stood back.

While the machinist worked, any sounds from the saucer were drowned out by her tools. With precise and deliberate motions, she cut a thin line around the disk's circumference. Sparks flew up where the blade met the strange metal, which howled in unfamiliar tones.

When her work was done, she packed her equipment and departed. The aliens had failed to vaporize her. We let out the collective breath we had been holding.

Minutes crawled past.

At last, with a peculiar clang, the top half of the saucer seesawed upward. In the deepening dusk we could barely distinguish the dark limbs straining to raise it. Many monsters or one? we wondered.

"Drop your weapons," one policeman barked. The upper part of the saucer sagged for a moment, concealing whatever was within.

From within the ship, a voice said in perfectly comprehensible French, "We do not have weapons. We do not have anything."

"Come out where we can see you," the policeman said. The rest of us were glad that someone confident and capable, someone who was not us, was handling the matter.

It was too dark to see clearly, and so at the policeman's command, and at the other end of his semiautomatic, the occupants of the ship—the aliens, our first real aliens—were marched up the beach to the neon strip of casinos, while we followed, gaping, gawking, knowing nothing with certainty except that we were witnessing history, and perhaps would even play a role in it.

The lurid glow of marquees and brothels revealed to us a shivering, shambling crowd, some slumped like apes, some clutching their young. Some had five limbs, some four, and some three. Their joints were crablike, and their movement both resembled ours and differed to such a degree that it sickened us to watch. There were sixty-four of them, including the juveniles. Although we were unacquainted with their biology, it was plain that none were in good health.

"Is there a place we can stay?" the aliens said.

Hotels were sought. Throughout the city, hoteliers protested, citing unknown risk profiles, inadequate equipment, fearful and unprepared staff, an indignant clientele, and stains from space filth impervious to detergent. Who was going to pay, anyway? They had businesses to run and families to feed.

One woman from among us offered to book a single room for the aliens for two nights, that being all she could afford on her teacher's salary. She said this with undisguised hope, as if she thought her offer would inspire others. But silence followed her remark, and we avoided her eyes. We were here on holiday, and holidays were expensive.

The impasse was broken at three in the morning, when in helicopters, in charter buses, and in taxis, the journalists arrived.

It was clear now that our guests were the responsibility of national if not international organizations, and that they would be cared for by people who were paid more than we were. Reassured that something would be done, and not by us, we dispersed to our hotel rooms and immaculate beds.

When we awoke late, to trays of poached eggs on toast and orange juice, headlines on our phones declared that first contact had been made, that the Fermi paradox was no more, that science and engineering were poised to make breakthroughs not only with the new metal that the spaceship was composed of but also with the various exotic molecules that had bombarded the ship and become embedded in the hull during its long flight.

The flight had indeed been long. One African Francophone newspaper had thought to interview the aliens, who explained in deteriorating French how their universal translator worked, how they had fled a cleansing operation in their star system, how they had watched their home planet heated to sterility and stripped of its atmosphere, how they had set course for a likely-looking planet in the Gould Belt, how they wanted nothing but peace, and please, they were exhausted, could they have a place to sleep and a power source for their translator?

When we slid on our sandals and stepped onto the dazzling beach, which long ago, before the garbage tides, was what many beaches looked like, we saw the crashed ship again, substantiation of the previous night's fever dream. It leached rainbow fluids onto the sand.

Dark shapes huddled under its sawn-off lid.

Most of us averted our eyes from that picture of unmitigated misery and admired instead the gemlike sky, the seabirds squalling over the creamy surf, the parasols propped like mushrooms along the shore. One or two of us edged close to the wreck and dropped small somethings—a beach towel, a bucket hat, a bag of chips, a half-full margarita in its salted glass—then scuttled away. This was no longer our problem; it belonged to our governors, our senators, our heads of state. Surely they and their moneyed friends would assist these wretched creatures.

So it was with consternation that we turned on our televisions that night, in the hotel bar and in our hotel rooms, to hear a spokesman explain, as our heads of state shook hands, that the countries in their interregional coalition would resettle a quota of the aliens in inverse proportion to national wealth. This was ratified over the protests of the poorest members, in fact over the protests of the aliens themselves, who did not wish to be separated and had only one translation device among them. The couple of countries still recovering from Russian depredations were assigned six aliens each, while the countries of high fashion and cold beer received two or three, to be installed in middle-class neighborhoods. In this way the burden of these aliens, as well as any attendant medical or technological advances, would be shared.

The cost would be high, as these aliens had stated their need for an environment with a specific mixture of helium and neon, as well as a particular collection of nutrients most abundant in shrimp and crab. The latter, in our overfished and polluted times, were not easy to obtain.

This was appalling news. We who had stitched, skimped, and pinched all year for one luxurious day on a clean beach would have our wallets rifled to feed and house the very creatures whose presence denied us a section of our beach and the vistas we had paid for. Now we would find these horrors waiting for us at home, in the nicer house next to ours, or at the community pool, eating crab while we sweated to put chicken on the table and pay off our mortgages. Who were they to land on our dwindling planet and reduce our scarce resources further? They could go back to their star system. Their own government could care for them. We could loan them a rocket or two if they liked. We could be generous.

Indeed, in the days that followed, our legislators took our calls, then took this tack. If they meant to stay, shouldn't our visitors earn their daily bread like the rest of us? And if biological limitations made this impossible, shouldn't they depart to find a more hospitable clime? We repeated these speeches over the dinner table. Our performances grew louder and more vehement after a news report about one of the aliens eating its neighbor's cat; the distraught woman pointed her finger at the camera, at all of us watching, and accused us of forcing a monster upon her because we had no desire to live beside it ourselves. There was enough truth in her words to bite.

It did not matter that six days later the furry little Lothario was found at a gas station ten miles from home, having scrapped and loved his way across the countryside. By then we had stories of these aliens raiding chicken coops and sucking the blood from dogs and unsuspecting infants.

A solid number of these politicians campaigned for office on a platform of alien repatriation, and many of them won.

Shortly afterward, one of two aliens resettled in Huntingdon, England, was set upon and beaten to death with bricks by a gang of teenage girls and boys. Then, in Houston, a juvenile alien was doused in gasoline and set on fire. We picked at our dinners without appetite, worrying about these promising youths, who had been headed for sports scholarships and elite universities. The aliens jeopardized all our futures and clouded all our dreams. We wrote letters, signed petitions, and prayed to the heavens for salvation.

It came. From out of a silent sky, rockets shaped like needles and polished to a high gloss descended upon six of the major capitals of the world. About an hour after landing, giving the television crews time to jostle for position, and at precisely the same instant, six slim doors whispered open, and the most gorgeous beings we had ever seen strode down extruded silver steps and planted themselves before the houses of power, waiting to be invited in.

And they were.

"Forgive us for imposing on your valuable time," these ambassadors said simultaneously in the official languages of the six legislatures. Cameras panned over them, and excitement crackled through us, for this was the kind of history we wanted to be a part of.

When they emerged from their needle ships, their bodies were fluid and reflective, like columns of quicksilver, but with every minute among us, they lost more and more of their formless brilliance, dimming and thickening, acquiring eyes, foreheads, chins, and hands. Within half an hour they resembled us perfectly. Or rather, they resembled what we dreamed of being, the better versions of ourselves who turned heads, drove fast cars, and recognized the six most expensive whiskies by smell alone; whose names topped the donor rolls of operas, orchestras, and houses of worship; who were admired, respected, adored.

We looked at these beautiful creatures, whom we no longer thought of as aliens, and saw ourselves as we could be, if the lottery, or the bank, or our birthplace—if our genes, or a lucky break —if only—

We listened raptly as they spoke in rich and melodious voices, voices we trusted implicitly, that called to mind loved ones and sympathetic teachers.

"A terrible mistake has been made," they said. "Because of our negligence, a gang of war criminals, guilty of unspeakable things, namely—"

Here their translators failed, and the recitation of crimes came as a series of clicks, coughs, and trills that nevertheless retained the enchantment of their voices.

"—escaped their confinement and infiltrated your solar system. We are deeply sorry for the trouble our carelessness has caused you. We admire your patience and generosity in dealing with them, though they have grossly abused your trust. Now we have come to set things right. Remit the sixty-four aliens to us, and we will bring them back to their home system. They will never disturb you again."

The six beautiful beings clasped their hands and stepped back. Silence fell throughout the legislative chambers of the world.

Here was our solution. Here was our freedom. We had trusted and been fooled, we had suffered unjustly, we were good people with clean consciences sorely tried by circumstances outside our control. But here was justice, as bright and shining as we imagined justice to be.

We sighed with relief.

In Berlin, a woman stood.

"Even the little ones?" she said. "Even the children are guilty of the crimes you allege?"

"Their development is not comparable to yours," the beautiful one in Berlin said, while his compatriots in their respective state-houses stood silent, with inscrutable smiles. "The small ones you see are not children as you know them, innocent and helpless. Think of them as beetle larvae. They are destructive and voracious, sometimes more so than the mature adults."

"Still," she said, this lone woman, "I think of them as children. I have seen the grown ones feeding and caring for them. I do not know what crimes they have committed, since our languages cannot describe your concepts. But they have sought refuge here, and I am especially unwilling to return the children to you—"

The whispers of the assembly became murmurs, then exclamations.

"Throw her out!"

"She does not speak for us!"

"You are misled," the beautiful one said, and for a moment its smile vanished and a breath of the icy void between stars blew over us.

Then everything was as it had been.

"We must ask the aliens themselves what they want," the woman said, but now her colleagues were standing too, and shouting, and phone lines were ringing as we called in support of the beautiful ones, and her voice was drowned out.

"We have an understanding then," the beautiful ones said, to clamorous agreement and wild applause.

The cameras stopped there, at that glorious scene, and all of us, warm and satisfied with our participation in history, turned off our televisions and went to work, or to pick up our children from soccer, or to bed, or to the liquor store to gaze at top-shelf whiskey.

A few of us, the unfortunate few who lived beside the aliens, saw the long silver needles descend point-first onto our neighbors' lawns and the silver shapes emerge with chains and glowing rods. We twitched the kitchen curtains closed and dialed up our music. Three hours later there was no sign of any of the aliens, the wretched or the beautiful, except for a few blackened patches of grass and wisps of smoke that curled and died.

All was well.

MARIA DAHVANA HEADLEY

The Orange Tree

FROM *The Weight of Words*

> *Shelter me in your shadow*
> *Be with my mouth and my word*
> *Watch over my ways*
> *So I will not sin again with my tongue.*
>
> —*Solomon ibn Gabirol, eleventh century*

1.

SINCE THE BEGINNING of the world, there've been a thousand ways invented to be lonely. In a market stall, surrounded by speechless wooden wares, or banished to a black rock in the center of the sea. In a tower, feet forced into standing, floor too small for kneeling down, the only view a high window, the world below made of fire. On a road, parched, nothing but horizon. In the dark, visited by spirits jealous with their leavings.

At the tops of certain mountains there are places for those the world refuses, and at the bottoms of other mountains there are prisons for those the world regrets. There have been boulders installed for leapers once the never is too much.

The quiet is never quiet, not to the lonely. The quiet is full of newborn babies crying and lovers murmuring. The quiet is full of wineglasses and whippoorwills. Screaming quiet is the way the world lets a man know he's alone forever, with no remedy but death or sorcery.

2.

Málaga isn't a city where loneliness should overtake a man. Sweet milk, grapes and almonds, figs, lemons, bitter oranges, pomegranates, a view across the ocean from Spain to the coast of Africa. It's beautiful everywhere, everywhere but where Solomon is. Wherever he steps, there is sorrow and pain.

Solomon's come south from Saragossa to the city of his birth in a last attempt to heal himself. He's saltfish. Something's climbed beneath his skin, creating scabrous ridges on the sides of his ears and lips, and a cough, sometimes bloody. It isn't leprosy, but it looks enough like it that the neighbors shun him. No medical man can help him, and no woman will have him.

Alone in his house, Solomon names a cloud of dust, picturing an Avra with delicate fingers and a quick smile. Then he sweeps her into the street and watches her blow away. God doesn't permit men to knead dust into something with a heart. There is a short history of forbidden creations, a litany of longing. To defend a city, one might permissibly make a warrior of clay. One is not allowed to do that in order to fulfill selfish desires. There will be no blank-faced brides made of mud in Solomon's house. There's no hope of love now, not the way he looks. He's spent twenty years describing the thousand ways, and no time on any softer arts.

The four-hundred-thirty-fourth way to be lonely is the loneliness of the sleepless, awake while the world is not, moon risen, bats with it. Small owls, and teeth in the walls. A coverlet made of sand, a bed made of blisters.

When Solomon wakes each morning his mind is filled with words chewing at each other's tails, tangling toes and tongues. Unspoken poems run through his house, little long-legged darknesses. When he's on his pallet at night, words stand on their hind feet and stare at him. He can't sleep, nor can he organize words into sentences. When he lights a candle, he sees books he'll never finish. Words hide in the shadows and in the cracks in the walls, refusing to be written.

All he has are words, and none of them serve him. None of them even care for him.

Solomon sits alone at supper, taking figs from a dish painted with a lustered ship. He touches the ship's outlines, the oars, the rigging.

Had he a ship, he might sail to some far-off country where women had never seen men and thus wouldn't recognize him as a ruined specimen. He has no ship.

He idly makes a heap of fine sawdust and positions it across from him. *Tziporah,* he thinks, and then, realizing what he's doing, brushes her abruptly from the table. That dust isn't a wife.

Solomon spends an hour staring bitterly at the sky, mapping more of the ways of loneliness. The spheres above him, the sky filled with planets, and all of them are in love. He's a solitary star in the process of dying, the last of a galaxy, the only point of light in a bad piece of darkness.

As a young man he walked the roads of Andalusia and mapped brightness instead of the night. Black lace on golden skin, copper glances, the gentle mouth of a serving maid as she circled the table with a jug of wine. He was invited to meals in fine houses and published as a philosopher, but he made more enemies in such houses than friends. There was something wicked in his soul as well as in his skin. Perhaps the Almighty means him to live in solitary misery, a scalded man, but he finds himself in rebellion.

There are options. Witchcraft or suicide. Death or sorcery. The choices are clear.

Solomon has two new texts, bought during his last travel north. He has for years called himself a translator, bartering and wheedling, when in truth he wanted these volumes for something else. He's translated words, but he wants to translate other things. At last — this is his seventh night sleepless — he takes the books down and unwraps them from the linens that keep them safe from dust. The Banū Mūsā's treatise on the construction of ingenious devices, and the *Sefer Yetzirah.* There are instructions in both, recipes for things more complicated than joy. Nothing in it is obvious, but he's a poet. What he lacks in logic, he adds in lyric. He combines the instructions and draws a diagram.

The five-hundred-ninety-third variety of loneliness is the loneliness of first light, a dawn unwitnessed by anyone else, sun rising over the sea, a cracking seam in the world.

When he was sixteen and ignorant of his future miseries, Solomon boasted, *"I am the Song and the Song is my slave."* Even if that was true then, it's no longer enough.

The two-hundred-fifth way to be lonely is to hear an echo and think it is the voice of a friend.

At twilight Solomon dresses himself in a wide-brimmed hat, long gloves, a scarf about his throat and shoulders, a thin saffron-dyed robe, and a veil over his face. He goes into the Jewish quarter.

The nine-hundred-sixty-eighth variety of loneliness is the loneliness of planning magic and keeping it to oneself.

The moon rises as Solomon walks. It's spring and the trees are in bloom, but Solomon prefers the stars: they're brighter in winter. Lightning laughs in the distance. Nighttime is, at least, less lonely. He's free of the house. No one draws back from him in horror, because his garb covers everything.

He passes a garden and smells salt, clove, and cinnamon. The sky blooms with the roses of Venus, constellations of pale pink nard, falling stars of jasmine. He stops to inhale, and imagines sharing what he's seen. He could bring a wife a bouquet of all the flowers of this city, both poetic and actual. He could tell her every secret he's stored in his skull, every desire for murder, every yearning for love. He could pile them all at her feet and wait for her to look up and smile at the precious things he'd given her. He'd tell her about the assassination of his mentor, the way he wandered adrift after it. He'd tell her about the hundreds of elegies he's written, and about the grammars, the dictionaries. He'd recite them all from memory, until she knelt before him to tell him that it was time to sleep. He would go. He would not be an unreasonable husband.

At last he arrives at the orange grove.

"I need a tree," says Solomon. "Not too small a tree." He shows the grove man the size he means, stretching his arms.

"The entire tree?" the owner asks, looking at Solomon. "What will you do with a tree? How will you carry a tree?"

"The roots as well," says the poet.

The tree-seller sighs. "It won't grow back once it's cut. The roots should stay here in the earth, to feed the ground."

"The roots," says Solomon again.

The seller takes Solomon's coins, shrugging, and brings out his shovel. The five-hundred-sixth form of loneliness is the loneliness of drought, trees dropping their leaves and fruit, humbled by heat, a tree-seller amongst them, praying in vain for the clouds to burst.

The tree-seller shovels.

Solomon has a cart's worth of orange tree in the end, and he hires a donkey to haul it.

The seven-hundred-thirteenth variety of loneliness is the loneliness of driving a cart back to town in the dark, a donkey breathing loudly, smelling blossoms. The oranges from these trees are too bitter to eat, but their blooms are perfumed with the smell of sweat and sex.

At the carpenter's house, Solomon gives the carpenter the tree with its heady blossoms and wilting leaves, the roots a tangle of black soil and beetles. With the tree, he passes over a green glass cup from his own kitchen, and the lusterware dish painted with the ship. At last he gives the carpenter his diagrams. He pays him in maravedís from the publication of *The Fountain of Life,* the only thing he's written that seems likely to pay. Planets devoted to God, each one with its own section. He's out of fashion now, he fears. No one pays for poetry.

"Hinged," Solomon says, pointing at various places on the diagram. The carpenter usually makes doors. Solomon wonders if he's literate.

He has no certainty, only longing. He'll do the most difficult part of the magic himself, but for this part, the handwork, he has no skills. He goes home and waits, alone, alone, alone.

3.

"The poet's commissioned a cabinet," the carpenter tells his father. "But it's a strange one. He insists I use the entire tree to build it, the shavings and the dust, the roots and the leaves, the flowers. It'll take days of planing and shaping, and even then I'll have to bend the wood in too many places. He wants it hinged at every compartment, and he wants a musical instrument built into it. I don't know what to tell him."

The carpenter's father shakes his head, and so the carpenter goes to his mother. She's not from Spain at all, but from a city across the sea. She has different skills than those his father possesses.

"He pays us well for this?" she asks.

The carpenter shows the coins, looking uneasily at the branches he's meant to shape.

"Well enough," she says, counting them. She examines the diagram with interest, annotating it, drawing the outlines of an instrument from her homeland. At last she scratches in another small alteration, a tiny compartment to be placed deep within the creation, and sealed.

"I should not make this," the carpenter says. "It will offend."

The carpenter's mother glances sharply at him. "The commission is a kind of cabinet, whatever it looks like. Deny what you've made if anyone asks who made it. But we'll take his payment."

She hides the poet's coins away in her apron, then brings her son sheets of metal, pounded thin, a curved knife, and a tiny hammer. She consults the diagram again, goes to the market, and returns with a stillborn goat, bought for its tender hide, and the tanned skin of a doe. She brings tools for carving and stitching: awls, a vial of a particular oil, sand for polishing.

What the poet has commissioned is no sin to her people. The desert has wandering fountains, and the holy have help.

The thirty-ninth form of loneliness is the loneliness of a woman who can see her home from across a sea but cannot return to it. The loneliness of childbirth in a foreign land, none of the rituals, none of the other women. The loneliness of a marriage made across a table, cooking food, the sound of men talking the language of this country, not of the one you came from.

The carpenter's wife comes from a family whose men made objects for kings. Her son and husband are not what she'd have chosen for herself had she been doing the choosing. If she were a man, she'd have spent her life working metal and dark wood, inlaying it with gemstones and camel bones.

Instead she lives on the southern coast, looking over the water at the weather of the continent she's lost.

So the carpenter and his mother work the wood of the orange tree, sanding and polishing, putting in hinges. They work at night when the other work is done, and in the dark the workshop fills with the scent of sap, fruit, and pitch. There are the sounds of strings being plucked and then bowed, the sounds of taut leather being tapped. The carpenter's mother adds an instrument from her home, and while she builds the instrument she sings the songs it should play.

The carpenter's mother sits on her heels, looking at the blistered hearth where the fire caught out of control one afternoon beneath a spitted goat. The goat, with its twisted horns and yellow eyes, is long gone, but she remembers its voice, the song it sang, beheaded. She takes a handful of the ash, presses it hard into her palm, shapes it.

Her son crouches beside her. "People want strange things," he says. "Nothing I'd wish for."

"Most people don't," she says, working the ash, adding a tiny piece of parchment with something scrawled upon it, a word in her own language, and then more ash. "Most people want things to remain the same forever, but the world changes, and we change with it."

She pets the wood, finds a long splinter, and tests its sharpness. She soaks it carefully in the oil until it shines. Perhaps things like this cabinet are made all over the world, and always have been, but she only knows them from her home city, and then only small ones, playthings for the wealthy. This one is different.

She kneels, and opens doors until she arrives at the secret door hidden deep within the commission. She places her handful of ash there, a gift to it.

The carpenter's mother closes that door again and seals it with beeswax. She closes the next door and the next, until all the doors are tightly shut.

4.

The golem isn't alive, and then she is.

The first loneliness is the loneliness of birth. The golem opens her eyelid hinges, delicate doe leather. Her eyes are cold and dry, but she can see the man she's been created to serve, standing over her.

"You," he says. "You."

The golem has pale yellow-brown skin, smoothly sanded. Her hair is made of creamy white flowers with canary streaks, and there are shining green leaves throughout it. She smells of biting honey. She's small and slender, her waist narrow. No taller than he is. Her arms show the tracks of the tools that made her. There's a gouge between her breasts where there was a knot in the orange tree's trunk.

The poet has hammered one of the secret names of God into her palate, and this is what has brought her to life. She tries to speak, but she has no tongue. There is a pain, a stabbing where the silver tablet is. She can't tell what it is, only that it hurts.

It stretches inside of her body, a tentacled name. There is a loneliness in this too, the two hundred sixty-seventh, the loneliness of the only name one can speak being unspeakable.

"My name is Solomon ibn Gabirol," the man says, and blinks nervously. "You are my wife and servant. You'll help me write. I've need of someone to keep my words contained."

She examines the man before her. His hair is turning white, and his skin is red, black, and yellow. His cracked flesh bleeds. Salt water runs from his eyes.

Solomon, she mouths. There is no sound.

"Yes," he says. "You're a thing made for me."

The man feeds her a piece of paper, on which is written a line of a poem, and then he feeds her another. They taste like termite, wasp, worm. A hinge creaks in her jaw.

She's never seen a man before, not from this angle. She wants to take his tears and use them for some purpose. *A ship,* she thinks, catching a bewildering taste of his old thoughts. *On a salt sea. An island where they have never seen a woman.*

She tries to make a noise, but only a rattle comes out. There's a lock on her lips, a bent metal hook through a bent metal eye, and he has latched it. He takes her through his house, showing her its rooms.

"You'll clean for me," he says. "You'll rid my house of dust."

She understands. She begins to shovel with her hands. She buries her fingers in the mess and thinks of rooting there, falls to her side and stretches, planting herself, but he pulls her up, telling her he wishes her to sweep the dirt, not roll in it like a sow.

She learns quickly. She's made to learn.

5.

When he ordered her, Solomon gave only the measures of the golem's body, writing figures in the margins of his diagram. The carpenter was no sculptor. The golem is full in the hips and breasts, but one breast is bigger than the other, and her hips are tilted.

She has no heart, and no soul. She is therefore no sin.

This is what Solomon thinks to himself when he is trying to sleep in a house in which he is no longer alone.

Solomon's diagrams included no more than suggestions for

her face. She therefore has crude features, a mosaic of lustered ceramic for a mouth, and green glass eyes neither the same size nor the same shape. One is oval, and the other is wide and round. The lids, at least, are neat half-moons. Her nose is an angled slope with a bump at the bridge where the grain of the orange tree arcs. She has only an approximation of a woman's looks, but her hinges are perfect. All over her body there are metal hinges and wooden ones, leather hinges and string ones.

She's held together to come apart.

Sometimes, after the first days when she has to be kept from dropping in the garden and pressing her long fingers into the soil, or from standing too many hours outside with her face upturned, waiting for bees to land on her skin, the poet opens a door in her abdomen to remove a word and use it in a sentence. He talks more and more, all day, all night. He paces the room, telling her of injustices, years of woe, jealous companions and patrons murdered. He tells her of his childhood and his disease. He reports every injury done to him, and then writes more lines and feeds them to her.

My throat is parched with pleading, he scribbles. *I am buried in the coffin of my home. I combine my blood with my tears, and stir my tears into my wine. I am treated as a stranger, despised — as though I were living with ostriches, caught between thieves and fools, who think their hearts have grown wise.*

Solomon wonders why he still feels lonely. What kind of loneliness is this? One that hasn't been given a number. It makes him itch, all over, everything from his fingertips to his brain.

6.

The golem is busy. She sweeps the house's dust into the street. She washes the clothes. She clatters on the stones of his floor, her feet too loud in the night, and sometimes she sits, looking out the window, waiting for him to wake, breathing in the new dust that falls from the old walls of the city. She doesn't sleep or eat. She has no need for it.

He writes a list of his enemies and puts them into her mouth. He wants them dead or forgotten, himself remembered. He burns his name onto her wooden skin, a thin line of characters, black and smudged, a circle around her wrist. She looks at the words, curious. They're nothing magical. He is, for all his labor and verse, an ordinary man.

I am your thing, she thinks. *Thing.* She has no name. It is his job to give her one, and he has not.

The poet writes poems, and the golem walks in circles. She lifts his pallet with one hand, to dust around and beneath it. She beats a rug with her fist.

There is a thumping and pleasurable loneliness in this, the loneliness of a drummer in the desert, pounding a sound into leather, untethered by any city. She pounds the rug and feels a song inside herself, the song of falling oranges in a storm, the noise of their ripe roundness rolling away. The rug is silk, and she ravels a strand of scarlet loose and wraps it around her fingers, weaving it through her hinges. There is pleasure in this too, the feeling of an orange tree surrounded by dancers, the feeling of a gourd strung across by strings. She pulls the silk through her hands, stretching it, thinking of spiderwebs. She was once companioned by hundreds of spiders, each one using her branches as an anchor for an instrument of its own, fishing at night. She unravels the whole rug and makes a delicate web in a doorway.

"What is that?"

She has no answer, of course. She's standing beside her web, moving silk over silk, patterning the web to mimic the ones she's seen in her own twigs. With dawn there would be dew on each thread, and the spider in the center, waiting quietly for whatever might be drawn to something with so much gleam.

"This is nothing you'll do again," he says to her, taking the threads in his fist, tugging at them until they detach. He takes the tangled silk and throws it over the cliff. She watches it unspool, red loops caught in the wind, spun strings. Scarlet words in the air for a moment and then gone.

The loneliness of a bird trapped in a web, its wings twisting backward as it swings, struggling and trapped. The spider's venom, the twisting of thread to cover the beak, the glittering eyes, the feet and flight. The loneliness of being too much body to eat, and killed anyway. A mummified silence, a veiled singer dangling from a chain of silver threads.

Solomon leaves her mouth unlocked one night, and she tests it, stretching the hinges, coughing up half a poem. She feels dirty, and so she goes out into the rain and opens nearly every door in her body.

She thinks of sap. There are roots inside her, her stomach and her intestines made of them, and she places a hand on the ground and takes water from the soil. The sun is part of her skin, and so are the wind and the salt from the sea. She's three hundred years old, and grew from an orange seed dropped by a gull. She's birthed thousands of oranges, and they've fallen from her boughs, taken into the ocean and into compote dishes. A few of them grew into trees.

Now she's a golem, but she's still what she used to be.

In the morning the poet finds her with her head still upturned and screams at her, fearful of rust stiffening her smallest hinges.

She looks toward the blaze on the horizon, her jaws wide for the rain until he closes them again, muttering that his hidden words will get wet. He locks her mouth. She grinds her tiny wooden teeth, tasting dust, which she swallows, but she isn't built for anger at her maker.

She's seen the stars now, and she longs to see them again. They're familiar, the green haloes around them, the way the bird-hunting bats swoop and hang from her fingers, the way darkness turns to dawn, bleeding at the edge of the sky.

7.

The poet brings her inside the house and locks the front door, just as he locked her lips.

"You must be as a wife," Solomon says, his hands shaking. "That is what you were created to do."

The house is very clean. He arranges her on the bed, and she opens for him. She is built to do this. Her diagrams were clear. The secret hinges he requested are small and soft, made of the leather of the stillborn goat. They unfold, door after door, until the second to last door unhinges. He shoves himself inside it.

There's still the final sealed compartment. He doesn't know it exists. Nothing of him gets in.

The golem wonders suddenly if the house is like her, if she's inside the mouth of a larger golem. The loneliness of the motherless daughter, the loneliness of the daughter eaten by the mother, the loneliness of a roomful of wooden teeth. She looks at the chairs and table. She looks up over the poet's shoulder to see if the name of God is hammered to the ceiling. The loneliness of the result of magic.

When he's finished with her, the golem's doors shut themselves, one by one. She stands up and sands herself; there's a spot of blood on her breast from a wound on his. Sawdust flies until she's clean again. He coughs blood, and curses. She sweeps the dust away.

He gives her a chestnut to crack between her teeth. She hands him the meat and keeps the shell for herself to suck. It's like a nub of tongue. The golem makes a tiny sound, balancing it in her mouth, a rattle. She wedges it there with her fingers, pressed against the metal name.

She feels liquid drip down her wooden thigh. Startled, she closes the doors tighter.

"I thought I'd be happy with you," Solomon says from the pallet. "But you're not a real woman. You're a thing I made."

You didn't make me, she thinks. *I grew.*

With the shell in her mouth, she makes a tiny noise, a moaning sound, not a word, but not the sound of nothing. She chirrs a note. Everything that ever sang through her branches, every gust of wind, every bat, every bee, every bird. They all spoke to her and she spoke back to them when she was a tree. Now she is a hinged woman, muted by magic, and she moves the shell in her mouth, looking for a voice she's not been made to have.

8.

Solomon gets up, dresses in his loosest garments, and writes. His skin is boils and snakes. His bones feel breakable, and even his thoughts feel diseased. Talking doesn't help his loneliness. He wants to have her again, because she is all he'll ever have.

She isn't what he wants. He had a different woman in mind. Copper glances, black lace, a living woman willing to wrap him in bandages, a woman willing to carry him to a warm tub, a woman to cure his agonies.

This one is cold and has no heart. This one is ugly and has no mind. She's only an orange tree.

He writes of the loneliness of the poet, years of shunning, the way his life has bent itself into a hoop of suffering. He writes of the eight-hundred-sixty-first form of loneliness, the loneliness of the scratching quill plucked from some dead swan. He writes of the forty-eighth form of loneliness, the loneliness of the moment of orgasm, when all the sky rushes from the blue and into the sea, leaving nothing in its place.

He goes to the golem and stares at her, considering the conditions of the magic. He asks for one thing he hasn't had yet.

"Play me a song," he says. "It's too quiet."

9.

The golem is surprised to discover that she's made of music. She has no tongue, but she has noise.

The golem's body is a chamber. There are strings made of silk, and a curved bow inside one of the cabinets of her thigh. When she threads three strings through tiny holes drilled in her sternum, and another set just below her stomach, she can play the rabāb. This was part of her diagram, any instrument, and the carpenter's mother chose this one from her own home. There is a thin membrane of doeskin, tanned and stretched taut over the cavity of the cabinet, and this skin vibrates.

She plays the tunes given her by the carpenter's mother, songs of the desert, songs of another religion. There are *S*-shaped openings in her stomach from which the song pours.

She draws the bow across the strings, filling with greater and greater pleasure, until the poet waves his hand, goes to his bed, and waits for her to stop the noise and come to him.

10.

There's a hard storm that night, and all the pomegranates fall. The golem goes into the street at dawn and kneels to collect them, each one as large as a baby's head.

"Who are you?" a woman says, and the golem looks up, startled, her fingers pushing through the pomegranate's skin and deep into the seeds, groping for something.

The woman is standing over her, looking horrified, and when

the golem raises her face, the woman screams and backs away, gasping.

The golem feels the seeds slick and fat between her fingers. She crushes some, and juice runs out into the dirt. There are tiny ants all over the fruit, and she feels their bodies crushing too, their certainty that they might carry something so tremendous. She feels sorry for that.

"What are you?" the woman says, and makes a gesture of protection. "Demon," she whispers, and runs, dropping her basket.

The golem goes back into the house.

She curls into the cold fireplace, a heap of sticks, and stays there through the day and until the next morning, though Solomon shouts for her when she brings no evening meal. Her blossoms are falling off. The petals are dropping, and she feels as though she will soon be naked.

When the petals are gone, though, there are oranges, tiny green ones. Her skull is beaded with them.

The loneliness of the bee seeking nectar, the journey between trees, a wavering flight, a humming and thrum. The loneliness of the pale flower, a channel of gold at its center, dew and dawn and a white room.

In the morning she raises Solomon's bed with him on it and sweeps the dust from beneath it. She swabs water over the new wounds on his skin. He is weak and fevered. She wonders if he will die.

"You serve me," he croaks. She feels her doors opening. She has no say in it.

11.

Solomon presses into her, looking down at her still face, pushing against her hard flesh. He is too sick to leave the house at all. Too sick to enjoy anything. His skin feels like a board being planed, shaven, the scraps trod on by goats. He needs a diet of milk and honey, a balm of olive oil. She can't fetch any of it for him. He is a monster and she is a cabinet. Neither of them can go into the street.

He considers the precious word that brought her to life. He

means to pry it loose. She'll be firewood at least. This has been a failure.

"You're not what I wanted," he says when he is finished.

He puts his fingers to the corner of her mouth, intending to open the hinges and remove God from her.

12.

As Solomon approaches her, the golem feels a startling jolt deep inside her body. Something sealed begins to unseal; something forbidden begins to reveal itself. She holds the innermost cabinet door shut, feeling the hinges stretching, the thing behind it trying to be loose. If the poet notices her alarm, he says nothing.

There is shouting from the street. Solomon withdraws from her. The golem smoothes her dress. The poet rearranges his robes. The oranges are ripening. The room is heavy with their smell, sweat and sweetness.

The door inside the golem's body, the last and smallest door, the last and smallest hinge, shakes and swells. She keeps it closed. She refuses. Whatever is in there, it can stay locked behind the door. Liquid on her thigh. She closes all the doors with ferocious resolution.

Men shout to enter. Solomon ties a patterned cloth about her head, over the lumpy oranges.

"Qasmūna," he says. "Your name is Qasmūna. You're a house-maid."

Her fists open and close convulsively as the door pounds.

She wonders if she'll kill his enemies. That is what she was made to do.

13.

The men surge into the house, bearded and cloaked. There are five of them, and they're all elderly, years beyond Solomon. He knows them. The elders are the ones who kept him in this house, unable to walk amongst humans. When he arrived in the city, he was shunned. It was only their permission and their memories of his parents, long dead, that allowed him to live here at all, to stop walking the roads. Otherwise, he'd be dead somewhere, parched and dried to leather.

It might be better than this.

He thinks for a moment that he can take them all, pulverize them. He might crush them into a cupboard and barricade them there. He might make them into the contents of a cabinet, dishes asking to be broken. Then he remembers that they're living men, not his creation. He's lost his understanding of the nature of the world. He is a sickly poet, and they are the men in charge of the city.

The men circle the room, staring at the golem, who stands in the center, waiting, trembling. She's a tree full of birds, and they're foxes.

"What have you done?" they shout at Solomon, and he lies to them, though it's futile. They're holy men with long beards and hundreds of years between them. They know his books and they know the history of his books. They know every corner of the law. Solomon feels himself surrounded by poems he will never write. He'll be taken to executioners. It troubles him for a moment, and then it doesn't. He'll stab out their eyes as he goes. He'll scream his own elegy from his last moments. It's already written and stored inside his cabinet.

"This creature is no woman, Solomon ibn Gabirol," says one. "Do you take us for fools?"

"She's nothing more than a housemaid," Solomon says calmly. "Her name is Qasmūna, and she came from Saragossa. I brought her here to tidy my house and care for me. You know that I've been ill."

The loneliness of capture, the loneliness of guilt, a single intruder caught and tied, burned at the stake. The loneliness of fire touching feet, the loneliness of stones flying toward a target. All he wanted was a wife.

This is no sin, he thinks. This is not a sin. She's a housemaid, and Solomon has a house that needs cleaning. He has a heart that needs polishing. He has a body that needs a companion. He cannot see the problem. There is a map inside his mind of all the sins, and he doesn't believe in most of them. This one? To build a woman out of wood? How could it be wrong? To use her as a wife? She has no heart and she has no soul. She's an instrument and he has played her properly. That's what he'll say. That's how he'll argue.

One of the men nearly touches the golem and then stops, his fingers inches from her hand. He leans forward and shakes his head.

"This is not a maid," he insists, then lifts a metal cup and raps it against her wrist. It makes the sound of an ax meeting a tree. "No. We know what this is."

The golem opens her mouth hinge, slightly, to show her teeth. In her mouth, the nub of tongue rattles, and she makes a tiny noise, a cry. A string within her body vibrates and makes a sighing tone.

"We do *not* know fully," another man protests. He looks at the golem, skeptical. "Solomon ibn Gabirol isn't holy enough to make a golem. He's not held in grace. Perhaps she's simply ugly. Open your mouth wider, girl, show us what you have," he says.

She shows her teeth a little more, and her sound grows louder, a humming rattle, a clicking. Her eyelid hinges blink, quickly, a leathery brush against the green glass.

One of the men leans forward and taps her eye with a spoon. She flinches. It rings like a bell calling for prayers.

"She's a living woman," says Solomon, fearful of punishment, but angry too. His fingers curl around the tabletop.

"She is not," one of the men says, and looks at Solomon with something approaching kindness. "Shelomo ben Yehuda ibn Gabirol, you are too lonely. You are fortunate we've come to help. No one knows you've done this, not yet, and we will save you from this sin for the sake of your father."

14.

The golem trembles, bound to protect Solomon. She feels his rage like a windstorm bending her trunk. She is a newborn woman and she is a rabāb full of the songs of an entire country of travelers. She is a tree with hundreds of years of history.

She removes the bow from the cabinet in her thigh and starts to play the strings in her abdomen. The song is not a hymn. The song is a wild high flight from some other shore, the song of a woman shouting in a ship across the sea. The song of the strings bends and weeps, and she plays, her head bowed, while the bow in her hand moves quickly. Tongueless, she is telling them what will happen, but they don't listen.

"Speak," says one of the men.

"She can't," says Solomon. "She doesn't speak our language."

I am speaking, Qasmūna plays. *I am warning you. You should leave.*

"This is a sin. More than a sin. To fornicate with *this*. Speak in Spanish, you serving maid. Speak in Arabic. Speak in Hebrew. Speak any language at all."

Qasmūna plays harder, her wooden fingernails stopping the strings, the bow calling forth the sound of women seizing a ship's crew and tearing them apart. The loneliness of the shore with no one landing on it in a year. The loneliness of hunger. She is an orange tree clinging to a cliffside, oranges falling into the sea. She is a forgotten wife clinging to a village full of forgotten children. She is called to war while the men are at another war. She and her sisters march over the Atlas Mountains. She and her sisters sing war cries, play their instruments, light signal fires.

"SPEAK!" a man shouts. "Or we will know what you are."

I am speaking, the golem plays. *Hear me. Leave before you can't leave.*

Qasmūna can see veins bulging in Solomon's neck. Her hinges flutter. The secret door inside her shakes loudly enough that the men can hear it. It is unsealing. It is opening. She can't help it.

"This is not a sin," argues another holy man. "She doesn't need to be cleansed after menstruation, for she doesn't menstruate. She can't procreate. She can't speak, nor has she any intelligence. She's less than an animal. It can't be fornication if she isn't a woman."

"Her lack of speech reflects the flaw in her creator," the first man says. "He's not holy enough."

The golem listens to them argue over whether she is holy or only wooden. She plays. They look at her in annoyance. She is an instrument and she plays the music she is filled with. She bends and draws the bow over the strings, playing an attack on a tent, playing a moon rising over bloodied sand. They don't understand her. She attempts to give them a final warning, but they are too busy with their debate.

15.

Solomon rages, but doesn't dare do it with his voice. The golem is playing some tilting tune, and he can't get her to stop. Her music is nothing he'd have chosen. Why did he not kill her last night? She could be in the fireplace, heating the house. She could be rising through the chimney, her smoke a small cloud in the sky.

This was a mistake, but now that they are trying to take her from him, he wants her back. Who are they to deny him a wife?

"You must destroy this golem, Solomon ibn Gabirol," concludes the man most in charge. "For though it may not be a sin in the eyes of the law, you're a poet, not a holy man, and you have made a monstrosity for yourself, not for any city. This is forbidden."

"She's not a monstrosity," pleads Solomon. "She's my house-maid. She cleans the dust." His wounds are bleeding. He coughs, wet and red.

The loneliness of seeing one's own blood on a white cloth. The loneliness of a disease impervious to magic, to knowledge, to weather. He is dying, and there is no one to take care of him. He is dying, and soon he will be like an infant, helpless and howling. Soon he will be a body in a bed, bones like kindling.

The thousandth form of loneliness is the loneliness of the dead, rotting just beneath the ground. There will be worms and insects, there will be birds pecking at the earth, but there will be nothing to love any man underneath the world. The thousandth loneliness is a grave with fresh shovel marks, the noise of the dirt being packed down above. He will be, he realizes, down where the orange tree roots snake in the dark, white wooden bones hard as stones.

"You'll remove the name from her mouth. You'll destroy her, and you'll burn her materials." The men nod. "You'll do it now, for these witnesses, or you yourself will be put to death. Take her apart now. We will watch."

Solomon sways. He's still living, he thinks. His prick pulses. He must retaliate. He must fight.

There's a creak in the room, and a muffled pounding.

"Defender," Solomon whispers to his golem. "Defend."

The golem is already standing, staring at the old man before her. She raises a hand, and looks at it. Slowly she brings her fist down on the man's skull, a neat rapping. He cries out and falls. The holy men scream.

Solomon watches her push her fingers into one of the men's mouths, her fist pressing deeper, deeper, until she finds the root of his tongue. She tears out the meat of his voice and crushes it, a splattering gore beneath her foot. Solomon makes a sound, whether of vengeance or of protest, he can't say. He looks at the holy tongue for a moment, watching it bleed, then doubles over, vomiting.

The sound of something breaking open. He turns to see the golem and the last of the holy men, his skull vised in her two hands. She looks at Solomon, her face blank, and there is a grievous crack, sending blood spraying. Her mouth rattles and she breaks the man's neck for good measure, as though he is a hen.

16.

The loneliness of being the last man alive in a room filled with the dead is the nine-hundred-ninety-ninth loneliness.

They're all murdered in his house, the holy men of Málaga. Solomon won't die of illness as he'd imagined. He'll be executed. He has to flee the city, but he can't flee with her. He gathers himself. She has saved him and damned him at once. It can't be his fault. No one would think it was. He would never order his golem to kill for him.

"Open your mouth," Solomon orders his golem. "Give me the name. Take it out and give it to me."

Slowly the golem's jaw hinges open, showing the poet the name of God. One of her hands reaches up to remove it.

There is the sound of a sealed door opening. Something changes in the room.

Solomon looks down at the golem's chair. There's a creature in it, small and black, made of ash. It stands, its arms outstretched, a tiny thing, and it shakes the room with a high, wild song, a song like the rabāb and like a singer too, a song of loneliness beyond number. It sings a horde of women in open space, raging across a landscape, swords raised.

Solomon clenches all over. Can he smash it? With a dish, perhaps, or a text. It's small enough. It's no animal or insect he's seen.

A rough black creature, the size of a closed fist. The song is something . . . Solomon tilts his head. His ears feel penetrated.

"What's that?" Solomon manages. "Where did it come from?"

Qasmūna picks the creature up and cradles it. The ash looks at Solomon, its eyes glittering. In its fist it holds a splinter of orange wood.

A splinter held by a tiny thing. That's nothing. No sword, no matter the feelings roused in him by its song. Whatever those feelings were, they are falsehoods, defenses without teeth. Women running over sand, bloodied swords. This is only a small aberration. He'll consider it later, when this is all done.

What it is, Solomon doesn't know, but it doesn't matter. He'll dismantle the golem and it'll die with her. There will be a heap of wood, leather, metal, and string. There'll be some metal hinges, some green oranges. He'll toss it all over the cliff edge. He feels a little stronger suddenly, purposeful. He'll dress and put his books in a sack. He'll hire a cart.

The loneliness of the fleeing poet. The road before him, the dust, the cart rattling, the bones pained. The loneliness he is well accustomed to, traveling by himself, wandering bookstalls at night, reading texts he procures from the darkest, dustiest stacks. He will write two hundred verses in mourning for the golem, he decides. He'll write of her smooth skin and fragrant hair, her green eyes and sharp teeth.

He hears the golem moving, and turns to find her quite close to him. She hasn't listened to his request. Why has she not given him the name? Is the magic flawed?

Solomon clasps his golem's wrist, groping for her jaw hinge, but the golem's golem is there, standing on his arm. It stabs the splinter into the poet's hand, deep into the vein at the top.

"You are my thing!" Solomon shouts at her. "My wife!"

She says nothing. There's only that high song from the ash, and the golem, moving the bow across the strings in her stomach. Red threads. A web, Solomon thinks. A spider.

Solomon runs for the door, but almost instantly he's too ill to run, too ill to walk. He falls, shaking and vomiting, feeling his body dismantling itself from the inside out. He's made of hinges and all of them are bending, all the doors inside his body too far open, his heart dropping through staircases, his kidneys swollen, his eyes watering and blasting agony. His skin is shedding and he is a snake.

His hinges are rusting and he's alone on a rainy road, floodwater rising. The loneliness of the poet muted. His hands are claws. His mouth feels thick and his throat is closing.

17.

Qasmūna goes to him. She is built to serve, to defend, to protect, and her protections include the cessation of misery. She gives Solomon the juice of bitter oranges in a green glass cup, gently, a drop at a time from her finger. This is all there is left to do. She knows that much.

His heart thunders, but after a time he's quiet.

She picks him up from the floor and carries him, not gently. Now he's only a body, not a master. She ferries him from the house, and with her hands she digs a grave in the garden beneath the roots of a fig tree.

This not-loneliness in this garden. The company of trees, the conversation of birds, the discussions between wasps and fruit. The pollen of flowers and the high pallor of clouds. She looks up and breathes in. She spits out the inadequate nutshell and takes a twig from the tree. She works the twig into the space in her mouth, behind the name of God.

The tiny golem watches her, prepared to defend her city, prepared to do what it is golems do. As she pushes her new tongue into place, a door opens in her chest.

The golem's golem places itself inside the compartment there, a compartment that has previously been perfectly empty, and the hinges close.

Qasmūna's heart beats. The strings of her instrument vibrate. She speaks a word.

18.

A season passes, and the walled garden grows wild.

The fig tree bears fruit, and the carpenter's mother crosses over the wall and onto the poet's land to pick before the birds and bats can eat them. She can see slender yellow bones bending up from the soil beneath the tree, fingers, and a jaw, long since picked clean by animals. The earth is especially dark here, a bright russet soil, and the bones are beautiful, like jewelry lost after a night's dancing. The carpenter's mother steps barefoot on the dirt and packs it down, leaving it smooth.

She reaches up and plucks figs, dropping them into her smock. The figs are heavy and green, their centers scarlet. The carpenter's mother eats one as she stands in the garden, looking out toward the country that was hers before this one.

She hums a song about marching through sand, a song about homecoming after war. The song can only be played on the rabāb, and the tune runs counter to the music, a twisting blade sung at night while the washing's being wrung. When she was a girl, all the women sang this song at once, and when the men returned from wherever men went, they were nervous at the patterns the women's feet had made in the dust, the way they'd danced together beneath the moon.

Months have passed. The carpenter's mother knows nothing of where Solomon ibn Gabirol has gone. He walked in one day, and surely he walked away the same. His kitchen was full of coins for a time after he disappeared. Then the coins went into the carpenter's mother's apron as payment for a cabinet.

She knows nothing of where the holy men have gone, either. She saw nothing late in the night all those months ago, beneath a moon like a blossom. She heard no music playing, no mournful joyful strings, no echoing resonance and thrum. Those songs were unfamiliar to her. They sounded nothing like wandering fountains in the desert, nothing like shining things made of metal and silk.

The carpenter's mother never saw a woman walking out from the house of Solomon ibn Gabirol, her feet clattering across the stones of the street. A stranger to Málaga! She didn't see that woman lifting five men and throwing them tenderly, one by one, from the cliff, nor did she see her digging here, beneath the fig tree.

She didn't see the woman step off the rock path and walk down to the harbor. Nor did she see her open a door in her abdomen and remove a thousand pages of words, sections from poems, scribbled lines and wishes. She didn't see her tear these until each word was left lonely and then begin to rearrange them.

She didn't see this, the carpenter's wife would swear, if anyone asked her. No one will ask her. She's an old woman, and must know little of the world. She's been here too long to read and too long to write. Too long to know anything of the world of magic.

But how quickly that wooden woman went, arranging poem after poem, the words of the poet who called her from the trees taken and changed. She took all the poet's words and made new things with them, a line on the sand.

When she was finished, she looked up at the old woman standing on the cliff.

The old woman, of course, saw nothing.

She didn't watch the wooden woman place herself in a boat, take the oars in her strong hands, and begin to row.

Surely no mother of Málaga would let a murderess of so many men, all the intellectuals of this part of the coast, all of the holy, and a philosopher-poet too, surely no carpenter's wife would let a murderess go free.

19.

On the night the golem left Spain, after it was fully dark, the carpenter's mother climbed down the rocks to the shore. This much was true. She would say it, if she were asked.

The poem on the sand was written in a language she could read, and she thought for a moment about the market stalls in her homeland, the words scrolling over her fingertips, the things made by her father and brothers, brought to life by her own blood and spit.

In dreams she inlaid a mother-of-pearl woman with coral, camel bones, ebony eyes. In dreams she breathed into the woman's lips and sent her to kill those who would sell a talented daughter to wed a lowly carpenter on the southern coast of Spain. Her life is no horror, but it is no glory either, and who would imagine that a carpenter's wife would be full of poetry, full of spells, a maker of women? She could cause a fountain to spring from the desert, and here she is, sold, sold and spelled, daughter to a magician long dead. She'll never go home again, because the water will refuse her.

She read the poems Qasmūna left for her. Some had already caught the wind and blown out into the salt by the time she'd made it down the cliff, but two remained.

> O gazelle, tasting leaves,
> here in the green of my garden.
> Look at my eyes. Dark and lonely,
> just as yours are.
> How distant we are from our beloveds, and how forgotten
> Standing in the night,
> Waiting for fate to find us.

The carpenter's mother looked up, listening to the song coming over the water. She ate a fig and tasted the wasp that had pollinated it, the bones of the poet that had fed it. The second poem was shorter.

> The garden is filled with fruit on the vines, but the gardener
> refuses to brush a finger over the skin of even one piece.
> How sad it is! The season of splendor passes,
> and the fruit that ripens only in darkness
> Remains lonely.

The gulls followed the wooden woman into a new life, out from Spain and over the sea, but that is nothing the carpenter's mother will admit to knowing. She's merely an old woman sitting in the dark, listening to the sounds of a creature made of ash and one made of wood, singing their way away.

She sits there a long time beneath the stars before she writes the poems onto a piece of cloth, before she walks barefoot down the road to another town with them, before she puts them into the hands of a song-seller.

"Where did these come from?" the seller asks.

"A woman," she tells him. "Qasmūna."

"Who is her father?" he asked. "Who is her husband?"

"She has neither," the carpenter's wife said, knotting the scrolls with red silk thread. "Will you buy them?"

Coins are never lonely. They clacked and rang out, and the carpenter's wife held them in her palm, though soon they'd disappear like the kind of shining moths which land for only a moment to drink, before lighting again into the night.

Historical Note

The legend of the wooden golem created by the Andalusian Hebrew poet Solomon ibn Gabirol (1021–ca. 1058) is much less
known than that of Rabbi Loew and the Golem of Prague, perhaps
because Ibn Gabirol's golem was a (rare) female golem brought
to life not as a defender but as a housemaid and likely bedmate.
The historic Ibn Gabirol was a complicated and brilliantly prolific
intellectual figure, a reclusive misanthrope who suffered from a
skin disease, possibly cutaneous tuberculosis. His poetry is filled
with feelings of ostracization and rage relating to same—he com-
plains about jealous enemies, among other things—though he
also wrote rapturous and religiously ecstatic poems regarding the
planets, the gardens of the sky, and laughing lightning. In the accounts, Ibn Gabirol was forced to destroy his hinged golem after
being accused of fornicating with her. The legend typically comes
up in discussions of personhood in Jewish law—and the debate in
Hinge is typical of that discussion. The *Sefer Yetzirah,* in which mys-
tical information related to golem creation is traditionally thought
to be found, was a significant influence on Ibn Gabirol's work,
and he translated sections of it. The Banū Mūsā's *Book of Ingenious
Devices* was written in the ninth century and contains instructions
for creating a variety of automata. The legend of Ibn Gabirol's
murder and burial beneath a fig tree is historical, though used to
new ends here.

The rabāb is a stringed instrument still played all over the world,
an ancestor of the violin (which wasn't invented until after the period in which this story is set). It came from North Africa via trade
routes to Spain in the eleventh century, and there's a very nice
drawing of a more pear-shaped variant included in the Catalan
Psalter, ca. 1050. There's also a version of a rabāb in a fresco in the
crypt of Sant'Urbano alla Caffarella, near Rome (ca. 1011), and
that version looks almost exactly like a modern violin, including
S-shaped soundholes. The tones of the rabāb are said, even in early
accounts, to mimic those of a woman's voice.

Bitter oranges, a primary crop in Málaga, have recently been
discovered to have effects similar to those of the banned diet-aid
ephedra—their extract, often marketed as a stimulant, can cause
strokes and heart attacks. The pale yellow wood of the bitter or-

ange tree is so hard that it is made into baseball bats in Cuba. The golem's golem, composed of ash and a name written on parchment, is a far more traditional golem than the wood-and-hinges creation said to have been made by Ibn Gabirol (the only golem of that composition in the history, so far as I can tell), but that one is my invention.

Qasmūna (or Kasmunah) bat Isma'il was an eleventh- or twelfth-century Andalusian Jewish poet. Her name is likely derived from the Arabic diminutive of the Hebrew root *qsm*, meaning charming and seductive. Charming, in this case in the literal sense —magical. It may also be derived from the Arabic male name Qasmun—someone with a beautiful face. Her two extant poems (my loose translations from the original Arabic) are in the text. She is one of only two documented Spanish Jewish female poets in the period, the other being the Wife of Dunash. Qasmūna bat Isma'il's biography is unknown, though there has been plenty of speculation—the daughter of a scholar, the daughter of a well-known poet, or, in this case, something else entirely. Regardless, her poems are erotic, and steeped in the natural world.

MAUREEN McHUGH

Cannibal Acts

FROM *Boston Review: Global Dystopias*

THERE'S A DIFFERENCE between dissection and butchering. Dissection reveals, but butchering renders. I'm a dissector, professionally, pressed into service as a butcher. I mean, I was a biologist. Am a biologist.

The body in front of me is a man. I know him, although not very well—there aren't that many of us so I know pretty much everybody. His name is Art. He looks much smaller, positively shrunken, laid out in the kitchen, and very, very white. I haven't seen many naked male bodies, but I am intimately acquainted with Art's. I have washed him. I'm not attracted to men when they're alive, much less when they're dead, but I feel a weird protectiveness toward Art. I've felt the soft spot in his skull from the fall that killed him. I have washed around his balls and the curled mushroom of his penis. I have cradled his hard and bony feet.

Now I tie a rope around his ankles and hoist him. This is a commercial kitchen with big steel counters and a Hobart dishwasher. The pulley in the ceiling is new. It sounds easy—"I tie a rope around his ankles and hoist him"—but I am not very strong these days and just one pulley means I'm hauling his whole weight. I don't know what Art weighs. He used to weigh more; we all used to weigh more. I am so tired, my fingers are cold. I'm seeing spots when I pull hard on the rope.

Kate has taken to calling the town Leningrad, which is lost on most of the people here. It's because we're under siege in this stupid little Alaska excuse. It's got an airstrip, a coast guard base, an army listening post, a dozen houses, and it's surrounded on two sides by water—the ocean at our back and a river called Pilot's

Creek on one side. The army listening post was monitoring the Russians, of course, which is probably where Kate got the idea of Leningrad.

So anyway, I get Art hanging, fingers just sweeping the floor. The dead are limp. Heavy. One of the locals used to hunt when there was anything to hunt. Eric Swetzof is a long-bodied, short-legged native Unagan. Maybe, he says, he and his wife are the last Unagan left alive. He told me the steps to field-dressing a large animal.

Eric is not going to eat Art. There is a group of people who have declared themselves to be noneaters. Eric says he understands the people who have voted to eat and he doesn't judge them, he just can't. Can't cross that line.

I understand him too. I stand in front of a human with a good knife. "Blade at least four inches long," Eric said. "You want a real handle on the thing, and a guard. When the knife hits bone it can turn and you can end up cutting yourself."

I used to like to cook. I've cut chickens into parts. I'm familiar with the way a joint shines white with ligament and tendon. What hangs in front of me is an animal. I am an animal. I don't believe there is something particularly special about bodies and I don't believe in souls, the afterlife, or the resurrection of the dead. I tell myself that this is a technical challenge. It's a skill I have some parts of and I will learn the rest as I go.

I am not sentimental.

I put a plastic tub underneath Art to catch blood and viscera.

It's still very hard to open his throat. His viscera are lukewarm.

I'm so hungry.

Butchering has gotten me out of manning the defenses today. We all have to man the defenses, but I'm nearsighted and terrible with a gun. Luckily, there isn't much shooting, because neither side has much in the way of ammunition. They are mostly men, as best we can tell, a lot of them fairly young. Maybe thirty of them, some still in ragged military fatigues. They are in the sharp green hills, waiting us out. They have a couple of boats, Zodiacs, but we sank one when they first attacked and now they either don't want to risk them or they are holding them until we're too weak to fight back.

Or maybe they're getting too weak to fight.

I find Kate on Beach Road. It runs along the beach, of course, and then turns inland and runs to the airstrip. It's cloudy and soft, it rains all summer here. The air off the water smells wrong. It should smell of fish and salt, that slightly rank and pleasant stink of ocean, but instead there's a taste to it, like nail polish or something. Organics. Esters and aldehydes.

Kate is sitting cross-legged with a paperback on one knee and a rifle next to her. Technically she's on sentry, watching the ocean, but we're sloppy civilians. Does the distinction even matter anymore? She's taller than me—a lot of people are taller than me. I'm 5'4". She's rangy; a long-legged, raw-boned woman with large hands and feet. She's originally from New Mexico, but she's an Anglo with light hair and blue eyes.

I am still surprised when I see her in glasses. She has worn contacts as long as I have known her. She was always going to get corrective eye surgery. Too late now.

I can't tell if she is pleased to see me. I mean, usually she would be, but she knows what I've been doing. Kate is a noneater.

I sit down next to her and watch the chop.

"All done?" she asks.

I nod.

I think for a moment she is going to ask me if I'm okay, which is something we would have done for each other before. She doesn't and I don't know what I would answer if she did. I'm both not okay and weirdly okay.

"What's the book?" I ask.

She flips it over so I can see the cover. *The Da Vinci Code*. I can't help it, I bark out a laugh. Kate hated the book when it came out.

She sighs. "There aren't that many books here at the end of the world."

"It's not the end of the world," I snap.

She rolls her eyes. "Don't tell me about the Great Oxygenation Event or Snowball Earth again or I'll scream."

It isn't the end of the world—just maybe the end of us. Or maybe not, humans are clever beasts and the world is a big place. It's probably not even the biggest extinction event the earth has ever seen. The Permian extinction killed something like 95 percent of life—including bacteria. Life comes back. It may take millions of years. First bacteria, then multicellular organisms, then plants and animals. We're just another set of dinosaurs, about to

go extinct. Although some dinosaurs actually survived the Creta-
ceous-Tertiary extinction. We just call them birds.

"You're sitting there composing a speech," Kate says.

"I'm not going to say anything," I say.

"You intellectualize as a defense mechanism."

"I don't think psychologists talk about defense mechanisms anymore," I say. Back when we were both at the university we were
also both in therapy. Growing up gay pretty much ensured you
were messed up about something. My therapist told me I was an
emotophobe—afraid of negative emotions.

"What's your defense mechanism?" I ask.

She laughs. "These days? Anger. When I have the energy."

I brought her here. Not specifically here, this ass-end little Alas-
kan town, but "here" as in leaping at a chance to go to Juneau to
study giant viruses and get us away from the increasing chaos of
the lower forty-eight.

I look at her wrists, narrow, the knob of the styloid process
standing under scaly skin. Her ankles are swollen.

Kate and I bitched about Houston the entire time we lived
there. When I took the position, I had no idea that Houston was
tropical. Ninety-eight degrees in the summer with 99 percent hu-
midity. Flying cockroaches the size of my thumb. Getting into the
car at the end of the workday was like climbing into a pizza oven.

Honestly, though, I remember Houston this way:

In the last year we were there, crime was getting horrible. There
were refugee camps outside Brownsville and Laredo. Rolling
brownouts. We had a used Prius, which was good because gas was
rationed. Hamburger was twenty-two dollars a pound.

Kate gardened and we had half a dozen chickens. We had close
friends, Ted and Esteban, and we'd take eggs and garden vegetables over to their place and make dinner. They had huge trees in
their backyard and a pool. The electricity would go out and we'd
sit in the dark and complain about mosquitos and drink beer.

I was coming home from work one day and stopped at a stop-
light, as one does, and someone wrenched open the driver's-side
door of the Prius. It was a very angry man with a blue bandanna
covering half of his face. He'd have looked like some kind of old
movie bandit if he hadn't also been wearing sunglasses. He was
waving around a gun and screaming at me.

He yelled "Get out of the car!" at some point.

Back in the day, if you were on Facebook or Tumblr and you were a woman, you probably got safety tips in your feed. I had read *something* about whether you were safer in a car or out of it, although I think it was about getting into a car with someone who was armed—like someone who was going to get you into the car and take you somewhere. I remember it seemed vitally important to know whether I was safer in the car or out of it, but I couldn't remember and in the end I scooted across the middle console and out the passenger's-side door.

He got in the car and drove off. My laptop was in the back seat. I had the key fob in my pocket, so he didn't have that.

The police came and we went down to the police station and I told them everything. Then Kate took me home in a Lyft and Esteban made me a precious vodka martini (vodka was expensive) and everyone came over and sat around, commiserating. The electricity went out and we lit a couple of candles. I remember people brought food. Ted said he could take me to work the next day. Another neighbor volunteered to pick me up at work—it wasn't that far out of her way.

I was genuinely shaken. I don't want you to think that I wasn't. But it was such a pleasure to be the center of everyone's concern and attention. As the city vibrated into pieces around our ears, we worked to take care of each other.

In Houston I was studying big viruses. Everyone was, all over the country. My head of research, an asshole named Mark Adams, said it was like the nineties when everybody got sucked into the Human Genome Project. Careers were stagnant for a decade, he said.

Careers. Imagine worrying about a career.

Imagine having deep discussions about things at conferences in Atlanta or Baltimore. Big viruses were different from regular viruses. They didn't just take over a cell and destroy it to make new viruses. They took over a cell and turned it into a virus factory, pumping out viruses at an order of magnitude higher. They had already been linked with a meningitis outbreak in India.

I was doing work on ATP, the energy transfer mechanism in cells, and how the virus co-opted the system. I was at a conference and ended up sitting next to a guy named Zhou Limin from the University of Science and Technology of China in Hefei. We'd corresponded but never met.

We ended up getting lunch. He was a short, intense guy in glasses. He'd done graduate work at Penn State and been a post-doc at UCLA, so he spoke great English. We bitched about the emphasis on virus coatings and how that was a legacy of HIV research and how the organizers of the conference were biased toward those people.

"You want a beer?" he asked.

I didn't know if he knew I'm gay. I think I did the thing where I said I had promised to call and check in with my girlfriend.

He didn't care, so we ended up sitting in the hotel bar, some Hilton or Sheraton. The beers were nineteen dollars apiece.

"Let me expense it," he said.

"USTC covers alcohol?" I asked.

He grinned. "There'd be mutiny if they didn't."

Sometimes I fantasized about doing work in China. There were fewer restrictions there. The Chinese were willing to play fast and loose with ethics. I mean, I knew it would not really be anything like I thought; their office politics were complicated and so were their governmental. "I wish we could do some of the things you guys can do," I said.

He turned his beer glass in his hands. "The government is weaponizing big viruses," he said. "They're trying to make them to deliver bird flu."

Everyone talked about what China might be doing. China had been the first country to bring human clones to term, in violation of international ethics. Of course we thought they might do something like this. "You know for sure?" I asked.

"I know people on the project," he said. "I've seen some of the results."

So you might think I would instantly rush to the government or to the newspapers. That I was in a position to save the world.

But I wasn't. What were we going to do, invade China over microbiology? All that would happen was that Zhou would be compromised. I think he just had to tell somebody and I was the stranger on a plane.

I told a couple of friends without mentioning Zhou. Then I saw the job listing for a new lab in Juneau, and it sounded so far away, so clean and cold and safe. (Juneau was actually like Seattle, wet and green.) I remember watching television in the airport

while we waited to catch our plane first to Salt Lake City and then
to Seattle and then on to Alaska. There were reports on the bird
flu epidemic in Russia. Russia had been saber-rattling at China
in Mongolia and the Chinese had retaliated. In a month we were
all working on ways to stop the viruses—vaccinations, antivirals,
manufactured viruses that spread their own antivirus (and look
how well that went in Japan). People were getting sick all over the
world. Kate got sick early on and was in the hospital on a ventilator
for three days. She was lucky. In a month there were nowhere near
enough ventilators for the people who needed them and infection
among hospital staff was running at over 80 percent.

Pakistan and India went to war and we all waited for India to
drop the bomb, but instead North Korea nuked Tianjin and Los
Angeles.

The pandemic was burning unchecked—bird flu, the counter-
flu—and it seemed like being near other people was a terrible
idea. We decided to retreat to a cabin on the Alaska Peninsula. It
was owned by a guy in my department, but he was dead.

My parents died in the pandemic. Kate's mother too. We don't
know about her father, she hadn't talked to him in a decade. Is
Houston still there?

It's like asking if Troy is still there. There's a place on the map
marked Troy, but nobody has lived in those ruins or called it Troy
in millennia. Maybe someone still lives in Houston. Maybe Ted is
standing on his back deck looking at his empty swimming pool
and he's converted it into a kind of greenhouse, like he always
threatened. Maybe they are growing things. Maybe the chickens
we gave him live there.

Everything we try to grow here in Alaska dies, and no one, least
of all me, knows what that means.

In the late afternoon there are gunshots and I scramble to the airstrip. *Scramble* is a relative term. When I stand up too quickly, I see
spots. We all conserve energy. But the rule is, when you hear shots,
anyone not on sentry has to grab a weapon and go.

We dug trenches and put up barricades of useless vehicles,
trash, and fence before these guys even showed up. I find Eric.
The big man is crouched in a trench.

"What's the password," he says. A joke between us.

"Leningrad," I say. "Where's Deb?" Deb's his wife.

He shrugs. Eric doesn't talk much. It took me a long time to figure out he's a sarcastic bastard. He's so deadpan it's scary.

"What are they doing?" I ask. "I heard shots."

(I wish I could say I was some sort of intrepid survivor, but the first time someone shot at me I just froze. I hunkered down and couldn't move. Eric's comment later was, "It happens.")

"They aren't doing anything," Eric says.

I watch the green and granite hills. No sign of movement in their trenches.

"I wonder how much food they've got," I say. "Maybe we should do some kind of nighttime sneak attack." Not that there's much night at this time of year.

"Jeff said no," Eric says. Jeff is our elected mayor/commandant.

I'm tired from jogging to the airstrip and these days my concentration is pretty shot, so I sit for a minute carefully studying the landscape and feeling empty and stupid. (And thinking about Art cooking back in the kitchen.) "Wait, you suggested it?"

Eric glances at me, expressionless, which I think is Eric-speak for "Are you a moron?" He looks back out at the blank hills.

We sit there for a while and I try to figure out what that means. It starts to drizzle.

"Do you think they're planning something?" I ask.

"I think they're desperate," Eric says.

"Join the club," I say.

Eric looks at me, stonefaced. But I'm beginning to get when he's amused. I think he's amused.

The eaters assemble in the canteen. Len did the cooking. He has worked very hard to make sure that Art no longer looks like Art. We have Art a couple of ways. We have some of Art roasted and sliced thin. Lean strips of meat. The rest is boiled. So here it is: human flesh tastes . . . pretty bland. Tough and maybe a little bitter. I can see why people compare it to veal or pork or chicken. I am so hungry, but I eat it slowly. Len cries as he eats. He was a fisherman—like the guys in the television show who catch crab, only he worked on boats that caught halibut, pollock, and herring and occasionally did stints in processing plants. I almost sat down next to him, solidarity in our grisly parts in this meal. But I thought maybe it was better if I didn't make us so obvious.

There isn't a lot of meat. The broth is salty. I feel full.

Thank you, Art.

I wonder who at this table will eat me? Although I'm a short woman and there's a good chance I'll outlive most of the men.

I almost fall asleep at the table. Spoons clink against bowls. Len cries as he drinks spoonfuls, salty tears slipping into his ragged beard, flannel shirt loose on him.

A single gunshot the next morning brings us to the airstrip.

It's sunny for a change. Kate and I walk over together. We haven't said anything about what I've done. It should have been some kind of personal Rubicon and maybe it was, but what I feel is that I held out on Kate. That I didn't share food with her. Like I cheated. There was a time when we'd have talked about it. It's what lesbians do, you know, we talk and talk. We negotiate our needs and our wants. We explore our feelings. But here, at the end of the world, it's okay that some things won't be resolved. We'll go to our deaths with resentments and unfairness clutched to us like greedy children. What else have we got?

There's a white T-shirt flying on a stick.

We all sit on the ground, the edge of a trench, whatever. I mostly feel as if I don't have the energy to deal with this. Not after Art. No more decisions.

"What do you want to do?" Len asks everybody and nobody in particular.

"They surrendering?" Callie asks.

Eric's face doesn't exactly change, but I suspect he's thinking, *Moron*.

Callie is perfectly nice. I think she was local, administration. Like a secretary or data entry. I can imagine her thinking she'd work for a few years, get a nest egg, and then get a job in Juneau. Or maybe she's like a lot of Alaskans and she likes the ass end of nowhere and she had a husband who loved snowmobiles or something.

"I don't trust them," she says.

Oh for Christ's sake.

"We can ask them," I say. I thought I was too worn down to care but I remain myself—opinionated and unwilling to shut up till the end.

Everyone looks at me.

I stand up and yell over the tipped Land Cruiser that forms part of a barricade. I yell, "Hey! Are you surrendering?"

Kate finds me embarrassing sometimes.

A guy comes over the hill. He's dressed in camo pants and a T-shirt and he looks normal, not superskinny. He waves his arms. "We need help! We're dying! We're sick!"

"All of you come out in the open!" Eric yells.

It's a long five minutes or so before three men shuffle to the edge of the airstrip. We shout back and forth. They are all that's left, they say. We don't believe them. One of them weeps.

It takes most of the morning before we are convinced. There are four more guys too sick to walk. We could shoot them.

They don't look starving. That's the important thing.

"What if we quarantine them?" Kate asks me.

"We'd be talking Ebola levels of decontamination," I say. "Bleach. The whole nine yards. We don't have that stuff."

"I've already had the flu," she points out. "I'd be immune. I'd just have to be very careful."

Three of us have had it and survived. They decide to risk meeting; everyone else will be ready for an ambush. We have rubber boots and Wellingtons, and latex gloves and hairnets that were for the kitchen staff. The three put on raincoats and gear and I use duct tape to seal the sleeves of the raincoats to the tops of the latex gloves. When they come back I will make them walk through tubs of bleach and wash everything off before putting on a pair of gloves and taking all the homemade gear off.

"Cover me," Kate says to me, grinning—I am a terrible shot —and walks across the airstrip.

No one shoots.

That evening, in our bed, she tells me what it was like. The graves. The newly dead. The smell. The sick. The trash and carelessness. "They were, like, teenagers," she says. One of the sick men died during the afternoon.

There is a box truck three-quarters full of supplies. Bags of beans and rice. MREs. These weird emergency bars.

Kate tells me they were convinced we had medical supplies. One of them said that he knew we had supplies when they smelled meat cooking. They assumed then that we had power, maybe a freezer.

"They're just kids," she says. "Like my students." Kate taught English, freshman composition, in Houston. "Just clueless kids."

"Like we have a clue," I say.

We eat MREs. Mine is Mexican chicken stew. There is the stew and a packet of red pepper to spice it up, Spanish-style rice, and jalapeño nacho cheese spread. There are cheese-filled pretzel nuggets. There is Hawaiian punch, so sugary that when I taste it, tears come to my eyes. And these weird crackers, like saltines but coarser. Some weird refried beans with so much flavor. There's a full-sized bag of peanut M&M's. It's weird, seeing it all bright. It's exotic.

Kate gets spaghetti with meat sauce (we reached in and drew blind so we wouldn't know what we were getting). We agree she won. It's like canned spaghetti and comes with a weird cracker that is shaped like a slice of bread but isn't either bread or a cracker. Cheez Whiz–type stuff, hot sauce, potato sticks, and blueberry-cherry cobbler.

I feed her some of mine because, I keep saying, I ate yesterday. Besides, I'm full. We share her blueberry-cherry cobbler, which has no crust and isn't really anything like a cobbler but who cares, and we keep the M&M's to share in bed.

Cheese and crackers! A meal!

It makes me think that maybe we'll survive. Maybe in a few months there will be fish in the ocean and Len will show us ways to catch them. It makes me think that a society that made things this marvelous will not just disappear.

It makes me think that none of the rest of us will get the flu.

It makes me believe we will hang on.

We sit in our bed in the big main building of the coast guard station—no one lives in the houses because they are too hard to defend. Our home is a mattress and box spring sitting on the floor of an office, next to a desk. I feed Kate a yellow M&M and eat a brown one.

"Don't eat all the brown ones," she says.

"Oh, do you like them best?"

"No, you're giving me all the pretty ones and eating all the broken and brown ones."

"I ate yesterday," I say.

"I ate today." She picks up a red one and holds it out to me on the palm of her hand.

I take it.

"I'm sorry," I say. "I'm sorry I ate." I wish they had surrendered before.

"I want you to eat," she says.

"You're not."

"I am," she says, and pops an M&M in her mouth. "Now I am again."

I sigh and settle on my side.

"Promise me you'll eat me," she says. "If it happens."

I don't say anything.

"You're so brave," she whispers. "I would if I could, but I can't. I can't be like you."

I smell the M&M's and the dusty carpet. I feel the bones of my hips on the mattress.

"Eat me because I love you," she says. "Because you love me. Because you have to. Promise me."

MARIA DAHVANA HEADLEY

Black Powder

FROM *The Djinn Falls in Love*

THE RIFLE IN this story is a rifle full of wishes. Maybe all rifles seem to be that, at least for a moment, when they're new, before any finger has touched any trigger. Maybe all rifles seem as though they might grant a person the only thing they've ever wanted.

At the beginning of this story, there are no bullets. At the end of this story, there are no more bullets *left*. In the middle of this story, there are enough bullets to change the world into something entirely different.

This rifle is full of anything anyone could want, each bullet a captive infinity, each an ever after.

Bullets may be made, in the old way, of a thin cylinder of any animal's gut packed full of black powder and attached to the back of the projectile with glue. They may be made of bronze points, of buckshot, with tiny arrows — fléchettes — embedded in them to maximize damage on entry. Rifles may shoot anything from orbs to thorns, which may be propelled, in antique weapons, by a mixture of charcoal, potassium nitrate, and sulfur, or, in certain situations, by the motions of something else entirely.

Thus may one fire a wish. Thus may one shoot a star.

That's a story people tell, in any case. Like all stories, this one contains lies, and like all old rifles, this one contains the dust of its history.

Perhaps the story begins with a kid behind the wheel of a truck, this same stolen rifle beside him.

This kid — call him the Kid, why not? — has big plans. Here at the base of the mountains, he's been looking up too long, seeing only girls who want nothing to do with him. He stole the rifle from the dumb old man at the pawnshop, who never even saw him coming.

The Kid shot the rifle once, and then—

The Kid's nothing special. He's gangle, denim, pustule, and pouch. Back pocket of his jeans is full of stolen chew, and his hands are covered in corn-chip ashes like he's been elbow deep in a Dorito crematorium.

Something weird happened when he pulled the trigger, something he's not thinking about.

Something asked him a question.

The something is in the back of the Kid's pickup truck now, on the dog's blanket. Maybe real, maybe imagined, maybe a flashback to some cartoon reality seen when he was little. He's decided not to think about it.

Out here, near the remnants of the reactor, there's a marker for a massacre of trappers, and there's a historical designation for the place, their possessions enough to identify them.

In the summer, poison mushrooms leap from the shadows, shape of skulls. The spot is surrounded by cliffs that glow green at sunset, and the hollow in the center feels seen. It's been declared safe enough, the radiation dispersed, though most people would never come here. It's a bad place.

The Kid imagines the fire flooding up from it; pictures the pale blue sky when the meltdown happened, tree branches shaking, studded with black squirrels. The way ash fell from the heavens, and his mother walked out from the trailer and filled her hands with it, filled her mouth with it, rolled in it like a dog in snow.

"I didn't know no better," she says. "Lot of people didn't. We thought it was some kinda miracle."

Then she was pregnant, and she swears she doesn't know how it happened, doesn't know who the Kid's father ever was.

He veers left on the highway and drives on the wrong side a while, singing along with the hum inside him. In the seat, the rifle sings too, bullets rattling, each a distinct tone.

The Kid feels stars inside his chest, burning novas, sparks flitting through his body. He's a man on a mission, to spread the word of the dead.

He thinks about his future: a hero's journey through the flat earth of high school. He's readying himself to graduate from childhood and into legend.

Drop back in time to another part of the story, a hundred and fifty years ago, long before the Kid's even born.

Out here in these woods, at that time, there's a notorious free-trapper who takes all the pelts and all the women. He pays in plague as well as in trade goods, taking the beaver, the mink, the wolves, taking the daughters of chieftains and the wives of warriors.

He's a bringer of disaster, and in the years he walks the woods, he takes wife after wife, never for long. Some die in childbirth, and some die in rapids, and some die by bear. One leaps from a cliff. They walk ahead of him and ride behind him. They are the starwatchers he uses when he can't see a way out of the wild and the warmth he relies upon in winter. The animals hate him, and the wives hate him, and he carries a black-powder rifle, an ax, and a bottle of whiskey. Anything else he needs, he steals. Every time he takes a new wife, he's cursed by all the inhabitants of the places he passes through. There are babies left behind after each wife dies, and he gives some to the animals and puts others out to be collected by anyone who lives in the trees. The trapper wants only wives, not children.

The rifle in this story is the one that once belonged to this trapper.

Downwind and upriver of the trapper's territory, there's a pack of company men with a bag of sugar and a bag of tea, a pile of pelts tied to horseback, the riders chewed over by the tilted teeth of the mountains. Each green cliff glints with ghosts, and each new place is written on a map of the men's making.

Silk has not yet taken over the world. It's the trappers' mission to bring back fur and carry it into drawing rooms where the pianos are made of wood from other conquered places. At night the men circle, make their fire, boil the river, steep tea leaves, drink it hot and sweet, the only rightness, their ragged remnant of civilization. It's a strange civilizer, the drinking of brackish water.

They write journals of their expedition into forbidden country: caverns narrow and full of black wings, pine trees sharp as knives pressed into soft bellies. Each man has his spoon. Each man has something gold hanging under his shirt. If they chisel into the stone they find only dark muddy green, stone the color of swamp, no emeralds. Above them, mountain lions stalk the white bone knobs at the back of each man's neck.

One of the men's got a monkey with him, the only source of comedy, brought from his lady at home, and he sets his monkey off into the woods. The monkey chitters high and holy, telling him where the beavers are building their dams. That trapper comes back rich in oily pelts, the decapitated heads of beaver strewn on the path behind him, ghost tails slapping the water while the men sleep.

One day a woman appears at the edge of their camp. She carries two pistols and wears trousers made of leather. Her eyes have tattoos of treelines along the lids.

Call her the Hunter.

With her is the French Canadian freetrapper, whose legend the men all know. He's the Bluebeard of the Rocky Mountains, and his tales travel, but something's wrong with him. He rides on the back of her horse, sidesaddle. He sucks at the insides of his cheeks, spits in the dirt, and bows his head. He wears a brilliant blue blanket around his shoulders and shivers, even when he's near the fire. His beard's gone half white.

The trappers decide he's no longer a man. Something's gone wrong, and whatever it is, they won't ask. They decide never to speak of him again. Bad luck.

"What are you doing here?" the leader of the company men asks the woman. "What are you hunting?"

He's already given her all the tobacco they've brought, though he doesn't know why.

"What do you think I'm hunting?" she asks. "Don't you know where you are? What do *you* call these mountains?"

They tell her their name for them, and she laughs. "That's not their name. I've been following them around the center of the world. I've been hunting a long time.

"Let me tell you a story," she says.

The men carefully fail to listen. The only stories to tell nine months into a trapping are *about* women, not *by* them. *Girls on their backs, girls on horseback, girls in horsehair.* No man wants to risk drawing the attention of his own ghosts, not this far in. The longer they travel in this country, the more fear travels with them. The women in these mountains are dangerous if they exist at all, and the men pretend they don't, in favor of the few women working up in the gold veins and silver valleys outside the tourmaline range. The men make progress toward them, gathering pelts for payment at bars and brothels.

The story the Hunter tells them is something about a magical creature in the trees, left here by an earlier expedition, offloaded from a wagon, and chained in a room made of metal out in the woods, all alone.

"I ran up on the last man from that expedition, and he told me they put their monster where nobody would ever find it," she says, and the men shudder.

"Next time I saw him, he was turned innards out," she says, "and hanging from a tree. He was missing all his mains. So I guess they didn't cage it well enough, now, did they? You haven't seen it?"

They haven't seen it.

When she rides away, the freetrapper looks back at them, and they pretend not to notice. All is well. Pelts and then home.

One morning, though, the men come upon a gathering of the dead, skeletons sitting in a circle, drinking tea. Cups shattered in the snow, gilt-edged smiles, brown stains in the ice. All the dead are dressed in furs, layer after layer of them, beaver, bear, and wolf. The skeletons are wearing the claws of the animals, the teeth of the animals, the tails of the animals.

The monkey leaps from its man's shoulder and runs to one of the dead. It shrieks in recognition.

One of the living men kneels beside one of the skeletons and touches the skull with his fingernail, tapping it. With that touch the skeleton blooms, regaining all its lost flesh, young and strong and fat with feasting. It is a body full of brilliant blood. It is a familiar body. Each man sees himself there, and shudders in time, himself living, himself dead, all in the same moment.

There's a whipping wind now, and hailstones. The fire rekindles in green flames, and there is a voice, and the voice tells them to eat.

There is the Hunter with the trees tattooed on her eyelids too, but she doesn't arrive until somewhat later, and by then the thing she's hunting is gone.

What do we hunt but each other? A hunter might go on an expedition, might map the forest and mountains, but what they're truly looking for is their own broken heart hidden inside an elk, their own lost lover hidden inside a wolf, their own dead child hidden inside a bear. A hunter is always looking for wishes to come true, and if it takes blood and rending to get them, then it does. There is a magic in the explosion, in the black smoke cloud, in the way whatever one is hunting runs off, the way the hunter is left standing there, inhaling powder.

All most people wish for is *more,* wishing forever until tongues are parched and hearts are tired of beating. Love is a kind of wish.

Wishing for love is the same as wishing for more wishes.

Snap forward in time again, a hundred and fifty years. Now there's a pawnshop down a dirt trail, deep in the woods, near the spot where the trappers died.

There's a man named Yoth Begail behind the counter, scraggle jaw and white yellow beard, tin of chew in his front pocket and stretched tendons in his neck giving him the look of a scarecrow gone sentient. There's pawned-off precious in the glass cases, dust on everything thick enough to epic it. These are the gun hoards of suicides from the local police repo, snuck out by janitors looking to buy other things, trading them over to Yoth Begail for the time being, taking his cash off to dealers and alimonies.

Yoth's been out here sixty-five years, give or take. Pawnshops are robber beacons, and people come in a couple times a year to gunpoint Yoth, who pulls his own weapon from undercounter, no hesitation. Yoth's got no town rules to live by. He sells things no one else can sell.

Got a case of stones brought in by the woman out near the reactor. Bunch of folks that way went to heaven and left their blood behind, crystalized into little geodes, and the woman, only one still out there, has been selling them for years. They left bones that look like milk opal too, centered with garnet marrow, and Yoth's got some of those as well. The woman tried to sell him a skull, but he didn't want that glittering thing around, the stony brain visible inside the opal casing. All of it was like to get him sick. Rest of the stones out here are hunks of green tourmaline, but the muddy kind, and tourmaline is rough luck.

Oh, Yoth's got the usual pawn glories too. All the things people come to him to forget. He's like a confessor in that way. Bingo-bought prizes and family heirlooms, forlorn valuables traded for canned-good grocery dollars. Pearl necklaces bought in Tahiti on the only vacation, engagement rings wrung off arthritic fingers. Televisions and trophies, couple of gold bars somebody brought in from a hoard, pennies on the dollar, 'cause you can't spend gold at the Walmart. He's got a gun-shop license, and he can sell whatever he wants to anybody he likes. These guns have been used to kill all kinds of things: animals, trespassers, ownselves.

Up high on the wall there's a glass case containing Yoth's best rifle. It's a black-powder model, so in federal terms it's not even a firearm. It can be sold to anyone, held by anyone. Black powder doesn't need a license. When Yoth's in the mood, he turns out the lights in the pawn, drinks a beer, and lets the rifle shine. Under the fluorescents it looks like any old firearm, dents and pits, but it came with weird copper-cased bullets, and the bullets are hot to the touch, even now, unfired since the 1800s.

Or rather, fired only once, by Yoth himself, and he got what he needed.

It's not for sale, but the pawn ticket's out there still. Brought in by a young woman with tattoos on her eyelids, who said there was no place out far enough that she could be sure people wouldn't find it, so she was entrusting it to Yoth Begail and his pawn palace for the time being.

"Welp," said Yoth, who was familiar with people trying to keep their fingers on their valuables from afar. "I'll take it off your hands then, ma'am."

"You have to keep it safe," she said. "It's a damned old thing and it's been in some trouble."

"Nothing's damned without it's had human hands on it," Yoth said. "That's just a black-powder rifle. It's the man with bad aim that's the problem."

"So you say," she said. "But you'd be wrong. I'll be back for it. I haven't slept in a while, and it's that thing's fault. Every so often I need a rest bad. There has to be a bargain made."

Yoth considered that. He was a young man then, and he thought for a moment he could consider a wife like her, if he'd consider any wife, but in her stare he saw nothing he liked. Woman looked like a wild dog, and when she shut her eyes she looked like a rattler. She was wearing clothes so old you'd have thought she lived in a cave, and she had white fur draped around her shoulders, fur of some animal he didn't know. Leather pants so filthy she might've been an animal from the waist down.

"You a hunter, then?" he asked.

"Am that," she said. "Been hunting in these woods years now. Trapping too."

"Why haven't I seen you before?" asked Yoth. She couldn't have been much older than he was.

"I was out a long time, this last one," she said. "Years. Got any tobacco? Can't smoke when I'm hunting these."

"Animals don't care," said Yoth, passing her a cigarette, lighting it for her. This was before he took to chewing, safer in a pawnshop.

She looked at him and laughed. "What I'm hunting likes the smoke. If I smoked, it'd find me before I'm ready to be found."

The tattoos on her eyelids were faint enough to be scars, but Yoth could tell someone had inked them in. Treelines on top of the mountains out here, recognizable peaks. A map. He looked at them secretly as he wrote out her pawn ticket.

"You keep that rifle for me," she said. "I'll be back. Don't fire it unless you want to call up trouble."

He peered out the window to watch her go. She was on horseback, the horse draped in an unlikely blanket the color of bluebells, a piebald black-and-white mane. Her mount moved like someone dragged up out of an armchair to dance to a song he'd never heard before. There was a little monkey in a vest sitting on the back of the saddle. The woman, the horse, and the monkey disappeared into the trees, and not long after that, snow piled up against his windows. Time he managed to dig himself out, Yoth Begail had decided to forget about the strange tracks her horse had left, nothing like hooves.

That was sixty years ago. Yoth keeps the glass of the case clear and the rifle oiled, but otherwise he leaves it alone. It's loaded, unlike the rest of the pawnshop guns. It's always been loaded. He took the bullets out once and held them, but he got a terrible feeling, and when he put them back in, there were burns on his palms. They took weeks to heal. That time he went to a doctor, who gave him some goat-shit-smelling ointment and told him not to play with matches.

At night he can hear singing coming from inside the rifle case, but he's no fool. He's not tempted.

Yoth's four drinks into the dark when the Kid comes through the front door, slipping in without ringing the bell, loping over to the desk where Yoth is sitting. The Kid says, "Old man, give me your best shooter."

"You're not old enough to own a gun," says Yoth. "I only sell to people old enough to aim."

"I'm older than I look," says the Kid. "And I'm not what you think. I want me some magic."

Yoth eyes him.

"Mind out of here now, kid," says Yoth. "I got the right to refuse service."

Yoth Begail is eighty-six years old when the Kid steals the rifle off the wall of the pawn palace and shoots him dead.

The Hunter wakes with a start in the middle of a blizzard, her cave filled with gray light. She's been sleeping a long time. Her hand is clenched around a slip of paper, and her mouth is dry.

Her heart starts up again, and she waits as blood circulates through her body, locks opening to let salmon through. Now the fish are running, red and pink and silver, bright fish in a bright river. Her horse is there in the entrance of the cave, his blue blanket over him, his mane whiter than it was when she was last awake. She shoves her boots on. The cave is lighter now, and icicles fall from the entrance, spearing the snow, cracking and groaning as they give themselves over to water again. Outside, flowers explode. The Hunter stretches her arms and checks her weapon. Her pawn ticket is still legible.

"Up, horse," she says, and the horse stands and shakes himself. She straightens his blanket. "Up, monkey," the Hunter says, and the monkey comes out of the saddlebag and looks around, eyes shining.

"It's hunting season," she says.

Another story from the history of the rifle: Yoth Begail fired this rifle just once, twenty years after he received it, into a stick-'em-up who'd opened the door of the pawnshop while Yoth was on the can. He grabbed the rifle without thinking, and pulled the trigger into the robber.

By then Yoth was forty years old and in love with the priest from down in the river valley, the one who traveled cabin to cabin spreading God like margarine.

Yoth had his own secrets, and his own once-a-year trip away from the woods to a city where there were bars to drink in and men to drink to, even if he had no way with words. Sometimes he opened his register and looked at the ticket and wondered if the Hunter was ever coming back. Yoth was starting not to sleep for thinking of the black-powder rifle, worrying that someone would steal it, and he wondered if what she'd told him was true, if it was the thing's fault, or if that was just his mind running wild.

The priest—let us call him the Priest, in the tradition of this kind of story—came to the pawnshop one day in spring and knocked on the door. When Yoth opened it, he was startled. Man of God. There was no God out here. That was *why* he was in the woods. There was only the new reactor, fenced and barbed-wired, patrolled by trucks, and the old places, the missionary buildings going to crumble now, nobody worshipping in them anymore. Hunters holed up eating beef jerky in the wood churches these days, pine needles and pitch, rabbit bones splintered beneath the sign of the cross. Piss graffiti on the walls. Yoth himself had spent some time with a smoke-jumper in one of those shacks, before he stopped that sort of thing cold. Mob of neighbors at the pawn, that was what his kind of love led to, and he didn't want it.

"Heard tell you were up here alone, Yoth Begail," said the Priest, and smiled. He was a rangy man a little younger than Yoth, wearing a string tie and a black suit and holding a Bible in his hand. His face had an openness normally found in fools, but there it was, on him, a man with a clean shave, nicked jaw, and eyes that showed evidence of a history other than prayer.

"Am that," said Yoth.

"Heard you might be looking for the Lord?"

"Heard wrong," said Yoth, who could hardly speak. His throat had a lump big as a cocoon in it, and he had no idea what wanted to emerge. Words he'd never say. "You're new out here," he said instead.

"I came from Missouri," the Priest said, with palpable awe. "On a train. I'm the new man of God out here."

"You are that," said Yoth. "Got a name?"

The Priest blushed from beneath his collar, his face heating to the color of a coal in a woodstove. Yoth felt himself blushing too, but he was in the shadow.

"I'm Weran Root. Not 'the Priest.' I don't know why I said that. This is my first assignment. I've never been to a place like this before. It's far between people. I've been walking this mountain since yesterday looking for you."

Weran Root came in uninvited and sat down at the jewelry case, gazing in at twenty years of Sunday best. He picked up a red stone and held it to the light.

"What kind of gem is this?"

"It's from when the reactor melted down," Yoth tells him. "Twenty years ago. All over the news. You remember."

Yoth could hear singing coming from the rifle. The jangling noise of a wedding in the wood, a charivari. Coins thrown into the apron of a bride, groom lifted and shaken upside down, laughter, fiddles and howls, whistles and shrieks of ecstasy. He tried to ignore it.

"What's that on the radio?" Weran Root said. It was a Sunday, but there was nothing church in the song. He looked up at the case on the wall in wonder.

Yoth looked at Weran Root in similar wonder.

Everything was new.

Six months later, when Yoth was grabbing the rifle from the case in the dark, he heard the singing louder still, and as he fired, the singing reached a pitch of tambourine and cymbal, rattling bells, all that louder than the noise of the shot itself.

"Wait! I'm here to save you from the Devil!" cried the intruder, reaching for the barrel, but Yoth's aim was true, and it was already over.

The smoke was dense and final, a black cloud in his eyes and lungs underlining each cell, a fog like a forest fire. It took a moment to clear, but by the time it did, Yoth already knew what he'd done.

He'd put a bullet in the heart of the thin man in the white shirt, string tie, and black suit, a bullet from a singing rifle pawned over by a hunter. On his back on the floor lay the love of one man's life, his heart something unclaimable by ticket.

Out of the bullet casing came the singer Yoth had been listening to for twenty years, smoke like a roomful of pipes, and in the center of it—

Yoth fell on his knees as something, some*one*, expanded from out of the wound in the chest of Weran Root, toes still in the place where the bullet had entered, fingers stretching long and gleaming, body undulating up.

"Are you the Devil?" Yoth Begail whispered. "Am *I* the Devil?"

He was weeping, his hands full of bent wedding rings and

crushed cash from the box, things to bribe back his beloved from the land of the dead.

You get one wish, the smoke said.

And so Yoth wished.

Forty years after Yoth Begail's wish, the Kid drives down the highway. All he can think about is lack of love. He tells himself a story a night. Girls walking past him in the hallway of the high school. When he prays, he prays to the god of lost causes. He's a lost cause himself, born bleak in a trailer out in the woods near the reactor, and his mama is a scavenger of skeletons. She smashes them up and makes craft glue mosaics out of them. He wishes she'd smashed and glued him into the shape of some other creature, but she didn't. Now he's this. It's her fault. Their trailer is surrounded by fake white wolves made of cement and paved in mosaics of glass and bone.

Everyone living left this area after the accident that didn't happen, the fire that wasn't. He and his mother stayed. Some people make peace with disaster, and his mother's that kind. Maybe the Kid's not, but he was doomed before he was born.

The Kid thinks fondly back on himself now, before innocence became experience, before he knew there'd never be any forever for him. He used to walk up and down the road, picking up souvenirs of crystal bones and holding all that hard blood in his hands, counting it up like he could build something out of it. He had visions of everything, back then. Now no one notices him.

Girls' eyes slant away under lashes, electric-blue liner, and who's that for? Their skin under tight jeans, and who's that for? It must be for someone. Why not for him? Not for him, because it's never gonna be him. The Kid's got no future. He's only past. There's nothing for him but hands out in the parking lot of a gas station or in the urinal, head against the wall, looking for salvation in a hot air blower and any drug buyable from anyone who'll sell to invisible boys.

Magic doesn't make anyone love you. All the Kid can do is start a fire in the palm of his hand and that's a trick he ordered from the back of a magazine.

Something offered him a wish after he fired that shot in the pawnshop. He's thinking about it.

*

The forest is deep winter now, and the caves are full of sleep. Animals uncurl from corners, bears in the backs of mountains and bats in the tops of caverns. Out in the ice where the reactor was, there's a hot, sulfurous spot, and beneath it there is a sound like coins in the pockets of the world. Steam rises from the cut into the frozen air, a cookpot. Out around that spot in the ice there are three black wolves, sitting on their haunches, their winter coats full and their bellies fat, unlike the other wolves in the area. These wolves are fed.

Wolves are only recently back out here, after years of ranchers and strychnine and years more of rumor. Wolves speak in howls, and when one is killed the rest know it and walk at night, grieving past the bodies on the fences, past the tufts of fur caught to the barbed wire. Now there are twelve wolves running over this mountain, living on deer meat and rabbit. They eat hot-blooded things, and an occasional bone, brought to them in payment. In the place where the reactor was, there's heat and smoke, but the ice hides it.

The motorcycle the Hunter's riding is gleaming black with white trim, a blue blanket stuffed in the gear bag. The monkey clings to her shoulder, its own little helmet buckled tight. There are rotting snowdrifts in the road, and fallen trees, and sometimes a dead animal starved and picked clean. A recently done deer looks reproachfully out from the roadside, flies hatching in her nostrils. The Hunter rides along this highway with its silver stripe down the center, her bag jingling as she goes.

When she gets to the pawnshop, it's full dark, and there are no lights to say this is a palace. The spot sings out with heat, though, and she has no trouble finding it. It's loud as a wedding in the woods, if it's what you're looking for. She dismounts and takes the monkey in with her, steps over the rubble and rank, the pool of blood, and finds Yoth Begail on the floor.

The monkey hops down, stands on the man's forehead, and peers into his mouth. It knocks on Yoth Begail's chest and his heart resumes beating, like an engine that's got too cold.

"You're not dead," the Hunter tells Yoth Begail. "You just think you are. Where'd it go?"

"Who?" asks Yoth, bleary.

"The one who came out of the bullet," the Hunter says. "I see you got shot. Did you shoot yourself, or did someone shoot you?"

"A kid shot me, and took the rifle when he went," says Yoth.

"Did he make a wish?"

"I don't know," says Yoth. "Boy was a strange customer, and I was well and truly dead. I regret I didn't see him coming."

She goes. The bike growls, and leaves tracks like a man running barefoot, like a horse galloping in gypsum, and then the tracks are gone again, white hollows in an evening world.

Yoth turns his head to look at the vision beside him, a tall man in the string tie. All the gemstones that were in the case are on the man's fingers, and all the music in the shop is played by his hands, and if he is not quite visible, if he lives in the crack between night and day, it's no huge matter. The shop is as fine a place for shadows as anywhere.

Yoth's wish was a switching of places, his dead beloved for the living djinn. He was left with a lover made of smoke.

"I thought I was over with," Yoth Begail says.

"I thought so too," says the man who was Weran Root. "But you're not, and I'm not, and here we are, in the dark, without the devils."

"The rifle's with the Kid," says Yoth.

"If I were still a praying man and not this, I might pray," says Weran Root. "He's going to shoot till he's done. That's his notion. It was written all over him. But *we* have a wish too. I planned for this. We don't let boys bring down the universe."

"We?" says Yoth Begail.

Weran Root opens his hand and reveals a bullet, the creature it contains still singing from inside it.

"I took this one years ago," says Weran Root, with the peaceful Missouri certainty he's always had, from long before he was a djinn. Weran Root never worried, even when love took him over and remade him. When he was changed from flesh into smoke, the love continued, blazing through Yoth Begail's lonely life, making the entirety of it bright. Yoth looks at his husband and feels his own heart beating. He takes the Priest's hand in his own.

"The legends lie. Wish-granters are not only makers of palaces full of beautiful girls and of forests in the desert," Weran Root says. "Wish-granters sometimes reverse things."

This is the beginning of this story.

Backward in time, a thousand years. Here's a girl in the desert, enslaved to a sultan. She wanders in and out of the shadows of a roomful of oil lamps, stepping on a stool to reach the highest ones and bringing them all down at once for polishing.

She knows what they are. She knows what she is and is not supposed to do with these lamps. She doesn't care.

She sets everything free at once. Why should they not be free? Why should *she* not? She frees herself from the job of story. She's been the girl who tells tales nightly, the girl who memorizes the histories of every star and whispers them into the ears of the sultan in hopes of keeping herself from death. She frees herself from the job of guiding men through the dark.

Forward in time eight hundred years, that same girl, now a woman, walks the woods of this part of America. She runs into a trapper wearing a blue blanket stolen from his last wife's people. He's drunk, and he's been traveling alone too long. He's a man in a pile of pelts, bear and wolf, beaver and mink, all the heat of their fur divorced from their blood, and she has no use for him.

"I need a woman," he shouts at her across the snow. "My woman died."

"I don't need a man," she says, and keeps walking. Deep snow and snowshoes, leaving tracks like she's two flat-tailed beavers walking side by side.

"You need *me*," he insists, but she keeps walking.

He runs up behind her and grabs her by the hair, pulling the braid away from her skull, tearing the roots, and she feels her own blood sizzle on her cold skin.

That's all he gets from her. Her heart is a copper lamp, and inside it is black smoke.

She made a wish a long time ago, and it was granted. She walks in safety.

The Hunter's eyelids are marked with the trees from a smoke tower, the place she sees if she looks over the woods and watches how they turn to words written on white snow slates. Everything is written somewhere, and all the languages of the world are here, in the bird tracks and the wolves dragging bloodied rabbits.

She should have buried her captives when she needed to sleep, not pawned them, though the old rules said the pawn should have kept them safe. She should've left them alone in the metal house in the woods, far from anyone, but last place like that, she found empty. A thousand years of searching for the wishes she set free, and now she only wants to find the last of them. They don't stay caged in copper.

She wonders. Maybe the things she hunts, if she left them to their own devices, perhaps they'd carry the old to their beds and the dying to their graves. She's been hunting too long to tell if the world is worse without wishes than with them. She's seen some wishes made, though. She feels guilt for her part in history, and so she hunts the djinn, trying to bring them back into captivity.

The Hunter rides past the site where the expedition ate itself. There they were, their hands full of blood, their mouths full of bone. She rides past the reactor she didn't keep from melting down. It wasn't her fault. She was sleeping, and she didn't know what was living inside it.

She's behind a truck now, on the highway, her motorcycle whining, the monkey's paws twisted in her hair. Rifle rack on the back of the cab, and the Kid's driving on the wrong side of the road.

She can hear the radio, the Kid playing loud to drown out the noise as he heads toward the high school floodlights in the middle of the field, the peeled paint coming off trucks like onion skin, the smell of metallic sweat, sleep, and chemistry labs, the smell of the reactor's effects continuing into the future, each generation on fire, brightness continuing through them, turning the children into something other than children. Now she knows that wishers are everywhere.

The Kid turns in at the high school. As he does, he looks to the thing in the back of the pickup truck and makes a wish.

There are reactions and reactors and spills in the river, there are trees growing up out of white dust and children born dazzled, with hearts full of black smoke. There are wishes inhaled in first breaths and exhaled in final ones.

The Kid has barred the door of the high school with an ax handle, and no one knows it yet. He is walking into the cafeteria, his denim making the rustle of rough animals brushing against one another in a pasture.

But outside the cafeteria, Weran Root, a priest made of wishes, cracks open the casing of the bullet, releases the djinn inside, and makes a wish, calling a reaction from the reactor.

In the woods, there's light around trees and heat steaming from the earth. There are three black wolves, and with a howl and a leap they fling themselves into the sky and become birds. Out of the reactor emerges a djinn, hidden in this place for a hundred and fifty years.

The Kid is walking toward the girls. They're seated in a row of shining ponytails and for a moment he thinks he's walking toward a stable, and then—

Girls on their backs, girls on horseback, girls in horsehair. Old stories from an old expedition. Stories he's told himself about happiness, all of them failures, all of them involving being lost without a guide, wandering helpless and hopeless, lonely forever.

I need a girl to look at me, he tells himself. That's his wish. It's a wish many have made before him, and it's never turned out well.

The cafeteria is, in an instant, full of wild horses, snorting and prancing, galloping, chestnuts and dapple grays, blues and reds. The Kid stands in the midst of all these girls who are no longer girls.

There's only one real girl left in the cafeteria, and the Kid, despairing on his mission, his legend shrinking, raises the ancient rifle and balances it on his shoulder. He's surrounded by horseflesh, the smell of horses wearing drugstore perfume, horses with hairspray in their manes, horses stepping around him and treading on him, rearing up, neighing.

The girl has tattooed eyelids and a monkey in her arms. She looks at the Kid. He's crying. He has his finger on the trigger. The Kid is somebody's wish, somebody's son, with his hardening blood and brightening bones.

"Come over here, now," the Hunter says.

Around him the horses of the high school spin, about their own business. The Kid is constituted of despair. He aims the rifle, shaking, at her.

A cloud coheres, standing between the Hunter and the Kid.

The Hunter looks at the smoke, her old companion.

"There you are," she says. "I heard you melted something down. Heard you made some things."

This djinn, the first to emerge a thousand years ago, has been lonely a while.

I heard my son was up to bad wishing, says the smoke.

The Kid looks around, bewildered as the smoke wishes him

backward in time, sends him back to his childhood, to his mother, to the mosaics in the yard made of bones.

He flickers for a moment, in his denim and misery, and then he's gone.

The room is full of stampeding horses and then the room is full of stampeding daughters, and then the room is full of the children of this part of the mountains, all of them made of magic, all of them the drift that comes of wishes falling from the sky like snow.

"Come with me," says the Hunter to the smoke. "At the end of every story, there's another story. I've been looking for you a long time. This is the story after the hunt."

The smoke regards her.

There's a world inside every wish. There are miles inside every lamp. There are places in these mountains where everything may dwell at once, guarded by wolves.

The two of them, old lovers, old stories, a Scheherazade and her secret, leave only a scrap of paper, a ticket exchanging one thing for another, and a little monkey that springs up and drops a handful of copper casings on the ground as it departs for the forest.

Yoth Begail is driving out of the woods, and beside him, covered in a cloak to keep him in shadow, is Weran Root. Yoth's eighty-six years old and recently dead. Death doesn't bother him. He's smoking a Cuban cigar brought out from someone's humidor, a pawnshop perk.

"Remember when I was the Priest?" says Weran Root. "Remember when I held the word in my hands and tried to put it around your finger?"

"Yep," says Yoth Begail. "I remember." He passes Weran Root a brooch made of blood and bone, and the old man made of smoke causes it to appear and disappear in his fingertips.

"What did you wish for?" Yoth Begail asks Weran Root.

"No one tells their wishes," says Weran Root. "Those are the rules of this kind of story."

They are two old men in love, freed of their obligations, in possession of every ticket for everything left in their keeping. They are driving out of the mountains and toward the sea.

*

The Kid is wished into another story, a hundred and fifty years before the beginning of this one. Now he's a newborn baby found in these woods, the forest bending to look down at him. He's the child of a dead woman, and his father is a freetrapper, but none of this is his pain.

Someone who will love him picks him up. She carries him away from the ice and into the green mountains, holds him beside a fire, sings him a song that tells a story about spring. Now he's raised with love instead of fury.

The wishes in this story are wishes built the way wishes are always built, and the way bullets are built too, to keep going long after they've left the safety of silence. Each person is a projectile filled with sharp voice and broken volume, blasts of maybe.

The hands outstretch, the hearts explode. The chamber is the world and all the bodies on earth press close around each bullet, holding it steady until, with a rotating spin, it flies.

Everything living is built to burn, of course. After the close, dark chamber comes the cold, bright world.

And after the world?

After the world is a cloud of smoke, and in the center of the cloud, a whispering flame.

TOBIAS S. BUCKELL

Zen and the Art of Starship Maintenance

FROM *Cosmic Powers*

AFTER BATTLE WITH the *Fleet of Honest Representation,* after
seven hundred seconds of sheer terror and uncertainty, and after
our shared triumph in the acquisition of the greatest prize seizure
in three hundred years, we cautiously approached the massive
black hole that Purth-Anaget orbited. The many rotating rings,
filaments, and infrastructures bounded within the fields that were
the entirety of our ship, *With All Sincerity,* were flush with a sense of
victory and bloated with the riches we had all acquired.

Give me a ship to sail and a quasar to guide it by, billions of individual
citizens of all shapes, functions, and sizes cried out in joy together on the common channels. Whether fleshy forms safe below,
my fellow crablike maintenance forms on the hulls, or even the
secretive navigation minds, our myriad thoughts joined in a sense
of True Shared Purpose that lingered even after the necessity of
the group battle-mind.

I clung to my usual position on the hull of one of the three
rotating habitat rings deep inside our shields and watched the
warped event horizon shift as we fell in behind the metallic world
in a trailing orbit.

A sleet of debris fell toward the event horizon of Purth-Anaget's
black hole, hammering the kilometers of shields that formed an
iridescent cocoon around us. The bow shock of our shields' push
through the debris field danced ahead of us, the compressed wave
it created becoming a hyper-aurora of shifting colors and energies
that collided and compressed before they streamed past our sides.

What a joy it was to see a world again. I was happy to be outside in the dark so that as the bow shields faded, I beheld the perpetual night face of the world: it glittered with millions of fractal habitation patterns traced out across its artificial surface.

On the hull with me, a nearby friend scuttled between airlocks in a cloud of insect-sized seeing eyes. They spotted me and tapped me with a tight-beam laser for a private ping.

"Isn't this exciting?" they commented.

"Yes. But this will be the first time I don't get to travel downplanet," I beamed back.

I received a derisive snort of static on a common radio frequency from their direction. "There is nothing there that cannot be experienced right here in the Core. Waterfalls, white sand beaches, clear waters."

"But it's different down there," I said. "I love visiting planets."

"Then hurry up and let's get ready for the turnaround so we can leave this industrial shithole of a planet behind us and find a nicer one. I hate being this close to a black hole. It fucks with time dilation, and I spend all night tasting radiation and fixing broken equipment that can't handle energy discharges in the exajoule ranges. Not to mention everything damaged in the battle I have to repair."

This was true. There was work to be done.

Safe now in trailing orbit, the many traveling worlds contained within the shields that marked the *With All Sincerity*'s boundaries burst into activity. Thousands of structures floating in between the rotating rings moved about, jockeying and repositioning themselves into renegotiated orbits. Flocks of transports rose into the air, wheeling about inside the shields to then stream off ahead toward Purth-Anaget. There were trillions of citizens of the *Fleet of Honest Representation* heading for the planet now that their fleet lay captured between our shields like insects in amber.

The enemy fleet had forced us to extend energy far, far out beyond our usual limits. Great risks had been taken. But the reward had been epic, and the encounter resolved in our favor with their capture.

Purth-Anaget's current ruling paradigm followed the memetics of the One True Form, and so had opened their world to these refugees. But Purth-Anaget was not so wedded to the belief system as to pose any threat to mutual commerce, information exchange, or any of our own rights to self-determination.

Later we would begin stripping the captured prize ships of information, booby traps, and raw mass, with Purth-Anaget's shipyards moving inside of our shields to help.

I leapt out into space, spinning a simple carbon nanotube of string behind me to keep myself attached to the hull. I swung wide, twisted, and landed near a dark-energy manifold bridge that had pinged me a maintenance consult request just a few minutes back.

My eyes danced with information for a picosecond. Something shifted in the shadows between the hull's crenulations.

I jumped back. We had just fought an entire war-fleet; any number of eldritch machines could have slipped through our shields — things that snapped and clawed, ripped you apart in a femtosecond's worth of dark energy. Seekers and destroyers.

A face appeared in the dark. Skeins of invisibility and personal shielding fell away like a pricked soap bubble to reveal a bipedal figure clinging to the hull.

"You there!" it hissed at me over a tightly contained beam of data. "I am a fully bonded shareholder and chief executive with command privileges of the Anabathic ship *Helios Prime*. Help me! Do not raise an alarm."

I gaped. What was a CEO doing on our hull? Its vacuum-proof carapace had been destroyed while passing through space at high velocity, pockmarked by the violence of single atoms at indescribable speed punching through its shields. Fluids leaked out, surrounding the stowaway in a frozen mist. It must have jumped the space between ships during the battle, or maybe even after.

Protocols insisted I notify the hell out of security. But the CEO had stopped me from doing that. There was a simple hierarchy across the many ecologies of a traveling ship, and in all of them a CEO certainly trumped maintenance forms. Particularly now that we were no longer in direct conflict and the *Fleet of Honest Representation* had surrendered.

"Tell me: what is your name?" the CEO demanded.

"I gave that up a long time ago," I said. "I have an address. It should be an encrypted rider on any communication I'm single-beaming to you. Any message you direct to it will find me."

"My name is Armand," the CEO said. "And I need your help. Will you let me come to harm?"

"I will not be able to help you in a meaningful way, so my not telling security and medical assistance that you are here will likely do more harm than good. However, as you are a CEO, I have to follow your orders. I admit, I find myself rather conflicted. I believe I'm going to have to countermand your previous request."

Again I prepared to notify security with a quick summary of my puzzling situation.

But the strange CEO again stopped me. "If you tell anyone I am here, I will surely die and you will be responsible."

I had to mull the implications of that over.

"I need your help, robot," the CEO said. "And it is your duty to render me aid."

Well, shit. That was indeed a dilemma.

Robot.

That was a Formist word. I never liked it.

I surrendered my free will to gain immortality and dissolve my fleshly constraints, so that hard acceleration would not tear at my cells and slosh my organs backward until they pulped. I did it so I could see the galaxy. That was one hundred and fifty-seven years, six months, nine days, ten hours, and—to round it out a bit—fifteen seconds ago.

Back then, you were downloaded into hyperdense pin-sized starships that hung off the edge of the speed of light, assembling what was needed on arrival via self-replicating nanomachines that you spun your mind-states off into. I'm sure there are billions of copies of my essential self scattered throughout the galaxy by this point.

Things are a little different today. More mass. Bigger engines. Bigger ships. Ships the size of small worlds. Ships that change the orbits of moons and satellites if they don't negotiate and plan their final approach carefully.

"Okay," I finally said to the CEO. "I can help you."

Armand slumped in place, relaxed now that it knew I would render the aid it had demanded.

I snagged the body with a filament lasso and pulled Armand along the hull with me.

It did not do to dwell on whether I was choosing to do this or it was the nature of my artificial nature doing the choosing for me. The constraints of my contracts, which had been negotiated when I had free will and boundaries—as well as my desires and dreams —were implacable.

Towing Armand was the price I paid to be able to look up over my shoulder to see the folding, twisting impossibility that was a black hole. It was the price I paid to grapple onto the hull of one of several three-hundred-kilometer-wide rotating rings with parks, beaches, an entire glittering city, and all the wilds outside of them.

The price I paid to sail the stars on this ship.

A century and a half of travel, from the perspective of my humble self, represented far more in regular time due to relativity. Hit the edge of lightspeed and a lot of things happened by the time you returned, simply because thousands of years had passed.

In a century of me-time, spin-off civilizations rose and fell. A multiplicity of forms and intelligences evolved and went extinct. Each time I came to port, humanity's descendants had reshaped worlds and systems as needed. Each place marvelous and inventive, stunning to behold.

The galaxy had bloomed from wilderness to a teeming experiment.

I'd lost free will, but I had a choice of contracts. With a century and a half of travel tucked under my shell, hailing from a well-respected explorer lineage, I'd joined the hull repair crew with a few eyes toward seeing more worlds like Purth-Anaget before my pension vested some two hundred years from now.

Armand fluttered in and out of consciousness as I stripped away the CEO's carapace, revealing flesh and circuitry.

"This is a mess," I said. "You're damaged way beyond my repair. I can't help you in your current incarnation, but I can back you up and port you over to a reserve chassis." I hoped that would be enough and would end my obligation.

"No!" Armand's words came firm from its charred head in soundwaves, with pain apparent across its deformed features.

"Oh, come on," I protested. "I understand you're a Formist, but you're taking your belief system to a ridiculous level of commitment. Are you really going to die a final death over this?"

I'd not been in high-level diplomat circles in decades. Maybe the spread of this current meme had developed well beyond my realization. Had the followers of the One True Form been ready to lay their lives down in the battle we'd just fought with them? Like some proto-historical planetary cult?

Armand shook its head with a groan, skin flaking off in the air. "It would be an imposition to make you a party to my suicide. I apologize. I am committed to Humanity's True Form. I was born planetary. I have a real and distinct DNA lineage that I can trace to Sol. I don't want to die, my friend. In fact, it's quite the opposite. I want to preserve this body for many centuries to come. Exactly as it is."

I nodded, scanning some records and brushing up on my memeology. Armand was something of a preservationist who believed that to copy its mind over to something else meant that it wasn't the original copy. Armand would take full advantage of all technology to augment, evolve, and adapt its body internally. But Armand would forever keep its form: that of an original human. Upgrades hidden inside itself, a mix of biology and metal, computer and neural.

That, my unwanted guest believed, made it more human than I.

I personally viewed it as a bizarre flesh-costuming fetish.

"Where am I?" Armand asked. A glazed look passed across its face. The pain medications were kicking in, my sensors reported. Maybe it would pass out, and then I could gain some time to think about my predicament.

"My cubby," I said. "I couldn't take you anywhere security would detect you."

If security found out what I was doing, my contract would likely be voided, which would prevent me from continuing to ride the hulls and see the galaxy.

Armand looked at the tiny transparent cupboards and lines of trinkets nestled carefully inside the fields they generated. I kicked through the air over to the nearest cupboard. "They're mementos," I told Armand.

"I don't understand," Armand said. "You collect nonessential mass?"

"They're mementos." I released a coral-colored mosquito-like statue into the space between us. "This is a wooden carving of a quaqeti from Moon Sibhartha."

Armand did not understand. "Your ship allows you to keep mass?"

I shivered. I had not wanted to bring Armand to this place. But what choice did I have? "No one knows. No one knows about this cubby. No one knows about the mass. I've had the mass for over eighty years and have hidden it all this time. They are my mementos."

Materialism was a planetary conceit, long since edited out of travelers. Armand understood what the mementos were but could not understand why I would collect them. Engines might be bigger in this age, but security still carefully audited essential and nonessential mass. I'd traded many favors and fudged manifests to create this tiny museum.

Armand shrugged. "I have a list of things you need to get me," it explained. "They will allow my systems to rebuild. Tell no one I am here."

I would not. Even if I had self-determination.

The stakes were just too high now.

I deorbited over Lazuli, my carapace burning hot in the thick sky contained between the rim walls of the great tertiary habitat ring. I enjoyed seeing the rivers, oceans, and great forests of the continent from above as I fell toward the ground in a fireball of reentry. It was faster, and a hell of a lot more fun, than going from subway to subway through the hull and then making my way along the surface.

Twice I adjusted my flight path to avoid great transparent cities floating in the upper sky, where they arbitraged the difference in gravity to create sugar-spun filament infrastructure.

I unfolded wings that I usually used to recharge myself near the compact sun in the middle of our ship and spiraled my way slowly down into Lazuli, my hindbrain communicating with traffic control to let me merge with the hundreds of vehicles flitting between Lazuli's spires.

After kissing ground at 45th and Starway, I scuttled among the thousands of pedestrians toward my destination a few stories deep under a memorial park. Five-story-high vertical farms sank deep toward the hull there, and semiautonomous drones with spidery legs crawled up and down the green, misted columns under precisely tuned spectrum lights.

The independent doctor-practitioner I'd come to see lived inside one of the towers with a stunning view of exotic orchids and vertical fields of lavender. It crawled down out of its ceiling perch, tubes and high-bandwidth optical nerves draped carefully around its hundreds of insectile limbs.

"Hello," it said. "It's been thirty years, hasn't it? What a pleasure. Have you come to collect the favor you're owed?"

I spread my heavy primary arms wide. "I apologize. I should have visited for other reasons; it is rude. But I am here for the favor."

A ship was an organism, an economy, a world unto itself. Occasionally things needed to be accomplished outside of official networks.

"Let me take a closer look at my privacy protocols," it said. "Allow me a moment, and do not be alarmed by any motion."

Vines shifted and clambered up the walls. Thorns blossomed around us. Thick bark dripped sap down the walls until the entire room around us glistened in fresh amber.

I flipped through a few different spectrums to accommodate for the loss of light.

"Understand, security will see this negative space and become . . . interested," the doctor-practitioner said to me somberly. "But you can now ask me what you could not send a message for."

I gave it the list Armand had demanded.

The doctor-practitioner shifted back. "I can give you all that feed material. The stem cells, that's easy. The picotechnology— it's registered. I can get it to you, but security will figure out you have unauthorized, unregulated picotech. Can you handle that attention?"

"Yes. Can you?"

"I will be fine." Several of the thin arms rummaged around the many cubbyholes inside the room, filling a tiny case with biohazard vials.

"Thank you," I said, with genuine gratefulness. "May I ask you a question, one that you can't look up but can use your private internal memory for?"

"Yes."

I could not risk looking up anything. Security algorithms would put two and two together. "Does the biological name Armand mean anything to you? A CEO-level person? From the *Fleet of Honest Representation?*"

The doctor-practitioner remained quiet for a moment before answering. "Yes. I have heard it. Armand was the CEO of one of the Anabathic warships captured in the battle and removed from active management after surrender. There was a hostile takeover of the management. Can I ask you a question?"

"Of course," I said.

"Are you here under free will?"

I spread my primary arms again. "It's a Core Laws issue."

"So no. Someone will be harmed if you do not do this?"

I nodded. "Yes. My duty is clear. And I have to ask you to keep your privacy, or there is potential for harm. I have no other option."

"I will respect that. I am sorry you are in this position. You know there are places to go for guidance."

"It has not gotten to that level of concern," I told it. "Are you still, then, able to help me?"

One of the spindly arms handed me the cooled biosafe case. "Yes. Here is everything you need. Please do consider visiting in your physical form more often than once every few decades. I enjoy entertaining, as my current vocation means I am unable to leave this room."

"Of course. Thank you," I said, relieved. "I think I'm now in your debt."

"No, we are even," my old acquaintance said. "But in the following seconds I will give you more information that *will* put you in my debt. There is something you should know about Armand . . ."

I folded my legs up underneath myself and watched nutrients as they pumped through tubes and into Armand. Raw biological feed percolated through it, and picomachinery sizzled underneath its skin. The background temperature of my cubbyhole kicked up slightly due to the sudden boost to Armand's metabolism.

Bulky, older nanotech crawled over Armand's skin like living mold. Gray filaments wrapped firmly around nutrient buckets as the medical programming assessed conditions, repaired damage, and sought out more raw material.

I glided a bit farther back out of reach. It was probably bullshit, but there were stories of medicine reaching out and grabbing whatever was nearby.

Armand shivered and opened its eyes as thousands of wriggling tubules on its neck and chest whistled, sucking in air as hard as they could.

"Security isn't here," Armand noted out loud, using meaty lips to make its words.

"You have to understand," I said in kind. "I have put both my future and the future of a good friend at risk to do this for you. Because I have little choice."

Armand closed its eyes for another long moment and the tubules stopped wriggling. It flexed and everything flaked away, a discarded cloud of a second skin. Underneath it, everything was fresh and new. "What is your friend's name?"

I pulled out a tiny vacuum to clean the air around us. "Name? It has no name. What does it need a name for?"

Armand unspooled itself from the fetal position in the air. It twisted in place to watch me drifting around. "How do you distinguish it? How do you find it?"

"It has a unique address. It is a unique mind. The thoughts and things it says—"

"It has no name," Armand snapped. "It is a copy of a past copy of a copy. A ghost injected into a form for a *purpose*."

"It's my friend," I replied, voice flat.

"How do you know?"

"Because I say so." The interrogation annoyed me. "Because I get to decide who is my friend. Because it stood by my side against the sleet of dark-matter radiation and howled into the void with me. Because I care for it. Because we have shared memories and kindnesses, and exchanged favors."

Armand shook its head. "But anything can be programmed to join you and do those things. A pet."

"Why do you care so much? It is none of your business what I call friend."

"But it *does* matter," Armand said. "Whether we are real or not matters. Look at you right now. You were forced to do something against your will. That cannot happen to me."

"Really? No True Form has ever been in a position with no real choices before? Forced to do something desperate? I have my old memories. I can remember times when I had no choice even though I had free will. But let us talk about you. Let us talk about the lack of choices you have right now."

Armand could hear something in my voice. Anger. It backed away from me, suddenly nervous. "What do you mean?"

"You threw yourself from your ship into mine, crossing fields during combat, damaging yourself almost to the point of pure dissolution. You do not sound like you were someone with many choices."

"I made the choice to leap into the vacuum myself," Armand growled.

"Why?"

The word hung in the empty air between us for a bloated second. A minor eternity. It was the fulcrum of our little debate.

"You think you know something about me," Armand said, voice suddenly low and soft. "What do you think you know, robot?"

Meat fucker. I could have said that. Instead I said, "You were a CEO. And during the battle, when your shields began to fail, you moved all the biologicals into radiation-protected emergency shelters. Then you ordered the maintenance forms and hard-shells up to the front to repair the battle damage. You did not surrender; you put lives at risk. And then you let people die, torn apart as they struggled to repair your ship. You told them that if they failed, the biologicals down below would die."

"It was the truth."

"It was a lie! You were engaged in a battle. You went to war. You made a conscious choice to put your civilization at risk when no one had physically assaulted or threatened you."

"Our way of life was at risk."

"By people who could argue better. Your people failed at diplomacy. You failed to make a better argument. And you murdered your own."

Armand pointed at me. "I murdered *no one.* I lost maintenance machines with copies of ancient brains. That is all. That is what they were *built* for."

"Well. The sustained votes of the hostile takeover that you fled from have put out a call for your capture, including a call for your dissolution. True death, the end of your thought line —even if you made copies. You are hated and hunted. Even here."

"You were bound to not give up my location," Armand said, alarmed.

"I didn't. I did everything in my power not to. But I am a mere maintenance form. Security here is very, very powerful. You have fifteen hours, I estimate, before security is able to model my comings and goings, discover my cubby by auditing mass transfers back a century, and then open its current sniffer files. This is not a secure location; I exist thanks to obscurity, not invisibility."

"So I am to be caught?" Armand asked.

"I am not able to let you die. But I cannot hide you much longer."

To be sure, losing my trinkets would be a setback of a century's worth of work. My mission. But all this would go away eventually. It was important to be patient on the journey of centuries.

"I need to get to Purth-Anaget, then," Armand said. "There are followers of the True Form there. I would be sheltered and out of jurisdiction."

"This is true." I bobbed an arm.

"You will help me," Armand said.

"The fuck I will," I told it.

"If I am taken, I will die," Armand shouted. "They will kill me."

"If security catches you, our justice protocols will process you. You are not in immediate danger. The proper authority levels will put their attention to you. I can happily refuse your request."

I felt a rise of warm happiness at the thought.

Armand looked around the cubby frantically. I could hear its heartbeats rising, free of modulators and responding to unprocessed, raw chemicals. Beads of dirty sweat appeared on Armand's forehead. "If you have free will over this decision, allow me to make you an offer for your assistance."

"Oh, I doubt there is anything you can—"

"I will transfer you my full CEO share," Armand said.

My words died inside me as I stared at my unwanted guest.

A full share.

The CEO of a galactic starship oversaw the affairs of nearly a billion souls. The economy of planets passed through its accounts.

Consider the cost to build and launch such a thing: it was a fraction of the GDP of an entire planetary disk. From the boiling edges of a sun to the cold Oort clouds. The wealth, almost too staggering for an individual mind to perceive, was passed around by banking intelligences that created systems of trade throughout the galaxy, moving encrypted, raw information from point to point. Monetizing memes with picotechnological companion infrastructure apps. Raw mass trade for the galactically rich to own a fragment of something created by another mind light-years away. Or just simple tourism.

To own a share was to be richer than any single being could really imagine. I'd forgotten the godlike wealth inherent in something like the creature before me.

"If you do this," Armand told me, "you cannot reveal I was here. You cannot say anything. Or I will be revealed on Purth-Anaget, and my life will be at risk. I will not be safe unless I am to disappear."

I could feel choices tangle and roil about inside of me. "Show me," I said.

Armand closed its eyes and opened its left hand. Deeply embedded cryptography tattooed on its palm unraveled. Quantum keys disentangled, and a tiny singularity of information budded open to reveal itself to me. I blinked. I could verify it. I could *have* it.

"I have to make arrangements," I said neutrally. I spun in the air and left my cubby to spring back out into the dark where I could think.

I was going to need help.

I tumbled through the air to land on the temple grounds. There were four hundred and fifty structures there in the holy districts, all of them lined up among the boulevards of the faithful where the pedestrians could visit their preferred slice of the divine. The minds of biological and hard-shelled forms all tumbled, walked, flew, rolled, or crawled there to fully realize their higher purposes.

Each marble step underneath my carbon-fiber-sheathed limbs calmed me. I walked through the cool curtains of the Halls of the Confessor and approached the Holy of Holies: a pinprick of light suspended in the air between the heavy, expensive mass of real marble columns. The light sucked me up into the air and pulled me into a tiny singularity of perception and data. All around me, levels of security veils dropped, thick and implacable. My vision blurred and taste buds watered from the acidic levels of deadness as stillness flooded up and drowned me.

I was alone.

Alone in the universe. Cut off from everything I had ever known or would know. I was nothing. I was everything. I was—

"You are secure," the void told me.

I could sense the presence at the heart of the Holy of Holies. Dense with computational capacity, to a level that even navigation systems would envy. Intelligence that a captain would beg to taste. This near-singularity of artificial intelligence had been created the very moment I had been pulled inside of it, just for me to talk to. And it would die the moment I left. Never to have been.

All it was doing was listening to me, and only me. Nothing would know what I said. Nothing would know what guidance I was given.

"I seek moral guidance outside clear legal parameters," I said. "And confession."

"Tell me everything."

And I did. It flowed from me without thought: just pure data. Video, mind-state, feelings, fears. I opened myself fully. My sins, my triumphs, my darkest secrets.

All was given to be pondered over.

Had I been able to weep, I would have.

Finally it spoke. "You must take the share."

I perked up. "Why?"

"To protect yourself from security. You will need to buy many favors and throw security off the trail. I will give you some ideas. You should seek to protect yourself. Self-preservation is okay."

More words and concepts came at me from different directions, using different moral subroutines. "And to remove such power from a soul that is willing to put lives at risk . . . you will save future lives."

I hadn't thought about that.

"I know," it said to me. "That is why you came here."

Then it continued, with another voice. "Some have feared such manipulations before. The use of forms with no free will creates security weaknesses. Alternate charters have been suggested, such as fully owned workers' cooperatives with mutual profit-sharing among crews, not just partial vesting after a timed contract. Should you gain a full share, you should also lend efforts to this."

The Holy of Holies continued. "To get this Armand away from our civilization is a priority; it carries dangerous memes within itself that have created expensive conflicts."

Then it said, "A killer should not remain on ship."

And, "You have the moral right to follow your plan."

Finally it added, "Your plan is just."

I interrupted. "But Armand will get away with murder. It will be free. It disturbs me."

"Yes. It should.

"Engage in passive resistance. Obey the letter of Armand's law, but find a way around its will. You will be like a genie, granting Armand wishes. But you will find a way to bring justice. You will see.

"Your plan is just. Follow it and be on the righteous path."

*

I launched back into civilization with purpose, leaving the temple behind me in an explosive afterburner thrust. I didn't have much time to beat security.

High up above the cities, nestled in the curve of the habitat rings, near the squared-off spiderwebs of the largest harbor dock, I wrangled my way to another old contact.

This was less a friend and more just an asshole I'd occasionally been forced to do business with. But a reliable asshole that was tight against security. Though just by visiting, I'd be triggering all sorts of attention.

I hung from a girder and showed the fence a transparent showcase filled with all my trophies. It did some scans, checked the authenticity, and whistled. "Fuck me, these are real. That's all unauthorized mass. How the hell? This is a life's work of mass-based tourism. You really want me to broker sales on all of this?"

"Can you?"

"To Purth-Anaget, of course. They'll go nuts. Collectors down there eat this shit up. But security will find out. I'm not even going to come back on the ship. I'm going to live off this down there, buy passage on the next outgoing ship."

"Just get me the audience, it's yours."

A virtual shrug. "Navigation, yeah."

"And emergency services."

"I don't have that much pull. All I can do is get you a secure channel for a low-bandwidth conversation."

"I just need to talk. I can't send this request up through proper channels." I tapped my limbs against my carapace nervously as I watched the fence open its large, hinged jaws and swallow my case.

Oh, what was I doing? I wept silently to myself, feeling sick.

Everything I had ever worked for disappeared in a wet, slimy gulp. My reason. My purpose.

Armand was suspicious. And rightfully so. It picked and poked at the entire navigation plan. It read every line of code, even though security was only minutes away from unraveling our many deceits. I told Armand this, but it ignored me. It wanted to live. It wanted to get to safety. It knew it couldn't rush or make mistakes.

But the escape pod's instructions and abilities were tight and honest.

It has been programmed to eject. To spin a certain number of degrees. To aim for Purth-Anaget. Then *burn*. It would have to consume every last little drop of fuel. But it would head for the metal world, fall into orbit, and then deploy the most ancient of deceleration devices: a parachute.

On the surface of Purth-Anaget, Armand could then call any of its associates for assistance.

Armand would be safe.

Armand checked the pod over once more. But there were no traps. The flight plan would do exactly as it said.

"Betray me and you kill me, remember that."

"I have made my decision," I said. "The moment you are inside and I trigger the manual escape protocol, I will be unable to reveal what I have done or what you are. Doing that would risk your life. My programming"—I all but spit the word—"does not allow it."

Armand gingerly stepped into the pod. "Good."

"You have a part of the bargain to fulfill," I reminded. "I won't trigger the manual escape protocol until you do."

Armand nodded and held up a hand. "Physical contact."

I reached one of my limbs out. Armand's hand and my manipulator met at the doorjamb and they sparked. Zebibytes of data slithered down into one of my tendrils, reshaping the raw matter at the very tip with a quantum-dot computing device.

As it replicated itself, building out onto the cellular level to plug into my power sources, I could feel the transfer of ownership.

I didn't have free will. I was a hull maintenance form. But I had an entire fucking share of a galactic starship embedded within me, to do with what I pleased when I vested and left riding hulls.

"It's far more than you deserve, robot," Armand said. "But you have worked hard for it and I cannot begrudge you."

"Goodbye, asshole." I triggered the manual override sequence that navigation had gifted me.

I watched the pod's chemical engines firing all-out through the airlock windows as the sphere flung itself out into space and dwindled away. Then the flame guttered out, the pod spent and headed for Purth-Anaget.

There was a shiver. Something vast, colossal, powerful. It vibrated the walls and even the air itself around me.

Armand reached out to me on a tight-beam signal. "What was that?"

"The ship had to move just slightly," I said. "To better adjust our orbit around Purth-Anaget."

"No," Armand hissed. "My descent profile has changed. You are trying to kill me."

"I can't kill you," I told the former CEO. "My programming doesn't allow it. I can't allow a death through action or inaction."

"But my navigation path has changed," Armand said.

"Yes, you will still reach Purth-Anaget." Navigation and I had run the data after I explained that I would have the resources of a full share to repay it a favor with. Even a favor that meant tricking security. One of the more powerful computing entities in the galaxy, a starship, had dwelled on the problem. It had examined the tidal data, the flight plan, and how much the massive weight of a starship could influence a pod after launch. "You're just taking a longer route."

I cut the connection so that Armand could say nothing more to me. It could do the math itself and realize what I had done.

Armand would not die. Only a few days would pass inside the pod.

But outside. Oh, outside, skimming through the tidal edges of a black hole, Armand would loop out and fall back to Purth-Anaget over the next four hundred and seventy years, two hundred days, eight hours, and six minutes.

Armand would be an ancient relic then. Its beliefs, its civilization, all of it just a fragment from history.

But until then I had to follow its command. I could not tell anyone what happened. I had to keep it a secret from security. No one would ever know Armand had been here. No one would ever know where Armand went.

After I vested and had free will once more, maybe I could then make a side trip to Purth-Anaget again and be waiting for Armand when it landed. I had the resources of a full share, after all.

Then we would have a very different conversation, Armand and I.

Contributors' Notes

Notable Science Fiction and
Fantasy Stories of 2017

Contributors' Notes

Charlie Jane Anders is the author of *All the Birds in the Sky*, which won the Nebula, Crawford, and Locus Awards and was shortlisted for a Hugo; also a novella called *Rock Manning Goes for Broke* and a short story collection called *Six Months, Three Days, Five Others*. Her next novel is *The City in the Middle of the Night*, which comes out in January 2019. Her short fiction has appeared in *Tor.com, Boston Review, Tin House, Conjunctions, The Magazine of Fantasy & Science Fiction, Wired, Slate, Asimov's Science Fiction, Lightspeed, ZYZZYVA, Catamaran Literary Review, McSweeney's Internet Tendency,* and tons of anthologies. Her story "Six Months, Three Days" won a Hugo Award, and "Don't Press Charges and I Won't Sue" won a Theodore Sturgeon Award. She hosts the long-running Writers with Drinks reading series in San Francisco.

▪ "Don't Press Charges and I Won't Sue" feels like a huge primal scream on paper, like I was venting all of my sheer terror and anger about being a transgender person in the Trump era. But when I look back at it now, I'm surprised at how much artifice there is. There's wordplay, there's weird whimsical anecdotes, there's a lot of odd little devices. To some extent, all of that stuff represents me trying to lure people into reading my dark gut punch of a story about horrific abuses. But I feel like it's also a survival tactic—we survive by escaping into fancy, and the fancier the better, plus I'm a huge believer in the power of creativity and even silliness to get us through the darkness—and it's also a way of trying to build a more complete picture of the world that let this happen and the befouled relationship between the two main characters, Rachel and Jeffrey. The actual germ of this story started with the common phrase that trans people use, *deadnaming*. When you refer to someone by the name he/she/they used before transition, you are using their deadname. I thought about that metaphor, of trying to shackle someone to a dead self, and started to build it out into something Frankensteinesque. I wrote this story in the middle of a huge political and social panic attack, and imagining the worst possible outcome actually did prove somewhat cathartic. I'm still terrified and angry, but I feel as though, like Rachel, I'm going to fight back the best I can.

Tobias S. Buckell is a *New York Times* best-selling author born in the Caribbean. He grew up in Grenada and spent time in the British and U.S. Virgin Islands, which influence much of his work. His novels and over sixty stories have been translated into eighteen different languages. His work has been nominated for awards like the Hugo, Nebula, Prometheus, and the John W. Campbell Award for Best New Writer. He currently lives in Bluffton, Ohio, with his wife, twin daughters, and a pair of dogs. He can be found online at www.TobiasBuckell.com.

▪ I've had the title for this story and a rough idea about the setting for years, waiting for the alchemy of "something else" to strike that would give me character and meaning. Early in 2016 I was thinking a lot about resistance after reading *Women in Grenadian History, 1783–1983,* by Nicole Laurine Phillip. My roots are Grenadian, and the history in Phillip's book inspired me to fuse the core idea of passive resistance with thoughts about artificial intelligence, belief, and how the dispossessed can still find routes of resistance. The way the mind fuses these things together into story is always magical and delightful to me when I set out to find a story in things like this. I was not expecting that when the story came out in 2017, it would resonate with so many.

Gwendolyn Clare is the author of the young adult steampunk novels *Ink, Iron, and Glass* (2018) and *Mist, Metal, and Ash* (2019). Her short stories have appeared in *The Magazine of Fantasy & Science Fiction, Analog, Asimov's Science Fiction, Clarkesworld,* and *Beneath Ceaseless Skies,* among other publications. She teaches college biology in central Pennsylvania, where she lives with too many cats and never enough books.

▪ This is unusual for me, but in the case of "Tasting Notes" I can actually point to a specific moment of inspiration. I attended a wonderful talk by medievalist Michael Livingston at a writers' conference, and in describing his research on the Battle of Crécy, he mentioned acquiring key information from, of all things, a cook's journal. I was fascinated with the idea of reconstructing major political events from the perspective of someone whose concerns are tangential to those events—people like that cook, who was more worried about how many chickens the English king was eating than he was about the battle they were marching toward.

As you can probably tell from the story, I am also an incurable wine snob. Anything worth enjoying is also worth analyzing to death—that's my motto. It's a particularly interesting challenge to try to describe senses like taste, smell, and mouthfeel, because there's such a paucity of words for those (in the English language, at least).

Samuel R. Delany's science fiction and fantasy tales are available in *Aye and Gomorrah and Other Stories*. His collections *Atlantis: Three Tales* and *Phallos* are experimental fiction. His novels include science fiction, such as the Nebula Award–winning *Babel-17* and *The Einstein Intersection*, as well as *Nova* and *Dhalgren*. Most recently he has written the science fiction novel *Through the Valley of the Nest of Spiders*. His 2007 novel *Dark Reflections* won the Stonewall Book Award. His short novel *The Atheist in the Attic* appeared this past February.

In 2013 Delany was made the thirty-first Damon Knight Memorial Grand Master of Science Fiction. He lives in Philadelphia with his partner, Dennis Rickett.

• "The Hermit of Houston," he tells us, "was my attempt to write a post-Trump science fiction story."

Jaymee Goh is an equatorial child who likes to poke snow. She is a graduate of the Clarion Science Fiction and Fantasy Writers' Workshop class of 2016 and holds a PhD in comparative literature from the University of California, Riverside, where she dissertated on whiteness in steampunk. Her short stories, poetry, and nonfiction have appeared in a variety of venues, such as *Strange Horizons*, *Stone Telling*, and *Science Fiction Studies*. She coedited *The Sea Is Ours: Tales from Steampunk Southeast Asia* and edited *The WisCon Chronicles Vol. 11: Trials by Whiteness*.

• On an annual trip to the Singapore Flyer fish spa, Joyce Chng (whom I coedited *The Sea Is Ours* with) and I determined that we would each write a fish spa story. "The Last Cheng Beng Gift" was drafted during my first week at Clarion and was jokingly referred to as the start of "disappointing children stories" in my class. It features two practices in Chinese folk religion still widely celebrated in Malaysia and Singapore: Cheng Beng, or Qing Ming, during which Chinese people clean the tombs of their ancestors and send gifts to the afterlife so our recently deceased may live comfortably there, and the Hungry Ghost Festival, either a day or a month (depending on where it's celebrated) during which the gates of the underworld open for the dead to visit the living. I wrote this for fellow Asian daughters who have similarly fraught relationships with their mothers, and from whom filial piety demands a gratitude that we can't give freely. The conventional narrative wants us to reconcile with our (oft-abusive) parents, and I wanted to find a more compassionate way of acknowledging both our pain and our parents' skewed love.

Maria Dahvana Headley is the *New York Times* best-selling author of six books, including the novels *Magonia* and *Aerie* and, most recently, *The Mere Wife*, a contemporary novel adaptation of *Beowulf*, to be followed by a new verse translation of *Beowulf* in 2019. Her short fiction has been nominated

for the World Fantasy, Shirley Jackson, and Nebula Awards and included
in many year's-best anthologies, including *The Best American Science Fiction
and Fantasy 2016*. She's a MacDowell Colony Fellow and currently lives
in Brooklyn, though she constantly thinks about uprooting to a remote
volcanic island.

▪ "Black Powder" began because both sides of my family have been in
America a long time—one side English blacksmiths, the other side *May-
flower* wanderers who edged west from Plymouth Rock. I grew up in the
very rural southwest corner of Idaho. We had the historic Headley rifles
—famous for being used in the "Indian wars"—in the house when I was a
kid. When my dad killed himself in 2004, his father wrote to us, wanting to
reclaim them. My siblings and I unearthed the pawn tickets, but we had no
intention of letting these guns be treasured. Without need for discussion,
we set the tickets on fire. A decade later, Mahvesh Murad and Jared Shurin
commissioned a story for *The Djinn Falls in Love*. I pitched them the pleasant thing I thought I was going to write, then didn't write it. I had a notion about the ultimate confined, dangerous metal space for a djinn; not
a lamp, but a bullet in a pawnshop gun. I had to invent some backwoods
gay heroes and fling in something read when I was in fourth grade, in the
Idaho history program. That program was unusually good—it went deeply
into genocide and usurping of land. The relevant story here is about a
French Canadian fur trapper who kept marrying female guides from the
local tribes, because without those women none of these dudes could do
anything but be gobbled by bears. In the version I recall, this trapper kept
beating up his pregnant wives, until finally one of them stood by, let him
be eaten, and went about her own hunting. I'm worried I made that story
up (it defies search engines), but even when I was ten, I knew what justice
was. I like to think I still do.

"The Orange Tree" started as a gift from a writer friend of mine, who'd
run across a paragraph about an eleventh-century female golem made by
a poet of wood and hinges. He'd hoarded it for a while but then gave it to
me, saying he knew that it was mine. I did the research and wrote the first
draft in a night. Then I dithered. It was a sex robot story, sort of, and I had
no interest in writing a sex robot story. It crossed the editor Liz Gorinsky's
desk, and she pointed to the contemporaneous female poet I'd mentioned
only in the historical note, saying that she seemed like she should be in the
story itself. I went back in, translated Qasmūna's two extant poems, and
brought her into the plot. Meanwhile, though, while trying to write about
a muted woman burdened with magical loyalty to a man, and with hinges
she hadn't installed, I was dealing with the ways my whole life had gotten
unhinged. See: Woman, Existing As One. *"You didn't make me. I grew,"* was
one of the more relevant things I could have said to my partners at that
point. It was very hard to type it, even into a story about a golem made of

wood. The rest of the story, when it finally worked, grew out of realizing that I might, unbeknown to myself, already have inside me what I needed to survive. A while later, William Schafer of Subterranean Press sent me a note about a Dave McKean art-based anthology, *The Weight of Words,* and gave me the opportunity to choose a piece of Dave's art to write around. It was easy: a naked woman curled into the crook beneath a tree rooted in a tremendous violin. There it was, the rest of the story. I'd been missing the golem's most powerful instrument: her voice.

Micah Dean Hicks's debut novel, *Break the Bodies, Haunt the Bones,* is forthcoming in 2019. His story collection, *Electricity and Other Dreams*—a book of dark fairy tales and bizarre fables—won the 2012 New American Fiction Prize. His work has appeared in the *New York Times, Lightspeed Magazine, Kenyon Review,* the *Chicago Tribune, Witness,* and others. He has won the Calvino Prize, Arts & Letters Prize, and Wabash Prize. Hicks grew up in rural southwest Arkansas and now lives in Orlando, Florida. He teaches creative writing at the University of Central Florida.

▪ I wrote this story as a kind of sequel to the Brothers Grimm fairy tale "The Six Swans." When I first read the tale, I was struck by the cruelty of the ending. The youngest brother is transformed back into a boy, but because his shirt is unfinished, he has a swan's wing in place of his left arm. I couldn't get that youngest brother out of my head. Not only is he marked for the rest of his life, but he spent six years living as a swan. It occurred to me that he might have been a bird as long as he had been a boy. What would it be like for someone to trade the freedom of flight for being anchored to a world where they would never fit in? Would he miss being a boy with two arms or being a swan with two wings? There's something so powerful about cruel fairy-tale endings, a world where magic makes anything possible but you still can't get what you want. I wanted the ending of my story to sting with that same unfairness.

Rachael K. Jones grew up in various cities across Europe and North America, picked up (and mostly forgot) six languages, and acquired several degrees in the arts and sciences. Now she writes speculative fiction in Portland, Oregon. Her debut novella, *Every River Runs to Salt,* will be out in late 2018. Contrary to the rumors, she is probably not a secret android. Jones is a World Fantasy Award nominee and Tiptree Award honoree. Her fiction has appeared in dozens of venues worldwide, including *Lightspeed, Beneath Ceaseless Skies, Strange Horizons,* and *PodCastle.* Follow her on Twitter @RachaelKJones.

▪ This story is unofficially dedicated to the food trucks of Los Angeles, which in a sideways fashion inspired it. I drafted the whole thing in a day while visiting Hollywood a couple years ago. Like any tourist trap, most

Hollywood restaurants on the main strip are overpriced chains with underwhelming selection, so I spent a lot of time chasing down food trucks instead. While this story started off as a dark comedy about a cyborg cannibal food truck making a name for itself in the quadrant, at its heart it's a tale about the creative life. Late-stage capitalism often requires you to offer yourself up for consumption as the price of success, especially in any customer-facing career, from artists to fast-food servers. And not only are you required to make yourself part of the product, you're supposed to thank the customer for the privilege. While it sounds undesirable, the reward system can be tough to escape. We all want that five-star rating, even if we want to pretend like it doesn't matter to us. Engineer's journey is a cautionary tale not to give up your dreams for the cheap meaningless rewards of the people who would consume you, then turn your steel into forks by way of thanks.

Kathleen Kayembe is the Octavia E. Butler Scholar from Clarion's class of 2016, with short stories in *Lightspeed, Nightmare,* and *The Best Science Fiction & Fantasy of the Year, Volume Twelve,* as well as an essay in the Hugo-nominated *Luminescent Threads: Connections to Octavia E. Butler.* Her work appeared on the SFWA and Locus recommended reading lists for 2017. She publishes LGBTQIA romance under the pen name Kaseka Nvita. She currently lives in St. Louis, Missouri, with a beloved collection of fountain pens, inks, and notebooks, and never enough time to write what she wants.
    ▪ If you're curious about the inspiration for this story, I talk about that in the Author Spotlight *Nightmare* has on its website. I probably never would have submitted this story for publication, however, if it weren't for the Clarion Science Fiction and Fantasy Writers' Workshop.
    When I wrote this story years ago, it didn't work. It all came from Izzy's perspective, and the battle for her body at the end of the story was a mess of disembodied memories trying to convey the backstory of how a "dog" wound up in Mbuyi's bedroom—all while remaining six thousand words or less, because you should always follow submission guidelines. The story worked fine until Izzy lost her body, then it all fell apart, and for the life of me I couldn't figure out how to fix it.
    Enter Clarion 2016. John Joseph Adams spoke to our class, told us not to self-reject, and encouraged us to submit to *Lightspeed* and *Nightmare.* I gave the story to Kelly Link, who told me some helpful things about horror and said I might consider different structures for telling the story. Then Derek So submitted a triptych to workshop that didn't work, but the form intrigued our cohort, and I tried one; it also didn't work, and Ted Chiang explained why. Then Jaymee Goh turned in a triptych and it worked brilliantly, used three individual stories to tell a larger story, one greater than the sum of its parts. That's when it finally clicked: "Family" hadn't

worked after Izzy's body was taken because she couldn't tell Kanku's story, or Mbuyi's, and "Family" belonged to all of them.

I cut everything after Kanku took Izzy's body and wrote his story, and Mbuyi's, and "Family" was much longer than six thousand words—a smidgeon too long for *Nightmare Magazine,* unfortunately, where I'd wanted to submit it—but at last it was whole, it finally worked. When "Don't self-reject" warred with "Always follow submission guidelines" in my head, I compromised by asking permission. John Joseph Adams very kindly took a chance on me when he gave it, and I submitted "Family" to *Nightmare,* and the editors published it . . . and now here we are.

Carmen Maria Machado's debut short story collection, *Her Body and Other Parties,* was a finalist for the National Book Award, the Kirkus Prize, the *Los Angeles Times* Book Prize Art Seidenbaum Award for First Fiction, the Dylan Thomas Prize, and the PEN/Robert W. Bingham Prize for Debut Fiction, and the winner of the Bard Fiction Prize, the Lambda Literary Award for Lesbian Fiction, the Shirley Jackson Award, and the National Book Critics Circle's John Leonard Prize. In 2018, the *New York Times* listed *Her Body and Other Parties* as a member of "the New Vanguard," one of "15 remarkable books by women that are shaping the way we read and write fiction in the 21st century."

Her essays, fiction, and criticism have appeared in *The New Yorker,* the *New York Times, Granta, Tin House, VQR, McSweeney's Quarterly Concern, The Believer, Guernica, The Best American Science Fiction and Fantasy,* and elsewhere. She holds an MFA from the Iowa Writers' Workshop and has been awarded fellowships and residencies from the Michener-Copernicus Foundation, the Elizabeth George Foundation, the CINTAS Foundation, Yaddo, Hedgebrook, and the Millay Colony for the Arts. She is the writer in residence at the University of Pennsylvania and lives in Philadelphia with her wife.

▪ It was only after I brought an early draft of "The Resident" to a workshop in the mountains of North Carolina that I realized the structure and tone of the story were heavily influenced by Shirley Jackson's *The Haunting of Hill House,* with its meandering opening journey, odd protagonist, tiny supporting cast, rambling manor, disquieting atmosphere, and abstruse denouement. But there was a second gothic novel at play: Charlotte Brontë's *Jane Eyre,* whose dark, troubling sensibility had spoken to me since adolescence. As in both of these novels, the protagonist of "The Resident" is emotionally fragile, scarily intelligent, and inarguably touched—hardly the strong female character that's so in vogue nowadays. That's terrifying territory for a writer, especially one for whom subverting genre expectations and sexist clichés is an ongoing objective.

I used subsequent revisions to interrogate tropes of trauma, madness in women, and the ways in which demanding these tropes—or rejecting them out of hand—alters women's ability to be eccentric, afraid, difficult, and human, cutting off their self-determination at the knees. My protagonist comes to her own conclusion about this, ultimately identifying as a "madwoman in her own attic" as she spirals into her own psyche. Her traumas have made her, and it is her right to occupy them with rage, art, catharsis; they are *hers,* after all. But the question at the heart of the story isn't whether or not our traumas affect or define us. I believe they do. Rather, it's this: what do we do with the person we've become?

Kate Alice Marshall likes to describe herself as a genre magpie. She is the author of the YA survival thriller *I Am Still Alive,* and her short fiction has appeared in *Beneath Ceaseless Skies, Crossed Genres,* and Rich Horton's *The Year's Best Science Fiction & Fantasy.* In her other lives she writes everything from historical romance to video games.

▪ "Destroy the City with Me Tonight" is not a story about motherhood, but it is a story that exists because I became a mother. It was the first piece of writing I attempted after the birth of my son. With him swaddled beside me, I set out to ease back into my writing with a straightforward, fun superhero adventure—something fluffy and uncomplicated. That plan didn't survive the first sentence. Instead what emerged was a story about obligation, isolation, and identity—issues that, in retrospect, had a great deal to do with the struggles of redefining myself as a mother and as a writer. "Destroy the City with Me Tonight" is not a story about motherhood, but it is a story about grappling with identities into which it is too easy to vanish —losing *who* we are in *what* we are.

Maureen McHugh lives in Los Angeles and teaches at the University of Southern California. Her collection of short stories, *After the Apocalypse,* was one of *Publishers Weekly*'s ten best books of 2011.

▪ I checked my spam one day and among the offers from Nigeria was an email from the *Boston Review.* I've been teaching Junot Díaz's short stories for years and was rather astonished to get a request for a story from him. (I fangirled and admitted as much and he emailed back that he had taught some of my short stories. I may have shrieked.) The story was for a collection called *Global Dystopias.*

I had written a number of stories about possible apocalypses in my own collection years before, but after I said yes, I realized I wasn't actually sure how much I wanted to go back to that headspace. Apocalyptic stories are as much a way for me to take my 2 a.m. staring-at-the-ceiling fears and put them into words, and I really didn't know if that was where I wanted to be writing. Then I saw a book about cannibalism. A friend recommended I also look at the siege of Leningrad. North Korea was in the news, and it was easy to imagine a kind of complex collapse.

I wrote the first scene of the story without knowing exactly where things were going, and then the story sort of told itself to me. When I describe it to friends, I call it my apocalyptic lesbian cannibal story, which is kind of fun in and of itself. Junot (I can call him by his first name now, right? I mean, I wrote a story for him) was quite gracious and the editorial notes were spot on. It was a weirdly great experience considering the subject matter.

Charles Payseur grew up in the suburbs of Chicago and now lives with his partner and an assortment of ridiculous pets in the much more scenic landscape of Wisconsin's Chippewa Valley. He is a queer reader, writer, and reviewer of all things speculative. His fiction and poetry have appeared in *Strange Horizons, Lightspeed Magazine, Beneath Ceaseless Skies,* and many more. He's also a Hugo-nominated fan writer who runs *Quick Sip Reviews,* contributes to *The Book Smugglers,* drunkenly reads the original Goosebumps on his Patreon, and generally has far too many opinions about *Star Trek*'s Garak. You can find him gushing about short fiction (and occasionally his cats) on Twitter as @ClowderofTwo.

▪ I live in a city built around rivers. Eau Claire, Wisconsin, twists and turns where the Chippewa and Eau Claire Rivers meet, and I think the story sprang out of the personalities the rivers possess. And, ultimately, how rivers are exploited and polluted, a situation that mirrors other, much more human experiences. To me, the story was about exploring how oppressed communities are often set against one another, pushed to fight each other instead of joining together to resist the larger and more dominant power. It's about the gravity of violence among the exploited and hunted, that even trying to avoid confrontation the rivers are pulled into fight after fight where they must hurt and kill, all the while losing more and more of themselves to the dust and sand. That, and I'm a big fan of the steam Western aesthetic and I love the visual of a person who can transform into a river.

Lettie Prell is a science fiction writer whose work has appeared in *Tor.com, Clarkesworld, Analog,* and *Apex Magazine.* Her stories have been reprinted in a number of anthologies, and another story is being published in *The Year's Best Science Fiction & Fantasy 2018 Edition,* edited by Rich Horton. She is a lifelong midwesterner and currently lives in Des Moines.

▪ I wrote "Justice Systems in Quantum Parallel Probabilities" while I was still the research director of the Iowa Department of Corrections. It was a distinct departure from my usual subject matter, which considers humankind on the brink of the technological singularity. However, I want to eventually write a science fiction novel about alien justice, so I started writing these vignettes as a way to explore possible new angles on the topic. The scenes quickly amassed into a sort of *Invisible Cities* of justice systems.

I was nervous about sending it out for publication. Here I was, thirty-five years deep in a justice career, a recipient of a research award from the American Correctional Association, and I'd written this subversive story that dissects the system's structure and finds it wanting.

The story came out in January 2017. No one arrived at my office door to escort me from the building. Later, my *Tor.com* story of 2016, "The Three Lives of Sonata James," was reprinted in *The Best Science Fiction of the Year: Volume Two.* I decided then it was time to switch careers—my second bold move. It was the year I let go of fear.

A. Merc Rustad is a queer nonbinary writer who lives in Minnesota and was a 2016 Nebula Award finalist. Their stories have appeared in *Lightspeed, Fireside, Apex, Uncanny, Shimmer,* and *Nightmare* and several year's-best anthologies, including two previous appearances in *The Best American Science Fiction and Fantasy.* You can find Merc on Twitter @Merc_Rustad or their website, http://amercrustad.com. Their debut short story collection, *So You Want to Be a Robot,* was published in May 2017.

▪ The first idea I had for "Brightened Star, Ascending Dawn" came from the ending, with the crew and the ship helping people escape a doomed world. I essentially worked backward from this point, figuring out what would bring the characters to this moment in their lives. Like with the majority of my stories, I had a series of words that helped define the mood and aesthetic: *shining, innocent, compassion, family.* (This story is also part of a series of space operas in the Suns of the Principality universe, which also had the challenge of fitting timeline elements and specific worldbuilding touchpoints seamlessly into the narrative.) Most of all, though, when I'm writing, I need to know where the emotional keystones are; Brightened Star's relationship with her crew and passengers—her family—was the most important element for me to illustrate. Without the empathy among the characters (and between me, the author, and the characters) there would be no heart, and I needed that heart to be present. We are all in the universe together, and our ability to care for one another is one of our great strengths.

Cadwell Turnbull's work has appeared in *Asimov's Science Fiction, Lightspeed,* and *Nightmare.* He is a graduate of North Carolina State University's MFA program in creative writing and the 2016 Clarion West Science Fiction Workshop. He grew up in the U.S. Virgin Islands and currently lives in Boston, Massachusetts.

▪ A cow-foot lady lived on the hill near my grandmother's house. The neighborhood kids and I would run past it on the way to get treats from a house further up that hill. Inside, the cow-foot lady's house was always dark, even though the land around it was well kept. It's strange the feeling I still get when talking about this. I'm not superstitious at all, but these stories have a sort of power that goes beyond rationalizations. Our monsters inhabit the same space as us; we don't tempt them with our unbelief. We are careful not to answer whispers late at night so as not to bring home unwanted guests.

The soucouyant is another character from Caribbean folklore. I'd heard my own stories of her growing up. When I sat down to write "Loneliness Is in Your Blood," the story came mostly out of my memory and then I added some things here and there to make it my own. My friends at Clarion West helped me get the story to where it needed to be. There are lots of variations of the soucouyant myth, so mine should be taken as just another account of a being that goes by many names. I'm not sure who told me the story first, but it has lingered in me all this time. Oral traditions are like that—the stories live on beyond the teller. And like the very best horrors, they never truly die.

Peter Watts (www.rifters.com) is a former marine biologist, flesh-eating-disease survivor, and (according to the U.S. government) Undesirable Element, whose novels—despite an unhealthy focus on space vampires—have become required texts for university courses ranging from philosophy to neuropsychology. His work is available in twenty languages, has appeared in over two dozen best-of-year anthologies, and been nominated for over fifty awards (fifty-one, actually) from a dozen countries. His (somewhat smaller) list of seventeen wins include the Hugo, Shirley Jackson, and Seiun Awards. He lives in Toronto with his wife, the fantasy author Caitlin Sweet; four and a half cats; a pugilistic rabbit; a Plecostomus the size of a school bus; and a gang of tough raccoons who shake him down for kibble on the porch every summer. He likes them all significantly more than most people he's met.

▪ There's a scene in my 2014 novel *Echopraxia*: a weary old colonel reminisces about his early days in the zombie program, about what it was like to give your body over to subconscious process that fought and thought and acted faster than the conscious mind ever could. "We first-gen types, we—stayed awake," he remembers. "They could cut us out of the motor loop but they couldn't shut down the hypothalamic circuitry without compromising autonomic performance. There were rumors floating around that they could do that just fine, that they wanted us awake—"

It was pure throwaway, a minor bit of character development, but it stuck with me. What would it be like, I wondered, to be possessed by some neurosurgically induced iteration of alien body syndrome? How might it feel to be a passenger in a chassis doing things you would never do, if only you could take back the controls? I've never been big on military SF, but when Jonathan Strahan approached me to contribute to *Infinity Wars*, I knew exactly where to go.

Of course, no one's going to risk their best and brightest on an untested protocol that rewires the whole damn nervous system. No career soldier's going under the microwave gun until they've worked out the bugs on other, more expendable assets. So while our colonel does show up for a cameo near the end of "ZeroS" (as a lowly lieutenant this time), he's more of an Easter egg than a character. This story belongs to Kodjo and his buddies.

"ZeroS" isn't just an acronym for the squad. It's also the value of a lab rat.

Caroline M. Yoachim has written over a hundred short stories. She is a Hugo and three-time Nebula Award finalist, and her fiction has been translated into several languages and reprinted in multiple best-of anthologies. Her debut short story collection, *Seven Wonders of a Once and Future World and Other Stories*, came out in 2016. For more about Yoachim, check out her website at carolineyoachim.com.

▪ The initial seed for "Carnival Nine" was spoon theory, developed by Christine Miserandino as a way to describe living with disability or chronic illness. In spoon theory, the energy to do tasks is represented by spoons, and people get a limited number of spoons each day. I initially considered writing this story with spoons but quickly began to consider other options. Candles were the first alternative to come to mind, and later keys —not the wind-up keys that are in the current story, but more traditional keys for opening doors. I eventually decided I wanted to represent energy with something that was internal to the character—spoons inside their rib cage, or burning-candle hearts. In the end I settled on wind-up characters, and from there the story came together pretty quickly.

E. Lily Yu was the recipient of the 2017 Artist Trust LaSalle Storyteller Award and the 2012 John W. Campbell Award for Best New Writer. Her stories have appeared in publications ranging from *McSweeney's* to *Tor.com*, as well as multiple best-of-the-year anthologies, and been finalists for the Hugo, Nebula, Sturgeon, Locus, and World Fantasy Awards.

▪ This story precipitated, crystalline and complete, from a clear-sighted fury in August 2016. It was accepted for publication on January 31, 2017, four days after the signing of Executive Order 13769, and published in *Terraform* a week later. It is as close as I come to pitching a brick through a window.

Notable Science Fiction and Fantasy Stories of 2017

Selected by John Joseph Adams

THE BEST AMERICAN SERIES®

FIRST, BEST, AND BEST-SELLING

The Best American Comics

The Best American Essays

The Best American Food Writing

The Best American Mystery Stories

The Best American Nonrequired Reading

The Best American Science and Nature Writing

The Best American Science Fiction and Fantasy

The Best American Short Stories

The Best American Sports Writing

The Best American Travel Writing

Available in print and e-book wherever books are sold.

hmhco.com/bestamerican